The Prince of Yanland
Kate Diamond

Copyright 2025 © Kate Diamond

All rights reserved. No part of this publication may be reproduced, stored or transmitted in any form or by any means, electronic, mechanical, photocopying, recording, scanning, or otherwise without written permission from the publisher. It is illegal to copy this book, post it to a website, or distribute it by any other means without permission.

This novel is entirely a work of fiction. The names, characters and incidents portrayed in it are the work of the author's imagination. Any resemblance to actual persons, living or dead, events or localities is entirely coincidental.

Also by Kate Diamond

The Cloudship Trader

Acknowledgements

Dedicated to my grandmother, who inspired me to love books.

Cover art by Sophie Anderson

Characters

Talland Royal Family
Seraphina Beran (Queen of Talland)
Isadore Beran (Crown Prince)
Celeste Beran (princess)
Abigail Beran (princess)

In the Palace
Marjorie Hammond (housekeeper)
Jonah Hammond (Marjorie's son)
Patrice Addison (head cook)
Ambry Jean (servant, Isadore's assistant)
Delia Williams (servant, messenger)
Ella Marsh (servant, cook)
Danny Dillon (servant)
Marion Willoughby (servant)
Erik Walsh (gardener, carpenter)
Alice Welles (servant)
Kieran Alder (postmaster)

Dominick Marshall (Isadore's guard)
Sylvia Marwen (Isadore's guard)
Lawrence Arnholtz (Isadore's guard)
Melanie Zeegers (secretary to Isadore)
Markus Avery (senior assistant to Melanie)
Sarah Laston (assistant to Melanie)
Minerva Corey (palace archivist)

In the City
Darby Allister (royal tailor)
April Winnifer (Darby's lover)
Aubrey Marks (romance author)
Florence Ostberg (newspaper chief)
Nathalie Collins (inventor)
Amalia Tobin (priest)
Rose Kirsten (Adrian's lover, barmaid)

Lenora Jean (Ambry's mother)
Polly Madder (Ambry's aunt)
Herrin Madder (Polly's grandson)

Ellis Hardy (gang leader, conman)
Jeanette Forsythe (construction foreman)
Hannah Dreisand (Captain of the Guard)
Sophie Laston (Willow St. resident, artist)
Dale Arman (Willow St. resident)
Connor Trapper (Willow St. resident)
Daisy Trapper (Willow St. resident)
Tara Hedley (City Council representative)
Raluca Travers (Education Minister)

Politicians

Sheridan Beck (Talland's ambassador to Arrawey)
Karin Miller (Talland's ambassador to Kivern)
August Teller (Talland's ambassador to Larsellan)

Sir Valentino Bressing (Arrawey's ambassador to Talland)
Lady Claudine Pennafor (Arrawey's ambassador to Kivern)
Lady Lauretta Martellan (Arrawey's ambassador to Larsellan)

Alaric Grenner (Kivern's ambassador to Talland)
Frederick Massan (Kivern's ambassador to Arrawey)
Willem Habb (Kivern's ambassador to Larsellan)

Kestrel na'Southwind (Larsellan's ambassador to Talland)
Sandry na'Briargate (Larsellan's ambassador to Arrawey)
Mila na'Greenwood (Larsellan's ambassador to Kivern)

King Daragh (King of Arrawey)
Queen Frida (Queen of Kivern)

Oswald Brennan (the elder Lord Brennan)
Edwin Brennan (the younger Lord Brennan)

Allen Tisdale (Adrian's father)
Adrian Tisdale (Isadore's friend)
Cedric Farndale (former friend to Isadore and Adrian)
Cynthia Mohren (wealthy lady)

Other
Lacey Penner (former assistant to Isadore)
Jasmine Marel (Lacey's wife)
Reed (sailor)
Arius (sailor)
Sigurd Michaelsen (explorer, researcher)

Chapter One

✧

Ambry had not slept in days. Not well, at least. Delia, who shared Ambry's tiny room in the servants' quarters of Talland's royal palace, had been ill all night, and had kept them awake long past midnight with her fevered tossing and turning. She was resting today, which meant of course that there was all the more work for the others.

The bathwater had been cold when Ambry got to it, and it had taken far longer than usual to tame their mass of reddish curls into something acceptable. Once their hair was passably tidy, they arranged their saint-scarf around their neck and pinned it in place with their royal servant's badge. They wore it less as a sign of religious devotion and more as a way to make their gender, or lack of it, clearer to a world that often did not know how to recognize it. At least here in the capital, the mark of Saint Astrenn of the Island was known to most everyone, as was the fact that the saint watched over those who did not fit inside the traditional boundaries of gender, including those like Ambry who found themselves to be neither man nor woman at all.

As they did every day, they ran their fingers over the initials carved into the back of the little golden pin. They would not forget the honor of their position, no matter how hard the work was. They were paid well for their labor, and it gave them the chance to catch a glimpse of Queen Seraphina, or of Prince Isadore, however unlikely that might be. Even the mages of Arrawey didn't bear such skills as the Tallandi royal family, or so it was claimed. The queen, it was said, could reveal lies merely by listening to someone speak. And the prince could heal wounds with a touch of his hands. Ambry had heard the stories the servants traded. How when the prince was only an infant the Queen had exposed a prospective nursemaid's treasonous plot against him after inviting the woman to a conversation over tea. How years later the prince had discovered his ability by healing his tutor's aching arthritic hands.

The twin princesses Abigail and Celeste were away at the University honing their own abilities, but these had not yet been announced to the public. The Queen guarded her own privacy fiercely, making only enough public appearances to stave off rumors of infirmity.

Some of Ambry's fellows, the senior messengers and tablemaids, worked directly with the royal family. But as the housekeeper Mrs. Hammond often told them, their work was just as important.

Ambry tried to remember that as they hurried from one task to the next in an exhausted haze. In the kitchen, Ella danced between the stove and the fire and the table, calling out orders to her fellow cooks. Danny looked up for a moment from carving a row of fat birds to wave cheerily as Ambry entered.

Ella walked by with a tray of buns ready for baking. "Morning, Ambry. How's Delia?"

"She was still coughing when I woke up," they said, fighting back a yawn. "She says she thinks she'll feel better by tonight."

"I hope she's right. She whines so much when she's sick."

"You don't have to be in the room with her." It wasn't quite fair to say, but they were too tired to care. "Is there anything you need me for?"

"There always is," Ella sighed. She adjusted her apron. "Can you fetch me the box of sharpening supplies from the cellar? Be careful, it's heavy."

"I'll get it."

"Good. It should be at the far wall of the second room."

Ambry climbed down into the dim and the cool of the maze of rooms under the kitchen. The box was easy enough to find. The hard part was getting it out from where it sat wedged between a collection of brooms and a stack of old washtubs without dropping it. They lifted the whole thing into their arms and started heading back up the stairs just as someone else came into the kitchen.

"Marion!" they heard Ella say. "You look happy."

"It's a very good day. I've got the latest issue of Bright Changes."

"Number fourteen? I thought it wasn't coming out until next week."

"It isn't." Ambry could hear the grin in Marion's voice. "But I know a fellow who gets them early."

Distracted by the conversation, Ambry misjudged their step and would have tumbled to the stone floor below if they hadn't managed to grab onto the railing at the last moment, somehow without dropping the box. Something in their wrist twisted further and harder than it was meant to twist; they choked back a cry of pain and found their footing again.

"Someone needs to fix that step," they said as they handed over the box, no small amount of chagrin in their voice.

"Erik says he'll get to it when he gets to it," Ella said.

"Whenever that is," Marion put in.

"Keep your chatter for your own time, there's none for it today," Mrs. Hammond scolded from the doorway. As intimidating as she looked, it hadn't taken Ambry long to realize that she was fair, as long as all those under her rule worked hard and missed nothing. "Ambry, I'm going to need you to take Delia's messenger shift. Ella, Danny, you'll be doing her washing. Go talk to Patrice as soon as you can."

Ambry hurried off to the messengers' post before she had a chance to complain. It was several deliveries later before they had a spare moment to examine the injury. They rubbed their wrist, wincing and cursing their misstep. They couldn't feel any swelling, but the pain hadn't faded, and there was no sign that it was going to fade soon. They spared a moment to be grateful that their work today consisted mostly of carrying letters and supplies. Hurrying about the palace and having to speak to so many people was not something they would usually enjoy, but at least it meant they didn't have to go about their cooking and cleaning and mending with that hand. Then again, if they had been assigned their normal work, they would not have slipped on the stairs and ended up in this position.

"You about ready to come down from your cloud?" came a gruff voice at their side. Postmaster Kieran, carrying a towering basket of letters. Without waiting for a response, he shoved it into their arms, setting their wrist twinging again. "Take these to Melanie."

Ambry blinked. "The prince's secretary?"

Kieran snorted. "Unless you know another Melanie Zeegers, she's the one. You know where to go?"

Ambry did, though they had never had reason to go anywhere near the prince's chambers before. They nodded.

"Good. Then get on your way." Kieran walked away, leaving them with the basket. They hurried through the hidden back passages that kept them out of the way of guests and up the heir's tower by means of the narrow servants' stair, which let out behind a blue-and-silver curtain in a lamplit antechamber.

A stony-faced guard stood watch at the entrance to the prince's study. His neatly-trimmed graying hair and spotless uniform could not have been tidier if he had been pulled out of a painting. He was missing most of his right ear, as if it had been mangled somehow, which lent him a grizzled, fierce appearance. Ambry drew to a halt before him. He ran his sharp eyes up and down their form, as if evaluating what threat they might pose.

"What is your purpose here?" he demanded of them.

"Postmaster Kieran sent me, sir," Ambry said, barely keeping their voice steady. "I have letters for Melanie Zeegers." They gestured with the basket of letters, and barely managed not to drop it when their wrist sparked with pain and threatened to give out. The guard noted their wince with suspicion.

"Dominick?" a woman's voice called. "If they're from Kieran, show them in."

A few moments more of tense silence, and at last the guard nodded to them silently and pushed open the doors onto a sunny six-sided room. Bookcases of warm wood lined two of the high walls, and a wide window on another lit the space so brightly there was no need for candles or lamps. There was a hearth at the far wall, clean-swept and unlit in the pleasant spring weather. Delia had often sighed over the beauty of the prince's study, and now Ambry knew that she was right.

To one side of the room a woman sat at a large desk covered with stacks of papers, books, pens, and ink. Her yellow hair was tied into a fall of curls down her back. Ambry had worked with her staff before, but never reported to her directly. Melanie looked up as Ambry entered and pushed her wheelchair back from the desk. They approached; she took the basket from their arms, piled the letters and packages onto her desk, and started sorting through them. "Thank you. I don't think I've seen you on mail duty before? What's your name?"

"Ambry Jean. Delia is ill today."

"Not too serious, I hope? Good."

She looked them over, clearly taking in the hair that was pinned and tied like a man's, the feminine cut of their sleeves, and the mark of Saint Astrenn on the short scarf at their neck.

A quick question, handled more swiftly and easier than most, and she'd confirmed that the ambiguous "they" was entirely appropriate.

"Good. Just wanted to be sure."

They appreciated the question. Here in the capital, nobody much minded their gender, or lack of it. It wasn't the same everywhere, though, which was why they and their mother had moved here from the southwest shortly after they'd discovered themself.

"Can you wait here for a few minutes?" Melanie asked. "I have some letters for you to take back with you, but they're not quite ready yet."

"Of course."

"Thank you. You can sit down over there." She gestured to the deep couch that sat at the back of the room, right under the great window that looked out onto the palace's courtyard, and past that, the city.

Ambry settled on the couch to wait. They looked around the room that Delia had so lavishly praised, curious about what they would find here. They were not disappointed. The shelves were filled with not only books but also little carved wooden figures: a couple embracing, a cat curled up asleep in a basket of laundry, a fox wearing a jester's pointed hat. On the top shelves sat intricate metal instruments made of rings within rings that Ambry could only guess were used for sailing or astronomy. Next to the main door there was a woven hanging depicting a wise forest dragon perched on a hill, casting beautiful images from her crystal staff. Her tail coiled around the slopes behind her and merged into the landscape itself, flower-draped spines steadily merging into berry bushes and then tall trees where birds nested. A map of Talland hung next to a curtained doorway on the inside wall, hand-drawn and labeled down to the smallest town. Ambry imagined that if they looked closer, they would find the tiny village in the southwest where they were born.

It was warmer here than in the rest of the palace, and quiet but for the scratch of Melanie's pen and the occasional rustle of papers, which made it all too easy for Ambry to lean back into the soft cushions and close their eyes for only a moment, let the dull ache of weariness in their head fade into a comfortable fog, let their thoughts drift away from the endless work that awaited them when they left here.

They blinked their eyes open again some time later, much rested and a little confused. Where were they? And then they saw the shelves and the map and the desk, and remembered their task. That comfortable puzzlement abruptly turned to dismay and no small amount of fear. Damn. *Damn.* How long had they been asleep? Had the angle of the sun through the great window changed? They were not certain. But they knew it had been more than long enough that they would now be late. And to fall asleep in the prince's study, with his secretary waiting on them! A humiliating first impression, to be sure.

Melanie glanced up from her papers. "You're awake?" she said, sounding amused.

Ambry's ears heated with shame. "How long?" they asked, fearing the answer.

"Nearly half an hour, no more than that. It was no trouble." She clearly meant it to be reassuring, but even so it struck Ambry through with dread.

"I'm so sorry," they managed past the knot tightening in their chest. "The letters—"

"Will not be harmed for waiting a little," Melanie finished for them. "If they were that urgent, I'd have sent a courier. The lords can stand to be a little patient." Even so, their gratitude could not completely tame their fear.

"Mrs. Hammond will be angry," they said, as a side door opened.

"No, she won't."

Ambry knew that voice. Of course they did, though they had only heard it a handful of times from the back of the crowd at New Year's speeches. And once, from the other end of the dining room while filling in for an injured server at the prince's dinner with some noble or other.

Prince Isadore came into the room, carrying a stack of letters in his hand. He was dressed in an embroidered shirt that drew the eye with patterns of twining flowers, rich purple and blue on smooth fawn. The jeweled pins in his hair glinted in the sunlight. Before now, Ambry had only ever seen the prince at a distance, and in newspaper sketches. This close, they could see why so many of the serving girls and no few of the boys talked about him the way they did. Warm, dark skin and bright eyes, and an inviting smile that still had the power to pin Ambry in place for fear of displeasing this man they could not help but admire. They should not have been surprised to see the prince, they realized, not with his guard at the door, but right now it was all they could do to turn and look up at him and try to regain some sort of dignified composure. They jerked to their feet and bowed, and to their relief Isadore didn't seem to notice how clumsy the motion was.

"Your Highness?" they managed, and to their relief their voice remained steady.

"Mrs. Hammond will have no complaint of you today, because you have been running errands for me for the past half-hour."

Melanie nodded, spoiling the secret with a grin. "They have."

Isadore shrugged, a small elegant motion. "She cannot challenge me if I wished to ask your assistance for a while."

"I–" Ambry stammered. "Thank you." They bowed again, hoping the prince understood some measure of their gratitude. They walked towards the door, not quite certain if they were allowed to move without permission. The mail basket, full again with letters, waited on Melanie's desk. They picked it up, forgetting about their injury, and winced at the pain that stabbed through their arm at the motion.

"Wait," Isadore said. "Your wrist."

Ambry paused, turned back. "How did you know?" Had it been that obvious?

"I can see people's pain, if I focus. I do not want it widely known, but–"

"I won't tell," they promised, too fast, and bit their tongue, cursing themself for interrupting.

"Thank you," Isadore said, as if he hadn't been so rudely cut off, and then, "I could heal it for you. It would only take a moment."

Ambry's eyes widened. They set down the basket on the corner of Melanie's desk.

Isadore stepped forward, reaching for their hand. "May I?"

Ambry held out their arm. Isadore gently pushed up their sleeve, then wrapped warm fingers around their aching wrist and closed his eyes. A few moments of heat, a flash of tingling numbness, and when Isadore drew his hand away, the pain was gone. Ambry stretched their fingers in wonder, twisted the joint and found it moved freely.

"There. Is that better?"

They almost forgot how to speak under the warmth of the prince's eyes. "Yes. Thank you."

Isadore smiled. "Good." He turned to talk to Melanie, and Ambry took it as a dismissal. They fixed their sleeve, gathered up the basket, and walked out the door and past the stern watch of the guard. They escaped down the steps, glad to be out from under the pressure of the prince's gaze, but also somehow missing it. Isadore had healed their wrist and saved them from Mrs. Hammond's ire, and for what? They were only a servant, and a low-ranking one at that. They only hoped they hadn't made a fool of themself. Though there had been nothing at all patronizing in Isadore's words or in Melanie's, no reason they would not have been honestly willing to help.

They met Kieran at the door where he was just finishing loading his cart with packages.

"Well now, you were gone a while," he said as he took the basket, not quite an accusation but demanding an explanation all the same.

"Melanie and Prince Isadore needed me to do some things for them," Ambry said, going cold at the fear that the lie might be uncovered. But surely Kieran wouldn't challenge the word of the prince?

Kieran studied their face for a few tense and uncomfortable moments, as if he were looking for a physical manifestation of a lie, and then gave up, grumbling. "Hmph. Tell him to get his own assistant next time instead of stealing people from their jobs." He waved his hand dismissively. "You can go. I'll be glad when Delia's back on her feet. She might have more fluff than brains in that head of hers but at least she keeps to a task when it's assigned…" He turned away, still muttering to himself of the faults of all those around him. There was no reason for Ambry to take the insult personally, not when most of what Kieran said on an average day consisted of complaints and insults, but it still stung a little, the insult to Delia even more so than the insinuation against them. She was just as intelligent and hard-working as the rest of them, perhaps even more so, no matter the gossip and fanciful imaginings she enjoyed that Kieran so disapproved of.

Ambry hurried back to the servants' hall to see what Mrs. Hammond needed of them. Isadore's message must have already reached her, because she didn't ask where they had been, only assigned them to their next task as if nothing at all had gone amiss.

They took the broom from its little corner and headed out to the courtyard to sweep, something that would no doubt have been all but unbearable before Isadore had mended their wrist with his gift. Now, it was pleasant to stand in the sun and brush the pollen and dust from the mosaic stones, glancing up every so often to the prince's window and wondering what he and Melanie were working on that required so many letters. So often they'd heard of the life of ease that the royal family lived. And they did not doubt that Isadore and his family had many more comforts than Ambry could ever dream of. But the daily work of governing, that seemed far from easy, and it was not something like washing or cooking which could be wrapped up at the end of the day and left until the morning to begin again. They doubted Isadore would be able to rest as he had allowed them to do.

Their wrist gave them no pain for the rest of the day or after. The only evidence left of the injury or its healing was a faint warmth that lingered where Isadore had touched.

✧

Isadore watched Ambry leave, wondering what he had done to earn that reverent astonishment. It felt good to have helped, but the fear that had flickered in Ambry's eyes when he entered had been unsettling. It had been far more pleasant to see them comfortable and deeply asleep, to whisper to Melanie to let them rest as long as they needed, that he would make certain they were not disciplined for it.

"You ought to consider choosing an actual assistant someday," Melanie said once Ambry was out of hearing. "You haven't made any attempt at finding a new one since Lacey moved to the coast to be with her wife."

"Well, since you won't loan me Markus…"

She laughed and shook her head. "I'm not giving you my best researcher, Isadore." She was one of the few people who dared to use his bare name, or speak to him like a friend and not a master. He wished more would. It was tiresome to be treated as half a saint every moment of the day. His teachers had, when he was a child, but he hadn't been able to appreciate it then. "I need him if we're ever going to get this treaty on the signing table. Besides, he's more than half in love with you already, it would be unfair to bring him so close when I know you're not interested. And unfair to you to have to deal with him making moon eyes at you every day."

He sighed. "I suppose. You think I should choose Ambry?"

She shrugged. "Perhaps. If they prove capable of it. It would be good to choose someone familiar with the comings and goings on the ground. I can ask among the staff and see if any show promise."

"And you didn't do that before, despite insisting almost daily that I seek someone for the position, because…?" he said, eyes twinkling with humor.

"Because you wouldn't have accepted it, and it's not worth raising some poor maid or undersecretary's hopes for you to reject them out of hand simply because they are not Lacey Penner."

He couldn't argue with that. "See what you find and I'll consider it."

"I'll hold you to that." She gathered a handful of letters from her desk and pushed them towards him. "Here. The first one's a report from Ambassador Beck on the situation in Arrawey."

"Hm. What does Sheridan have to say?" He unfolded the paper and studied Beck's neat handwriting. They insisted on writing all their official correspondence themself, which Isadore appreciated. It was good to know the words came direct and not through an intermediary. It was probably a little hypocritical of him to think so, given how much he relied on Melanie, and, before she left, Lacey, but that was a matter for another day.

"They seem pleased overall with the progress on the treaty, but they're concerned about the level of influence King Daragh's trade minister seems to have in the proceedings." She pressed her lips together. "Her brother owns a company that would benefit greatly from the provisions Arrawey's Grand Council wants added, and Beck suspects she is conveniently leaving out a lot of not-so-pleasant details that the King might want to hear before he makes his final decision."

Isadore nodded, folded the letter away. "That's not good. I'll consult with Mother and have a reply by the end of the week. She has a good relationship with King Daragh, she might be able to send a message to him directly."

Melanie noted that down and moved on.

"Is there anything from Ambassador Miller?" While working with Arrawey could be tricky at times, it was nothing compared to working with the famously stubborn Kivern. Miller had made progress with them before on numerous smaller agreements, but it would take a miracle to get this treaty signed without giving up key parts of the text.

"Nothing yet. And nothing from Grenner either." Kivern's ambassador to Talland had stymied almost every one of Isadore's efforts so far. "So you're spared that headache for another day, But I think you'll be happier about this: Captain Michaelsen has sent a report of his latest expedition to the northern ice-lands. I glanced over it, it's very interesting. He's got a way of making everything exciting without being ridiculous about it like so many of his fellows are."

Isadore smiled. "I'll read that tonight."

She set the thick packet aside for later and turned to the next item. "Lord Tisdale wants to consult with you on a change to the import tax laws."

If it was anyone else, he'd assume that such a suggestion was self-serving and hardly worthy of attention, but Tisdale tended to have good ideas on that front.

"Send it to the finance minister for review and give me his report and the original when he's done."

"Noted." She made a face at the next item on her list. "And it seems Lord Brennan is trying his very hardest to start a feud with Florence Ostberg."

Isadore frowned. "With the newspaper editor? Why?"

"Let's just say he's rather unhappy with her reporting on the Spring Festival debacle."

Isadore raised an eyebrow. "The Spring Festival debacle where he demanded tribute from all the market stalls, got incredibly drunk on said tribute, and was found asleep behind the Guard stables?"

Melanie grinned, holding back laughter. "The very same." Isadore sighed. "He wants her arrested for slander. And he wants to forbid the sale of her paper in his province."

It was far from the first time Brennan had raised a fuss about things that were entirely his own fault. "He'll have a hard time finding a magistrate who'll convict her, I'll wager, not unless they want every petty gossip dragged in afterwards. He's within his rights to do the latter, but he should know that neither I nor the Queen will look fondly on it when it comes time to reevaluate his status in the court." They could not be rid of Brennan, his family held far too much power for that, but they found ways to censure him as best they were able.

"I will make sure he knows that."

Isadore read the next letter as Melanie filled another page with tidy notes. They continued in this way, slowly working their way through the pile until the stack was nearly finished. As much as he complained about the work, he didn't resent it. His mother had far, far more to handle. He was grateful for the chance to hold some responsibility before he took the throne, even if much of it was tedious things. Such was how a kingdom was run. There was enough time left for personal projects, at least. He couldn't have done a fraction of it without Melanie and her staff.

The distant chimes of the city bells drifted in through the window. Isadore glanced outside. There was somebody sweeping in the courtyard. Was that Ambry? He thought he recognized the long reddish curls. He pulled his attention back to the room and set down a rather boring report from the Captain of the City Guard. "What else do you have for me today?"

Melanie didn't even need to consult her schedule to tell him. "You have a luncheon with Lady Mohren in half an hour in the Blue dining room, and after that you're back here for an appointment with Darby Allister so they can fit you for a summer jacket."

He didn't roll his eyes, but he wanted to. "Don't I have enough jackets?"

"Not in the new style."

His mouth twisted. "With the ruffles? It looks ridiculous."

She shrugged, unconcerned at his plight. "You can argue that with Darby if you want. Don't expect them to listen. I will decline to have an opinion."

He nodded, smiling. "Wise decision."

✧

"You saw him?" Delia exclaimed that evening when Ambry told her of their unexpected meeting. They'd come into the room with her dinner to find her reading in bed, but she'd set aside the book to talk. Fortunately, she'd declared herself well enough to return to work the next day. The rest had served her well. Ambry nodded. "He healed my wrist. I'd hurt it while I was fetching supplies for Ella."

She sat up, causing the fat kitchen cat curled by her feet to open one annoyed eye before closing it again and covering it with its striped tail. "Tell me you're making this up."

Ambry shook their head. "It was real. That's what happened." If they'd been making it up, they thought but did not say, they would never have been foolish enough to drift to sleep while waiting in the prince's study. They gestured towards the tray and bowl of soup on her lap. "Eat, before it gets cold."

Delia sighed and twirled the spoon in her fingers. "I will, I will. It's just that I've been up there dozens of times and I've barely even caught a glimpse! He's always in meetings, I suppose. Lucky!"

They were lucky, they agreed with her on that, but not for the reasons she said. Meeting the prince, now that had been indeed a gift. But Isadore covering for their mistake, now, that was what they were truly grateful for. And the healing was a pleasant warm memory they could return to on long, wearying days. They were more proud than ever to serve in the palace now that they knew how the prince cared for even the most minor among them.

"What else happened while I was asleep? Did you saddle a unicorn too?"

They snorted. "Check the stables. His name is Edward." Ambry grinned, pleased with themself. Usually Delia talked far too quickly for them to come up with any clever responses.

Delia grinned back. "Ha! Making jokes too. That's how I know you had a good day."

It had been a good day, Ambry thought, despite the pain and exhaustion with which it had begun. Delia continued talking between bites of soup, asking them about every detail of their day.

"It's beautiful up there. You were right."

"Of course I was. When am I ever wrong?"

They eyed her. "I can think of a few times…"

"Oh, pish. Those don't matter."

"Even the time you baked a cake with salt instead of sugar and Patrice didn't let you back in the kitchen for a month?"

She mimed throwing the half-empty bowl at them. "Forget that happened!" she ordered.

Ambry shrugged dramatically and looked to the ceiling. "What saint decreed I would have perfection as a roommate? I should want to thank them."

"Tell them to send a little more luck my way while you're at it. And a handsome lover. And maybe an extra off-day or two."

"You just spent all day in bed!"

She sighed. "It's not the same when it's because you're ill."

Ambry could agree with that. Delia sopped up the rest of her soup with a hunk of bread and set aside the tray. She curled on her bed with a dog-eared book borrowed from the little library the servants had made for themselves. Ambry made use of it often too, and when they could, contributed a volume or two bought from the little shop in the city. There were books of poetry, a handful of histories, a stack of those flimsy adventure serials sold for a chime or two each month on paper that grew raggedy almost as quickly. But most of the collection was made up of tales of romance. Most were sweet, some almost sickeningly so, but a few were steamy enough to set Ambry's ears burning from only a glance. They'd had their share of secret encounters and youthful sweethearts, but nothing they'd done had been like what was in those pages. Some of their friends liked even stronger stuff, like Marion's treasured Bright Changes: illustrated books that came wrapped in thick paper that somehow made no attempt whatsoever to hide what they were for, but the owners of those traded them in secret and kept them in hidden drawers and at the bottom of clothes-chests where they would not be accidentally stumbled upon.

Ambry would be lying if they tried to claim they'd never looked at those, since they mostly preferred the adventure stories, especially those that involved sailing to magical lands. But there were a few romance authors that had caught their eye. Delia knew, as much as they tried to hide it. She'd surprised them once with a New Year's gift of their favorite author's new series, rebound into a sturdy volume by a friend of hers who worked in the court archives. Sometimes she daydreamed out loud about printing her own tales, but even she knew the archives would never have time or paper to spare for that.

They took that book from the chest at the foot of their small bed and lost themself for a while in the tale of a weaver's apprentice and the noble lady who became enchanted with her work. It was a beautiful story, one that usually sufficed to pull their thoughts away from anything that occupied them. But by the time Delia leaned over to blow out the lamp, their thoughts had turned again to Isadore, and they wondered if they would ever come so close to him again.

Chapter Two

✧

Adrian's letter had been very welcome indeed after a week of ineffective meetings and tedious formalities. It was good to get out of the palace and into the city sometimes. Even with one of his guards not-so-subtly tailing him at all times, there was some freedom to be found out here.

Few people recognized him. Some thought they did, peered at him curiously and whispered to their companions, but they were too uncertain or too shy to say anything aloud. And after a few moments in the busy crowd that filled the streets, they lost their chance to try.

Pleasant days meant the performers came out to beg for a coin in exchange for a cheery song. Jaunty tunes rippled through the square. Children danced to the music as they followed their parents through the streets. At the southwest corner a one-armed street musician played a foreign string instrument with his feet, grinning at the astonished faces of passersby. Isadore walked close enough to drop a five-lind piece into his cup without earning a comment from his guard. The large coin clattered against the pile of smaller one- and two-chime coins he'd earned so far. The musician smiled up at Isadore, winked – did he know? – and played a few snippets of the royal anthem. Which was more than enough to tip off his chaperone as to what he had done.

It was Lawrence on duty today. He was smaller and less noticeable in a crowd than Dominick, but just as quick and strong in combat. Like Dominick, he had known Isadore since he was a child and had transferred from his mother's guard to serve him when he came of age. Unlike Dominick, though, he had not seemed to notice that his charge was no longer a young boy in need of lessons. Lawrence said nothing, but Isadore was sure he was smiling under his mustache.

Isadore made his way through streets strung with lanterns to Adrian's favorite tavern, a stout building tucked down a side street, high-class enough to ensure there was little risk of brawling or of questionable food, but common enough that few would expect to find them there.

Lawrence, of course, would have far preferred he summon Adrian to the palace to dine in private where there would be no chance of their conversation ending up in the pages of Florence Ostberg's next printing. She did try to keep her publication free of petty rumor, but when the public clamored for more, it was difficult to refuse. Her paper, therefore, had earned the unusual distinction of being the favorite of nosy gossips and haughty politicians alike.

Despite the risks, he liked meeting Adrian here for personal business. If they were discussing anything that needed more privacy, he would agree with Lawrence and seek the palace walls, but not today.

He received a knowing nod from the proprietor as he stepped through the door. She knew full well who he was, even if her staff did not, and had many times helped to make sure that secret was kept. She did it out of loyalty, Isadore was confident of that, though the coins he handed over to thank her for her discretion couldn't hurt matters.

Adrian was waiting for him at a table in the back. Isadore slid into a seat, glad to let the rumble of voices wash over him. Here, he could go unnoticed in the flow of people and set his responsibilities aside for a short while. Lawrence took a seat two tables away, keeping Isadore and Adrian in sight, and sipped weak cider under a graying yet still impressive mustache. He would not be permitted to enjoy himself tonight, but Isadore would make sure he had an evening to himself later in the week.

"Well, you look ragged," Adrian said by way of greeting. "Don't tell me you've been working all week straight." He adjusted his blue cap to uncover his eyes. He had his long blond hair tied back today, and his cheeks and chin were shaved clean where most days there was a faint stubble there. If he'd gone to that trouble with his appearance, it usually meant he wished to catch someone's eye. He waved over a serving girl and ordered them hearty steak pies and tall mugs of beer.

"No, but it certainly feels that way. Certain customers are being especially difficult as of late."

Even here where people were unlikely to be listening to the conversation of two seemingly unremarkable young men, it would be unwise to speak directly about delicate political affairs. Adrian and Isadore had long ago devised a code that made it possible to refer to issues without letting secret details slip.

"Hm. Count yourself lucky that it'll be a long time before your mother will hand over the family business." Adrian took a deep swig from his mug. "Father still has me at bookkeeping every day he can. I try to stay out of sight, that way he can't think of more work. Or more lessons. I am so desperately sick of the lessons and tutors and books…"

Privately, Isadore thought Adrian would do well to study more. Perhaps he would not be the expert on trade that his father wished him to be, but even so Adrian had areas he excelled in. Of course, that would require that his father bothered to listen. It was no secret that Lord Tisdale thought his son lazy and far too fond of spending nights with friends and games and lovers. He had kept his grumbling quiet since the previous year, when through his affairs and gossip Adrian had discovered and foiled an attempt on his father's life, but the tension was still there. That incident was still not enough for Tisdale to accept that there was gain to be found in listening to one's fellows and the city gossip, but it had helped.

And it could hardly hurt matters that Adrian was close friends with the heir to the throne. Not that Isadore or Seraphina would ever let that translate to any substantial extra favor, but having the prince's ear could be useful even so.

When the server returned with their pies, she lingered a few moments longer than was strictly needed. And then Isadore caught the coy smile she cast at Adrian.

He raised an eyebrow. "You know her?"

"A little," Adrian said. "She started here last month. Her name is Rose, she likes cherry cakes, and her brother is a lieutenant in the Guard." He smiled, a light coming to his eyes, and added, "But I plan to learn more, if she makes an invitation."

"I wish you luck in that."

"I hope to have it! And you? Has anyone caught your eye?"

"Not recently." In truth, he'd been far too busy to think of such affairs.

"Nobody, truly?"

"I haven't had the time. It isn't like university anymore." It had been so easy then to find eager companions, to enjoy each other without fears of gossip, without the responsibility of his position to shoulder. "I still consider myself lucky my mother isn't troubling me or my sisters about marriage yet."

Adrian laughed. "I'm not talking about marriage. That can come later, and I'm certain you'll find the best wife in the kingdom when it comes time for it."

"So I hope."

"But now isn't the time for that. What about enjoying yourself? And enjoying other people? Have you never danced with a girl at a fair and taken her to a quiet inn after?"

"I think my guards would have a thing or two to say about that," Isadore said, eyeing Lawrence, who, to his great relief, didn't appear to be able to hear their conversation. Or at least was pretending he did not.

"Or swept up a sweet maid from her cleaning and made her squeal with delight?"

"No, saints no." Isadore shook his head. "I would never put anybody into a situation like that." He recoiled from the thought.

"Not to force them. Heavens, not that. But if they wanted it?" Adrian pressed.

"There are any number of reasons why they might not. I cannot risk it."

Adrian laughed. "Do you think so little of yourself? I assure you, there are many people who would dream of sharing a bed with someone like you."

Isadore studied the bubbles in his glass. "It's nothing to do with me, and everything to do with my status." He sighed. "People might believe they have to please me for their own safety, or they might seek to gain favors or learn secrets."

"Do you truly go whispering your secrets to every beauty you meet?" Adrian scoffed. "There's no harm in sharing a little fun where you can find it."

Isadore took a long drink and set his cup down on the table. "I will not do what Cedric did."

Adrian winced at the name. He shook his head. "Cedric was a fool. You're nothing like him. *You* would have seen that Marjorie only tolerated him for the gifts he bestowed to gain her favor."

"Did she even have a choice in the matter? And what good were all those gifts when he left her on the streets with her baby?"

Adrian sighed, and for a moment his eyes drifted somewhere far away. "It was a terrible thing he did. But she's doing well now, isn't she? Better she be in your employ than his."

He nodded. "She is, and her son is thriving." He hadn't even needed to think about that decision. But he would have far preferred it had never been necessary.

"And I'm sure you would do that for any other unfortunate happening."

He would, if it came to that. But he hoped it would not. "I'm still not going to leave some poor girl pregnant."

Adrian hummed. "Find a boy, then? Not to my taste, but I know some who would be interested. That actor, Wake, was it? From the dance comedies they've been playing at the Northwind Theater. Though perhaps you'd prefer someone more discreet."

"Weekes. Nazario Weekes. And I happen to know he's been seen getting cozy with that troublemaker Ellis Hardy." Even if he wasn't, Isadore didn't find his tall bony frame and ostentatious dress attractive in that way, though he certainly could admire him on stage. And he knew Nazario would never keep his mouth shut about an affair with the prince.

"Ah, him," Adrian grumbled, flicking a few crumbs sullenly across the table. "I wouldn't trust him an inch. Bested me out of a good sum of money at cards a few weeks ago. I'm sure he cheated."

"Serves you right, for playing a known trickster." Hardy was known the city over for his bad behavior, and for his cruel friends who pursued darker criminal persuasions at his command. Isadore eyed Adrian suspiciously. "Or you were too deep in your cups to play well?"

He got a snort in reply. "You best me in a set and then see what you have to say."

Isadore pretended to consider it. "A proposition I might take up another day."

"You won't, because you know I'll win."

"That hasn't stopped me playing you before."

"Playing sober. I think of all my best strategies after a few drinks of whatever elixir this place serves." As if inspired, he caught Rose's eye and ordered another round.

She leaned close to Adrian as she set down the brimming mugs and whispered in his ear, not quite softly enough so that Isadore couldn't hear, "Stay until I'm free?"

He caressed her chin, bringing a gentle blush to her cheeks. "Always, for a girl so lovely as you."

Isadore couldn't help but laugh at the glow that lingered in Adrian's face once Rose left to serve the next table. "You really like her," he said, shaking his head.

"I do," Adrian said, none of his characteristic coyness in his voice this time. He finished the last bites of his pie and pushed aside the plate. "You don't need to deny yourself, Isadore. You truly will not take any of those starry-eyed maids who adore you so much?"

Isadore shivered. "I do not even like to imagine it. But…" He grew thoughtful. "But if there was a lord or lady visiting from afar, who wanted nothing other than shared pleasure… that, I would not refuse."

Adrian grinned, raised his cup. "I can drink to that."

✧

"He's not going to, you know," Ella said.

Ambry looked up from their washing. "What?"

She laughed and smacked them with the brush she was soaping. "Take you to bed. In case you were wishing, which I know you are."

Ambry felt their ears go red.

"What's this?" Marion asked. Once a man, for a short while a woman, and now neither of those, they were the only other found-person among the main kitchen staff. The others usually expected them and Ambry to share similar thoughts.

Ambry liked Marion, and the two of them were perfectly friendly, but Ambry still found themself drawn more to Delia and Ella's company. Marion had plenty of other friends in the palace and the city, so Ambry didn't feel guilty about it.

Marion pulled a ribbon from their pocket and tied up their long pale hair into a tail before starting their work. They gave Ambry a conspiratorial grin. "Tell me more."

"Ambry met the prince," Delia said. "Lucky, lucky thing they are. And now they've been having *thoughts.*" She raised her eyebrow and grinned in a way that left no doubt as to what she meant.

Ambry was very glad that the steam hid their face. Were their thoughts truly so transparent? They had thought of it, idly, but no more than that. After Isadore's kindness to them, it did not feel right to use the memory of his gentle touch for something so base as that. Their fellows, though, had no such qualms.

"It's not going to happen," Delia promised. "He's far too proper for that. It's romantic, in a way."

Ella snorted, shook out a dishtowel with a snap of fabric. "Not romantic enough, if there's no bedding involved."

Ambry splashed their hands into the tub to grab another shirt. "No, I wouldn't, I mean– he wouldn't–"

Delia laughed. "You've been dreamy-eyed ever since you saw him. Don't tell me you haven't imagined it."

"Not everyone's as lovestruck as you are, Delia," Patrice sighed as she came through the door. "Give them some space." She thunked a basket of laundry onto the floor. She was right, Ambry thought. For as many of them who adored the prince, there were as many who had their sights set on others, or on nobody at all.

"Marion, pass the scrubbing board," Patrice ordered. They did so, but not before pretending to throw it, making Delia duck. She glared, they laughed. Ambry was glad of the distraction, because if Marion and Delia were arguing, it meant the others were not paying attention to them. Or prodding them for the vague imaginings they had indeed entertained of earning the prince's attention and regard.

Ella shook her head. "He's far too high and mighty for the likes of us."

"No, it's not like that," Marion said, wringing out a cloth into the tub. They shook their head. "It's that he thinks he'd be forcing you."

Delia hummed. "Maybe I wouldn't mind being forced, if it was him."

"It wouldn't be forcing, then, would it?" Ella said, smirking.

Delia tossed her dark hair over her shoulder. "Oh, I don't know. I could wriggle a bit, make him hold me down…"

Patrice rapped on the washtub. "You enjoy your bedplay imaginings on your own time, Delia," she scolded. "Some of us are trying to get work done."

Delia stuck her tongue out. "I can imagine and work at the same time."

"Not unless you want more laundry to do," Marion teased, splashing her with the soapy water.

She spluttered, spitting out suds. "Hey!"

Ambry took Marion's meaning and looked away, remembering trying to pretend that they did not hear her squirming against her hand in her bed at night. Was it Isadore she thought of then?

They were glad Mrs. Hammond wasn't nearby to hear Delia's dreaming. She never spoke of it, but they had heard it whispered more than once that her son was the product of an affair with her previous employer, Lord Farndale, and that he had not been pleased to find out. They shivered at the thought of ever finding themself, or Delia, or any of their friends, in that terrible situation.

"I'm grateful he keeps his hands off of us," Marion said. "I had enough of that with Lord Brennan."

Ambry winced. While their own previous employer, Lady Mohren, had certainly been unkind, nobody in her household had targeted the servants in that way.

Delia sniffed. "Doesn't harm no one if I dream."

"Enough," Patrice ordered. "You've got more to do after the washing, so best get to it."

Delia and Marion silently kept up their argument for a while longer, exchanging mouthed words and raised eyebrows, but they soon tired of it and joined the others' conversation, which had turned, to Ambry's relief, to town gossip. Ordinary things good for a laugh and whispered guessing, things that did not force them to think of how they viewed the prince or what they might want from him in their most secret thoughts.

"Brennan's going to get what's coming to him eventually," Ella said. "Or you could say he already has. Did you hear about what happened at the Spring Festival?"

"Who hasn't?" Marion snorted. "Word is he tried to fondle a dancer's bosom and got kicked in the stones for his troubles."

"And then got drunk as a brined duck to take the sting out of it," Patrice continued, showing she was not above the gossip she derided, "and fell over in the field like a brain-smashed foal."

Ella smirked, a dangerous expression on her usually steady face. "I heard he pissed himself too."

Marion crowed. "Oh, that's too sweet. Wish I could have seen it. Maybe he'll try it again in the summer and fall off the tower or something and do himself in."

"It's a nice dream," Ella said. "But I'd rather look at what's real instead of chasing after wild unicorns. And what's real is he's made such a fool of himself I doubt he'll be hosting any festival celebrations for a long time yet."

Patrice nodded agreement. "As Hammond says, unicorns won't get the cleaning done, or the shopping, or the baking."

"On that note," Ella said, pulling her hands from the water and toweling them off, "I've got a hankering for some sweets. If someone else does the washing up afterwards, I'll make currant buns for tonight."

"I can do it," Ambry said. Washing dishes was simple and mindless enough, and Ella tended to give her helpers first pick warm from the oven.

"I'll help," Delia added. She winked at Ambry, who braced themself for yet another round of questions and innuendo. At least this time it would come with Ella's currant buns, which were certainly sweet enough to make nearly anything worthwhile.

As it turned out, they didn't need to worry. Whether by virtue of her distractibility or because she had taken pity on them, Delia spent most of the evening telling them about a new serial she was reading, a tale about teachers at a magic school in the neighboring kingdom of Arrawey.

Ambry listened politely even though they knew none of these characters or anything of their stories. Delia promised to lend them the first two issues just as soon as she got them back from a friend. They enjoyed listening anyway, both hearing her enthusiasm and trying to puzzle out the plot of the books from what details she shared.

Ella swept through the kitchen to retrieve the tray from the oven. The smell when she set it on the table was heavenly, all butter and fruit and sweetness. As promised, Delia and Ambry got to snag their treats before she piled the rest into a basket to take out to the others. They grinned at each other as they juggled the hot buns from hand to hand, nibbling bites where they could. The taste was worth the burned fingers.

⇧

The treaty negotiations were not going well. After nearly three years, Larsellan and Arrawey at least had agreed to the core proposals, but Kivern did not and was refusing to budge, and continued to quarrel with Arrawey on the last details of their deal. Which was only one small piece of the whole. Which all four countries wanted this finished by the end of the summer if it was going to be finished at all. But none of them seemed certain of that, despite the bravado that filled their letters.

Isadore had spent most of the day in meetings with ambassadors and advisors. This was only the second such treaty he had handled on his own, and he was determined to satisfy his mother. He'd known for years how crucial this treaty was, and yet it all felt rather pointless, like going around in circles with a blindfold on while leaving real issues unsolved. But Seraphina was counting on him, as were numerous ministers, and the people of Talland who would gain greatly from the new trade agreements. If they could finish the text and get the other parties to agree, that was.

Not for the first time, he and Melanie worked late into the night on the mountain of documents and letters that seemed to grow rather than shrink as they drew papers from it. The teapot had long since gone cold, and neither of them had pulled themselves away from the papers long enough to refill it.

"I swear Grenner writes his letters to be as impenetrable as possible," he grumbled.

"Of course," Melanie snorted. "He thinks it makes him look intelligent. How else would he keep his post except by convincing Queen Frida that he knows absolutely everything in the world?"

"It makes him look like a stuck-up obnoxious—"

A knock on the door. Markus peered in a moment later. "Melanie?"

She raised her head, brushed hair out of her eyes. "What is it?"

"Sarah and I found some interesting things. Records from a few decades ago when Larsellan tried a similar arrangement to the Atworth Proposal. But Minerva doesn't want them to leave the archive. Can you come down?"

Isadore might be the prince, but within Talland's archives, Minerva Corey's words were law.

Melanie didn't argue. "I'll be right there." She capped her pen and passed her notebook to Isadore. "Here, take these. I've gotten through most of the Fira Weln treatise he wrote a few years ago. It's not much, but it might help us get a better idea of his priorities." She lifted her cane from its place by the desk. She used her chair most of the time, but sometimes she would walk when she had the stamina to manage it.

He nodded. "Go on, I can keep reading here." And tomorrow would be yet another conference with their own ambassador before she rode back to Kivern with their newest set of proposals. He wondered how long it would be this time before Queen Frida refused them.

Unfortunately, Talland was not in the best of positions to argue with Kivern. For better or for worse, Queen Frida tended to weigh her personal opinions of other leaders heavily in deciding how willing she was to negotiate on such agreements. She was still angry with King Daragh of Arrawey for refusing a marriage between their children five years ago. And she was even less friendly with Queen Seraphina, for reasons that Seraphina had never completely explained to Isadore. He wondered sometimes if that was because she had a role to play in it. She could sometimes admit her faults in personal matters, something she had taught Isadore to do as well, but she was utterly firm in political matters, never admitting weakness or blame. That manner had gained her many admirers, and many opponents.

But Isadore was determined to find a way through to all of them. He kept at it, reading and rereading, filling papers with notes until his wrist ached. He eased it with a touch, which only added to his growing fatigue. Any one of Melanie's staff could have acted as scribe, but he'd far rather have them at work in the archives and spare himself the dry throat from dictating. If only Lacey were here to assist him. Something as simple as bringing him tea before he thought to ask or having ready all the papers and pens and seals he might need to use, small things like that, would have made this far more bearable.

He could of course summon any one of the servants to assist and nobody would challenge him, but he didn't want to draw them from their work all the way to the heir's tower for what could no doubt be an awkward situation. He knew full well that he was prone to showing his frustration when he was tired, and he didn't want to inflict that on anyone who wasn't used to it. Melanie deflected it with jokes when it happened, but he still cursed himself every time. And as much as it pained him to criticize them, the servants had a tendency to gossip, and much of the things he and Melanie worked on were things that for various reasons needed to be kept quiet. So he continued on his own, occasionally sipping the cold tea when he forgot that it had gone cold.

Sometime later, he pulled himself from the work, rubbed his sore eyes and cramping neck. He turned, and saw Dominick still standing there at the door, quiet and proper as always. Yet there was tension in his form, and pain. He had been on duty since the morning, Isadore realized with a sharp pang of guilt. Dominick saw him looking and said nothing. But Isadore had known him long enough to know that his silence did not mean all was well. He took a breath and let the vision come to him, though summoning it only added to his growing headache. He saw the aching weight of exhaustion behind Dominick's eyes, a dry throat and empty stomach, and, most urgently, a desperately full bladder just beginning to threaten humiliation with tight surges of need. He gave Dominick leave to take care of that last, and the flush of embarrassed gratitude on his face when he returned shamed Isadore. If he had not seen, how long would he have forced Dominick to stand there, forbidden to rest or eat or even to relieve himself?

Isadore set down his pen and turned to Dominick, hoping too much of his concern did not show on his face. "How long have you been on duty?"

Dominick lowered his head and gave his answer. Far too long, Isadore thought. He winced.

"Where is your alternate?" And cursed himself that he was not certain whether it was Sylvia or Lawrence who ought to be on duty now. His guards shuffled their schedules often, for security purposes they said, so that an assassin could not learn their patterns. Isadore thought it entirely unnecessary, but for once in his life this was something he did not command and could not hope to. So, he let them rotate around him like so many distant moons and did not interfere. But even if it was not his to manage, at the very least he should keep track of his protectors' ways.

"Ill, today," Dominick said, expressionless. He hadn't heard. He should have asked.

"And no time to assign another?"

Dominick tilted his head, the closest he ever got to a shrug. "If the armsmaster has, he has not come."

"When will the next shift arrive?"

"Another hour. It will be no trouble for me to serve that time."

Isadore did not argue, for to do so would be to question Dominick's competence and his ability and Isadore would not do that to him. A few moments of silence passed between them. And then Isadore asked, "Would you have said anything?"

"Highness?"

"Would you have asked for relief?" He had needed it badly enough to warrant it.

Dominick glanced away. "When the right moment came. I did not wish to interrupt your work."

Confronting him on it would only make him uncomfortable. But Isadore needed to know he understood. "For your needs, you are more than allowed." He all but owned this man, he would treat him well. How could he be worthy of his position if he did not?

"I understand. Thank you." Dominick straightened his back and returned to his watch, and Isadore pressed him no further. All of them, Dominick, Sylvia, Lawrence, even old Theodora who had guarded him as a babe and retired before he moved to the heir's tower, they gave so much of themselves to him. They deserved to be cared for in return, and to not be put in unneeded pain.

Melanie came in with another sheaf of papers in her hands, leaving him no more time to consider it.

Chapter Three

✧

Spring flew onwards, warming as it went, and as the season blossomed, so too did the work. The warmth gave them the chance to work outside, to bring larger things out to the courtyard to wash. To pack away the heavy winter things and bring out lighter ones for summer.

Ambry didn't see the prince again in those weeks. They hadn't expected to, now that Delia was back on her mail shift for Kieran. Though there was the day that she told them Melanie had asked after them. Their heart lifted – they hadn't thought she would remember or have any reason to think of them. Delia had smiled, eyeing them in that searching way she had, and mentioned that there had been whispers that Isadore was looking among the servants for a new assistant. But that had been over a week ago, and since then Ambry had tried to move their thoughts on to other things. If none of Melanie's staff were suited for the job, maybe Isadore would choose Delia to work with him. How she would love that!

Today was one of those valuable sorts of days where there were no visitors to prepare for, the laundry loads were light, and the gardens plentiful. The sort of day that could be used for mending and cooking, and preparation for future days that might not be as gentle. Mrs. Hammond was away today, visiting the city with her young son Jonah. As the oldest and longest-serving of the staff, Patrice had taken command in her absence, shouting commands from her place in the kitchen, and the others scurried to obey.

Ambry was just finishing packing away the blue-edged winter dishes into boxes and replacing them in the cabinets with the flower-patterned ones for spring when Erik came in from the gardens with the vegetable hamper piled high with peas and lettuce and radishes. Ella and Danny were busy at the stove preparing large pots of jam from the delicate early berries. It was a specialty of the palace, loved by everyone from the Queen to the gardeners, and they always made as much as they could. Ambry could smell it from across the kitchen. They hoped there would be enough to grace the servants' tables through the next winter. They could survive waking in the dark if it meant they could enjoy fresh warm bread with sweet jam.

Patrice walked past, noted their progress in a slim book that she slipped into her apron pocket. "Delia, Ambry, start polishing the silver. Danny, take those first jars into the cellar and put them on the back shelf."

Danny, a gangly and cheerful man who had gained Patrice's eternal favor by speaking little and complaining less, nodded at her order. With quick motions of his bony hands, he packed the sealed jars away neatly into wooden boxes, stacked them, and gathered them and their precious contents into his arms.

One of the kitchen cats twined around his ankles. Patrice shooed it away. "Get out before you trip him up, little furball," she scolded.

"Come on," Delia prompted, pulling Ambry's attention back to their own work. "If we take the tub out to the yard, we can enjoy the sun while we work. And maybe Patrice will forget about us." She winked.

"I heard that, Delia!" Patrice called, but she was smiling. "Don't think you can get away with that silly tactic, not under my watch."

Delia ignored her. "Let's go."

She and Ambry lifted the tub together and brought it out to fill at the pump.

"Are you going to go to the Spring Festival?" she asked as they worked the pump.

"I hadn't thought about it." There'd been so much work, they'd barely had time to think about what they'd do on their rare free days. The seasonal festivals were often louder and busier than Ambry was comfortable with. But they always enjoyed watching the lights at night, hearing their friends' stories afterward and sharing their treats. "I hope so."

"I'm saving up for a new dress and earrings," Delia said as she spread a dishtowel on the stones and laid out the silverware. "Maybe I can find a dancing partner this time."

Erik, pushing the wheelbarrow behind them, laughed aloud. "What, you're giving up on being Princess Delia?" He mimed an elegant curtsy that might have suited a fine court lady a hundred years ago.

She shook a finger at him. "Oh, you just wait."

"Would rather not, else I'll be waiting a very long time!" He continued on with the wheelbarrow towards the gardens without turning to see the faces Delia made at his back.

Ambry resisted sighing. Delia's humor didn't irritate them as much as it did Erik and Patrice. Without her, their daily work would be a lot more tedious.

"I wonder who he's going to choose for that, when it comes time," Ambry pondered.

"I've heard it might be a princess or noble's daughter from Arrawey," Delia said. "You know, to celebrate the bond between the kingdoms or something like that. I wonder if she would bring her own staff."

"It could be someone from Arrawey," Ambry agreed. "It's not as if their child would be heir anyhow. The throne passes through the closest female relative, so even when Isadore's king, the heir would be Abigail's or Celeste's oldest."

"It's still romantic."

Ambry dipped their cloth in the tin of polish and picked up a candlestick. "I hope she's friendly."

"I hope she's pretty!"

Ambry laughed. "You're not the one marrying her."

"You never know, I might marry a princess. That'll make me a princess too, which'll be just as nice as—" She was cut off by a tremendous crash that rang out from the hall.

Delia jumped. "What was that?"

Ambry dropped the cloth and ran with her towards the source of the sound – the door to the kitchen cellar. They gasped aloud at what they saw there. Danny lay in a crumpled heap at the foot of the stairs, the boxes of jars he'd been carrying now a splintered mess on the steps behind, jagged shards of glass gruesome with golden springberry jam.

Ambry rushed down the steps and crept close to his fallen body as the others hurried around and drew back in horror at the sight of the blood that soaked his pale hair and dripped onto the stones of the floor.

Delia, following beside them, shook his shoulder and got no response.

"Don't move him!" Patrice snapped, hurrying in from the kitchen with Ella and Marion following behind. "And don't crowd around. Give me space." She swept her skirt out of the way and knelt at his head, examining the wound there with practiced fingers. The others waited in silence, fearing the worst.

"He's breathing, at least," she announced, after too many painful moments of waiting. "But this is bad. Give me a cloth."

Ella scrambled to untie her still-clean apron. Patrice wadded it up and held it to Danny's head, trying to staunch the bleeding.

"What do we do?" Delia asked, white with shock.

"I don't think there's anything we can do," Patrice said, and the fear in her voice sent shivers down Ambry's back. "If he doesn't wake…"

And then the memory of a warm touch on their wrist came to them. "The prince," they said. "He can help."

"What are you doing? You can't possibly expect–" Ella protested, but Ambry was already running. Through the back hallways, pushing past the pages with their mail pouches, the maids carrying linens and laundry baskets. They pounded up the stairs towards Isadore's study, slowing their pace only enough so that they would not risk sharing Danny's fate.

The guard at the door, a woman this time, tall and broad and no less intimidating than Dominick, barred their way. "What is your purpose?" she demanded, when she saw they had no letters in their hands. "The prince is very busy today and should not be interrupted."

Ambry coughed, struggling to catch their breath. They might well be punished for this, but it would be worth it if Isadore would aid them. "Someone's hurt, I need help…"

The door was open; they peered past the guard to where Isadore sat across from Melanie, the two of them working through a tremendous stack of letters and papers.

The guard stepped forward, forcing them back. They went cold, stomach clenching. This had been a mistake. How could they have thought they could simply pull the Prince of Talland from his duties to help an injured servant?

But they had to try. "Please, we need–"

Isadore looked up in alarm. "Sylvia, what is it? Let them in. Ambry?"

Sylvia moved aside without protest. Ambry stepped into the room, sparing only a moment to wonder that Isadore had remembered their name, and nearly lost their breath again under his eyes. They managed to speak again for Danny's sake. "Your Highness, I'm sorry, we need help. Danny fell down the cellar stairs, he's bleeding and he's not moving. He hit his head and we can't wake him."

Isadore was already on his feet before Ambry could even finish the sentence. "Take me there."

Ambry remembered little of the journey back, only the pounding of footsteps behind them and the little gasps of surprise from those they passed on their way back to the cellar. And the fear that they would be too late for even Isadore's gifts to do any good.

Voices echoed up the stairs: Patrice and Erik, arguing.

"I can go for a doctor in the city," Patrice was saying.

"That'll take too long. We need to carry him there."

"And addle his brains even more? No! We can't mo—"

She fell silent mid-word when Isadore stepped into the doorway and hurried down the steps with Sylvia close behind, deftly avoiding the broken glass under his feet.

"What—" Ella began, before Patrice shushed her and herded the servants out of Isadore's way.

He knelt on the stone floor and lifted Danny's head into his lap, heedless of the blood that dripped down to stain his fine clothes. Isadore set his fingers against the wounds, bent over until his forehead almost touched Danny's, and then there was a long, long stretch of silence in which none of them dared speak, only watched their prince at his work and prayed for his success.

Ambry had begun to fear all hope was lost when at last Isadore gasped a breath and raised his head. Danny stirred faintly under his touch, as though dreaming. Isadore pulled his hands away, set Danny's head gently back down onto Ella's requisitioned apron, and moved to sit on the bottom step out of the way as the servants moved to examine Danny.

"There. He'll be well when he wakes, but a day or two of rest will do him good."

Patrice drew a deep breath of relief, as did no few of the others. She was the first to speak, drawing herself up before bowing her head in respect. "Highness. Thank you. We cannot say enough how grateful—"

Isadore raised his hand. "There is no need. Tend to him well, and that will be enough for me. Please send word if there are any more issues." He paused for a moment, and then asked her, "What is your name?"

She straightened her apron. "Patrice, Highness."

"Patrice, tell me, what happens when one of you is hurt or ill? Is there nobody you can consult?"

She lifted her chin. "We tend to ourselves, Highness, and share the work when it's needed." She hesitated, as if weighing the risk of saying more. Isadore waited, until she drew herself up yet again and said, making no attempt to keep the bitterness from her voice, "There was a doctor once, but he was lost to his bottles half the time and chasing the maids the rest. Mrs. Hammond sent him away two years ago."

"I see. And there has been none since?"

"No, Highness. There are healers in the city who will treat us, for a cost, but it is a difficult trip to manage when there is work to be done."

Isadore's mouth tightened, a barely noticeable thing Ambry only noticed because they hadn't looked away from his face since they returned. "I understand. Thank you."

Patrice stood staring at him for half a moment, and then nodded. She and Erik lifted Danny together and carried him towards the dormitory. Ella, ever practical, fetched a brush to scrub away the blood and set Delia to sweeping up the glass and jam. Ambry managed to pull themself away for long enough to fetch a damp towel so Isadore could clean the blood from his fingers. He took it mechanically and silently, as if his thoughts were leagues away.

One by one, the others who had gathered, whether to gawk at Danny's injury or to catch a glimpse of the prince, scattered back to their work, but something held Ambry in place. Did none of them see the strain in Isadore's eyes? He still sat on the step, breathing hard, as if he'd been running all day. Several of his glittering hairpins had come askew, colors winking in and out of the dark waves, but he didn't seem to notice. And then he stood and stumbled. Ambry moved to support his arm without even thinking. Isadore took the assistance without a word, and only a cough from Sylvia warned Ambry of the impropriety of what they were doing. They stepped back, as Sylvia reached out to help.

Isadore waved her away. "It's all right, Sylvia. I can manage." He looked to Ambry. "Come with me." And with that Isadore set off up the stairs, Sylvia close by his side. Ambry followed. If they were not in trouble... what did Isadore want of them?

Isadore was silent as they walked the halls. The main halls, not the tight servants' passages. If Ambry were walking alone, they might have dared to pause to study the tapestries and paintings that decorated the walls, but the prince's pace left no time for that. He brought them through the dining room where the royal family took their private meals, along a curving veranda that offered a beautiful view of the gardens, through another passage lined with artworks, past a supply elevator that served the tower, and up an elegant stair.

Melanie waited for them in Isadore's study with a pot of tea, a crock of honey, and three cups. Had she expected Ambry to return beside Isadore? She didn't press them for news. No doubt she could read in their faces that it had at least not been a tragedy, and she could wait for further details.

Isadore accepted the cup she offered and drank deeply before he spoke. "That was bad, but I was able to treat him in time. He'll be fine, with some rest."

Melanie nodded. "That's good. I'm glad."

Isadore wasn't done. "Have a doctor sent to the servants' dormitory tomorrow morning. And I want to arrange to have one in residence there against future need. A competent one, not a drunken lech," he added, an edge to his voice that might have been frightening if it had not been in the servants' defense. "And arrange a meeting with Marjorie Hammond later this week."

"As you command," Melanie murmured, smiling, and wrote something in her notebook.

A doctor could not have saved Danny, Ambry had no illusions about that. But a doctor could provide much future aid for the minor injuries and illnesses that the palace staff suffered in the course of their work. Ambry had been lucky enough never to meet the man Patrice had described, but they had heard Delia speak disparagingly of his wandering hands and his lecherous winks. That Isadore cared, that learning of it had upset him so, that was something Ambry could not have expected. They thanked whatever spirits had pushed them from their frozen horror and made them run for Isadore's help.

But it was done. Danny was safe, and Isadore had work to return to. Ambry stood awkwardly in the center of the room, unsure of what to do.

"Sit, drink," Isadore prompted, gesturing with an unsteady hand. After a moment's hesitation, they took the second cup from Melanie and joined him on the couch.

For a while there was nothing but the sound of Melanie's pen and the taste of sweet lemon tea. Did the prince expect them to talk? Finally, Isadore turned to Ambry, who paused under the force of his attention.

"Ambry. You did very well. You saved a life today."

Ambry shook their head. That credit didn't belong to them. "You healed him."

"And if I had been any later in arriving," Isadore said, serious and solemn, "I don't believe I could have saved him. But you kept yourself steady, you came and found me, and you insisted I help. Without that, I could not have done what I did."

He meant it. A small glow of pride lit in Ambry's chest, all the brighter for who it was who had praised them. Mostly, though, they felt relief, and gratitude.

And then Isadore's expression grew darker, and he asked, "What other problems are there that I don' t know of?"

Ambry hesitated. "Highness?"

"If I cannot manage my household to any appreciable degree, how can I hope to manage my kingdom?" The bitterness in his voice shocked Ambry.

Melanie spoke next, saving Ambry from having to search for answers to that most strange of questions. "That's why you have housekeepers and secretaries and advisors. And…" she turned a meaningful look at Ambry, "…assistants."

Ambry blinked, tried to hide their confusion in a sip of tea, and barely avoided choking on it.

Isadore sighed again. "I'm sorry. I don't mean to press you. I only wish to do the best for you and all the rest who serve in the palace."

Ambry swallowed, searched for words. How strange it was, to have the prince looking to them for advice. They had to do this right. "Highness. Our jobs are good, most of the time. We're well cared for here. It would be good to have more hands for the work…" They fiddled with their royal badge as they spoke, twisting the little golden thing back and forth.

Isadore nodded. "I will see that more are hired."

"And many of the kitchen and laundry things are worn out."

"Then you will have new ones."

Perhaps they were a little light-headed from the drama of the day, because that could be the only reason they dared to add, a hitherto-unknown mischief touching their voice, "…and we'd all like berry cream cakes every day?"

Melanie barked a laugh, surprisingly loud in the small room. Apparently, Ambry had startled her. They didn't know whether to feel proud or embarrassed about that.

Isadore smiled, eyes bright after the dullness that his labor had put into them. He seemed to relax for the first time since Ambry had arrived breathless at his door. "That might unfortunately be beyond my means. But we can see."

Ambry found themself smiling too, partly at the joke and partly at how the prince had cheered and how the exhausted tension in his face had eased. It felt good to help Isadore, even a little, after what he had done for them. Isadore stood, walked to the bookshelf, and studied one of the figures there. A stag wearing a tiny crown, with a rabbit sitting on its back and birds perched in its branching horns.

And then he turned to them again, and Ambry could not look away from the intensity in his gaze. "You have shown yourself strong of mind today, and quick of action," he said. Ambry would never have described themself such, not with the fears that preyed almost constantly on any comfort they could find. But if Isadore thought so, how could they not believe him? "I've been looking for someone with those traits." Was that what Melanie had meant? No, he couldn't possibly want them as an assistant. "I need someone I can trust to be honest and discreet. You might be summoned at odd hours. And I will need you to be able to tell me when you believe I am following the wrong path." Ambry's mouth went dry even as their heart leapt. "If you prefer your current post, I will not push you. I won't demand an answer now. I can give you time to consider it–"

"Yes. I'll do it." Ambry accepted before their fears could get the better of them.

Isadore blinked. "Truly?"

Ambry nodded. "Yes. It's an honor."

"Good." Isadore smiled. "I'll make arrangements for your things to be moved."

"Moved?" Everything was happening so quickly.

"It'll be easier if you're closer to the tower. And you might have to deal with sensitive documents, so it'll be better if you're not in the dormitory. Is that all right?"

"Yes, that's fine." Their few possessions could probably fit into one trunk, so moving wouldn't be too great a difficulty. They would miss Delia and the others, but they knew they would be an absolute fool to refuse this. And Delia would never forgive them if they did.

"You won't be completely removed from them," Isadore reassured them. "But most of your work will be with me. It won't be all glamorous work either. A lot of everyday things in between the interesting ones." Even everyday things could be interesting, Ambry thought, if done in this beautiful tower to help their prince in his duties.

They found their voice again. "I understand."

Isadore smiled. "Right then. Report here tomorrow morning after breakfast, and we can start."

Ambry bowed and departed, and as they passed under Sylvia's watchful eyes again, they could have sworn she gave them an approving nod.

✦

Isadore sighed and dropped back onto the couch, leaning his head back against the cushions. They had been lucky today, very lucky. A few minutes more and… he did not want to think about it. But he must, for that was what would happen if his people were not properly cared for. Today had proven what a poor job he had done of that so far. He thought back to Ambry asleep on this very seat, their exhaustion and their aching sprained wrist, and vowed that nobody in Talland's royal palace would have to suffer without respite again. He would make certain Marjorie knew that she and her staff could seek his aid and fear no reprisals for doing so.

His head ached from the effort he'd expended in mending Danny's cracked skull. But he welcomed the pain. This was the first thing he'd done in weeks that felt useful, that directly helped another, had a result he could see rather than waiting months more for dry reports from advisors that might or might not indicate that some policy or other had helped some situation halfway across the kingdom. He knew the importance of such things, and valued it, but it was good to do smaller, closer things as well.

Patrice's words echoed in his thoughts. And his teachers', scolding him for being so improper as to subject Ambry to their prince's half-rhetorical ramblings, which they surely did not want or need to listen to.

"Isadore." Melanie's voice roused him from his darkening thoughts. "You've done well. Far, far more than most in your position would. It's not your job to supervise every movement in the palace."

That didn't matter. "I will not have my people preyed on. They should be safe within these walls."

"And they shall be. But you should not blame yourself for things that happened years ago that you had no knowledge of or control over."

She was right, but part of him resisted still. "I should have known. Or at least asked."

She shook her head. "Marjorie took care of it."

"After how long?"

"It does nobody any good to fret over it." How could she say it so coolly?

"This is important!" he snapped before he could stop himself.

Melanie, very deliberately, set down her papers and pen. "Believe me, Isadore, I understand. I've met my share of perverts. They'll chase anyone they can, daft knees or not." He fell silent under her piercing eyes. "You're doing the right thing. But you can't change the past."

He forced himself to be calm again. It wouldn't be fair to her if he didn't. "Melanie, I'm sorry. It's… it's just hard to hear."

"I know. It's hard for me to hear too. And it means the world to me that you care. But I also know that it will only hurt you to look at the past. Even the saints can't change what has already happened. You must look to the future and use your energy there, for good. And let us who serve you help in that." And now, he had another to help him. He had no doubt Ambry would prove a very good assistant.

"You're right. And I should thank you for it more than I do."

She tilted her head, smiling, "Oh, you do plenty, though I wouldn't object to more."

He eyed the papers on her desk. "The treaty…" The mere thought of reading through all that tiresome language yet again set his head pounding anew.

Melanie pulled the papers closer to her. "I can finish reviewing it and have notes for you when I'm done. We'll need another few days to work out everything Kivern has managed to weasel in here in any case." She watched him for a few moments, giving him the strange sensation that she could see right through him to everything he tried to hide. "You need to rest. I don't need your magic to know you're near to falling over and your head is aching something terrible right now."

This time, he didn't try to argue. A few moments to gather his energy, and then he stood. His head spun when he rose, proving her right. Gratefully, he opened the side door and headed through the corridor, climbed the steps to his bedroom with Sylvia following behind. He pulled the curtains to darken the room, undressed and unpinned his hair, and climbed into bed, trying to shake the feeling that he should be doing more. Easing his headache with his own magic took several long minutes, after which he could do nothing but fall into a dazed sleep.

Chapter Four

✧

Personal assistant to Prince Isadore! How had they come into such fortune? Why had he chosen them, of all people? Whatever the reason, they must not fail. Visions came to them of foolish mistakes, Isadore shaking his head and casting them away in disappointment, visions that quickened their breath and clenched their heart. But they forced that down, for it could do them no good to dwell on what might go wrong. They would need to put all their focus into learning what was right.

The rest of that day passed in a daze, a forgettable series of tasks performed while their mind danced elsewhere. The rest of the staff were subdued after Danny's accident, so there was little of the usual chatter and gossip in the air to distract them from their thoughts.

Delia nearly burst out of her skin with delight when they told her of their assignment. "Oh! That's incredible. I'm so happy for you."

It wasn't quite the reaction they'd expected. "I thought you'd be jealous."

"Oh, I am," she replied, rather bluntly, "but I'm also happy. I know you'll be good at it." In a conspiratorial whisper, she added, "You'll have to tell me everything. And all those delicious secrets!"

They shook their head. "I don't know if I'll be allowed to see anything that's secret."

She shrugged. "What else are assistants for? If you're around royalty long enough, you'll learn secrets. That's just how it happens."

Maybe she was right. But they didn't want to get their hopes up that this would be anything more special than cleaning and fetching. If they did somehow come into possession of any secrets, they thought, if they were trusted enough for that, they would protect them with their life.

Somehow, they slept that night, though it was a tentative thing punctuated by uneasy dreams of failure at tasks they could not understand, and with still stranger dreams of Isadore drawing them close, running his hands through their curls and stripping the thin shirt from their chest, pressing warm touches along their body until they hummed all over with the heat of it.

Ambry blushed at the thought when they woke and pushed the memories into some faraway recess of their mind where they could not trouble them in their work. They dressed in their cleanest clothes and joined the early shift at the breakfast table and ate without tasting. When the plates were clean, they climbed the stairs to Isadore's study, heart fluttering in their chest. They pushed aside the curtain, ready to announce themself to the guard there, only to find the door open and unprotected.

"Come in," Melanie called, as if she'd been waiting for them. Uneasily, Ambry stepped inside. Melanie smiled apologetically at them from behind a tall stack of books and thread-bound reports. "Isadore's been delayed. There was an urgent courier from one of the governors. He sends his regrets – he'll probably be a few hours yet."

"Oh." Maybe they should have been relieved that they'd have a chance to learn their role before Isadore could judge their work, but they were only disappointed.

"It happens," she added, sympathetically. "He really did want to be here to see you."

Ambry nodded. "That's all right. Er, what should I do?" Of course, they scolded themself silently. The Prince had far more important duties to attend to than leading a new assistant around by the hand.

"I can get you started. He'll be pleased if he comes back and finds some of the work done already."

That was enough to lift their hopes and straighten their shoulders. "Yes, I'm ready." If there was a chance of impressing Isadore, they would take the challenge and hope to prove equal to it.

Melanie rolled herself out from the desk and led them over to the bookshelf. "I've been meaning to go through these, but it never seems to be the right time. I want you to look through the books and pull out any that need repairs."

Ambry nodded. "I can do that."

"Isadore sometimes leaves his notes in the books. If you find any, don't take out the papers, but set the books aside on that table." She motioned to an elegant wooden desk at the side of the room. It hadn't been used much, judging by the flawless shine of the polished surface.

"I understand."

"Good. Don't hesitate to ask if there's any issues."

She returned to her work, leaving Ambry to start pulling books from the shelf. Most of the books had been very well kept, with no stains or tears or other damage under the fine bindings. They searched the spines one by one for signs of insects and fortunately found none. Ella's father ran a printing shop in the city and she had told them how often he complained about how difficult those were to be rid of. They did find a few books where the glue was starting to come apart or the threads of the binding had snapped and stacked those on one side of the little table.

Ambry couldn't help but admire the collection as they worked. Some of the books were tightly printed, some lavishly illustrated. There was philosophy both ancient and new, books on architecture and war and politics, histories of

Talland and of neighboring Arrawey, Kivern, and Larsellan. Not all of them were in languages Ambry recognized.

Every so often they would come across folded pieces of notepaper tucked between the pages, covered in Isadore's tidy handwriting. They hoped there were no secrets hidden in these papers that they were not supposed to see, for it was difficult to keep from reading bits and pieces of Isadore's commentary, even if most of it was an unrecognizable blur of names and dates and the sorts of words they had only seen before in the most tedious pages of the city broadsheets.

They were tugging a heavy volume from a shelf just above their head when it knocked into one of the little wooden figures and sent it tumbling to the floor. It struck the floor hard and broke into three pieces. Ambry choked back a curse and knelt to gather them up, heart pounding. So much for impressing the prince. Maybe they could pay for it, or mend it somehow...

"Oh, you've found the puzzle?"

Ambry jumped. They spun to face Isadore, who was watching them with amusement on his face.

"I'm so sorry. I knocked it off the shelf." Worry surged through them again. Isadore only smiled and held out his hand to take the pieces.

"You haven't done anything wrong. It's a puzzle, it's supposed to come apart." With a deft twist of his long fingers, he slid the three parts together again. "Not such a challenge once you know how to do it, but it's beautifully made." Now that they knew, they could see the smooth edges on each part.

Melanie snorted. "Not a challenge? As I recall, you were fidgeting with that thing for weeks before you could get it to work."

"As I said, it's very well made."

Ambry found their breath again. They silently blessed their luck as they waited for Isadore's command.

"I think that's enough of the books for now. Can you take the ones that need repairs down to the archives?"

"Yes, Highness."

"I'll have someone show you the quick way," Melanie said. She reached over and pulled a bell cord. One of her assistants arrived at the inner door a few moments later, a young woman with her black hair cut short. "Sarah, can you take Ambry to the archives?"

"Of course." Sarah turned to Ambry. "Come this way." She hurried off at a pace Ambry was hard-pressed to follow, back through the side door, around a curving corridor, and down another set of steps. She continued through the servants' passage behind the guest chambers until finally they reached a door that opened onto a small room tight with shelves. The air was noticeably dry, and all the lamps were carefully shielded.

"Here you are," Sarah said. "Better remember it, the prince sent Lacey for boxes from the archives all the time."

"Lacey?"

"His old assistant. You didn't know her?" She laughed. "Guess that's a good thing, means you don't know what you've got to live up to. He's been missing her ever since she married that chef from Kivern and moved to the shore to open an inn."

Ambry swallowed. Of course they couldn't measure up to that. But they could do the best they could, and hope Isadore found it to be enough. They turned to look for an archivist, and when they glanced back, Sarah was gone.

"Are you looking for someone?" The woman who had spoken was sitting at a table studying a sheet of paper pressed under glass.

"I– yes. Prince Isadore sent me with some books that need mending." They held out the stack. The woman pulled off the thin gloves she was wearing and took the books, turning each over carefully to study the bindings.

"I see. Hmm, this shouldn't take more than a few days. We'll send word when we're done. Thank you." It was clearly a dismissal, so Ambry retraced the path Sarah had taken, trying to commit it to memory as they walked. A guard waited at the door when they returned, not Dominick or Sylvia but a short man with a large mustache on his lip and larger blade at his belt. He eyed Ambry from under bushy brows and waved them into the room.

"Good, good," Isadore said when they reported back. He motioned for Ambry to follow him back through the side door. "I should show you the other rooms up here."

There were far more little spaces nested into the tower than Ambry had expected. The curving passage spiraled up the tower, letting out onto maybe half a dozen large rooms, each of which seemed to have several little hallways tucked away that led to hidden spaces. Isadore led them through the storage rooms and then the series of small chambers where Melanie's staff worked copying documents, writing letters, and reading through ancient laws. They wondered for a moment how she navigated the levels when she used her chair, and then Isadore pointed out the clever lift platform and other mechanical devices. Years ago he'd hired genius inventor Nathalie Collins to turn the rickety goods elevator into something usable, and her work now served them every day, not just Melanie but anyone with heavy packages or other needs.

Up at the top of the tower, Ambry knew, sat the prince's private rooms. Ambry couldn't help but wonder what they looked like. Delia would certainly want to know, to better furnish her imaginings. They shied from that idea. Whatever she – or they – might want, Isadore deserved some privacy when he gave so much of the rest of his life to his people.

Isadore introduced them to some of Melanie's assistants who they hadn't met before. There was Markus the researcher, with his long braided hair and wire spectacles.

Mira who worked the printing press, a tall woman who wore a skirt embroidered with dozens of tiny butterflies. The couple who managed the accounts and filed through receipt-books and checking stock so fast they looked like dancers in a play. And so many other names and faces that Ambry hoped they could remember.

And then Isadore showed them into a little round room near the bottom of the tower.

"This will be yours," Isadore said. "It was originally built to house a nursemaid for the heir's children. But I don't have any, so it had been empty for a long time when Lacey decided she liked it. So now it serves as the assistant's quarters. I had everything cleaned and prepared, but if there's anything else you need, don't hesitate to ask."

"Thank you. This is wonderful." There was a small bed already made up with a blue and green quilt folded at its foot. The window looked out onto the gardens; Ambry could spot Erik hard at work among the fruit trees with his wheelbarrow and rake. Against the walls stood a bookshelf and a little desk, and there was a hearth too, with a rack beside it for wood. They would be grateful for that come winter.

"I'm glad you like it," Isadore said. "I'll let you get settled. I have a lunch with my mother and another meeting with the ministers after that. You can go see Melanie when you're ready, but—" He smiled, and there was a hint of mischief to it. "Let her know that she's not going to claim you so easily."

Ambry couldn't tell quite whether Isadore was joking, so they merely nodded and waited for him to continue.

"I should be back around two, as long as nothing else comes up. Which is never a certainty here." He gave Ambry a last smile and headed off down the hall, leaving them to their new quarters.

Their things were waiting there by the bed. When they opened the clothes-chest, they found everything neatly folded – no doubt that was Patrice's work – and there was a stack of books sitting there on top of their shirts. And a note from Delia wishing them well, complete with a little sketch of them and Isadore riding unicorns across a flowering field. At least, that's why they thought it was supposed to be. Delia's drawings were sometimes a little difficult to interpret. Not that she particularly cared what other people thought. She and Marion had made a game of exchanging amusing drawings back and forth, each adding yet another ridiculous touch to the image.

Ambry ordered the books on the shelf, along with the few other small things they owned that were worth displaying. Trinkets from long-ago adventures with their cousins. A few good luck charms from the Winter Festival – they didn't believe in such things themself, but Delia and Ella had convinced them to buy them. They looked pretty if nothing else. And a necklace from their mother. They should send her a letter and tell her what had happened. They would have to ask Melanie's assistants for some paper, since Delia had taken the packet they'd had as payment for bringing over their belongings.

Even with all their things laid out, the books still looked lonely with so much space around them. Perhaps they could find something in the city markets to decorate the empty shelves. They sat on the bed for a while, thinking through the morning and all they had seen, and then they rose, and went to see what Melanie needed from them.

✧

"I hear you've been involving yourself in matters of the household," Queen Seraphina said as her maid served them roast duck and slivered roots. It didn't surprise Isadore that she knew already. Though she took pains to appear removed from the daily bustle of the palace, little happened in Isadore's life without her inevitably learning of it. They were sitting in her private dining room where not even guests were invited. The food was impeccable, but Isadore found himself wishing he was back in his study with Melanie, carving out a break with the more amusing stories from the city papers.

"It's important, Mother."

She held up a hand and he fell silent. "I don't disagree, Isadore. I only mean to remind you that someday you will be the master of a far greater world than the one within our walls."

He nodded. "I understand."

"Managing a great number of people, seeing their needs and how they intertwine, that is a valuable skill. Very much so. As is the ability to see what duties are left unfulfilled and decide how best that might be remedied." He let the praise go a little way to soothing his lingering doubts. And then she continued, "But you will have to learn how to delegate these roles to others and trust their vision and their answers without taking every detail into your own responsibility."

Again he thought of Ambry. "I have been doing something like that, of late," he said. "I've hired an assistant. They started work today."

She smiled, a subtle thing that he recognized only because he had known her all his life. "That's good. I have no doubt you will have many loyal advisors and helpers in your life, if only you will allow them to help you."

He nodded, hoping only that she was right.

By the time he returned to the heir's tower, Ambry had a new stack of annotated books for him to review and had set one aside to be rebound by Minerva's people in the archives. They were sitting in his chair at Melanie's desk, sharing a platter of sausage rolls as she read out an article from Ostberg's paper.

"The thief claimed that he was the bank's new night watchman," she was saying, "and he'd forgotten his uniform and his keys. When he was unable to describe what the watchman's uniform looked like, the guardswoman became suspicious and summoned the district chief, who confirmed that the man was the fugitive Peter Roberts, known associate of notorious criminal Ellis Hardy."

Ambry snorted. "You'd think sneaking around the vaults at night was suspicious enough."

Melanie folded the paper back. "They mention that too. Apparently, there'd been an incident a few months back where the guard actually arrested the night watchman and wouldn't let him go until they'd pulled the bank manager out of bed to vouch for him."

"That must have been embarrassing," Ambry laughed.

"I'll bet." Melanie looked up and saw Isadore. "How was the meeting?"

Ambry jumped up when he walked in. "Welcome back."

"Productive, surprisingly. It's all right, you can sit down. We'll need another chair. I'll ask for someone to get one."

Melanie laughed, and Isadore couldn't imagine why.

Until Ambry blinked, opened their mouth, paused. "Er– I think that's my job now?"

That had been the whole point of choosing an assistant, hadn't it? To have someone ready and waiting for those sorts of errands. "That it is," he said. Ambry made as if to go to the door, but Isadore ushered them back. "You can finish eating first, it's not urgent."

A little uncertainly, they sat back down and nibbled the half-eaten roll sitting on a napkin in front of them. To show that he truly wasn't troubled by it, Isadore sat down on the couch. Melanie turned to talk to him.

"I'm interested to hear what 'productive' means when we're talking about Captain Dreisand," she said, pulling out a piece of paper. Isadore handed her his notes. "She never agrees to anything if it wasn't her own idea."

"Captain Dreisand still favors the harsher policy, but I think Sergeant Harlow can talk her into a compromise. Mostly by letting her take all the credit. Which is an acceptable sacrifice considering the circumstances."

"Hopefully before the end of the year…" Melanie grumbled.

"She's starting to unbend a little. I know, it surprised me too. But Harlow showed her the reports from when Arrawey started doing it. No surprise, criminals tended to come back to jail less often if they were treated like they belonged in society rather than as aberrant monsters."

Ambry raised their head. Isadore might not have noticed it if he hadn't been looking right at them. But now that he was, all of it was plain on their face. He watched them fight with themself over whether to speak. Something held him back from asking directly. If they wanted to speak, he would listen, but he wanted to see if they would start on their own.

Melanie copied something from his paper to her own. "I do agree with you, but her current standards aren't that bad."

"Try asking anyone who's been through the process," Isadore returned, dry. "It's harsh, especially on first-timers." As he'd seen countless times reading through petition letters from the families of such unfortunate prisoners.

Ambry's courage won out. "You're talking about prisoners?"

Isadore nodded. "And what to do with minor criminals who get caught working with bigger ones."

Ambry watched his face for a long moment as if looking for permission, and then said, "When I was young, one of my older cousins fell in with some thieves in the city." They paused, and then when neither Isadore nor Melanie stopped them, went on. "It started with small things, trinkets from shops, but then their projects got bigger and bigger. And then they got caught. He tried to run. His friend stabbed the guardsman."

Isadore sucked in a breath. Melanie winced.

Ambry continued. "The Guard judge decided my cousin hadn't done as much as the others, but they threw him in prison along with the rest of them anyway." They looked down, but Isadore caught their bitter expression even so. "It was a short sentence, but when he was let out, he'd lost his job as a shopkeeper's assistant and nobody else would hire him. He came back south and lived with us for a while. My mother welcomed him back, but not all of my aunts did. He had nightmares about the prison that were so bad he could barely sleep."

Isadore nodded solemnly. "That's what we're trying to change."

"I'm glad," Ambry said, smiling gently. They stayed like that for one long warm moment, and then they stood, gathering up the plate and sweeping the crumbs to the center so they wouldn't spill. "I'll go take the plate down and get a chair."

Melanie tucked away her notes on the prisons meeting and brought out a stack of letters: legal disputes that Isadore was expected to advise on. This, he enjoyed: getting a feel for each case and searching through his books and the archives for the statutes and precedents needed to resolve it. As the heir, he had the ability to override the precedents when they were clearly unjust, but he was cautious with that power and weighed it every time he used it.

Today's cases were tricky ones that required him to delve deep into his library. At times he ended up sitting on the floor with four or five books arranged around him while Melanie used the desk to consult another stack. He kept Ambry busy fetching books from the shelf, taking dictation for notes, and supplying bits of colored ribbon for bookmarks, so that he barely had to look up from the pages as he worked. After having handled most of the books just that morning, Ambry found each requested volume easily, sometimes faster than

Isadore might have himself. Once or twice, he sent them over to the archives for a text; they returned promptly each time.

Ambry kept fairly quiet for the rest of the day, as if they'd used up all their words in telling him of their cousin. Isadore found he liked listening to them and hoped they'd speak more in the coming days. Together, they got through four cases, when usually he could only manage two or three in an afternoon. Isadore set the decisions aside to review and send out in the morning.

"Well?" Melanie said that evening, just before she left for the night.

Isadore looked up from his book. "What is it?"

"What do you think of your new assistant?"

"I'm very pleased."

"And?"

"And," he laughed, "you were right. They were a very good choice."

She nodded, satisfied. "You should listen to me more often."

"Don't I? I recall your policy recommendations forming a large part of the New Landing code…"

"And it was a great success for all involved. That's exactly why you should."

"I'll remember that."

He returned to his reading. It was good to have an evening where he had energy enough to read for pleasure, rather than trawling through more legal documents and letters. As much as he complained to Melanie, he did enjoy the work often, when there were answers to seek or things he could do. But even when it was enjoyable, it was still tiring. A few minutes later, he noticed Melanie was still there. He glanced at her. She had a thoughtful look on her face, one he knew well. One that usually came before some breakthrough in a complex political manner or a phrasing for a speech that would please both sides.

"Do you remember," she said, "that fairy tale about the princess who challenges all her suitors to move the palace gardens from one plot to another using only a single spoon?"

Isadore rubbed his neck and yawned. "Which telling? I can think of three off the top of my head. There's always a twist to it. One suitor completes the task as ordered, but she rejects him for his lack of creativity and will. Or he completes the task and then rejects *her* for demanding something so pointless and ridiculous. Or the man who uses a giant spoon wins, or he finds a hidden treasure in the garden and goes off on another quest…"

Melanie waited, amused, for him to trail off. "The one where the man attempts it, and then after a few days asks why she doesn't make the gardener do it with the proper tools."

Behind them, Sylvia laughed. When Isadore looked at her, she said, "There's a version of that tale in the Guard, but in our version, the suitor who complains that the task is pointless also fails, because you should never challenge orders from a superior, no matter how ridiculous they seem."

"I'm not surprised," Melanie said. "They're very particular about that."

"What was your point?" Isadore asked.

"I was wondering how Ambry would respond, if given a ridiculous assignment."

"From what I've seen, I suspect they'd ask why you were doing it, and then recruit the palace gardener to help," Isadore said. "Which in my opinion is the best way of going about it, so long as you're dealing with a reasonable master and not that bully of a princess."

"They're practical," Melanie agreed. "I like that. Sometimes we need more of that in this room."

"Are you saying I'm impractical?" Isadore would have been offended, if it hadn't been Melanie telling him so.

"I'm saying that you have high ideals, but you don't magically know the best way to get there, or who to call in to help. That's where an assistant will help."

"By fetching chairs and tea?"

She shook her head. "We both know that's not what you appointed them for. You want advice, and they're willing to give it, because they care as much as you do, but they haven't spent their whole life lost in this puzzle you call royalty."

She was right. Isadore needed more than a quiet maid or page who would fetch and carry, or a scribe to take notes in meetings. That was why it had taken him so long to consider replacing Lacey. So far, Ambry seemed a worthy candidate, but then, it had only been a day, and an easy one at that. It remained to be seen how they would handle more complicated duties, or the intricacies of politics, or the pressure of Isadore's sometimes chaotic schedule.

Isadore nodded. "I worry they're a little overwhelmed." They had hid it well today, but he had been paying enough attention to notice how tense they seemed at some moments, how they had always hesitated before asking for help.

"Of course they are," Melanie said, sliding the desk drawer shut and locking it with the little keys only she and Isadore had. "But that'll change over time as they settle in."

"I just hope they'll say something if anything's wrong."

"Even if they don't, with all of us watching them–" she gestured towards Sylvia, including her and the absent guards in this– "we can take care of them."

"Yes. I will make certain of that."

Chapter Five

✧

Ambry's new quarters at the base of the heir's tower were very comfortable. Though they missed Delia's presence and her laughter and gossip, they appreciated the quiet. It was far easier for them to relax when they were alone, without anybody around who might judge them or force them to speak. It wasn't that they didn't want to interact with their old fellows. Maybe a week into their new duties, Isadore dismissed them early in the evening so that they could join the rest of the servants for supper.

"So, the hero returns!" Delia exclaimed when they came into the kitchen. "Tell us of your quest, O great voyager?"

"I haven't– I haven't gone away!" Ambry choked, before dissolving into laughter. "I've been right here in the palace all week!"

"But very far removed from us," Patrice said. "We're not asking you to share anything secret–"

"Though we'd love it if you did!" That, of course, from Delia.

"–but we're all interested to hear how your days have been."

"It's been good. Busy." They looked around, searching for a face. "How is Danny? I don't see him…"

"Right as rain, and very grateful for it," Patrice told them. "Was up and about only a day after the accident and hasn't seemed to have suffered overmuch for it. He'll be along shortly."

As promised, Danny came into the room barely a minute later bearing a plate of steaming rolls. If Ambry had not seen it for themself, they would never have believed he had ever been injured.

There was a new face there too, a shy young woman named Alice whose dark hair floated around her face like an enchanted cloud.

"I've mostly been helping Erik in the gardens and doing the washing so far," she said. "Patrice won't let me in the kitchen yet."

"Not till you've proven you can manage it and not be in the way," Patrice said, blunt but not harsh. Ambry had learned very quickly not to take her attitude personally, and it had made the work a great deal easier once they had. They were decidedly not skilled at cooking. Nearly everything they touched ended up undercooked or burned, so when they were given work in the kitchen, it tended to be in chopping and fetching and cleaning rather than anything that might risk ruining a dish.

"Enjoy it while it lasts, Alice," Delia teased. "The kitchen feels like a hellpit in summer, especially when there's baking going."

"But it's very pleasant in winter," Ella added, defending her domain. "And there's nothing better than warm buns after working outside in the snow."

"Maybe by the winter I'll be helping you with the baking," Alice said, a little smile on her lips.

"Ah, probably sooner than that, if you impress me," Patrice told her. Alice must have already done so, for her to talk like that. "But I make no promises."

Mrs. Hammond did not join them. She was far too busy with her account books, Patrice reported and sent Alice to her chambers with a tray. When Alice returned, they took their places at the table and passed around the platters: roast fowl, marrows stuffed with rice, a pie made from roots and the trimmings of the more expensive meats that went to the queen's table. Ambry had enjoyed far finer food over the past few days. They'd been eating mostly with Melanie, and with Isadore when he was not hosting guests. Fine food, but eaten quickly between tasks, without time to appreciate the flavors. The servants' rough table felt like home, and they wouldn't have traded the warm chatter and friendly faces for the best food the Queen's personal chef could offer.

"Did you hear about the fight in the square last week?" Marion asked.

"Which one?" Ella put in. "There was the one after the schoolboys raided the sweetseller, and the one where Nathalie Collins accused Ellis Hardy of stealing shipments to her workshop."

"I hadn't heard about Collins!" Delia said. "What happened?" she prompted, looking up for a moment from the task of picking out the morsels of bacon from her beans and pushing the greens to the side while Patrice watched disapprovingly.

"Turns out he hadn't," Marion said with a shrug, "but you know it's exactly the sort of thing he would do. She chased him out of the crafters' district with a mechanical dragon at his tail. Last I heard he still had bite marks on his hand!"

"I heard they were on his arse," Erik put in, giving a vicious grin. Ella and Marion laughed uproariously.

"I bet they were! He deserved it too."

Ambry could easily imagine Collins building a dragon to defend her workshop. Once Isadore had taught them what to look for, they'd noticed her machines all around the palace, making life easier in ways big and small. They also learned that she had designed Melanie's wheelchair to match her own, allowing Melanie to navigate uneven ground or small steps with the same ease with which Collins moved around her workshop.

"I'm looking forward to seeing her presentation at the Midsummer Festival this year," they said. If they had the spare time to visit, they thought.

"Knowing her, she'll be showing half a dozen," Erik said. "Remember that climbing monkey from last year? The one that was supposed to help clean chimneys?"

"I remember it got stuck when its joints were too full of soot," Marion snorted. "You'd think she would have thought of that. I suppose even a genius will have some stinkers."

"And the rotating spoon rack for cooking?" Patrice said. "What a frivolous idea."

"Well, I thought it was useful," Ella said. "Makes it easier to find things when you've got four pots going and no time to spare. If there's anything new kitchen-wise in her collection this year, I'm buying it."

"So long as it comes out of your own pocket, I won't stop you," Patrice said.

They talked all through the meal of too many things to count: gossip, trading unwanted duties, remembering past fairs and planning for upcoming ones. Ambry didn't contribute much, but they were perfectly content to listen and laugh and enjoy the evening. The others did ask them many, many questions about their new position and about Isadore – most of them coming from Delia. But to Ambry's relief they didn't press for anything they couldn't share. It wasn't that they didn't want to share, but the idea of disappointing Isadore or damaging an important political move through lack of care was too much to bear.

"What's he like?" Ella asked. "In person, I mean, when he's not on official duty."

"He's always the prince," Marion interrupted. "But it's a different thing in public and private, at least I expect. He probably doesn't dress like he's on parade every day if he's not making an appearance."

"I hope not," Erik said. "Those things never look comfortable." He turned to Ambry. "Is he taking you to meetings with lords and such?"

"No, but I help him prepare his things for those meetings. Pens, notebooks, folders, that sort of thing."

"Sounds dull. Well, you're closer than most of us will ever be."

"I heard what happened with Danny," Alice said. "Have you seen his healing magic again since then?"

"Once," Ambry confirmed.

She leaned forward. "What did it feel like?"

They shook their head. "It wasn't on me, it was for Melanie. Her knees were aching." They hadn't wanted to ask what kept her in her chair, and hadn't minded not knowing, but they'd ended up learning anyway that while she wasn't incapable of walking, she had some sort of condition in her knees and hips that made it very painful most days. Something that not even Isadore could permanently heal, though he could ease the pain on days when it got too bad for her to focus.

Alice looked a little disappointed, so they added. "I did feel it once, though, when I'd sprained my wrist. It's warm and a little tingly. It's like it washes away the pain and makes whatever was hurt feel whole again."

"That sounds amazing. I wish I could feel that."

Patrice snorted. "Let's hope you're never hurt badly enough to need it."

Delia was giggling again.

Ambry looked at her, trying to glare and failing. "What is it?"

"You're all starry-eyed again! Just from talking about his magic. Want me to hit you before you go back? Then he could heal you again."

Erik shook his head. "You couldn't hit hard enough, lassie. Leave it to me." He brandished his fist, making Ambry blink. Erik laughed, turning the gesture into a shrug. "Naw, I suppose not, wouldn't want to cause a stir. Or have him hunt me down to save your honor."

"Oh, now that's romantic," Delia laughed.

When the meal was over, to everyone's delight, Ella brought out a blackberry tart dusted with sugar and decorated with curling bits of candied lemon peel. Patrice cut thin slivers for each of them, setting them on scraps of baking paper so that they wouldn't have another round of plates to wash. Delia and Erik finished their slices within moments, but Ambry ate theirs in tiny bites, savoring the buttery crust and sweet filling. Patrice clucked at Delia when she dropped some of the filling onto the royal badge at her neck, wiped it off, and licked her finger clean.

"Does Isadore like blackberry tarts?" Delia asked suddenly, ignoring the scolding. "I know the Queen does."

"I'm not sure. We had berry shortbread with lemon cream one day at breakfast."

"Mmm, that sounds good, I'm jealous." She glanced at Ella. "Make me some of that?"

Ella laughed and pointed her fork at Delia. "You be glad you're getting this. I haven't got time to make you special treats. Unless…" She tipped her head, grinning. "Unless you do all the cleaning and take my laundry for the day."

Delia eyed her. "I'll think about it."

Just before Ambry departed for their bed under the heir's tower, Danny pressed a letter into their hands. "For the prince," he said.

Ambry handed it to Isadore the next morning. As he read, his face settled into an expression Ambry could not interpret, save for that there was determination in it. He took a slow breath and tucked the letter away in a desk drawer. Ambry had never seen him do that before – most documents went into the mail basket, or one of Melanie's many folders and cases.

"Thank you," he said, looking into the distance.

Ambry fought with themself for several long moments, before asking, fearing it might be the wrong thing to say, "You… you don't seem happy."

Isadore let out a heavy breath. "Is it truly so astonishing that I would take the time to heal a dire wound in my own household?"

Ambry bit their lip. "You have so many duties. We don't want to be presumptuous." And the Queen had for so long set a standard of holding herself and her family apart from the household.

Isadore shook his head, pained. "For somebody's life? For somebody to go about their day without avoidable pain? That wouldn't be presumption."

Still, in the absence of an urgent matter, the idea of coming all the way to the tower and interrupting Isadore's work was distasteful. They shouldn't ever demand that he ease all their cuts and aches. *And how long could you bear it, when it wears you so thin?* Ambry thought but did not ask. They knew their fellows would not ask more than Isadore could give, but when he buried his fatigue in stubborn determination, it would be hard for them, and impossible for others, to tell when he was near to breaking from exhaustion. And would others care so much for his own condition when he could ease theirs with a touch?

"There'll be a doctor soon," Ambry reminded him. "So we will be taken care of." Not "we" anymore, technically, but they still could not separate themself from their friends and fellows.

Isadore nodded, "Marjorie is already reviewing candidates. The post should be filled before the month is out. But if I could do more personally…"

Melanie had kept quiet through most of their conversation, intently focused on writing a letter. As she pressed down the seal, she looked up at them with an expression that told Ambry she had indeed been listening to every word.

"Healing people is an incredible thing," she began. "But you're a leader first, and not a healer. You can touch far more people by governing than by wandering around the palace in search of bruises."

Ambry thought that harsh, but Isadore only shook his head sadly.

"My mother said much the same thing recently," he said.

Ambry frowned. "Maybe there's still a way, for emergencies. And," they went on, more confident in this idea and determined to make up for the previous one, "you could give the doctor permission to send people to you when you have time."

"Would they, though?" Isadore asked, echoing Ambry's doubts. Most of them, Ambry themself included, would likely rather work through their pain than risk disturbing their prince.

"To be fair," Melanie said, "you haven't exactly worked on making yourself more approachable. Up here in your tower with your guards at the door, how's anybody supposed to think they're permitted to speak to you?"

Isadore sank into his seat and rested his head in his hand. He looked heartbroken. All Ambry wanted to do in that moment was find some answer to it, some way to cheer him, but they'd spoken far too openly already. Part of them wished bitterly that Danny had not given them that letter, though they could hardly blame him for any of this.

"It's becoming all too clear to me," Isadore said, voice grim, without looking up, "that I have failed this household tremendously." It hurt to hear him so bitter and sharp and hopeless. Ambry wanted to protest, but before they could, Isadore went on, "If Ambry hadn't thought to come to me when Danny was injured, he might well have died. I never knew the servants' doctor was a useless pervert. A few weeks ago, Dominick had a double shift and damn near pissed himself because he didn't think he could ask me for a few moments' rest, and he's served me for years. How did it get to be like this? What have I done so wrong? And why didn't I see it before?"

"Because things are not usually so dire," Melanie said coolly. "There are vanishingly few deathly injuries in the palace. The servants kept their business to themselves and handled it accordingly. And Dominick is far too stubborn and stoic for his own good, you know that."

Ambry had a moment of thinking it unjust that she should soothe him after upsetting him so, but they pushed that aside. Whether her words were harsh or kind, Melanie was always honest. And she knew Isadore far better than Ambry could ever hope to.

"Here in the palace," Ambry said, "we can take care of each other. And if there's a new doctor, they can help too. But there's places in the kingdom that need more help. You can pass laws to do that." They hoped they didn't sound ridiculous.

"It needs to be better," Isadore agreed, still not looking up.

"Then you need to work towards it," Melanie said, stern but not unsympathetic. "You can't change the way things are done with one gesture. You can't fix everything in a day, or in a week. It takes time, and it takes work, and it takes adjustments along the way. It's just like what you always say about sailing – you need to adjust your course as you go, or you'll end up somewhere far afield of where you planned. You know that. Stop waiting for the perfect answer to fall out of the sky and start working on it."

Isadore nodded, took a deep breath and blew it out. "Very fair. Where should we start?"

Melanie cleared a space on her desk and pulled a notebook from a drawer. Isadore didn't see her smile, but Ambry did.

"We could ask people personally what issues they face. And you could find someone to compile responses and seek out other problems in need of mending." She hummed thoughtfully. "Though the problem there would be in finding someone who'll see things as they are and as they could be and not try to shape them to their own personal ideals."

"I can help," Ambry said, almost before they realized they were speaking, or how important a post they were volunteering themself for. They didn't want to seem arrogant, but if they could help Isadore and everybody he wanted to help…

Isadore at last looked up and smiled at them, that light coming back into his eyes. "Then that's what we'll do."

◆

Isadore had wondered for a time and scolded himself for being so inconsiderate as to do so, whether selecting a new assistant would only remind him painfully of the perfection that had been Lacey Penner. That he would judge Ambry not for their own merits but on the differences from what he was accustomed to. But so far, that had not been the case. True, he had to ask for things where Lacey would have known what he wanted from a glance, and sometimes before even that, and Ambry sometimes needed – though less frequently, as time went on – to ask for help in finding something or to learn how exactly Isadore wanted something done, but at some point within the past weeks, they had found a rhythm to their days.

He took an early breakfast with the Queen most days, and headed to the tower study right after if he had no morning meetings scheduled. While the city mayor and Captain of the Guard preferred to meet as early as possible, most of the Council kept their engagements to the afternoon when there wasn't a full session scheduled. By the time he arrived, Ambry had done some minor cleaning of whatever needed it, and Melanie was ready with the earliest deliveries of letters and the morning papers. He'd walked in more than once to her reading an article out loud to hear Ambry's opinion.

The position of assistant had always been intended as something more of a servant than an advisor. By all tradition, Ambry's role should have been to fetch books and carry pens and make tea, but how could Isadore not listen to them when their words lifted his spirit so?

Sometimes he lifted his head from the endless letters and simply watched Ambry work, all long red curls and clever, compassionate brown eyes. He hadn't thought he wanted a new assistant when Melanie had pushed the issue, but something about Ambry, about the way they moved and the way they spoke, set him at ease when they were there. Ambry seemed more comfortable around him recently too, which pleased him. No longer did they duck and hesitate and look away, and Isadore suspected they were sleeping better as well. Whether that had to do with their satisfaction with their new role or simply with sleeping somewhere away from the servant dormitories and the noisy kitchen, he didn't know, but he was glad of it.

As they grew more comfortable, they talked more too, joked more, offered suggestions to the issues he and Melanie wrestled with. Most of them could never be implemented, regardless of how good they might be, but they led to intriguing conversations. His work seemed less, when Ambry was there, and not simply for the help they provided. It was good to have those moments of brightness during otherwise tedious days.

Melanie occasionally cast curious looks between them, as if searching for something in the air, but always demurred when Isadore asked her what she meant. It was unusual for her not to answer with either something direct or a clever remark, but Isadore didn't linger on the question. If it was important, she would share.

He worried sometimes that Ambry might find the work demeaning, given how much of it was ordinary things: cleaning, fetching, carrying. And that they might not protest even if they did, for fear of offending him. But Melanie assured him that was far from the truth. Isadore had become more comfortable commanding them and reading their expressions.

On the rare occasions that they were not immediately needed, Isadore let Ambry sit by the window and read. They were making good progress through a set of Arraweyan histories that Isadore had particularly enjoyed, and he stole moments here and there to talk about them with Ambry. He had to send them from the room sometimes, when he and Melanie were discussing something too secret or sensitive for them to hear, but they didn't protest.

Meanwhile, the work continued. There were always more disputes begging for his recommendation, more than he could ever address, even if he worked on them and only them for every moment of the day. Melanie's staff chose the most important and interesting of the lot to bring to his desk, but still he could not help but think of those that languished unresolved for lack of time. And of course there was the treaty, the treaty that had been a weight on his shoulders for nearly three years now, ever since Ambassador Beck raised the possibility to Queen Seraphina and Isadore had asked to be allowed to manage it. At the time he'd done it as much to prove to her and to himself that he could as he had to ensure the treaty's passage and that the contents of the agreement would be beneficial to all involved. If they could see this through, it would improve life immensely for those who lived on the borders of the four kingdoms, and would make trade between them easier, binding their sometimes-tenuous alliance all the tighter. Talland and Larsellan were already in agreement on most of the points. But it remained to be seen if Kivern and Arrawey would be as willing.

There had to be some answer that would suit them all. Some arrangement of the terms that all four would see as a victory. He was sure that if he worked hard enough, he could find it.

Adrian sent him another letter, full of the usual things: complaints about his father's lofty expectations and his tutor's irritating tendencies, news from other friends from their university days, and rather too much detail on his time with Rose, who, Isadore gathered, was very pleased with his company. He was glad for them, truly. Adrian had grown a lot since university, where he had tumbled into beds for the sheer fun of it and rarely sought a deeper relationship. As entertaining and exhilarating as Adrian had found it, he'd often complained to Isadore and Cedric that he felt unfulfilled, missing something he couldn't yet find. Perhaps he had found it now with Rose.

And then a line caught his eye, carefully buried within the rest. An offer to introduce him to a visiting nobleman Adrian was quite sure he would get along well with. In that, if in nothing else, Adrian was subtle. Isadore hadn't expected he'd truly go through with his offer of seeking out a partner for his friend. It warmed him that Adrian had thought of him, even if it was in this teasing way. But somehow, the idea didn't interest him anymore, not now that it was a real offer and not simply a fanciful imagining between friends. He tried to imagine it and found he didn't want to bed a stranger, didn't want to have to fumble through learning what each other liked while not having any existing bonds to guide them, or any reason to remember for later what each found most pleasurable. And without that care, it would be purely physical, no matter what pretense of affection they brought into it.

There were certain people in the city who could simulate such affection to the level of an art form. It served them very well, so long as their customers understood it was merely an illusion, shared when convenient for pleasure and nothing more. But of course, Isadore could not seek them out in any case, for fear of shameful gossip. And he would not want to, for as he had told Adrian, he did not know if they would be willing to refuse him. Things had been so much less complicated before Cedric.

He put the letter aside. He'd write a response once he'd gathered his thoughts.

"There's another letter from Ambassador Beck," Melanie said by way of greeting when he came into the room. Ambry wasn't there, probably off on some errand or another. "They say they had a brief conversation with Lady Pennafor, Arrawey's envoy to Kivern. She thinks they're going to try and remove the Lynwood Provision, and she says Arrawey won't stop them."

Isadore sighed, rubbed his head against the ache that threatened there. "I thought Arrawey wanted the Provision?"

"They do, but not as much as they want Kivern to stay at the table."

"Kivern can't be threatening to back out now?" Isadore sat up, alarmed.

"Not yet," Melanie assured him. "But if we want them to agree to the Greenstone Law, we're going to have to bend somewhere."

"We're not sacrificing the Atworth Proposal."

Melanie shook her head sadly. "We might have to, for the sake of the rest of the agreement." She'd been saying it for days. Ambry thought the same. Isadore didn't want to believe it, but it was becoming harder to deny that they would have to compromise somewhere.

"We worked hard for Atworth," Isadore said, frustration sharpening his voice. "But without the Lynwood Provision, this whole thing is meaningless." All three years of work, wasted. It would be an embarrassment for Talland and only a tiny gain for Kivern.

"I know." Melanie leaned back, drummed her fingers on the desk. "I think it's going to come down to one or the other. We can leave the Proposal for another time. And stepping back from that might earn us enough goodwill with Kivern to keep all six points of the Lynwood Provision. As long as Larsellan backs us, which isn't a given at this point."

"Is there anything from Miller or Grenner?" But he knew better than to hope that their ambassador to Kivern had heard differently, or that Kivern's envoy to Talland would do anything to get in the way of a possible advantage for his Queen. "Or from Larsellan?" Their relationship with Larsellan was pleasant mostly by virtue of being very uneventful, and both sides of that particular communication were laconic and direct in their letters. At least someone was, Isadore thought.

"Nothing yet, but I wouldn't be surprised if we get something in the next few days. Grenner will want a meeting before he rides home for Kivern's Summer Conference."

Isadore nodded. "Let me talk to my mother and the Council, and then we can work on a response."

Ambry came back into the room with their lunch, a platter of roast pork and various pickled vegetables. It was one of Isadore's favorites, a dish from Larsellan that he had developed a taste for on a state visit there with his mother and asked the cooks at the palace to recreate. They'd done well, even sending away for the right sort of spices.

He noticed Lawrence watching the dish as Ambry passed by. Had he eaten recently? Isadore doubted it. Dominick would never accept something like this, but Isadore knew Lawrence would. He folded a portion of the meat and pickles into one of the buns and wrapped it in a napkin.

Lawrence looked at him. "Highness?"

"You can eat, if you want. We certainly have enough."

"You don't have to do that," Lawrence protested, but he took the bun and ate it one-handed while keeping his watch, and Isadore suspected it was something more than Guard manners that prompted him to finish every crumb.

Satisfied, Isadore turned back to the letter, frowning at the words as if he could force them to change through pure force of his displeasure.

"Larsellan agreed to Lynwood and Atworth months ago," he said. "But you're correct that they might back down if pushed. It maddens me that we can't get them all in a room together until *after* all of this has been agreed. Maybe if we could talk face to face instead of through letters and short meetings, we'd work this out in a day or two."

Melanie gave a sharp laugh. "I thought you'd given up chasing unicorns, Isadore. Doing this through official channels means that Grenner and Habb can't force their points through with pure bluster." Willem Habb was Kivern's ambassador to Larsellan. Decades of contact with their culture had taught him to be a little more flexible than Grenner, but that still wasn't much.

"And Beck can't use their charm to wring any concessions," Isadore sighed.

Ambry listened patiently to the exchange; bright brown eyes slightly narrowed in thought. Even though they hadn't attended most of the meetings with the ambassadors, they'd picked up the points of the treaty remarkably quickly from listening to Isadore and Melanie discuss it and had even offered a few useful thoughts here and there. Seeing the whole tangled thing from a new perspective was more of a boon than Isadore had ever expected.

"Is Grenner demanding more changes?" Ambry asked.

Melanie smiled. "When isn't he?"

"He's certainly trying," Isadore said. "But we will manage it." They had to, for he didn't think he could bear it if they failed.

Chapter Six

✧

"I'd like you to accompany me to the city today," Isadore said to Ambry one morning in summer. "I have some people I need to meet. And I want to buy you new clothes."

"Is there something wrong?" Had their attire displeased him? Their shirts were worn but well-kept, and the hems of their trousers were clean, though the knees had been patched more than once.

Isadore frowned. "Is that all right? I thought you would like to have something new."

Melanie laughed over her ever-flowing basket of letters. "It's a gift, Ambry, take it."

How could they refuse that? They hurried back to their room to get ready. When they reached the courtyard with their bag and boots, Isadore was waiting there, wearing what was for him a plain coat, though a close look at the materials would have betrayed its value. He'd removed most of his jeweled hairpins, and Dominick behind him was also dressed in commoners' clothes rather than his Guard uniform. Despite the unremarkable dress, the sword at his belt was unmistakable, as was his strength and watchful eyes.

"I don't like to be conspicuous in the city if I'm not on official duties all day," Isadore explained. "It tends to cause a fuss."

Ambry wondered how anybody in the capital city could think that this beautiful man was anything other than their prince, especially when he was followed by a guard who as far as Ambry knew had never been inconspicuous in his life, but they didn't protest. They could understand why Isadore might not want to be noticed, even by people who adored him and meant him no harm. Especially by people who adored him, they thought, remembering Delia's fantasies.

But the streets past the palace gates were busy enough that the three of them could blend in without too much effort. Once they were through the gates, Ambry removed their royal badge at Isadore's command and slipped it safely into a pocket. This was a day when it would help to not be recognized as part of the royal staff.

They joined the flow of people heading towards the city center. The Midsummer Festival had ended just a few days before, but the capital's inns were still full of visitors hoping to enjoy the season. Despite their earlier hopes of visiting, Ambry had almost forgotten the festival in the rush of letters needing responses. Summer was the time when Arrawey's king appointed new diplomatic officials, and all of them were apparently very eager to send their introductions to Isadore and Seraphina. Add to that the flooding in the west and the reports of bandits on the southeast border with Kivern. These were bandits who attacked both kingdoms' people with little discrimination, leading both to accuse the other of sheltering the criminals, and neither they nor Isadore nor Melanie had had much time to think of celebration. But today, there was finally space to breathe. It was good to be outside in the world. There was something to the air that just wasn't there in the palace courtyards or gardens.

"Who are you meeting?" Ambry asked.

"Adrian, for one. He's Lord Tisdale's son. We went to university together. We'll meet him for lunch after I introduce you to Darby. And then the Guard commanders at the North Gate have some things they want to discuss, and after that Education Minister Travers wants to show me a new school building."

Even what had seemed at first glance like a rest day was full of appointments. But Isadore didn't seem too troubled.

"You don't have to come along for the afternoon if you'd rather not," Isadore added. "You could head back after lunch and I'm sure Melanie could find something for you to do." That, said with a hint of humor.

"No, I'll stay. As long as I'm not in the way." They were only an assistant; they couldn't expect that they'd be allowed in every meeting today.

"You could never be in the way," Isadore said, a sudden earnestness to his voice and in his eyes that nearly stopped Ambry mid-step. He looked away, and the moment was over. "You'll take notes. That way Melanie won't complain when I don't remember everything that was said."

Ambry had gotten rather good at shorthand after several weeks of teaching from Markus. If they kept their focus, they stood a fair chance of being able to record every word if they wanted to. But they'd also learned that what was most important in the few meetings they'd been allowed to attend was not the exact words spoken, but each person's motivations and goals. It was far more important to know that the Captain of the Guard might be swayed by an appeal to public safety and social stability than it was to know that she had a penchant for horse-related idioms. Hidden in that friendly banter was the fact that the Lands Minister disliked risk but the Finance Minister was willing to chance it if the potential gains were high enough. Isadore was better at reading those sorts of things than they were, and Melanie better still, but they were learning fast. They were starting to understand what drew Isadore to it, as exhausting as it was: the puzzle of it, of finding answers between the stubborn stances and far-reaching desires. Of knowing when to push and how, and how to make each party feel as if they'd gained something in the bargain. The gain to the people was what made Isadore dive into these things again and again, but the satisfaction of seeing it through was what kept him at it, even when it became tedious and disheartening.

Ambry worried about those times. Sometimes Isadore's definition of success was so narrow that nothing would please him, and it took all of Melanie and Ambry's efforts to get him to move beyond planning and into action, knowing the attempt would fall short. It reminded them of something their grandfather used to say, back when he still spoke to them. *Half a basket of clams is better than no clams*, he'd repeat whenever Ambry or one of their cousins balked at the size of a chore.

Isadore must have noticed how Ambry's thoughts were drifting, for he said, "The work comes later. For now, we can enjoy the day."

And a marvelous day it was, sunny without being exceptionally hot. Enough clouds drifted through the sky to allow for comfortable shady spots, and a light breeze from the river cleared the dust from the air and set the flags proudly rippling.

They passed an old woman pushing a wooden cart before her, selling little woven charms made of, so she claimed, the discarded sails of old ships.

"They've traveled all over the world," she said, smiling a toothless smile. "And that means they've spent all their lives soaking up the magic of faraway places. They'll bring you good fortune and safe travels."

Most of the ships at Talland's ports were fishing boats and trading vessels, not diplomatic craft or adventurers' ships, whatever the thrilling novels Ambry loved would have one believe. Ambry privately wondered if the ships from which the sails had come had ever traveled farther than the Crested Islands that sat far off the southern coast.

Whether or not Isadore shared their doubts, he was clearly delighted with the charms and bought two of them without pausing to haggle over the price. He had no need, of course, but if the woman had not already guessed his wealth from his fine clothes, she knew now.

They continued on, heading towards the river. The City Guard had their buildings only a street away from the Stonebridge, as close to the center of the old walled city as they could be without being in the water. A young officer was on duty watching the traffic that passed over the bridge. In more troubled times, she might have focused her efforts on watching for those who meant harm; today it seemed her job consisted mainly of providing directions to lost travelers and warning off minor fights when the narrow road by the river became crowded.

From there they entered North Moon Square, where a little park sat at the center of a wide tiled plaza. Children played among young trees, waving their hands to try and catch the birds that flitted safely from the branches to nearby roofs. Older children sprawled on the grass with books or games while parents and caretakers watched their charges.

Dominick glared at the pair of toddlers splashing noisily in the fountain but said nothing. If the weather had cheered him, he did not show it in his face. Then again, he probably disapproved of Isadore wandering the streets with only a single guard for protection, even if Dominick's strength and sight was clearly more than enough to keep the prince safe from anyone who might seek to harm him. Any of his three guards could, but at least Lawrence and Sylvia sometimes had a sense of humor about it.

Isadore led them past the square and to a little shop down the far end of a shopping street far too luxurious for Ambry to have ever thought of coming here on their own. A gorgeous dress sat in the window, ripples of blue shading down to white at the skirt, the sort of thing that Delia would absolutely adore. A similar dress in shades of purple sat next to it, the pair angled towards each other as if they were two ladies sharing a secret, or perhaps a kiss. Next to those was a deep brown tunic with gold stitching and embroidered lions curling up the sleeves, draped in a long dark cloak that held in its depths subtle patterns that changed as Ambry moved their head.

Ambry had a moment to dream that Isadore meant for them to have something as grand as that, a moment to hope that he *didn't*, and then they were through the door and into a wood-paneled front room. Here there were a few more richly-dressed figures, a shelf of ribbons and buttons and thread that were probably used for mending and altering, scissors of various shapes hanging from pegs, and on the edge of another shelf, a little dish piled with pieces of chalk.

On the one wall that was not covered in cabinets and shelves hung two beautiful banners, each embroidered with a saint-mark, every stroke of the symbols garlanded with extravagant flowers and fans of leaves. One was the sign of Saint Kessi of the Loom, patron of tailors, spinners, weavers, and all who worked with cloth or thread. The other was unmistakably the mark of Saint Astrenn.

Behind a wide desk spread with papers and drawing tools and scraps of fabric sat a tall and thin and elegant person of no particular gender, with a sharp nose and pale hair cut short and combed to perfection, sketching on a pad of paper. Unhurried, they added a few last sweeping lines to the page they were working on, and looked up, revealing bright eyes behind angular spectacles.

"Darby Allister, the royal tailor," Isadore said.

"My prince! How good to see you." Allister stood and bowed. Their gray suit both caught the eye at once and seemed almost a natural part of their body. Ambry noted the angles and ruffles and colored accents that Ella and Marion talked so much about. It was only fitting that a tailor should dress themself in the latest fashions. Or perhaps it was Allister's designs that had started the fashions in the first place. Ambry suspected that even when the trends changed, the outfit would still be attractive.

Isadore put a hand on Ambry's shoulder as he introduced them; the touch was almost enough to distract them from examining Allister's clothing. "This is Ambry Jean, my new personal assistant. I want them to have a daily suit that'll be comfortable but appropriate, a formal outfit, and something suitable for outdoors and sailing. They'll be coming with me to the Crested Islands later in the summer."

The Islands? Isadore hadn't mentioned that before. He was planning on taking them with him on the royal family's yearly holiday? They didn't have time to think about it. Allister wrote on a tiny notepad as Isadore talked, and when he was done they tore the page out with a flourish and ushered Ambry behind a curtain into what could only be their workshop. All around them stood a crowd of dressmaker's models wearing half-completed creations, looking like dancers at a fairies' ball. Off to the side sat several tables strewn with offcuts and ribbons and buttons. Rolls of fabric in every color and pattern imaginable were piled into a honeycomb of deep compartments on the wall, each bolt tagged with a number and a few words in a looping hand. A glass-fronted cabinet displayed too many spools of thread to count. In one corner, a black-and-white cat slept lazily in a padded basket, a scrap of green ribbon caught between its paws.

Allister had Ambry strip to their underclothes and stand on a block to be measured. It might have been strange or uncomfortable to be measured and examined so, and nearly naked while doing it, but Allister put them at ease within the first few moments. The touch that might have been unnerving was utterly proper. They barely felt Allister's hands on them, just heard the swish of their tape in their ears.

"Right, that shouldn't be too difficult," Allister announced. Ambry hadn't thought they were even halfway done. Ambry spun around to follow them as they dashed over to a table to note down the numbers. "You can get dressed now," they called back.

When they were done, Allister led them through a whirlwind of fabrics, pulling the rolls out one after the other like an alchemist with their compounds. Ambry followed, giving startled opinions when asked. Yes, they liked the deep green; no, the silver waves seemed gaudy, but the gray and blue crosses were pleasant.

Then Allister continued on to a long row of drafters' cabinets, thin drawers filled with pages upon pages of patterns and sketches. They pulled out one sheet, and then another, and then a third, not even pausing to consult the labels on the drawers. Allister kept talking all the while, questioning Ambry on which sorts of styles they found comfortable and which they disliked, what sort of work they did and what leisure activities they enjoyed, even the sorts of underclothes and breast bindings they preferred, an exchange that was over and onto the next before Ambry could even think to be embarrassed.

At last Allister declared them done and returned to where Isadore waited at the front. They grinned at him, the picture of delight. "This should be most enjoyable. It's been a long while since I've had a project like this! Most people, they come in and they think they know exactly what they want, and then I am merely a tool of their limited imagination, rather than an artist working alongside them." They shook their head mournfully as if this was a truly pitiable state. "But today!" They brightened. "Today I am tasked with crafting a vision suitable for a companion to the Prince!"

Isadore smiled indulgently at Allister's theatrics. "I'm glad you're so pleased. The usual rate, and have them delivered when you're done?"

Allister frowned. "Hmm, I should like to see the fit for myself, in case any last alterations are needed."

"So, I see even perfection such as yourself needs finessing?" Isadore said, and it was a moment before Ambry realized he was teasing.

"Everything needs finessing, my dear Prince, or what would we have to strive for?" Allister returned, equally playful.

"Very well said. Is the usual schedule enough time?"

"Only if you want to contend with some very angry dancers. I've been charged with making costumes for the Springleaf Opera's winter show. A story about little songbirds going to war with a massive gnarled crow, and I'm afraid they want the costumes a little more literal than I might have liked had I had my own way about it. The time needed to sew the feathers alone!" They shook their head in dismay. "But I am sure I can make room in my schedule for you and this charming fellow by your side." They fixed Ambry with a look flirty enough to set them blushing.

Very soon, Isadore and Allister reached a deal. "Send a note if there's any trouble. Bring the finished things to the palace when you're ready."

"That's a deal." Allister noted it down with a flourish in one of many, many notebooks. "And you over there, all handsome and strong and silent?" they called towards the doorway. "Perhaps a new coat is in order?"

Ambry had almost forgotten Dominick was there, they realized with a touch of guilt. It surprised them how easily Isadore's guards, once so intimidating, faded into the background now that Ambry spent most of the day with them. But they supposed the same skills that allowed them to pass unnoticed also made them excellent protectors.

"I thank you for the offer, but I am satisfied with what I have," Dominick said, utterly formal but for the hint of surprise in his voice. Isadore looked from him to Allister with a thoughtful look on his face. He was planning something. Ambry would have to ask what when Sylvia came on duty.

By now the sun was well overhead and Ambry was beginning to feel hungry. Good, then, that their next appointment was for a meal. They followed Isadore from Allister's shop and back towards the square, passing a group of ladies studying the window display with great enthusiasm.

"Thank you," Ambry said. "When you said a new suit of clothes, I wasn't expecting anything so grand." Not that they had expected anything cheap, but Allister was the royal family's personal tailor; it would have been the height of arrogance to assume they'd receive something crafted by such an artist.

"I wouldn't have anything less," Isadore said. "Besides, Darby would never have forgiven me if I'd patronized any other tailor for dressing my assistant." He smiled. "You'll look striking in their creations, I'm certain of it."

Ambry didn't doubt it for a moment.

They arrived at a tavern on Fairwinds Street, somewhat finer than those Ambry and their friends frequented, but not so much so that they felt grubby entering it. If Isadore had hoped to find somewhere he could pass unnoticed, he had chosen well. The clientele here ranged from people in fine dress who they supposed might be minor nobles and well-to-do merchants to fishers and guards enjoying some time away from their ships and their posts.

A man with golden hair and a blue summer jacket waved to Isadore from a table at the back of the hall. "Where have you been hiding all this time?" he accused when they reached him. "Has Melanie been keeping you prisoner?"

Isadore winced. "The letter – Adrian, I'm sorry, I truly meant to reply."

"But you were busy. It's all right." Adrian sighed, waved a hand to invite them to sit. "I hear you've had some difficulty with shipping contracts. Business partners not playing along."

He must mean the treaty, Ambry thought, and the odd phrasing would keep their discussion from turning any stray ears.

Isadore frowned. "I didn't think that much was public. Where did you hear?"

"There are newspapers from across the border, you know. And merchants who aren't quite as circumspect with their knowledge as you are."

"The trouble we've been having with the Kivernese party alone…" Isadore groaned. "We'll have to talk about it somewhere else if you want the full story."

Adrian snorted. "Oh no, I'm staying out of it. Lest you draft me into some sort of position where I'll have to carry your stock."

"I couldn't do that, what would Rose say if I stole her man away to do my bidding?"

Adrian grinned. "She would fight you, and it wouldn't matter to her whose son you are."

At last Adrian seemed to notice Ambry. "Now, you haven't introduced me to your friend here."

"This is Ambry, my new assistant."

"So it seems this *is* a business meeting after all?" Adrian put his hand over his heart and pouted dramatically. "I'm hurt, Isadore. I thought you were above tricking a fellow like this."

"Oh, be quiet. You're the one who mentioned business in the first place."

"I'll know better in future. Well then, an assistant?" He eyed Ambry in a curious way. "Or something else as well?"

Ambry looked down, ears going hot.

"None of that, Adrian," Isadore said, as if they had had similar conversations many times before. And what did that mean? That Isadore would never look at them in the way they wanted? They might have lost themself to that thought if not for Adrian's next words.

"I know, I know. So, Ambry, how are you liking it? Is he working you to the bone?" This said with a sideways grin at Isadore.

"It's..." *–amazing, perfect–* "It's been very good. I like it. It's a lot of time, but it's not too much work."

Adrian nodded. "Or you're just the sort who's built for it. Wish I could steal you for Father's accounting. I just don't have the patience for it."

"You don't have the patience for anything," Isadore laughed.

"That's not true," Adrian complained, in a way that reminded Ambry of Delia. "I like hunting, that requires patience."

"Except you talk the whole time and scare away your prey."

"Oh, you and your obsession with unimportant details."

A girl came by with mugs of beer and a dish of little crusty breads. "We're serving roasted river-wings today, with salted onions," she said, "and there's the usual beef stew with beans if you'd prefer."

"I've heard it's a good season for river-wings," Adrian said.

"The fishermen are bringing in crates and crates of them," the girl said. "Cook's running out of ways to prepare them. But they're all delicious, so we're not complaining yet."

"Well, we'll be glad to take a few off your hands. How does that sound?" He looked around at the others.

"I have no objections," Isadore said. Ambry nodded agreement, and the girl hurried off with their order.

"Speaking of hunting," Adrian said, "Father is organizing a trek to the lodge at Bard's Hill next month. You're welcome to join us. It'll get you away from your boring tower for a while. I think I can keep the others from hassling you about politics. I know you're not that fond of hunting, but it has to be better than whatever you're doing now."

"Hunts, no. But skill shooting, I'll join you for that, and you would be wise to prepare yourself for a challenge." Somehow it didn't surprise Ambry that Isadore might dislike hunting but enjoy target shooting. They'd read descriptions of some of the courses, both on horseback and on foot, in their books. Would they ever get to see Isadore enjoying himself at such a sport?

"So, you'll come?"

Isadore sighed. "I don't think it'll be possible. There's already the Islands trip in a few months. We wanted this bargain sealed by the end of summer but every day we're getting two or three couriers with something new we have to wrestle into the deal." And every hour they spent with those letters meant that the rest of the work piled up, the judgements and the policies and the ministers' reports that needed to be reviewed no matter what.

"Oh no, don't you start." Adrian shook his head. "Maybe next season, then. I miss when it wasn't so difficult to claim some time to ourselves. I thought having an assistant would help you with that."

"It has. Ambry's already helped a great deal," Isadore said. Beside him, Ambry hid a proud smile. "But as I haven't chosen to spend all of that time with you, I suppose you wouldn't have noticed."

Was that a reprimand or simply a friendly jab? From the way Adrian laughed, Ambry decided it probably was the latter.

"You've made the wrong choice, then."

"I think I can live with it."

Adrian shook his head and looked as disappointed as he could manage, reminding Ambry a little of Delia. She too acted like a child sometimes, though she could be serious when it counted. They were still considering that comparison when he looked at them and smiled. "No need to be so quiet, Ambry! Isadore might keep you too busy to talk, but I'm here now, and I'll listen."

How much did Isadore expect them to speak? They didn't want to interrupt his meeting with a friend. He got little enough opportunity for that as it was. And they didn't want to say something to reveal their ignorance on all the matters Adrian and Isadore cared about that they knew so little of.

"You're not going to steal me that easily," they dared, and were rewarded with a grin from Adrian and a satisfied laugh from Isadore. "I've heard better wooing than that in the kitchens."

"Ha! You haven't heard me when I'm trying," Adrian returned.

Thanks to Adrian's insistence on not talking about politics and his tendency to jump from topic to topic based on whatever caught his interest, the conversation quickly turned to things Ambry knew from servants' gossip and Delia's letters. Nathalie Collins's inventions, both the successful ones and the dramatic failures. And the tale of the traveling dancers who'd come to town for the Spring Festival and then, instead of leaving, set up a theater for the year.

"I've heard they've got the most astonishing musician," Adrian said. "One flute, and yet he makes you feel like you're really there in an enchanted wood, watching the spirits come to life."

"Ella and Danny saw them a few weeks ago," Ambry said. "They were impressed."

The serving girl returned with three platters balanced across her arms. Ambry's mouth watered as she set theirs down. A whole fat fish sat on the plate, big enough for its tail to hang off the edges, salt-dusted skin curling and crispy, the meat flaky beneath. Steam rose up as they cut into it, smelling of spices. The first bite was perfection, all salt and crisp and soft, rich meat. The thin rounds of preserved onions on top lent a sharpness that made the meal taste all the better. Ambry made certain to catch a little piece in each bite.

Their upbringing in the south meant they had no trouble picking morsels of fish from the bones, and between eating and listening and adding contributions where prompted, there wasn't a great deal of space for worrying about how they sounded.

"I told you it was a good season for river-wings," Adrian said, sounding very pleased with himself though there really wasn't any reason for it. "It's the weather – the spring had just the right amount of heat and rain that the fish had enough food for their broods to grow big and fat. That doesn't mean the fishers are completely happy, though, because if there's more fish they sell for less money, and buyers might get tired of them. But I think it's a good thing, because it means we get more dishes like this. What?" Isadore was staring at him with an amused look on his face.

"It looks like you've picked up some of your economics lessons after all. And natural science, you've always liked that. Remember the explorer who gave that seminar in our second year? The one with the imprints of ancient animals?"

"Of course. I'm still subscribed to the journal. Have you seen any of the rubbings, Ambry?"

"I haven't. But that sounds interesting. Ancient animals?"

"Very, very ancient. Some of them are older than mountains, or at least that's what the experts say. Animals that died in bogs. Somehow their bones become part of the stone. Explorers dig them up piece by piece and reassemble them. I just wish Father would let me go on one of those expeditions. I've even sent letters to Captain Michaelsen, but I've never heard anything back."

How could anything be older than mountains? Ambry had a momentary image of gigantic skeletal beasts roaming the forest. Was it truly possible that one could see so far into the past simply through rocks and bones?

"What do they look like?"

"Oh, they're ferocious things. Huge teeth and claws and spikes all down their backs. If you want, I can send Isadore some of the things that've been published. There's some detailed illustrations of what they might have looked like. You know those serpents on the Crested Islands? The ones Saint Baven is supposed to have sent to bite sinners? The researchers think that thousands of years ago, they had legs. Can you imagine that?"

Before he could go on, a man stormed through the doors, flushed with anger and drink. One of the servers approached him timidly. "Sir, do you need something?"

He shoved her out of the way without even looking, sending her stumbling against a table. The woman sitting there gave her a hand up, cursing at the man, but he paid them no mind. He scanned the room like a hawk after a mouse. His eyes narrowed when he spotted Isadore's table and he staggered forward, brandishing a knife, yelling, "You! I've been looking for you and your little friends. How dare you come here, looking all high and mighty, like you're—"

Before he could even finish his sentence, Dominick had him pinned over a table with a dagger at his throat. The knife fell from the attacker's hand and clattered to the floor. The other diners gasped and scrambled out of the way. The man fought Dominick to no avail, swearing and shouting all the while. His flailing hands caught a glass of beer and sent it tumbling across the table; it fell off the edge and shattered, spilling a puddle across the floor. The man continued to writhe uselessly for a while and then fell still.

Whether in punishment for the broken glass or her own indignity, the girl who he'd knocked to the floor crept up behind him with another mug of beer and dumped it over his head. He sputtered; she leapt back from his furious snarl and Dominick's disapproving glare.

"Who's your dog, Tisdale?" he hissed, eyes burning. "Too afraid to face me on your own?"

Adrian cursed. Isadore stood, sheltering Ambry behind him.

"Highness, please sit down," Dominick ordered.

The man he held went pale, his eyes widening in recognition as he stared at Isadore. "Your Highness."

Whispers spread through the tavern like wildfire. So the drunk man had been so intent on attacking Adrian that he hadn't even recognized the prince. But why? The horrified look on Adrian's face confirmed Ambry's fears.

"He wasn't here for you," Adrian said, without turning away from the astonished would-be attacker.

Somebody must have had the sense to run for the Guard, or the noise had been enough to be heard from the street, for an officer came through the door with her blade drawn and strode up to where Dominick had the attacker secured. She bowed to Isadore and then turned to Dominick. "Thank you, Lieutenant Marshall. I'll handle this and send you a report."

Dominick wrenched the man upright and let the officer bind his hands. He remained oddly silent through it all when Ambry would have expected him to protest and threaten. The other people, though, were not quiet at all, and the whispering continued even after the Guard officer left with her captive. A chill passed over Ambry despite the warm weather. If Isadore hadn't been here with Adrian, if Dominick had not caught the man in time…

A hand on their shoulder brought them back to themself. "Ambry. Are you all right?"

"I… I think so, yes," they managed around the knot of unease squirming in their stomach. They took a deep breath and forced it down. They were safe now, thanks to Dominick. And Isadore needed them to stay steady.

Dominick approached their table, sword still drawn and ready. "Highness, we must return to the palace at once."

"I have a meeting with the commanders at two," Isadore protested. "Do you honestly think I'll be in danger with half the City Guard around me?"

It didn't help. "I'm sorry, but we must return to the palace," Dominick repeated, implacable and not at all apologetic. "You can send couriers when we arrive. I'm sure the commanders will forgive your absence."

"He was threatening Adrian, not me. He's the one who needs protection." But Ambry already knew that nothing Isadore said would convince Dominick, not when he had protocol to follow. And from his half-hearted pleading, Isadore knew it too.

"We can bring him with us," Ambry said, cutting the fruitless debate short.

Dominick nodded. "That would be acceptable. He will stay until we can determine it is safe for him to leave."

Isadore sighed. "Very well. Adrian?"

"I'm certainly not staying here by myself," Adrian said with a shaky laugh, still looking at the wrecked table and the mess around it.

Isadore found a server – it wasn't hard, as they were all staring at him – and said, "I'm so sorry for all this."

The girl glanced around as if expecting that he was talking to somebody else. "It's—it's all right, Highness. We've had worse brawls in here before, believe me. We know how to deal with it."

"Good." He pushed a pouch of coins into her startled hands. From her expression, it must have been a lot more than their meal had been worth.

Before she could stutter her astonished thanks, Dominick called for him again. "Highness. This way." Staying close so that he could keep them all in his sight, he ushered the three of them out onto the street.

Chapter Seven

✧

Isadore would have interrogated Adrian as they walked if not for the way Dominick glared at him as soon as he so much as whispered a word. He understood the need for security, and he was of course very grateful for Dominick's protection, but this seemed a little too much. But it wasn't worth pulling rank on him with the palace gates so close ahead of them. The one circumstance under which Dominick would refuse to follow his orders was when he thought his prince needed protection.

But as soon as Dominick shepherded them into the tower study and explained in a few gruff words to a very startled Melanie what had happened at the tavern, there was nothing stopping Isadore from turning to his dearest friend and demanding, "Adrian, what in all the hells did you *do?*"

Adrian opened his mouth to argue, closed it, and then dropped into a chair and rubbed his eyes, all that bravado draining away. "I... I might have started a feud with Ellis Hardy and his friends."

Isadore stared. He knew Adrian could be impulsive, could sometimes seem utterly ignorant of the risks he took, but he'd never thought he could be this impossibly foolish. "And how exactly did you manage that?"

"I didn't think they'd take it this far! It was just a few games of cards." At least Adrian had the good grace to look embarrassed. "Or at least it started that way. Then I lost a few hands. I wanted to win the money back so I wouldn't have to ask Father for more. I was drunk, I wasn't thinking straight. I might have told him I had friends who would hunt him down if he cheated me, and then he said his would get to me first. I thought it was all just in jest."

"Apparently not. Or at least, not to that fellow who attacked us. I thought you said you thought better when you were drunk?" Isadore said, letting sarcasm drench his words. He'd truly expected Adrian would know better than to challenge a gang like that. Hardy might not be much of a threat on his own; while he was a notorious cheat he rarely resorted to violence. But some of his friends had no such compunctions. The Guard had never been able to pin him to any of their crimes despite years of trying.

"Maybe I don't." Adrian scrubbed a hand across his forehead. "I'll need to send word to my father. He's expecting me back soon."

Without needing to be asked, Ambry handed Adrian a pen and a sheet of paper.

"We can take care of that," Isadore said. "Sit, wait, and please try to stay out of trouble for at least a few minutes." This, kinder than before, but heavy with authority. It was a testament to how serious this was that Adrian didn't try to answer with a joke. He scrawled a few lines onto the paper, folded it, and handed it to Melanie to tuck into an envelope and stamp with Isadore's seal.

She gave it to Ambry, along with short and apologetic notes to the Captain of the Guard and Minister Travers. They took the letters and hurried off to the messengers' post, nearly colliding with Sylvia as she came up the stairs.

"Dominick, what happened? Why are you back early?" she demanded.

Dominick repeated what he had told Melanie.

"He wasn't targeting me," Isadore put in when Dominick paused for breath. "I don't think he even recognized me at first."

"It makes no difference," Dominick said. "He would have harmed you if given the chance."

"Well, we'll see what the Guard gets out of him," Sylvia said. "I don't think we need to wake Lawrence." Lawrence had started his career as a Guard investigator, and while he would certainly want to look over the reports, there was precious little to review as of yet. Isadore idly wondered what the Guard would turn up, but he doubted it would be of much interest. Likely the man had been nothing but an angry drunk bent on avenging some imagined slight against a friend.

Sylvia and Dominick wasted no time planning shift changes, extra guards at the gates, and reports to the city commanders. It was no use arguing with them. The only thing to do for the foreseeable future was to be quiet and let his guardians fuss over him. But first, he had to take care of them.

"Dominick, are you all right? You weren't hurt at all?"

Dominick paused before replying, which was how Isadore knew he had not escaped unscathed.

"Only a scratch. From the broken glass, I think. It's nothing to be concerned about."

Isadore winced as Dominick peeled his torn sleeve from the wound. It looked worse than it was – not deep, but it had bled a great deal before scabbing over and the dark fabric around it was stained and stiff.

"Were you planning on telling me? So I could mend it?" He didn't want to discomfit Dominick in front of the others, but it would be best to act before the wound had a chance to become diseased.

"I… you have enough to deal with already. It's minor."

"Still. Let me help?"

Dominick, expressionless, held out his arm as if for the Guard doctor. Isadore placed his hand over the cut and poured energy into it, feeling the skin knit together and the pain fade away like footprints on the shore. He couldn't do anything for the blood or the torn shirt, but Dominick could easily claim a fresh one from Guard stores if he needed it.

Dominick's face did not change, but there was warm devotion in his voice when he pulled away. "Thank you, Highness."

Isadore studied Dominick for a moment more, looking for any signs of pain or injury, and saw none. Good. Satisfied, he stepped back to let Dominick and Sylvia continue their planning. He searched through the cabinets until he found the folding wooden chess set Abigail had given him last New Year's, dragged out the little table so he and Adrian could play, and started setting it up.

"Good idea," Adrian said. He watched Isadore for a few moments, then made a sound that was almost a growl of frustration. "My heart won't stop pounding."

"After someone just tried to kill you in broad daylight, it's hardly surprising," Isadore said, a touch of concern tempering his tone. "You'll be fine, it'll fade."

"Hmm." Adrian tilted his head, hiding a smile. "No, it's pretty bad. I think I'll have to stay here all day. Father will just have to get someone else to review the exchange reports."

"Now I know you're all right," Isadore said fondly. If Adrian was still thinking about ways to get out of work, then the situation today clearly hadn't affected him too seriously. Hopefully, at least, it would teach him not to go around with cheats.

But he was worried about Ambry. They were hiding it well, but the incident had shaken them badly. Things had been so peaceful for so long that he hadn't thought when he hired an assistant that they might be exposed to such violence. This time, it hadn't been meant for him, but he could never be certain that they wouldn't be caught in the middle of something far worse, especially as Isadore grew bolder in proposing and implementing reforms. He could all too easily imagine an angry lord paying someone to remove the outspoken heir who wanted to hold them responsible for the wellbeing of their people. Or a devotee of the Southern Order who believed his ways heretical, or some foreign adversary looking to weaken Talland's position. Whatever the motive behind its wielder, a stray knife or arrow could do worlds of damage, and though Isadore's healing abilities were great, and he was thankful for them every day, they might not be enough to repair a grave wound...

"Your move," Adrian prompted. Isadore blinked, studied the board for a distracted moment, and moved a piece.

Adrian tsked. "Not a very good move. You sure you're all here? If anyone here's got a right to be shaken, it's me, you know."

"I just hope Ambry–" He didn't get to finish, for at that moment Ambry came in with a tray of tea and a dish of Mrs. Hammond's cheese biscuits. That brightened his mood a little. Marjorie didn't bake often, but when she did she unerringly managed to craft tasty little creations that somehow never went stale and so were hoarded in tins by their lucky recipients. Even Sylvia was tempted enough to steal one from the tray before heading back downstairs.

"You got anything stronger than tea?" Adrian said, only half-joking.

"Wasn't that what got you into this situation in the first place?" Melanie scolded, rolling her eyes. "Ambry, come help me with these reports. We can leave the boys to their game."

At another time, Isadore might have protested her blatant misuse of her power and obvious attempts to steal his assistant away, but he couldn't muster the will for it. They finished the game; Adrian won, mostly thanks to Isadore's distraction.

"We need to do something about Hardy and his gang," Melanie said while Adrian reset the board. "Counting cards might not be illegal, but threatening people with a knife certainly is."

"The Guard's been trying to catch him out for years now, but he's always been ready for them. I have no doubts that this man will be sentenced, but I don't know if that'll be enough for them to reach back to the others. Most of them are minor cheats anyway and it'll be hard to argue they're worth the time." Isadore moved his knight with perhaps more force than was necessary. "They run underground deals and then don't deliver, and they make sure their victims are too embarrassed to complain, or they target people who are also criminals so that protesting would reveal their own dealings. I think the public actually finds it rather alluring."

"It's the whole bandit king image Hardy has about him," Adrian said. "It's supposed to be sexy. Or so I've heard."

"In books, I suppose," Ambry said, looking up from Melanie's desk. "There's always a secret cave filled with treasure. And clever outcasts fooling the arrogant lords. But outside of a story? It's frightening, not attractive. You can't trust that they're going to turn out to be the heroes."

"Attractive or not, he managed to seduce you, at least," Isadore said to Adrian.

"Because I wanted to beat him, not join him," Adrian protested, clearly offended.

"Same difference, in the end. You lose your money, and he gets away with it."

A knock on the door. "Or maybe not," Melanie said. "Come in!"

Captain Hannah Dreisand of the city guard strode into the room and bowed to them. She was a tall and well-muscled woman who managed to radiate intimidation with every step. This was the sort of person with no patience for troublemakers of any sort. "Highness. Lieutenant Marshall."

Isadore stood. "Captain. You didn't need to come all this way."

"Trust me, Highness, this is far more exciting than everything else on my desk today. And as I suspect your guards are keeping you stabled in here for the rest of the day, I thought it would be worth my coming to you personally."

She gave a rare smile. "You're not going to get out of our meeting that easily." She looked between him and Adrian. "All right. You were both there?"

"And my assistant, Ambry Jean." Ambry had moved themself out of the way as she entered and was currently standing at the bookshelves, searching for something in one of the fat volumes of law codes.

"Not me," Melanie put in cheerfully. "I've been here all day, staying out of danger."

"At least somebody is," Dreisand said.

What followed was a very long conversation that told Isadore very little he didn't already know but was hopefully helpful to Dreisand's investigation. Finally, she saw fit to tell them what she knew.

"We think he's telling the truth about not recognizing you, Highness. Which means this is probably not politically motivated. He was focused on Tisdale, who he believed had threatened his brother, who is one of Hardy's closest accomplices."

"It was just a game," Adrian pleaded. "I wasn't serious about it."

"We're not accusing you of anything, Lord Tisdale" Dreisand said, while giving him a look that said she probably blamed him for at least part of it. "We'll be asking him some more questions once he's sober, but I expect he'll spend at least a few weeks safely locked up. He's got a record of doing this sort of thing, but he's never been so bold as to use a knife instead of his fists."

Would she go to such trouble if this man had attacked a table of commoners instead of Allen Tisdale's son and the prince of the realm? Dreisand was an upstanding and dedicated woman and Isadore could easily believe she would come down hard on any sort of violence in her city, but if this case had not involved him, it might not have reached her desk in the first place to receive such dedicated attention.

"Ambry?" she asked, turning to them. "Did you see anything that wasn't already mentioned?"

They thought, clearly surprised to be asked. "He wasn't holding the knife correctly. I don't think he knew what to do with it." They held up a hand to demonstrate.

They knew enough about knife fighting to recognize the difference? Isadore was surprised by that.

"Hmm. That's interesting," Dreisand mused. "If he's inexperienced, that could mean Hardy is recruiting new blood, or encouraging his followers to violence they hadn't been a part of before. How did you know?"

"My cousin taught me once," they replied stiffly, as if expecting a challenge. The cousin who'd been harried by the Guard?

She asked them a few last questions and noted down their responses. "Thank you, I think that's all I need. I'll send the full report when it's finished." She tucked away her notes into her bag and brought out a second folder. "And now, about the meeting we were supposed to have. Lord Tisdale, Ambry, could you leave us in private?"

Isadore cut in. "Ambry can stay, they're going to be taking notes."

Dreisand peered at Melanie. "But your secretary is right here."

Melanie coughed. "I've got other work to do. And it's worth the practice."

Dreisand weighed this. "Very well, they can stay."

"I suppose it's safe for me to leave now?" Adrian asked, sounding rather disappointed about it. He unfolded himself from his comfortable seat.

"Go back to whatever you're avoiding," Driesand told him. "Your father will appreciate it."

"Right." He made a last move on the chessboard, not that it really mattered, as Isadore was winning this time, stretched lazily, and headed through the door, nodding to Dominick and Dreisand as he passed.

Ambry arranged themself with paper and pen at the side of the desk, and dutifully recorded the proceedings.

Dreisand's stony face turned somehow even more bitter. He knew Hardy had been a thorn in her side for nearly a decade, outwitting two predecessors in her office. "He's gotten bolder lately. It seems every day there's more reports of something he's got his fingers in, but he's as quick as a runaway stallion. He knows how to keep himself clean enough that the Guard has no fair reason to bring him in."

"There must be something you can do," Isadore argued. "If all these people have confessed to his involvement, you should at least be able to question him."

"If we could even find him," Dreisand said. She rubbed at a scar on her hand he knew she'd received in a fight with one of Hardy's thieves. "He has a dozen aliases, and he keeps himself safe behind armies of loyal followers. He helps the bandit gangs on the border sell their stolen goods, and that keeps him in enough gold to bribe anyone who might think to sell him out." Her voice darkened with anger. "I don't doubt some of my officers have taken his lind, and once I find them, they'll regret it."

By the time Dreisand declared them finished for the day, Ambry had several pages of notes on the rising threats the Guard was investigating and plans for how to address them. The lawbooks they'd retrieved earlier helped a great deal. They hadn't gone through all of it – the Guard didn't share all of their business with the Crown and Isadore and Seraphina certainly wouldn't have time for it if they tried. But it was enough for them to advise each other on how they wanted to continue.

Dreisand offered a few more formalities, then bowed and departed. Isadore leaned back in his seat, casting a rueful look at the clock. "I'll have to reschedule with Minister Travers."

"I'll handle that," Melanie said. "She'll be in the city next week for the Council session. I think we can work in some time then."

"There must be something we can do about Hardy's gang," Isadore said, without truly listening.

"Someday they'll be bold enough to do something he can't weasel out of. Something more than just defrauding other fraudsters. And then they'll find themselves in far more trouble than they can talk their way out of."

Isadore nodded. "I can only hope that's before someone is killed."

✧

Despite Dreisand's assurances that there was no immediate threat to Isadore's life, or for that matter Adrian's, Dominick advised Isadore against returning to the city that day. Isadore didn't protest. Secretly, Ambry was glad of it. The day had been exciting enough so far; no need for any more adventure.

Ambry expected Melanie to take the opportunity to shove several more baskets of letters and cases awaiting opinion at him, so it was a surprise when she instead pulled out a small stack of folded notes from a drawer.

"I've been keeping these for when we had time. They're from the servants and archivists and secretaries, all about how they've found your reforms."

Isadore brightened. "Oh?"

"From Ella Marsh and Patrice Addison, their thanks for the new kitchen supplies."

"That's good. And it's made a difference. I could have sworn the food has been even better than usual recently."

"There's a letter here from Marjorie, if you want to listen." What did Mrs. Hammond have to say? "She's pleased so far with Alice – that's the new girl – and she's asking if she can hire two more."

"I don't see a problem with that. The budget should allow for it." Isadore frowned in thought. "These should be her decisions, not mine. She knows what she needs far better than I ever could. I need to make sure Marjorie knows she has control over the budget to buy new supplies and hire new people when they're needed."

"You should tell her that, then."

"I will. And you, Ambry? Are you happy with the changes?"

Ambry smiled. "Yes. It's even better than I could have imagined."

"How are you liking your room?"

"It's very nice. I'm glad to have the quiet. I liked rooming with Delia, but she'd stay up late with the lamp lit reading and she'd try to talk when I wanted to sleep. And then I was never sure how much I could move around without disturbing her." They shook their head. Isadore didn't need to hear all that. "Having my own bath is the most wonderful thing." They had to laugh at themself for that. Such a small thing, and yet it had made their days so much easier. "There is one thing…"

"What is it?"

"May I have another table? The desk is a little small."

"Of course. You can take whatever you want from storage."

"I can ask Erik about it tomorrow. He does a lot of mending furniture and things like that." They ought to have thought of that themself, but they'd gotten into the habit of making do with what they had. When they'd worked at Lady Mohren's estate, her housekeeper had harshly punished anyone who dared to claim even the most worn and aged items from the storage closets. And the table had not been so much trouble that they'd been spurred to address it.

"Mending and gardening both? Perhaps we should hire a carpenter."

Ambry laughed. "I don't know if Erik would like that. He enjoys mending and building. And he has enough assistant gardeners to take over the work when he's busy."

"Very well, I won't interfere." Isadore sighed. "How did it get to this point?"

"It would have been a lot of small things," Melanie said. "But it took a long time to notice, because everyone was working so hard to keep it running. And they didn't want to ask for help. After a while I suppose it just seemed normal, and nobody wanted to go out of their way to change it."

So Ambry had not been alone in simply trying to make do instead of looking for the causes of their trouble. But Isadore would not settle for that. Not when things could be so much better, and all that was needed to get there was a little work and dedication.

"Mrs. Hammond will probably have everything in order within a few weeks, now that she has the extra hands," Ambry said. "She's good at that."

"I'll be certain it's done right this time," Isadore promised.

True to his word, he spent the next few days meeting with Hammond and Erik and the other senior staff, figuring out what else they needed and how best to organize and assign all that needed to be done. Ambry recorded page after page of notes, filling the margins with little reminders to themself of things they'd noticed in their own work.

After nearly a week of this, with Melanie carefully fitting time into his already busy schedule, Ambry would have expected Isadore to be pleased, even revitalized and energetic. The determination was there, to be sure, but it was quiet and shadowed with something darker that Ambry finally recognized was shame.

"I think we've done a lot so far," they said. "People are happy about it. Delia sent me a letter about how much she likes the new furniture in her room. Especially the desk with the secret drawer."

Isadore sat back, twirled his pen in his fingers. "Hm. I didn't know it had that. I might have asked for it if I'd known."

Ambry laughed. "Maybe that's why it's a secret. I can imagine the advertisements: The newest development in carpentry! Cabinets invisible to royalty!"

The joke sounded even worse out loud than it had in their head, and Ambry cringed in embarrassment. But Isadore didn't seem to mind, and Melanie smiled.

"This is good," she went on. "People are happier when they feel that they're being listened to."

"I only wish we could have done it earlier," Isadore sighed.

"We all wish that for one thing or another," Melanie said. "What matters is we're doing it now, and we're not going to let anything hold us up."

"Yes. I won't rest until this is a good place to be."

Ambry had to protest that. "I never felt it was a bad place to be. I know I didn't want to go anywhere else. Things were good, even if they were difficult. They were good because of what you provided."

"They were good in spite of the little I provided."

"It wasn't your place to provide it," Melanie put in. "And in some ways, it's good you didn't stick your nose in it right away. People might like to be listened to, but they also don't like to be tightly managed by someone unfamiliar with their lives."

"Very true," Isadore admitted.

There was a knock at the door. Isadore sat up and motioned for Dominick to see who it was. One of the Queen's messengers stood in the doorway. She wasn't carrying a letter, so whatever it was must be a brief message.

"Highness, the Queen wishes for you to join her table tonight," she said.

"Thank you. Tell her I'll be there." The messenger bowed and departed. "That's not too long from now. I ought to get myself ready."

⟡

"I'm delaying our trip to the Islands this year," Seraphina said.

Isadore raised his head, his fork stilling at his plate. "Mother?"

"There's far too much that requires our presence here. Once the treaty is completed, then we can sail." She continued to watch him, as if waiting for his response so she could judge it worthy.

He let out a breath that was not quite a sigh. "I understand." She was right. They couldn't in good conscience leave the work unfinished, not at this stage.

He took another bite of herb-crusted steak, thinking of how he would tell Ambry. He'd been looking forward to spending some leisure time with them and with Melanie, looking forward to getting them all away from the tower and the endless work for a few sweet days of freedom.

"I've already sent word to Celeste and Abigail," she continued. "I believe they might be secretly pleased when they get the letters. They've been telling me about some of the University's summer events. Neither has outright asked if they could stay, but it was very much implied."

"I remember. Adrian told me about the equestrian competition. And our friend Petra loved having the free time to explore the archives. I think Abigail would enjoy the art festival. They have several painters from the city come in and try to work in each other's styles, it's supposed to be a lot of fun to watch."

Seraphina smiled. "Good. I'll be looking forward to hearing their tales of it over the New Year's holiday."

Other than the summer sailing excursions and the winter holiday, the princesses didn't visit home often. From their letters, Isadore gathered they were enjoying the University and the freedom it offered far more than anything they had at home. It didn't surprise him. Celeste had always yearned to explore the world, and Abigail had been desperately bored with life in the palace with all its rules and its very few escapes to the city.

That wasn't the only thing keeping them busy. Celeste, with her magic-blessed ear for languages, had found her skills very much in demand by her teachers. He remembered one particular letter she'd sent right after starting classes, how excited and pleased she'd been. She so loved to be of use to others, and more importantly, she loved to discover new things and learn the old secrets hiding in cryptic texts. Abigail, on the other hand, was less certain of what she wanted to pursue. So far she had gone from class to class for nearly two years without finding a one true passion. But there was time aplenty for her to explore, and her family would support her in what she eventually chose. And there wasn't truly a need for her to choose any one thing – a well-rounded education could be just as useful as a narrow and deep one.

His sisters would be expected to serve as his advisors when he took the throne. And his heir would be the first of their children. He would welcome their help and their wisdom with open arms, but if they found something else that called to them even louder, he would not stop them from pursuing it.

He expected to hear a lot about their classes and friends and new adventures when they did visit. It would be better, he reasoned, to enjoy the holiday without the treaty and the summit hanging over them.

That was, if they could even get to the point of holding a summit.

Chapter Eight

✧

The position of assistant to the prince came with a generous stipend. Ambry didn't expect they'd have much time to spend it when the work kept them in the palace most days, but they found little reason to complain. Isadore made certain they were provided with everything they needed. They certainly couldn't complain after being promised clothing designed by Darby Allister, they thought, still hardly able to believe it.

Even on slower, more ordinary days, the work was good and useful, and to see the prince every day, to speak with him and help him in his duties, that would have been worth twice the work he assigned.

They had a day off every week, though Isadore usually dismissed them early once or twice more. On those days they usually joined the servants for supper and played games with Delia and Ella and Marion after, or if they were too tired for that to be appealing, sat in their little room with one of the books Delia had insisted they borrow. It was still too warm to light the fire most nights, but they expected to be very grateful for it come winter.

On one of those early nights, just before a free day, they returned to the tower room to find a letter and a package waiting on the bed. The package was a small thing, covered in brown paper and tied with a long braided ribbon, bright yellow against the plain wrapping.

They opened it without tearing the paper, which turned out to be a good idea because the inside was covered in little sketches: cats and dogs and flowers and crowns.

Inside there was a small tin of their favorite butter biscuits, and a set of hair ribbons in green and blue. On top of all that sat a note in Delia's curling handwriting: *Don't try to do anything in exchange! I like making gifts for friends who've moved away.*

"Moved away" wasn't exactly true; the pair still saw each other at least once a week. But in practice it was as good a way as any to describe it. Ambry was very glad the others hadn't thought them arrogant for their sudden advancement.

They set the items on a shelf, considering how to reply. The last time someone had sent Delia a gift in response to one of hers, it had turned into a competition of sorts, with each sending more and more elaborate packages, trying to outdo each other. Finally, her friends had joined in, sending the boy in question a tremendous box of treats, to which he had replied with a note and a single pressed leaf – a symbol of concession. Delia still had it in the box of treasures she kept under her bed.

The letter was from their mother. Aunt Polly was visiting for a week and wanted to see them if they had any time to spare for a visit. That would be a good use of a free day, they decided.

They picked a book from the little shelf and draped themself over the chair by the window to read. The book was one they'd borrowed from Isadore. It had been a gift from the Larsellan ambassador to Talland, Kestrel na'Southwind, and told the tale of the ancient Larse families who had famously taken down the wall between their fields and bred the line of horses that still pulled Larsellan's plows to the present day. When Ambry had asked if the Ambassador meant to imply anything by the choice of story, Isadore had shaken his head. "The Larse are proud, but not in the way the rest of us are proud. They don't need to shout their achievements from castle turrets. They're content to keep to themselves, using thousands of years of knowledge to keep fields and towns quietly prosperous for generation after generation. When they tell their stories to you, it's because they trust you to respect them."

Ambry had heard some say that Larsellan had no great schools, but from what Isadore said, and what they read in the book, that was completely false. Their knowledge might be passed down in other ways, from parent to child and master to apprentice, but they had it in plenty.

The story was certainly not boring, but it was slow and thoughtful, and when their eyes started to slip close, they set the book on the table and went to bed. They needed the rest if they were going to wake up early enough to make the walk to their mother's house to surprise her in time for midmorning tea.

The next morning, they set off early just as they'd planned, nodding to the sleepy gate guard as they left the palace. Ambry crossed the West Bridge, carefully keeping out of the way of the carriages rattling past taking goods to shops and bringing bottles of milk and baskets of fruit in from the neighboring farmland.

The last time they'd visited, they'd gotten caught in a rainstorm just past the gate that'd churned the piles of dirty old snow along the road into sticky, cold mud. Today the weather was much more pleasant, with enough clouds in the sky to keep off the heat of the sun, but still bright and cheerful.

Their mother lived in Grovewood, a small village just beyond the north edge of the city. It had a small church, and a small school, and a few weaving workshops that took in the wool from the sheep raised on the nearby hills. When they'd moved here from the southeast, the spinning women and the weavers had welcomed them into the community with open arms. And, most importantly of all, they'd welcomed Ambry for who they'd found themself to be.

There had only been one found-person in their old village, an old man who mostly kept to himself, selling smoked river fish at the market and turning an uncaring ear to the rumors whispered about him and what he kept or lacked under his clothing. Here, there were several, and they didn't hide themselves away. Two of the weaving women had found themselves, one as a child and one later in life. One was married to a builder who, like Ambry, had found they were neither man nor woman.

While Ambry helped them with weaving, the women told them stories of others like them, from everyday farmers to ancient saints, who'd led lives normal and extraordinary, not limited by ill-fitting bodies or others' disapproval. The women had taught them about Saint Astrenn of the Island, and the story of how in ancient times Astrenn guided people like Ambry to find their true selves and gave them the courage to show themselves to the world as they were and not how others wanted them to be.

The Southern Order hadn't recognized any saints of unusual gender, and only one who'd partnered with someone of their own sex. But the River Order had a few among their canon, along with others Ambry had never heard of in their grandfather's sermons.

The village kept the newcomers sheltered and fed for the few weeks it took them to get settled in their new home. They probably could have relied on that help for longer than they did, but Ambry's mother had been determined to fend for herself. She'd wasted no time installing herself at the old potter's abandoned cottage. Once she'd fixed up the kiln, her wheel hardly ever stopped spinning, and Ambry had secured a position in Lady Mohren's kitchen shortly after.

There had been a found-man working there who Ambry had briefly thought might become a friend, until they'd learned what a terrible bully he was. But he and most of the others had accepted Ambry as they were, and for a long time, that had been all they'd asked for.

Now, they thought, they had the chance to reach for more.

A few hours' walk brought Ambry past the old city wall, past the gate, and down the well-traveled dirt road to the grove of trees that had given the village its name. Their mother's house stood near a pair of willows. She had always called the hollows created by their draping branches fairy nests, and the village children could often be found hiding in them.

As they walked up the path, a familiar figure rushed out the door towards them, apron flying behind her. "Ambry!"

Lenora Jean was a small woman whose eternally wispy dark hair held only a trace of the rich color that adorned Ambry's, but she had all the grace they had never quite managed to acquire. To hear Aunt Polly tell it, she'd been the favorite of all her sisters, beloved and doted on, but it hadn't made her in the least spoiled or spiteful.

She smiled adoringly at Ambry and ran her hands over their shoulders, pausing to brush her fingers over the golden royal badge at their neck before pulling them into a tight embrace, which they returned happily.

"It's good to see you. So much has happened."

"You'll have to tell us! Come in, come in! There's tea, and the buns are almost ready. Polly's just inside, and Herrin's playing somewhere in the garden." Polly adored her grandson and always came along to watch him while his parents were busy on a building site in the city.

They went inside, where Polly was sitting at the old wooden table the village builder had made for them. A chipped mug of tea waited for Ambry. They picked it up, smelling their mother's favorite blend of honey and herbs.

"Now, did you take the bridge or the ferry?" their mother asked. "I've heard stories of things going missing on those ferries. Jewelry, scarves, loose chimes out of people's purses…" She shook her head. "What am I saying? You'd never be that careless." As she talked, she adjusted her saint-scarf, a worn but bright piece of blue cloth bearing the sign of Saint Mayri of the Hearthfire.

"I took the bridge," they reassured her. They hadn't heard that rumor about the ferries. They distantly recalled Patrice complaining about a missing scarf after a visit to the city, but things went missing all the time with no malice behind it.

"Assistant to the prince! How amazing," Polly sighed. "You must be proud of yourself. I hope the work isn't too hard. I told Lenora I didn't think you'd have any time to come all this way to see us."

"You'll have to tell us all about it," Lenora said.

"Have there been any problems because of your…" Polly started. She didn't say it directly, but Ambry knew what she meant. She asked about it every time she saw them.

"No, none," Ambry said, feeling a warmth of rightness in their chest. "Is– His Highness and Melanie, his secretary, they understand. The prince's tailor is like me too."

"Don't harp on it, Polly," Lenora scolded. "It's not the same here as it is at home."

"True, true. The city's always been a haven for strangelings of all types, I suppose. I always said, Lenora, I think you were secretly pleased after growing up with five sisters," Polly laughed.

"I would have been pleased no matter what," Ambry's mother said. "As long as they were happy."

It probably helped that Ambry's new post brought in enough coin to send a few more lind home every week, but they weren't going to mention that in front of Polly. They knew Lenora would be carefully keeping the money in the worn wooden box with the tarnished lock she said their father had made while he was courting her. Sometimes they wondered what he would think of them, if he'd lived past their childhood. They hoped he'd be proud.

Polly and Lenora continued to ask questions, which Ambry answered in between sips of tea. After a few minutes, Polly got up to take the tray out of the oven and peered at the cakes.

"You keep your oven too hot, Lenora," she said. "You should have told me, I'd have done a better job of this."

Lenora wasn't concerned. "It won't hurt anything. You always underbake them anyway."

"Underbake? Another few minutes and we'd have char on these." Polly glanced out the window. "Herrin! Tea is ready!" she called.

A few moments later, a young boy rushed into the house atop a raggedy hobbyhorse, muddy shoes leaving hoofprints on the floor. He smiled up at them under a crown of twigs and leaves, and brandished a little wooden sword.

Polly patted Ambry's shoulder. "You remember Ambry, don't you? They work for the Prince now."

The little boy's eyes went wide. "You do? Do you get to wear a crown?" he asked.

"No. Isadore doesn't wear a crown except when he's making public speeches," Ambry told him.

"Do you get to fight people, like Prince Aben and his army fought the pirates?"

"No, there's no fighting. He has guards to protect him."

Herrin's face lit up. That had caught his attention. "What are they like? Do they have swords?"

"They do. There are three of them. One of them's a big, tall man who's a little scary." They did their best impression of Dominick's stern, statue-like pose, which wasn't very good, but it was enough to make little Herrin giggle. They went on. "And one's a short man who's old but he notices everything." They put their hands up to their eyes like they used to do while playing finder when they were Herrin's age. "And the other one, she's big and strong, and she's very quiet, but when she says something it's always something funny."

"But if you don't fight or wear crowns, what do you do?" Herrin asked.

"It's a lot of reading old legal documents and listening to politicians," they said.

Herrin scowled in disapproval. "That sounds boring," he insisted. "Do you want to play bandits?"

"How do you play bandits?" Ambry asked.

The little boy puffed out his chest, clearly pleased to be asked. "You look around until you see something nice. Like, like this!" He took a bun from the table and pushed it into Ambry's hand. "Then you ride up really fast, so they don't see you, and you take it!" He snatched the bun back and stormed back out into the garden.

Through the open door, Lenora and Ambry watched Herrin run about, yelling at invisible compatriots and slashing at foes with his sword. Lenora frowned. "I'm not sure if bandits is the best game for a little boy. Whatever happened to chase and rangers and finder?"

"Oh, he plays those too. But he really loves anything about ruffians and troublemakers. He and his friends have spun all sorts of tales about Hardy's gang." Polly sighed and shook her head. "I'll be sure to check his pockets before we head home, so there's no need to worry about your things, Lenora."

"It's not the thievery I'm worried about. I heard that Prince Isadore was attacked in the city last month," she said, eyes deep with concern. "By someone working for Hardy."

"We were fine, Mum, I promise. The attacker didn't even know who he was. He was going after his friend. And Dominick – Isadore's guard – caught him before he could do anything." To their relief, neither of them asked for more details, and Herrin was too far away and too wrapped up in his game to hear.

But the concern in their mother's face only seemed to grow, settling into the few thin lines that creased her face. "I'd hate to see you wrapped up in any of Hardy's business. He's a brutal man. The stories in the Chronicle are dreadful."

Polly scoffed. "Oh, he's not that bad. What's stealing a few trinkets from people who don't keep their purses shut up tight enough?"

"But when the Guard gets involved?" Lenora asked.

Polly sniffed. "In that case they probably deserve it. You don't just fall into that sort of thing."

Ambry wanted to protest the contradiction. How could she brush off thievery and yet care so little for those caught up by the law? They nearly bit their tongue to hold back a protest about their cousin who'd suffered so much for even a brief association with thieves. From Lenora's expression, she was remembering the same thing.

"It's still not something to celebrate, Polly," she said. "It's not like the stories. What he does to people who owe him debts…"

But Polly wouldn't be moved. "Herrin's barely more than a babe. Of course he's going to chase flights of imagination. His mother was the same when she was a little one, and she turned out just fine. And I seem to recall that when you were that age, you wanted to be a wild cat that hunted in the forest all night long."

Lenora smiled. "And Ivy always said you wanted to be a butterfly witch who lived in the trees. Until you climbed on top of the barn and Father had to get you down."

Ambry hadn't seen their Aunt Ivy in years, not since they'd told her they weren't a girl, but they remembered that she'd always been full of stories about her sisters. Generally, ones that made her look like the most refined of the family.

"Let children play," Polly said. "They'll figure out what's right in good time."

"I suppose you're right. It's not something to worry about on such a fine day, when our family's together."

True to her word, she didn't bring it up again, and the three of them talked for the rest of the day until Ambry finally had to pull themself away to head back to the palace before nightfall.

⟡

When Isadore came into his study one summer morning to find the desk empty but for a note and Ambry sitting awkwardly by the window, waiting, he knew something was wrong.

"I'll go see how Melanie is doing," he said.

"There was just the note," Ambry said. "There's been two baskets of mail so far. I sorted them by their seals, but I haven't opened or read any."

"Good. Take a look through the newspapers, I'll be back shortly."

He made his way to Melanie's chamber, knocking softly on the door so that he wouldn't risk waking her if she was asleep. No such luck. She invited him in, and he entered the room to find her in bed but awake, face exhausted and drawn. A tray of food was going cold on her side table with maybe a few bites taken out of it but nothing more.

"Isadore? I left a note with Ambry."

"I saw it. Is it a bad day today?" He hardly needed to ask; one look revealed her joints bright with pain that spread in sparks and aches down her legs and up to her hips.

"Bad is one way to describe it. I don't think I can do much of anything today. I'm sorry."

He shook his head. "Don't be. I can read my own mail for a day. Or call in Markus if I need him."

"I suppose I'll allow that, but only for today," she said, managing a small smile on a face tight with pain. "Ambry can handle the mail and the newspapers. I wasn't expecting any more letters from the ambassadors so soon, but if any have arrived, well, they probably know the treaty back to front by now."

"You shouldn't worry about the treaty today," he insisted. And then, when the pain in her knees flashed bright again, "Let me do what I can. Please." They both knew that wasn't much. Whatever he did to ease her pain, her body would find a way to undo before long.

"I don't want to drain you. At least make me sleep?"

Isadore frowned. "You'll be even more tired when you wake. I've heard my great-grandmother had the power to cast true sleep, but I certainly don't."

"I know." She made a gesture that would have been a shrug had she been upright. "But it'll help for a bit, and I can fall back asleep myself when I wake up."

"If you're certain."

"Please?"

How could he refuse? She settled herself into the most comfortable position she could manage, and then he put his hands to her head. A few moments later, her eyes drifted closed and the pain lessened ever so slightly as she fell into a heavy sleep. Isadore sent a note to the doctor to attend to her when she woke and returned to the study.

"She'll be all right," he told Ambry. "She has bad days sometimes; it's the least I can do to let her rest."

Ambry nodded, but their eyes were still concerned. "Is there anything I can do?"

"She'd say the best thing we can do right now would be to get as much work done as possible," Isadore said, without much enthusiasm. "If she feels well enough later, I'll send her a book to read."

Ambry glanced at the newspapers on the desk. "There's a writer for the City Chronicle who writes a weekly column about all the bizarre and funny things that've happened. Last time there was a man who called for the Guard because he thought the dog going through his trash was a demon and a traveler who demanded their horse get its own room at the inn. It's the way he tells the stories that really does the magic."

Isadore nodded thoughtfully. "She's read some of those to me, they're good."

"We've been too busy the past few days to look at it. I can pull that section out for her while I'm reviewing the papers."

"That would be perfect."

Ambry smiled. "I'll work on that while you're meeting the education minister this afternoon."

Isadore raised an eyebrow. He'd almost forgotten that was planned for today. It was good that Ambry had remembered. If all had gone well, he should have met Minister Travers weeks ago, but every time, something got in the way. First it was an emergency she had to attend to, then a change in Isadore's schedule, then the attack on Adrian in the city. Travers certainly understood unpredictable schedules, everyone on the Royal Council did, but Isadore wanted to give her and her concerns the attention they deserved.

"I see even with Melanie abed I'm not going to be able to let things slip from my schedule?" She'd trained them well.

"She wouldn't forgive me if I did," Ambry returned.

"I see." Isadore sighed in mock disappointment and settled himself on the couch. "Well, I suppose you'd better make use of me while you have me."

They started with the basket of letters the messenger had brought up while Isadore was away. Ambry's handwriting wasn't quite good enough for them to write replies as Melanie did, but they prepared drafts for her to copy when she was able. Only a few of the letters were important enough to warrant Isadore writing a reply in his own hand. He set aside the personal letters to read later when he had more time. There was one from Adrian, and one from his sister Abigail, among a few others. Abigail's was thicker than the others. He wondered if she'd included a few pages of ink drawings with it, like she had last time she sent a letter.

After the meeting with Minister Travers, he had meant to spend the afternoon in the city and give Ambry the rest of the day off, but the weather had quickly made that impossible. Dark clouds gathered over the city, rumbling like the displeased mountain trolls of legend. The sky went nearly as dark as night and the rain came down in sheets, drumming against the tower in an endless wave. Ambry went around the room and lit the lamps so there would be light to read by. The two of them worked through one particularly odd case: a complaint from a construction chief building a temple on the south river. She'd bought an order of supplies for the project from the esteemed Francis James Company, only to receive subpar materials. It had turned out that she'd ordered not from the real Francis James Company, but a different and far less trustworthy one that shared the same name. She, and the real Company, claimed the other's use of the name was deceit, but the owner had said that because his name was indeed Francis James, he had the right to use the name, and if the chief had had any doubts, she ought to have done more research before signing the contract.

"They're clearly angling to confuse people into believing they're the original," Isadore said. "On the other hand, they certainly have the right to set up a building company of their own, and it was a legal and binding contract."

"But signed under false pretenses?" Ambry put in. They had a good mind for this sort of work, Isadore had learned. Empathetic, but with little patience for ill intentions.

"Very true. But there's two questions here: that of this particular contract, and that of using a well-known name to give your business a reputation it didn't earn."

The rest of the evidence presented a strong enough case that the company was indeed attempting to fool their clients, so Isadore decided in the chief's favor and wrote his recommendation.

The next file proved not nearly as clear-cut. It was an inheritance case, filled with conflicting documents and unclear bloodlines. Neither side was willing to give an inch, and both considered the other to be irresponsible and weak-moraled cheats trying to steal their rightful property. Isadore wondered snidely if they were both right in those opinions. He kept himself interested by reminding himself of the real people behind the letters. However unpleasant it seemed, there was family who wanted to see this settled fairly.

He left the room for a moment to ask Markus to look up a marriage record when he came back in to find Ambry sitting on the couch rubbing their head, a book sitting forgotten on their lap. How long had they been hurting? He picked up the book before it could fall and set it on the side table as he took a seat next to Ambry.

"Are you all right?"

"Just a headache. It's the weather. I'll be fine." A few moments of quiet, and then they glanced up at Isadore. "Could you…?" They trailed off, as if not quite sure if it was appropriate to ask.

"Of course. Come here."

Ambry shifted closer, and when Isadore held out his hands, rested their head against his palms. The motion was surprisingly tender, and it struck Isadore with the sudden desire to hold them close, run his hands through their hair. He pushed that thought aside before it could go any further. Instead, he slowed his breath, narrowed his focus to Ambry and nothing else, and when he opened his eyes he could see shimmering there the dull ache that was clouding their thoughts with pain. He soothed it as if rubbing away a sting, felt the tension melt away under his hands. "There. How's that?"

Ambry lifted their head and smiled. "That feels a lot better. Thank you."

They sat that way for a long moment, neither wanting to get up just yet, as Isadore wondered what to say.

Lightning struck somewhere nearby with a tremendous crash, rattling the lamps in their stands. Ambry yelped and jumped, laughed at themself for it, and then turned towards the window to watch the flashes of light.

"That's incredible. I've never seen a storm from this high up before."

Isadore stood beside them. "It's pleasant, in a way. I just hope nobody's outside in this."

"Me too. That would be terrifying."

"The Guard will be out in the morning to assess the damage. We've been fortunate so far this season, but I'm still concerned about flooding. The river's been high lately, and this isn't going to be helping matters."

"Is there anything we can do?"

Isadore sighed. "Well, Captain Dreisand wants me to talk to the city council again about enforcing the building code. And on the face of it, I completely agree. There should be standards about where and how people can build, so that they don't end up underwater when something like this happens. And so that fires don't spread, and so that roofs aren't falling in from having too many things stacked on top."

Ambry frowned. "What's the catch?"

Isadore sighed. "There's a lot of people who can't afford housing that's up to standard, and certainly can't afford to rebuild what they have."

Ambry nodded. They thought for a few moments, then said, "Can you focus on the builders and landlords, then? Make sure they can't sell anything that's unsafe."

They were so bright, so thoughtful, when they were comfortable enough to speak. "That's exactly what Melanie and I decided on. But then the landlords started threatening to raise rents if we enforced the rules." That had been a bitter shock to a young leader so sure of himself and his plans. "And so the Council backed off."

Ambry grumbled. "That's not fair. If anybody should be responsible for this, landlords should be."

"They said they would have to do it to pay for the construction needed to meet standards."

"It still doesn't seem right. People shouldn't be afraid of being hurt by their own homes. And wouldn't paying for better buildings now help them in the future?"

"I agree with you. I completely agree. But it's difficult. In any change, there's so many competing priorities to balance. And stubbornness, and tradition, and often greed. Very often greed."

"That's why you do things like this, so you can make a difference somewhere."

Isadore smiled. "It's part of the heir's duty to resolve disputes. But you're right. Sometimes it feels like the only worthwhile thing I do."

"I think Melanie would disagree with that."

"She would, she would." He hoped she was resting now. "Back to the books?"

Ambry sighed and reached for the legal text again, but they were smiling.

Without Melanie there to remind him, Isadore quickly lost track of time. He only noticed how late it was when he glanced outside and realized that the drumbeat of rain and wind against the walls had slowed, and the darkness through the window was not stormclouds but the night sky.

"It's getting late," he said. "I'm sorry, I should've let you leave ages ago."

Ambry laughed; a pleasant, relaxed sound. "I suppose I forgot too."

"You should eat." Between the cases and the weather, he'd completely forgotten dinner. He thought vaguely that something should have been sent up, but he hadn't asked, so he supposed he shouldn't be surprised that it hadn't.

"And you. I could go fetch something for both of us."

"That would be perfect, thank you."

They headed through the door and down the stairs. Isadore took the time to slip bookmarks into each of the open volumes and pile them in a tidy stack on Melanie's desk. They could pick up the work tomorrow. Nobody would be looking for urgent legal judgments tonight.

Ambry returned a little while later with a tray and a concerned expression. "There was some confusion. They didn't know if you were going to be here tonight, and then when you didn't call for anything, they assumed you were away." They held out the tray. "I hope this is suitable."

Two large bowls of soup swimming with meat and roots, four thick slices of seed-speckled bread, and two piles of carrots roasted in honey and spices. Rough food, but no worse than he and Adrian ate on their escapes to the city. And no doubt delicious, for the kitchens could prepare nothing less.

"More than suitable," Isadore reassured them, taking the tray and setting it on a table. "But this didn't short somebody else a meal? I can wait if that means there'll be enough for everybody else to eat. They've been working harder than we have."

"No, it's all right. Patrice and Ella made a lot tonight. Some of the laborers the gardeners hired were stranded here by the rain, so they ate with the rest of the servants. They had a lot left after the meal so they kept it warm in case someone else needed it."

"Good, good. And the laborers have shelter for the night?"

"Delia and Marion are working on it. They're going to lay out bedding in the old Guard training hall."

A brief swell of pride rose in him that the people of the palace would do such a thing and think nothing of it. "Good. Do they have everything they need?"

Ambry took a portion of food from the tray and pushed the rest towards Isadore. "I think so. At least, they seemed fairly calm about it, and I know Delia would have said something if she needed help. I hope the storm hasn't given them too much more work to do."

He tried the soup first and found it almost as rich as stew. Across the table, Ambry was tearing their bread into pieces to soak in the thick broth. "I'm looking forward to seeing the gardens finished. I haven't had much time to look at the plans but what I did see looked beautiful."

"Erik's preparing to put in a hothouse and more winter plants. He says Princess Abigail suggested it. They want to have it ready for when she returns for the New Year celebrations." There wouldn't be much progress made today, but there was ample time before the princesses came home for the winter holidays.

Imagining Abigail's face when she saw brought a smile to his own. "Is it a secret, or can I mention it in my next letter to her?"

Ambry smiled. "I was about to say. It's meant to be a surprise."

"How exciting! She'll be delighted. I'll take a look when they're not so busy." They would be busy for a long time with everything that might need mending after all the wind and rain. But they were used to such work, and knew the secrets to it that Isadore could never learn.

"I won't keep you from your bed any longer," Isadore said when the meal was done and the last of the papers had been put away or left on the desk for later reference. "You did very good work today. If you want to sleep a little more tomorrow, I'll allow it."

Ambry shook their head. "I'll be fine. I've had later nights than this. But thank you." They piled the empty dishes onto the tray and departed, leaving Isadore to watch out the window as the fog slowly cleared and sparks of light flickered in the wet city streets as the first few lamplighters dared to venture out into the darkness.

Chapter Nine

✧

The next morning, Isadore insisted on going out into the city to survey the damage. Dominick, predictably, objected to the idea of the prince traipsing through the mud, but together Melanie and Isadore managed to convince him that Isadore being seen among his people was politically advantageous enough to be worth it. Ambry didn't miss the way Isadore's face tightened in chagrin as Melanie and Dominick argued.

Melanie didn't miss it either. "Don't be like that. It's not as cold-blooded as you think. It's a victory for everyone: you get to be involved, and you get to be *seen* being involved, which'll gain you favor when it comes time to argue for stricter building codes."

Ambry remembered. "We talked about that yesterday."

Melanie smiled. "He talks about it every time there's a storm like this, or a fire, or any sort of crisis. This time, he might finally do something about it. At least now we have the Guard on our side."

Isadore nodded. "And if enough of the public insists on it, we'll have a better chance of getting it done."

Ambry fetched their oldest boots that were still watertight, and Isadore donned a long raincoat, for there was indeed an awful lot of mud and damp to be found. This time, Ambry wore their royal badge proudly on their collar.

The sluggish sun had not yet managed to show itself through the fog that still enveloped the city. Most of the few people who were out and about in this mess picked their way down the streets, careful to avoid muddying their shoes. The workmen busy clearing the roads, on the other hand, took little notice of the puddles as they hauled carts loaded with debris. A few of them looked up as Isadore passed; one even saluted, which his fellows reacted to by pulling him back to his work.

"You're doing good work," Isadore said. "Thank you."

"Would be doing less if someone had trimmed these trees in the past year," one of the men muttered. Another one, horrified, smacked his arm.

The man shrugged. "Apologies, Highness, but it's true."

Isadore nodded. "Thank you for telling me. I'll be sure to talk to the city council."

They continued on through the puddle-strewn streets, past a pair of workers replacing a battered street sign, towards Kings' Square, where the repair work seemed to be based. In the center of the square stood a woman with a guild leader's badge shining on her expensive coat and a sheaf of papers tucked under one arm. Even without the badge, it was clear she was in charge. Every so often, a worker or pair of them would come up to her and she'd send them off in a different direction. Ambry couldn't get a clear look at the saint-scarf pinned to her shoulder, but they thought it might be the sign of Saint Luten, one of at least three saints favored by architects and builders.

Isadore was looking away, talking to another group of workers, but Ambry caught the flash of irritation in the woman's face before she smiled broadly and bowed her head in greeting.

"Good morning!" Isadore called as they approached. "I trust I can assume this is your work I'm seeing?"

"Indeed, Highness," she replied. "Jeanette Forsythe, I'm the director of the repair efforts. You needn't trouble yourself to come out here, we'll send a full report when we're done."

"It's no trouble. How goes the work?"

"Everything is well under way. We've got crews working all the way from Northgate Street to Green Park. In a few days' time, you'll hardly know there was ever a drop of rain."

"What about west of the park?" Ambry asked before they could think better of it, pointing off in that direction, where a church steeple rose above the roofs, missing tiles visible even from here.

Forsythe frowned, looking to Isadore for an answer. "You mean the lower districts?"

Isadore said nothing, only waited for a response. Finally, Forsythe cleared her throat and said, still not looking at Ambry, "Well, you see, we prefer to work with people who have the initiative to address their own problems. Most people of the city have already begun contributing to the repair efforts. But the people of the lower districts have so far been content to leave their homes and businesses in shambles."

That was monstrously unfair. "It's a working day today," Ambry insisted. "They don't have the *time*, they're working from dawn to dusk. And most of them would rather spend what little money they have on food or medicine."

"Or drink, or the dice table, or other vices," Forsythe said, shaking her head. She finally deigned to look at Ambry, giving them the sort of pitying expression one would give a naive child. They longed to argue, but they had said too much already. "Charity is all well and good," she said, "but you must understand the reality of the situation. If these were truly the responsible, dedicated people you claim them to be, they would not have ended up in that lamentable situation in the first place. And we respectable folk certainly don't have the means to fix their situation for them." She turned impatiently back to Isadore. "Now then, Highness, if we could return to business?"

But Isadore was unswayed. "No, I would like to hear more about why your plans neglect a full third of the city's lands."

"Highness..." Forsythe protested.

"They are as much my people as any other, and they should experience the same benefits." He paused, and then offered, coolly, "If the Guild is lacking adequate funds, they can be provided."

Forsythe drew herself up in affronted pride. "We have the funds, Highness," she ground out.

Isadore smiled. "I'm glad to hear. I shall be expecting your report."

"It shall be delivered." She bowed politely, if rigidly, and returned to barking out orders to her teams.

It wasn't until they were a few streets away that Ambry fully realized what they had done and felt sparks of anxiety break through their fury. But they couldn't regret what they had said.

"That was good, Ambry," Isadore said. "I couldn't have said it better myself. Thank you."

"She was wrong. They're not irresponsible. They don't *want* to live in shabby houses and work all day long." They forced themself to stop before anger could consume them again.

"I know." Isadore's steps slowed as they approached the crossroads. "I want to see for myself what the lower districts have suffered." He gave Dominick a meaningful look, half asking permission and half daring him to refuse.

Dominick considered it. "I would recommend against it, but if you insist, then you must stay close to me, Highness. Most of the people of the lower districts are good-hearted and hard-working, true, but those of lesser morals and more destructive tastes also gather in those streets. Many would wish you harm."

"I understand. And I trust your skills," Isadore said.

"Then come this way." Dominick set off down a narrow side street. As they walked, Ambry studied the smudged sheets posted on the walls, offering a range of services from the unremarkable to the less-than-legal.

"I patrolled these streets as a new recruit," Dominick said, stepping around a pile of sodden rags. "It was difficult work. The residents here do not appreciate the Guard's presence in their business."

"I would imagine not," Isadore said.

"There is a great deal of crime here."

"Out of desperation!" Ambry interjected.

Dominick silenced them with a sharp look that sent tremors through their stomach. He shook his head. "Whatever the cause, it is unacceptable." What could be said to that? To someone so rigid and unfeeling… "Some within the Guard," Dominick went on, "care only when it begins to spill out into more respectable districts, but the duty of our order is to protect all of the city's people, and that is what I had been tasked to do."

"And you did it well," Isadore said.

"Well enough to be promoted out of it near as soon as I had at last found my footing," Dominick said, a trace of sarcasm in the words. "It took a friend of mine to teach me that it is a far better deterrent to crime to befriend them than it is to make yourself their foe. When they know that they have recourse against abuse, they are less likely to resort to it themselves."

Ambry found themself still tense, still searching Dominick's words for insult, whether he deserved the scrutiny or not. They hadn't expected such a compassionate and intelligent analysis from someone they knew only as a stern guardsman. And they still weren't sure what to make of all he had said. But Isadore trusted him, and Ambry had no reason or right to question that.

At the southwestern corner of Green Park stood a small temple to Saint Lanisa the Peacebringer. A few worshippers had gathered in the yard, offering silent prayers to figures so worn they would have been unrecognizable if not for the unique poses and symbols of each.

It was painfully obvious that the interior of the structure was no longer used for worship out of fear that the whole thing might collapse at any moment. The door was barred, and a spider's web of cracks split the walls into an ugly mosaic of rough, crumbling stone. The damage wasn't new, either; green tendrils of insidious weeds poked their heads here and there through the crevices. It might have been pretty if the harm done to the structure wasn't so clear.

"Those walls should have been repaired years ago," Ambry said.

"But without the money or the time," Isadore observed, "other things take precedence." He sighed. "Something has to be done. And soon."

A few paces onwards, the street opened up into a wider lane lined with tight-crowded wooden houses. Children hurried back and forth with brooms or baskets, gathering up the debris and sorting out what items might be salvageable. Workers on ladders reinforced broken beams with stronger scraps of wood and fastened tarps over holes in the roofs. So much for Forsythe's comments on how the people here didn't take responsibility for their homes. They might not have the same tools and resources as the Guild, but they cared, and worked harder than most with what they had.

Ambry saw many places where the residents had made ingenious use of what wealthier people might consider trash. A cracked cart frame had been stood up against a wall and repurposed as a rack to dry clothes. In one lot, chickens pecked at seed inside a fence made from discarded fishing spears with nets strung between them. Under the windows of another building hung glorious creations of patchwork fabric, each an image of a different animal picked out in tiny scraps of color: an eagle, a dragon, a lion.

A woman – the artist, perhaps? – watched them from an open second-floor window, eyes narrowed. When she noticed Ambry looking, she disappeared, only to stride out the door a few moments later. She stood in the street, blocking Isadore's path, and stared him down.

Isadore stopped to look at her. "Good morning," he said.

Where anyone else might have stepped back or at least bowed politely, she stood firm. "With all due respect, if you've come here to gawk, we'd prefer you leave. We don't need your help," she insisted.

"You're doing very well on your own," Isadore said. "But as a resident of this city, you're entitled to assistance. That's why the Builders' Guild is out mending the damage from the storm."

The woman scoffed. "The repair teams won't come here."

"I have corrected that. They will no longer be permitted to overlook you."

She raised an eyebrow, cautious. "Good. And so you've come here to seek our gratitude?"

Melanie's talk of political advantage began to ring hollow in Ambry's head.

"I'm here to make changes," Isadore said, unperturbed. "I wanted to hear from you what you think should be done."

She glared at him. "We have enough work to do without being politicians too. And don't tell us we haven't tried. We send representatives to the city council just the same as the districts you and your friends walk in."

She was testing him, Ambry thought. Seeing if he was quick to anger when challenged by people such as she.

Isadore didn't take the bait. "You should have a better chance to be involved," he said, calm and steady.

"And let you speak for us? It's your people and their greed that traps us here. Prices higher every month, and every law that would help left on the council clerks' floor. We need more than scraps from your tables."

Ambry bit their lip unhappily. Her hostility chafed and stung, and they were not even its true target. She was utterly justified in her rage, but such unkindness could easily drive away those who sought to help. But then, wasn't that the purpose of it? To ensure that any powerful people who wished to help did so on her terms rather than for their own benefit or vision. That hostility was what kept her people from slipping under the heels of others.

Yes, they saw the point of it, but they still didn't approve. Ambry had seen far more good come of people reaching out in friendship than they had seen come of rage and unkindness. Progress would be all the slower if the people involved could not trust each other. Isadore had to prove that he could be trusted, that he would listen. Only then would his people listen to him.

She went on. "Most of these buildings are owned by folks who live their whole lives on the other side of the park. You want to do something for us? Make our landlords do more than just send their underlings marching in every week to collect rent."

Ambry had planned on staying quiet, feeling they'd exhausted their store of courage in front of Guild Master Forsythe. But they couldn't help but say, "They should at least live in the district if they're going to own a lot of property here. That's how it works in the southern cities."

The woman nodded towards them. "This one knows what they're on about. That'll be a start. They'll find ways around it, of course. Probably hire people to live here and collect the money and not much else."

Isadore nodded. "But at least *someone* will be there, and they'll have to handle complaints."

"And hopefully," said a large man wearing a worn cap on top of tangled pale hair, "handle them before they end up like Daisy and Connor's house."

"What happened there?" Ambry asked.

"Come this way," the first woman said, setting off down the street, pausing only a moment to see if they were following.

Isadore asked her questions as they walked. After that first meeting, she seemed more willing to talk. They learned that her name was Sophie, that she had indeed sewn the window-hangings, and that it brought in just enough money to pay her ever-rising rent and keep her meager pantry stocked with enough to feed her family. But like all her neighbors on Willow Street, she feared illness or injury that might keep her from her work. She feared fire, which could ravage her workshop and turn her beautiful beasts to ash in moments. And she feared storms, which could tear her home apart or send debris shooting through her windows.

That was what had happened at the house she brought them to. The door had blown off its hinges; the windows gaped open and shattered. If they had not been told, Ambry might have guessed this ruin to be as old as the one that they had seen by the park.

"They got out with the baby, but they lost everything else," the man said. He'd introduced himself as Dale.

Isadore stared into the ruins. Ambry stood beside him, studying the jumble that had once been a home. Chairs reduced to firewood. A baby's cradle, painted sides splintered and scratched. A small rug, drenched and filthy, sprawled across the floor.

"Something took off a good portion of the roof," Sophie said, though the sight hardly needed explaining. "They'd known it was weak. Connor had already asked several times for it to be repaired. But nobody came. And he couldn't do it himself, not in his condition. And once the wind and rain got inside…" She shook her head.

"There's not much you can do then, not in that weather," Dale said. "The wind carried some of their things clear across the street."

"The rest of us on Willow Street are doing what we can to help," Sophie offered, "but when we barely have enough for our own families, there's not much to spare."

Dale's face darkened. "It won't be long before Hardy and his gang are crawling over here, selling stolen goods and trying to lure the youngsters in." He shook his head. "Sometimes it feels like folks like Hardy are the only ones who can make things happen around here."

Beside them, Ambry saw Dominick's eyes narrow in disapproval. They remembered what he had told them about places like this and the criminals who profited from people who had no other choice.

"I won't buy from him," Sophie declared. "And my boys know to stay well away."

"Some of the others see him as a hero," Dale said. "I'm not saying it's right, but they want to be tough and daring, just like those stories they tell about him."

Isadore turned to face her. "I promise you, something will be done."

Ambry would never have thought to doubt the determination in Isadore's eyes. But Sophie did not have the same trust.

"I hope you're right," was all she said before she turned and walked away, leaving them there in front of the ruined house.

✧

The cleanup efforts continued for another week before the city council was satisfied with the work. As much as they would have liked to declare the work done, signs of the storm lingered for longer than that, especially in the poorer districts where the residents were expected to mend their own homes, and few could spare the time away from their jobs to do so. Jeanette Forsythe's workers had indeed entered the districts, but there was too much to be done for even dedicated builders to finish it before they were pulled back to other tasks.

At least the knock-on effects in nearby streets served to drive home the point that something had to be done about the building code. Willow Street's somewhat wealthier neighbors quickly grew tired of the eyesore of broken shutters and cracked roofs hastily swaddled in tarps to keep the rain out. Their complaints, on top of Isadore's letters and the lower districts' representatives' speeches, were at last enough to spur the council to consider the matter where the struggles of the residents themselves had not. It was a distasteful reason, but it was better than nothing.

If they were going to get anything done, they had to act now. Two weeks after the storm, Isadore met with the representative from the Hawkgate district, one of the hardest-hit areas of the city. Representative Tara Hedley, a short woman with iron-gray hair and a face carved into sharp lines by years of bitter and determined political battles, hummed in surprise when she saw who else was waiting in the room. Arranged around the table were Captain Dreisand of the Guard and architect Calvin James, who was very grateful to Isadore for preserving the honor of his grandfather's name.

"So, I see you're finally taking this seriously," she said, taking the seat Ambry directed her towards.

"The safety of my people has always been a serious matter," Isadore replied coolly.

Hedley snorted. "You say that, and then you back away at the first sign of criticism." She spread out a thick stack of papers on the table. "I heard about your visit to Willow Street. Very nice, that. But it won't mean anything if you continue to take the landlords' side over ours."

He was about to protest that he had never taken the landlords' side, but he already knew what she would say: that leaving things the way they were was as good as ruling in their favor.

"You can't make everyone happy, Highness, and you'd do well to remember that. Somebody's always going to be upset at your choices. You have to decide if doing the right thing is worth the consequences. Until you do, your efforts will remain ineffectual."

From the side of the room, Sylvia tensed at the disrespect. Isadore didn't reply for a few moments, during which the others' silence hung heavy in the air. Hedley didn't back down, didn't look away, only waited unperturbed for a response. Finally, Isadore sighed and said, "Well, I suppose I deserved that." He met her eyes. "I shall defer to your experience. Will you help me make some people unhappy?"

She smiled. "Let's get to it."

The meeting began in earnest. Isadore laid out the plans he and Melanie had spent the past weeks researching. Hedley, Dreisand, and James gave their own opinions and advice, correcting what wouldn't work and improving what would.

Ambry took notes, passed around papers, wrote out Mr. James's arithmetic on a chalkboard as he recited the numbers at astonishing speed. In most meetings of this sort, the guests took little notice of them, which Isadore knew suited them just fine. This time was different, with Hedley and James offering whispered thanks every so often as Ambry handed over a folder of papers or set a platter of treats on the table or refilled glasses. It pleased him. Ambry deserved the credit, even if they were equally happy to fade into the background.

Hours later, armed with Representative Hedley's accounts of years of suffering in her district and the Francis James Company's calculations on the savings sturdier buildings would offer, they had the foundations of an argument with which to confront the rest of the city council on the twin issues of high rent and neglected buildings. Not just an argument as to why the current situation could not be allowed to stand, but also a plan with which to remedy the issues.

"Which is going to take a while," Isadore said to Ambry once their guests had left. "They're not going to have time on their schedule for at least another month."

"Even for you?" Ambry asked, handing him a cup of dark, smoke-scented tea, a Kivernese blend he was rather fond of.

"Even for me. The ministers and representatives who worked for their positions don't have much patience for those of us who came by them merely by our birth." And they all knew that if not for the treaty, he would be even now sailing to the Islands instead of presenting to the council, while they worked through the summer with nary a break. Perhaps some good might come of the delay after all.

Ambry nibbled on one of the leftover pieces of herb bread from the table. "I didn't think it was fair, what Hedley said," they began.

Isadore shook his head sadly. "No, she's right. I've retreated too many times. I've been afraid of making enemies, and because of that I've gotten nothing of any significance done."

"The people whose cases you've been reviewing wouldn't say that," Ambry insisted. "You're trying to make a compromise. That's a good thing." They passed the last of their notes to Melanie, who would sort them for her assistants to copy.

"There's a time and a place for compromise," she said. "And there's a time and a place for demanding change. This storm has shown us that this is one of those times."

She was right. "We can't let this happen again," Isadore said. "Not when lives and livelihoods could be lost because builders and landlords want to scrape every penny from people who can barely afford it. If there was a fire!" He recoiled from the thought. "We need to fix this. But the landlords are going to protest. They'll find some way to raise prices."

"So we'll write laws about that," Melanie said.

"You know some of the representatives won't be pleased about that."

"So? They can deal with it."

Ambry looked thoughtful. "Sometimes you can't help that you're going to make people unhappy. Sometimes you should listen. But if they're wrong about you, and they won't listen in return, then you have to do what you know is needed instead of letting them stifle you. I've had to do that myself."

It took Isadore a moment to realize what they must mean. "Did people give you trouble when you declared yourself?" he asked, and immediately regretted prying.

Fortunately, Ambry didn't seem to mind the question. "Not most people. My mother accepted it right away. She said she'd guessed for a while. Most of my cousins had no problems with me. But two of my aunts, and my grandfather..." They bit their lip. "They stopped talking to us. Said we were embracing ungodly frivolity."

Isadore still could never understand how anybody could turn away from their own family members for something like this. "I'm sorry, that's terrible. Was it because of the Southern Church's rulings?"

Ambry nodded. "My grandfather was a follower of the Southern Order his whole life."

"Disgusting." Isadore shook his head. "I'm so sorry. We've tried to censure the cruelest factions of the Church, but it's been difficult." He winced as he heard the excuse come from his mouth.

Melanie looked up. "That's a battle that won't be won in a day. For now, we must make sure they know their bigotry is unwelcome in Talland."

If there was anything Isadore wanted to fight, it was this. It offended him down to his bones that these people who claimed to follow divine goodness could see people like Ambry and Darby as sinful. Could make them feel worthless and wrong simply for daring to be their true selves, when they harmed no one by doing so.

But what could he do about people frightened by difference and change, who believed themselves to be right and valorous and the world around them to be corrupt and lazy? As much as he despised their wrongheaded cruelty, returning it with unkindness and impatience could only make things worse. And to preach and scold those well-meaning but uncomfortable with having their sense of the world challenged would only drive them faster towards those who decried difference as wrong.

His displeasure must have been visible, for Ambry continued, "Things are a lot better here in the capital. My mother went looking for a temple after we moved to the city. She joined one overseen by a found-woman who used to be a priest of the Southern Order, before she discovered herself."

Isadore winced. How it must have hurt, to find herself the subject of all her order's hate! "I'm glad she escaped that."

They'd never truly enjoyed going to the temple, no matter the subject of the sermon, and they'd stopped going as soon as they'd left the schoolroom and started work. But they had fond memories of Amalia Tobin's stories.

"I can't imagine how hard that must have been. She talked about it in her sermons. She said you can't make people change by screaming at them, or telling them they're worthless. That'll just add mortar to their walls. 'All we can do is live in spite of them. Continue to be kind, successful people living in this vibrant world. Invite them to change and embrace them if they do.'"

Such beautiful words. "Do you believe that?"

Ambry shrugged. "It's a good thought. I hope she's right. There were a lot of people at that temple who'd left the Southern Order. Some had family members who'd discovered themselves, some had just stopped believing that they were so dangerous. So sometimes people change." They gave a lopsided smile. "But I don't want to deal with more small-minded people than I have to."

Isadore laughed. "I don't blame you. I feel the same."

"Unfortunately," Melanie said, "you have no choice. Otherwise we'd have to get rid of at *least* half the Royal Council."

That got a laugh out of all of them.

"Let's get to it, then," Isadore said, getting to his feet and reaching out for the folder Melanie handed him without looking up from her reading. He knew just from the heft of the thing that it would be a complex case, requiring much reading and even more interpretation before they could arrive at an answer, and whatever answer that was, it would leave all parties with some measure of dissatisfaction.

Those were, unfortunately, the sort of situations where patient deliberation and compromise would produce far better results than stubbornly insisting on one plan. Now if only Kivern could see that truth, he thought bitterly.

But as it turned out, his vindication was very near at hand indeed.

A few days later, Isadore was poring over the books he had lying open on the table, flipping from one to the other, searching for the lines he knew he'd marked out weeks, or maybe months, before, knowing they'd be useful someday.

He scribbled another note on a sheet of elegant stationery that was probably too fine for the purpose, but he liked the feel of the paper under his pen. And as a printing error had rendered this batch unusable, unless by some chance he became prince of the Kingbom of Tailanb, he might as well make use of it. Some poor typesetter's apprentice had probably lost a job over that, even though the Palace had still bought the batch. At a reduced cost, of course. Ugly stamps on the top of each sheet ensured it would never accidentally go out in the guise of anything official.

He pulled yet another book from the stack on the side table and turned to a page Ambry had marked with a ribbon, lifting his eyes from the text for a moment to savor one of the very few times he was alone, without an endless stream of letters and work demanding his attention. Alone, at least, except for Dominick. Who of course would say nothing unless it was absolutely required, and who affected a polite disinterest in Isadore's work, though Isadore knew he was silently noting every detail in case it might someday hold any bearing on the security of the land or the palace.

Melanie and Ambry were off in the archives reviewing some old tax maps, hoping to settle a territory dispute between two farmers in the north. Heavy rains had caused the stream that marked the boundary to change its course, enlarging one holder's lands at the expense of the other. Now the more fortunate farmer argued that she should be able to claim the new territory on the basis that the stream was the legal boundary, while the old wanted to keep the original borders. To complicate matters, the Crown's surveyors predicted that the stream would shift yet again in the coming years. By all rights this should be the governor's problem to solve, but one of the landholders was his daughter's husband's uncle, which had been deemed an irreparable conflict of interest, and so the case had fallen on Isadore's desk.

Dominick pushed open the door and cleared his throat. "Highness, Ambassador Karin Miller is here to see you."

A tall, slim woman stood in the doorway, wearing riding clothes in the southern style, her brown hair tied back and decorated with a crown of thin braids.

Isadore set down the book and stood. "Already?" He hadn't been expecting the ambassador to Kivern for another two days at least.

"I rode fast," Miller said, grinning. "Kivernese mountain horses are the finest out there. I can wait if you need me to."

"No, come in, come in. Did you not have a chance to rest?" Still in riding clothes with sweat on her brow… something had hurried her here, but if it was dire news, surely she would already have said, and she wouldn't be nearly so cheerful about it. Could it be?

"That comes later. First, I have news." She slipped the pack from her shoulder and withdrew a leather document pouch stamped with Kivern's royal seal: an image of a mounted warrior battling a bear.

"Good news?" Isadore prompted, his heart already light with hope.

"Very good news. Queen Frida finally settled on the last revisions."

"And the ambassadors agreed?" There was more astonishment in his voice than he'd meant to express, but he hardly cared. He undid the ties on the folder and slid the papers into his hands. There, in front of him, in ink and paper, was everything he'd worked towards for so long.

"At long last, they've agreed. Alaric Grenner wasn't completely happy about it, but I can't remember the last time my counterpart was happy about anything, so I wouldn't pay him much mind."

"I know. His letters are always a headache, even with Melanie to help. But he doesn't seem as bad in person, so maybe we'll be lucky."

"Oh, he's just as bad in person and you know it," Miller warned him. "But as long as he signs the papers, it doesn't matter how much he complains."

"So we've got all the details tied off and finalized?"

"Aye. All that's left is the treaty signing. By their laws, nothing's strictly binding until then, but in practice it's merely a formality. Technically they could still demand changes, but it would be seen as a dirty move."

"Do we have a date for the signing?"

"Larsellan is requesting the middle of next month. It's an auspicious day for them, if I remember correctly. It'll give them time to visit home and bask in their leaders' congratulations. Kivern's already agreed to the date, and we're waiting on word from Arrawey but I can hardly imagine they'd complain. And all of them have agreed to come to Talland for the signing."

This was better than he'd dared to hope. "You've done good work. The kingdom thanks you." If he had his way, Miller and Beck and all the rest of the ambassadors and their advisors would be honored for their work, but he knew that history would remember only the rulers as architects of the treaty and not those who had made it happen.

Miller snorted. "It can thank me with a hot bath and some good food. I've been riding for days and I've got grime in places you couldn't imagine."

"That's a wish I'll be pleased to grant. I'll have someone take you to the guest chambers?"

"I know my way. I can show myself there, as long as your guards aren't too unhappy with me wandering around unprotected." She made a cocky salute at Dominick, to which he gave no reply. "I'll take that as a yes, then."

"Will you join me for dinner?"

"Of course. But you ought to prepare yourself for endless stories about my travels on Kivern's North Canyon roads. There's all sorts of ancient sites there."

"Oh? I didn't think you were interested in ancient history."

"Well, I'm not, but they've got some very interesting carvings. You see, the ancient people of the canyon worshiped a fertility god. So of course all of the artwork celebrates his…" She grinned. "Natural gifts."

He nodded sagely, hiding a smile. "Perfect dinner conversation then." He wasn't about to tell her to be proper. She had spent more than enough time in Kivern, where formal behavior was even more heavily judged than in Talland. She deserved a chance to enjoy herself unguarded.

"Of course. There's nothing better."

"I'll see you then."

He spread the documents on the table. Here at last, in writing, Kivern's promise to uphold the Lynwood Provision and all the rest of the treaty. He'd had to give up most of Atworth to get it, but looking at these documents that were the product of years of work, Isadore thought it was worth it.

He tucked them back into the folder and closed it, studying the seal for a long while. Stubborn, proud Kivern, land of mountain strongholds and mighty horses, impeccable manners and fearsome warriors. He hoped this treaty would improve their relations. Kivern would be a powerful ally. Or, if they chose, a formidable enemy. This treaty should ensure the former for decades to come.

Isadore took the folder and headed down the hall to the archives to deliver the good news, Dominick at his back.

Chapter Ten

✧

The next few weeks went by in a whirlwind of plans and invitations. As Melanie was sure to warn Isadore, while sealing the treaty had been its own mountain of challenges, the preparations for hosting the signing were another beast entirely. He read through letter after letter while Ambry hurried all around the palace, making sure everyone knew what they had to do and that it was proceeding according to schedule. There was hardly a moment that they hadn't been hurrying back and forth between the tower study and all corners of the palace, delivering notes and arranging schedules. To Mrs. Hammond's little office, to discuss plans for rooms and meals for the ambassadors and their staff. The archives, to check on the printing of the final documents, ready for four kingdoms' seals and signatures. The gardens and laundry, to see what decorations were being prepared to greet their guests. And all this in between the usual notetaking and fetching and giving advice when Isadore asked. He made a silent promise to give them a day to rest at the first opportunity.

But there were bright spots amid the work, chances to breathe for a moment and appreciate all they'd accomplished. The best of these was when Darby Allister strode into the palace carrying a large case, followed by an assistant in a billowing green and gold dress carrying even more packages in her arms. The assistant's hair was done up in such a gloriously elaborate fashion that it could only be a wig, but if so it was a wig of the finest sort, indistinguishable from her own hair.

She hung back politely as Darby stepped forward. They were wearing a sharp-angled silver and blue coat like a fanciful version of a Guard officer's uniform, and under that a long night-blue skirt embroidered with glittering constellations of flowers and birds, split up the side to reveal pale stockings.

"My prince!" they exclaimed. "And Ambry! I am so glad to see you both." They grinned, and it wasn't for show; they were honestly delighted. "And I promise that you will be pleased with what I have to show!"

Isadore greeted Darby and turned to the woman behind them, who Lawrence was surreptitiously studying for potential threats. "And who have you brought with you?"

"April, Highness," the woman said, with an elegant curtsy that might be better suited to an opera stage than the halls of government.

"Do not let her sweet looks fool you, Highness," Darby warned, casting a suggestive glance at April. She blushed and returned it with an even steamier one. "She's a brilliant demon with a needle, and utterly unforgiving with her hands…"

They would have gone on, to April's obvious pleasure, but Melanie came into the room before they could start in on another round of praise.

"You're looking good, Darby," Melanie said, a light and playful note in her voice that Isadore rarely heard in quite this way. He more than suspected the two of them of having conducted an affair at some point in the past. He would not press Darby on the question, and Melanie, of course, told him nothing. All he knew was that Darby was one of those who frequently entertained many lovers. Unlike many of those, they did so with the knowledge – and often the eager encouragement – of those lovers.

"And you are looking perfect today. That jacket, is it one of mine?"

"You know that without even asking. And this," she said, nodding to her elegantly-carved cane. "Tell me, what do you think of the fashion of the nobles in Arrawey of chaining songbirds to their heads to perch on their hair?"

Darby scowled. "I wouldn't wear anything that still had a mind of its own, and I certainly wouldn't keep a bird from its rightful place in the skies. They starve those birds, you know, to prevent... natural processes."

"I'd wondered. Poor creatures. Well, you needn't worry about me taking up that trend. I don't know how they get anything done with all the squawking."

"By virtue of having very little of consequence to do in the first place, I imagine. It'll be gone by next season, living on only as a bad memory, like the short-lived trend for ornamented codpieces in the western provinces. I warned my clients that the lacquers were unsafe for skin, but they refused to listen. So many otherwise intelligent men going around with itchy–"

"Enough of that," Melanie interrupted – mercifully, Isadore thought, for Ambry had gone pink at the slightest hint of lewd talk. "I want to hear about April. How did you meet?"

"My sister is a frequent client of Darby's," April said. "She introduced us, and we found we shared quite a lot..." This with a knowing smile back at Darby.

Isadore had half a mind to leave them all to their flirting, but he knew that if he did that, there would be no end to it.

"You can put those papers away, Ambry," he said. "This is probably going to take the rest of the day." He didn't have the heart to blame Darby for it. In fact, he was secretly relieved. He might not like the fuss of new clothes or of Darby's insistence on adjusting and adjusting until they were perfect, but it was at least something to get him away from his desk for a few hours. And he was very much looking forward to seeing Ambry attired in the finest of Darby's work.

"Yes, let's get to it." Darby swept through the inner door as easily as if the palace was their own home. Isadore followed, ushering Ambry along, Lawrence close behind. All of his guards had long ago given up being frustrated at

Darby's irreverence. Isadore found it a welcome change to deference and formality, though he was sure he would tire of it if it wasn't a quality unique to Darby.

"How is the work for the opera going?" Ambry asked as they made their way down the tower stairs to their chambers.

"Oh! Do not remind me of the opera!" Darby sighed long-sufferingly. "I tried once more to talk them down to feather cloaks, but they foolishly refused to budge. It shall be humiliating, to have my name next to such a thing when their dancers take to the stage in the monstrosities they've had me construct."

Isadore nodded, not bothering to hide the indulgent smile that came to his lips. Darby could go through enough theatrics in a day to carry an opera trope for an entire season. "I see. I hope they're paying you enough to make up for it."

"Mhmm, that's one bright light in all this, to be sure. Yes, they are indeed paying me well. Enough to give my dear April the treasures she deserves."

"It is treasure enough to know you, my love," April said. Shameless, the both of them.

Darby set their case down on Ambry's bed and unclipped the lid, hovering protectively over the contents.

"Not ready for your eyes yet," they scolded Isadore when he attempted to lean over and look inside.

"Don't be so timid," April admonished Ambry, pushing them towards the mirror. "Today is your day."

Ambry hesitated with a hand on their shirt buttons. They met Isadore's eyes through the mirror. His face heated. Had he truly expected to make Ambry strip down to underthings here in front of him? He hadn't thought of it, so accustomed was he to undressing in the presence of others.

"Ah, right. I'll step out."

Lawrence raised one bushy eyebrow at him but said nothing – now what could that mean? Pushing aside an odd sense of disappointment, Isadore stepped outside. He studied the hanging in the hall as he ordered his thoughts and tried not to overhear Darby and April's chattering from inside.

"Such a fine form!" April exclaimed. "Simply a pleasure to dress."

"I told you they were a treasure, my dear." Darby must have known he was listening, that was the only way to explain the all-too-tantalizing talk. They were certainly making no effort to keep their voice down.

"I see my dear prince has neglected your boots," he heard Darby say. "You've done a good job of keeping those, but the soles are just about worn through."

"I should have bought new ones. I haven't had time." Ambry said. Isadore could imagine the touch of anxiety on their face and wished he had thought to notice.

"Nonsense!" Darby insisted. "Your appearance is my responsibility now, and I won't have you patronizing just any common cobbler!"

"I'll send a note," April promised.

"Mhm." Isadore heard the clink and snip of Darby's scissors. "Another stitch here, trim that thread there... and we're ready. What do you think?"

"It's incredible," Ambry breathed.

"You look very good indeed. I should like to work with you again sometime." If only Isadore could see the smile that must have followed those words!

"This must have taken so much time."

"Work for my prince is always worth it, though don't tell him I said that, lest he pile more projects onto my already demanding schedule!"

April giggled. Saints, how long would they keep him waiting?

"Come and see!" Darby called to Isadore.

Isadore stepped back into the room to the sight of Ambry staring at their own form in the mirror as if they couldn't quite believe it themself. They wore a fine cream shirt and light jacket in rich browns and greens. Embroidered vines snaked around the sleeves, a scattering of bright flowers peeking through their tangles. Dark trousers with silver stitching finished the outfit, and unlike their old pairs, didn't need to have the hems rolled up to fit. They were taller than many women, but Isadore guessed that men's patterns were usually too large to fit without some tailoring. Darby's creations suited their body better than anything else they had ever worn. All of it was elegantly cut, but in soft and comfortable fabrics that wouldn't hinder Ambry's motion.

"And that's the formal wear?" Isadore asked, raising an amused eyebrow.

Darby put a hand on their heart. "You underestimate me! Go, go, the best of my work is yet to come!" They pushed Isadore back out into the hall with their hands on his shoulders. Isadore let them do it; Lawrence merely cast him yet another amused expression.

As promised, the second outfit was finer still. Ambry turned around to reveal a long slate gray coat lined in cream over a burgundy vest, the breast of which was decorated with a delicate lattice of gold curls. April had braided Ambry's hair into a heavy plait that fell past their shoulders and fastened it with a gold ornament in the shape of a bird's wings.

It wasn't nearly as extravagant as Isadore had feared; in fact, he imagined it would look all the better next to the ostentatious eyesores that the nobles favored that season. The slightest of white frills at the neck drew Isadore's eye, making him long to pull the ties open and see the smooth skin beneath… No. Shame bit into him. He shouldn't even be considering such things. Not about an assistant who needed to be able to trust him to keep his hands off of them.

However much he wanted to touch, to hold, he would not let himself be like Cedric.

But there was no doubt Ambry looked stunning in Darby's work. What would ministers and lords and ambassadors say, to see such beauty? Would they take Ambry for one of their own, rather than merely a servant or assistant? He smiled at the thought.

The others were waiting for him to speak. "That's marvelous," Isadore said. "Fine work, Darby, I'm impressed."

Darby preened at the praise. "I had the finest of canvases to work from," they said, uncharacteristically modest. "And there's more to see, if you can bear to tear your eyes from this perfection."

The last of Darby's creations – the sailing outfit – seemed deceptively simple after the splendor that had been the formal suit. Light without being revealing, colorful without being gaudy, it consisted of a light shirt, short trousers, and a cap to keep the sun from their face. Isadore was very glad he'd asked Darby to prepare it, even though he hadn't been at all sure back then that they would even make it to the Islands this year. Maybe they wouldn't be sailing at the height of summer's beauty, but the late launch would be all the more wonderful for what it represented.

The work was almost done, Isadore reminded himself. All that was left was the summit and the signing. And after the treaty was signed, the ambassadors stuffed with a feast and wine and sent on their way, then he and Ambry could sail away for a few days of freedom.

Darby had done good work. The only alterations needed to make Ambry's new clothes perfect were simple ones that didn't require taking the suits back to their workshop. Isadore hadn't expected anything less. But he hadn't been sure that Darby wouldn't manage to find some invisible fault to wail and mourn over like an opera heroine over her lover's demise. Perhaps that was April's doing, he thought, watching her beam at Darby and their creations. He'd always known them to be more confident in their talent when they had someone to admire it.

When the last few stitches were tied off and the garments safely stored away, Melanie was waiting in the study with tea and butter shortbread.

"I hear we have reason to offer you congratulations," April said. "Ostberg says the treaty will be signed within the month."

"So it will," Isadore agreed, letting pride color his words. "It took years of work, but we finally found something all four kingdoms can agree on."

"All four kingdoms, and Alaric Grenner, so I hear," Darby said.

"I'd be thankful never to see his signature again, once it's on that treaty," Isadore said. "But I suppose dealing with him is preferable to displeasing Queen Frida. I wonder what she sees in him."

"Someone to stubbornly argue her cause, most likely," Melanie said. "Enough politics. We have enough of that as it is. How have you two been?"

Darby shook their head. "It hasn't all been good news, I'm sad to say. Just last week, dear April caught two ruffians attempting to break into my workshop!"

"A robbery?" Surely he would have heard from the Guard if Darby had been threatened.

"They didn't get their dirty hands on anything, April made quite sure of that." Darby grinned. "She flew at them with the shears like a warrior angel, and I'm sure they nearly wet my floor as they ran."

This time, April didn't try to look humble. Her eyes lit with defensive anger as Darby recounted their tale, and she followed up their praise with a vicious, "I'm certain they were looking for gold and jewels. I found them pawing around the cabinet where Darby keeps their royal badge."

Darby nodded. "There's not as much gold in those little badges as people think. But of course people like that would never have held one for themselves."

"Did you report it to the Guard?" Melanie asked.

"Of course. They said they already had enough patrols on my street." They sighed. "But I am not concerned. After all, I have April to guard my treasures."

They sounded certain about that, and quickly swept the conversation on to brighter topics. But it didn't ease Isadore's concern. He would have to speak to Captain Driesand again. The thieves in the city were getting more and more daring, and he didn't want to see where that might lead if they didn't find a way to stop it.

✧

The work continued with barely a moment for Ambry to breathe. Most of it went well, which somehow made the handful of issues feel all the larger. First there was the mouse nest found in a wardrobe in one of the rooms where Mrs. Hammond planned to house the Arraweyan delegation. Then came a message from the palace doctor asking Isadore to mend a gardener's broken arm after he'd fallen from a tree he was trimming. And the stains on the tablecloths, the cracked lamps, and a dozen other little things that needed Ambry's attention.

And then there came a beautiful morning in mid-autumn, just as the treaty preparations were drawing close to completion. Ambry woke early to a note on the door telling them that they had the morning free so long as they returned to Isadore's study after lunch. Ambry read the note over twice more to be sure they were correct, then gratefully climbed back into bed and slept a little longer. When they woke up maybe an hour later, they bathed leisurely in the private washroom near their quarters, and headed down to the kitchens to see what breakfast they could construct from the others' leftovers.

Delia and Ella, when they heard of Ambry's good fortune, insisted they go into the city together. The two of them begged the rest of the morning off from Mrs. Hammond, who reluctantly agreed, once they promised to scrub the washrooms when they returned.

A few minutes to gather coats and purses and then they stepped out into the crisp, refreshing air that came in from the fields, laden with the scents of the harvest. They passed Danny raking up the leaves that gathered in the courtyard, humming a festival tune as he worked. He waved to them.

"I'll bring you some sugared nuts," Delia called out to him, earning a wide smile in reply.

"Shh, don't yell," Ella warned. "Or you'll get everybody wanting some."

Delia shrugged. "If they pay me back, I don't mind."

"The nuts aren't nearly as nice when they're cold," Ambry said. "They all stick together."

"It's better than no sweets at all. And banging them on the table to break up the clump is fun."

"True," Ella conceded. "Danny will like it in any case. For such a skinny fellow he sure eats a lot. Last time I made buns, he took three of them."

"That's because your baking is magical."

"You're just saying that because you want more treats."

"I mean, that would certainly be nice."

"How's this, if you buy me a package of lemon sugar, I'll bake us a tart tonight."

"Deal." Delia smirked. "Maybe I'll get you some candied oranges too, and then you'll have to make *two* tarts."

"Be my guest. Just not cherries. Last time I had those, my face went all red and itchy."

"I remember. We'll avoid those. I don't like cherries anyway. Too many pits."

"And you spit them all over the floor." Ella reminded her with a grimace.

"You don't complain when the boys do it." Delia protested.

"Oh, I do, you're just too busy eating to notice."

"I like tarts," Delia said. "You'd better prepare for a lot of baking with the bounty I'm going to find for you."

They passed through the palace gates and onto the road that led down to the city. Delia dashed ahead, flying down the slope. When she reached the bottom she spun in place, letting her ruffled skirt float around her in a halo.

"She's going to do it, you know," Ambry commented.

"Oh, I know," Ella said. "But remember this, I promised nothing more than a lemon tart."

"What are you doing up there?" Delia called back to them "Come on!"

Ella and Ambry hurried to catch up, and even Ella couldn't help but laugh when they finally rejoined Delia at the Northgate.

It looked like half the city had had the same idea they did. Shoppers and passersby crowded the streets. Children chased after leaves that fell from the ceremonial trees planted at each corner. Friends called out to each other, musicians played for coins. When Ambry looked up, they spotted a few colorful kites among the rooftops in the brilliant blue sky. The smells of festival food drifted through the air even though it was a few weeks yet before the Autumn Festival proper descended on the Capital in a blaze of color and music. But the preparations were already there: garlands wrapped around every available lamppost and rail. Little flags in red and gold fluttered in the breeze, every second one stamped with Talland's royal seal.

It was a market day today, so the city square was lined with stalls selling all manner of treats and trinkets. Delia hurried after the earrings and the sugar sweets while Ella studied the ribbons and textiles. Mrs. Hammond had forbidden the servants to be ostentatious, but even she allowed some decoration. Delia had a dragon's hoard of bright jewelry stashed away in a little wooden box under her bed – most of it glass, but there were a few true jewels there too, gifts from a wealthy aunt that she wore only on festival days. Ella took scraps of bright thread and embroidered flowers and birds onto her scarves and dresses and some of her closest friends' too. For a while, Ambry had braided their hair in elaborate patterns with Delia's help, but they'd eventually tired of the inevitable tangles and headaches and nowadays they usually kept it back with only clips or ties. Their collection of pretty ties was dwindling, though, as one after another they'd been traded away in exchange for treats or to convince someone else to take an unwanted chore.

Ambry had already walked down two lanes of stalls, intending to simply observe, as they usually did, when they remembered the coins in their purse. After several months of their new salary, and almost no chance to spend it, they had enough now to buy nearly anything they wanted without fearing it would be too dear an expense. They paused before a woodcarver's stall, wondering if Isadore would like any of the figures to add to the collection that graced his bookshelves, but shook off the idea as foolish. Certainly Isadore would want finer ornaments than these to display, even in a private space.

They lingered a moment more to admire the artist's work, then headed on to a display of little creations of wire and beads. There were pendants and hairpins, charms and rings, and most strikingly, little trees rooted in stone whose whorled branches glittered with crystals like something out of a fairy tale.

"Do you like them?" the man behind the table asked. He had a set of what could only be jeweler's tools in his hands, which flew through the motions so fast Ambry couldn't see exactly what he did, only watch as a sparking little ladybug took shape between his fingers.

"They're beautiful." Ambry's eyes caught on a dragonfly hairclip with wings of green and blue on silvery wire. Its arching antennae were tipped with golden amber. Whether the artist had intended it or not, those were the colors of the royal house. It would be all too perfect for them to wear that while they served Isadore. And the trees… Isadore would love to see those. Ambry could imagine it: a surprised smile, eyes going bright just as they did when Ambry offered some clever joke or appeared at his elbow with exactly what he desired just as he turned to ask for it.

They bought the clip and a tree of brass wire and amber-gold glass, managing not to wince at the price. They could afford it, now. The artist slipped the hairclip into a little pouch, and the tree he packed away into a box of paper-thin wood so that there was little risk of the branches being accidentally crushed.

They tucked the two packages away in their bag and, still half-lost in imaginings of seeing the tree on Isadore's bookshelf, they followed a delicious scent to a baker's stall. There they bought a honey cake and rejoined Delia and Ella in front of a stand displaying a variety of books and news and comic pamphlets.

Ella reached for a pamphlet wrapped in thick brown paper, marked with nothing but initials and a number.

The shopkeeper raised his eyebrows. "Ah, now, that's not for innocent eyes like yours."

Ella glared at him. "If you think I'm innocent, maybe you need to get *your* eyes examined."

The man shrugged. "Suit yourself."

Ambry peered over her shoulder as she slid the book out of the paper and opened it. And then looked away, face burning, as they realized what was inside.

"Half a lind?" Ella muttered, glancing at the price. "The other shop sells them for three chimes each."

"Oh, is that Bright Changes?" Delia said. "Marion told me about that series. It's about a half-demon spy who has a magic ability to shapeshift whenever he comes." If the shopkeeper had doubted the women's experience with lewd novels, now he had no doubts at all. "They've been looking for the next issue. Their usual fellow didn't have it." Ambry privately thought the premise a little crass, but they supposed that was the point. Delia ignored their hesitation. "I borrowed the first two issues from them. I like it."

From the look on her face, Ella liked it too. She read a few pages, grinning all the while.

"You gonna pay for that?" the shopkeeper prompted. Ella sniffed and handed over a half-lind coin without looking away from the book. Apparently an extra chime wasn't too steep a price for her to pay to get a new issue before Marion did.

Delia gasped and grabbed something from the shelf. "Look! Aubrey Marks has a new book!" she exclaimed, pushing it into Ambry's hands. "It looks really good too. And, oh, this is *perfect*, it's about the duchess from *The Singing Princess* after she takes command of her uncle's ship on the Wild Seas. Oh, that's going to be beautiful!"

Ella picked up another from the display. "It's been printed in three parts. Looks like they've got the first and third, but not the second."

"That's awful," Delia whined. She turned a baleful look on the shopkeeper. "What do you mean by this?" she accused, only half in humor. Marks was her favorite author, a romance writer fond of tucking shockingly erotic beddings into long interludes of sweetness, intrigue, and adventure. She'd been enchanted enough by Marks's works to write little stories of her own featuring the same characters and shared them with her friends.

The shopkeeper peered at them, a not-altogether-kind gleam coming into his eye. "Hmmm. You know what, you're a sweet lassie, I believe I could *possibly, somewhere—*" he stretched the words into a tantalizing sing-song "find you my last copy of that second part." He grinned, showing teeth. "For a price. Say, three lind more?"

The little marks on the covers of each of the others read only one and a half lind, already more than most things on the stall.

Delia considered it, staring at her purse for a long while, and then sighed. "Forget it, we'll find another bookseller and buy it there."

The shopkeeper snorted. "Ain't no one else got it yet. It's either buy it here or wait three weeks 'til the others pick it up."

Delia hesitated. She was still holding the first issue in her hands. Her heartbroken expression when she set it down forced Ambry forward.

"I'll take all three for six lind." Perhaps buying the little tree had emboldened them, for they spoke without hesitation, as if for a moment they had become someone else entirely, untroubled by fears.

Ella pulled on their arm. "Ambry, the man's a cheat," she hissed in their ear. "You don't need to do that."

She was absolutely right, but… "It's only a few extra lind."

The shopkeeper studied them. "Seven. And only because it would be very sad if you could not impress your lady-friend."

"That's a deal."

The man took the money and handed over all three parts of the book. Ambry peeked inside the cover of the second to be sure it was actually the book in question and not something else made up to look like it and passed them to Delia. "There. Saved you half a lind."

Delia threw herself on them in a hug.

"And paid two and a half more than you would have from an honest retailer," Ella put in, unimpressed.

"But I have the book!" Delia said, holding it to her chest. "I'll lend it to you when I'm done."

Ambry fought back a sudden wave of anxiety that it had indeed been a foolish decision. But one look at Delia's face proved otherwise.

"Oh, I'm so excited,'" she said, already flipping through the first volume. "I hope the duchess brings Ilse with her on the ship, she's the maid who fell in love with her when the duchess saved her from the bandits."

Ella finally gave up on being displeased and sighed. She elbowed Ambry. "Ha. Lady-friend. If I didn't already know you didn't fancy her I'd think you had *motives*."

"Motives!" Delia protested. "Ella, stop it."

"I know, I know. Their only motives are towards Prince Isadore."

Ambry went pink. "I don't. I mean, I couldn't." But hadn't they just a few minutes ago bought Isadore a gift? The little tree felt heavy in their bag, and they spared a moment to be very grateful that they hadn't shared it.

"It's always safe to imagine!"

Ella blew out a breath. "No, they're right. Now that they're actually working with the prince, it's best to keep all that as proper as possible."

Ambry bit their lip. They had thought the same, and yet, it seemed being near Isadore most of the day only heightened the hopes they had thought to bury. They wanted to cheer him, make him laugh, and help however they could with his problems. They wanted his attention. They wanted his touch…

The city bells rang overhead, putting an end to that line of thought.

"We've got an hour before we need to be back," Ella reminded them. "Let's get some food."

"The Moonlit Cat?" Delia suggested, tucking the books lovingly away into her bag. The Cat was her favorite tavern. Ambry preferred The Swimming Turtle, because it was quieter and closer to the palace, but the Cat had better food for sharing.

"That's across the river," Ella said. "We'd have to get the ferry."

"There's time." Delia looked to Ambry for approval. They didn't see a reason not to give it. They pushed down a spark of worry that they'd be delayed and wouldn't make it back in time, and set off for the little dock where the nearest ferry ran day and night.

There was one waiting, with more than enough seats spare for the three of them. As they boarded, they dropped two-chime coins into the pilot's waiting cup to pay the fare. The little boat filled up soon after, and the pilot walked to the wheel, pushing roughly past Ambry as he went. A moment later, the ship's horn rang out as they pushed off from the shore.

Delia chatted merrily about Aubrey Marks's books for the entire time, pausing here and there to let Ambry and Ella offer opinions.

"I can't wait to see what they find on the Wild Seas," she said. There's so many strange things out in places like that. Even in real life. Did you ever hear about the goldstrike snakes on the Crested Islands? If they bite you, you'll be killed or driven mad." She sounded delighted by the idea. Ambry thought darkly for a moment of the stories of those snakes hunting down so-called sinners who didn't act in accordance with their sex, but they didn't want to linger on such thoughts with their friends around them.

Delia was still talking. "I wrote a story last year where a princess goes to an island and there's these parrots that speak your true love's name if you feed them special berries."

Ella giggled.

"What?"

"That's exactly the sort of thing you'd write. And let me guess, one of them falls down a cliff or something and needs to be nursed back to health."

"Of course!" Delia said, as if it was the most obvious thing in the world. "How can you have a romance without that?"

"It's the best part," Ambry agreed. Again they thought of Isadore.

"Oh, I think the best part is the bedding," Ella countered, "but healing is pleasant too."

She was still talking about the books when they arrived, about how the duchess had grown from shy to strong under the care of her uncle, how she had refused a lofty post from the corrupt King, choosing instead to sail the seas in search of new lands.

Just as they were stepping onto shore, Ambry reached up idly to touch the royal badge on their collar, and found nothing there. They stopped dead. Someone behind them walked into them, swore, and stormed off.

Frantic, they tried to go back and check the ship, but the pilot shook his head at them and ushered them on their way with an officious, "Nothing here. If you've left your jewels, the fish have them now. Move along, I've got fares waiting."

Even if there was something they could have said to convince the pilot to wait another minute, they couldn't have gotten the words out. Mouth dry and hands cold, they let Ella and Delia guide them across the street

"It must have fallen in the water," Ella said. "I'm sorry, Ambry."

"I'll have to report it to Mrs. Hammond," they said, stomach knotting at the thought. She wouldn't be at all happy. Of all the things she despised, carelessness was chief among them.

"No, you don't," Delia said, her face suddenly inexplicably bright.

They frowned at her. "What do you mean?"

"I have a spare! I lost mine ages ago, and when I reported it they gave me another. I lost three days' pay and Hammond had me scrubbing washrooms for a week, and then I found the old one behind the bookshelf."

"I remember you complaining about it," Ella said. "I was surprised you got off so lightly."

"I'm blessed by the saints," Delia said. "Don't worry about it, Ambry. I'll give it to you when we get back. The guards know us, we won't have any problems with them checking names at the gate."

Ambry breathed again, blessing their good fortune. "That'll be perfect. Thank you."

"And now I've more than repaid you for those books," she said. "Remember that."

"And now that that's sorted, let's hurry," Ella said. "I don't want to have to rush away from lunch."

The Moonlit Cat was only one street away. Ambry settled themselves at a cramped table with cups of cider and a large platter of potato-and-pork fritters between them. The smell was enough for their appetite, chased away by the earlier fright, to return in full force. Ella showed off some of the fabrics and brightly-colored thread she'd found, carefully so as not to get any grease on them. Delia was a lot less cautious with the paper bag of sweets she'd bought alongside the promised lemon sugar, spilling them out across the table in a colorful jumble and letting her friends take first pick of the bounty. Ambry selected a handful of honey balls and taffy twists, intending to take only a few, but Delia smiled and pushed another pile towards them in thanks.

They left enough time for a comfortable walk back to the palace, full of good conversation and even more of Delia's sweets. The guard at the gate waved them in with barely a glance, and Delia fetched her spare badge from her room and fixed it to Ambry's collar.

But by the time Ambry reached their room in the heir's tower, all that earlier confidence had drained away, and all that was left in its place was Ella's voice reminding them to be proper. They weighed the jeweled tree in their hands for a long time before finally putting it back in its box and sliding it under their bed. How would they present it to him without seeming foolish? Or worse, too forward? Isadore didn't need his assistant turning moonstruck and spoiling the relationship they had built together. True, Isadore had commissioned them clothes crafted by his own tailor, but surely that was only to ensure they looked respectable when seen beside him. They could not assume it meant more than that.

The hairclip, however, did not risk being seen as a love-gift, so Ambry tied their hair back and pinned it into place at the back of their neck before heading up to Isadore's study.

"That's pretty," Melanie commented when she saw. "Is it new?"

"I got it this morning,"

She smiled. "Appropriate colors too." So she'd noticed.

Isadore came into the room a moment later, a thick book under his arm. "What's this?"

"Ambry's taking after you," Melanie said, gesturing to the ornament. "Soon there'll be so many jewels in this room nobody will be able to see anything for all the glitter."

"Oh, that wasn't what I meant." Their face heated, and there was nothing they could do to hide it.

Isadore saved them. "Let me see?" Ambry turned, glad to look away for a moment and regain their composure. "That looks very nice. Good choice. I'm glad you enjoyed the morning." His face told Ambry that the rest of the day would not be nearly so relaxing. "Unfortunately, there's a lot of work to be done this afternoon. I've mostly finished final preparations for the presentation to the city council about the building code tomorrow. But then we're meeting with the Lands Minister about the storms to the west and then with the Seas Minister to talk about maintenance of the fleet. Usually that sort of thing would be handled by my mother, but she has no space in her schedule."

"We can handle it," Ambry found themself saying. They'd been in meetings with the Seas Minister before. "As long as we have our research all in line and let him talk himself dry, the Minister will listen."

Behind her papers, Melanie was grinning like a cat. "I've taught you well!" she crowed. "They're right, Isadore. You can handle the Seas Minister."

"He reminds me of one of my tutors. Master Robin, the old one with the shaved head. No patience for anything but facts." He shook his head. "I fought with them for so long. And then I finally started studying like they'd taught me, and I learned more than I'd ever thought I could fit in my head."

Ambry tried to imagine Isadore as a troublesome student and found it utterly impossible. They had heard several times now of how he had disliked his lessons, made clever answers that bordered on rude without crossing over into anything punishable, but it was hard not to see him as he was now: polite, refined, attentive, curious.

They thought for a moment about mentioning the missing badge, but Isadore had so much on his mind already, and Delia's spare was good enough for now, even if it was her initials carved into the back and not theirs. During the meetings, Ambry listened and took notes dutifully, yet their thoughts drifted again and again to the jeweled tree lonely in its box. They so wanted to see Isadore's face when he opened it, when he saw the light glitter on its branches.

From the glances he gave them, Isadore might have noticed something was off in their manner, but he did not comment. Usually, if it were anyone else, Ambry would have preferred to pass unnoticed. But part of them wished Isadore would say something. Would see them as he did in their dreams, would invite them to stay long into the evening. But those were not thoughts they could entertain here.

When they returned to their room, they pulled the box from under their bed, drew the tree from its nest of crumpled paper and set it on their desk, adjusting each glittering branch until the leaves caught the sunset and cast a scattering of golden light across the tabletop.

Chapter Eleven

✧

Ambry woke early the morning of the city council meeting, pinned Delia's spare royal badge onto the collar of the formal suit that Darby Allister had crafted, and spent a good hour reading over the notes on Isadore and Hedley's speeches. As it turned out, they needn't have bothered. The city council steadfastly refused to allow Ambry onto the debate floor without a signed invitation, which it seemed none of them had thought to issue. Isadore's face grew stern at the refusal, and Ambry cursed themself for not asking if anything like that would be needed.

"Rules is rules, even for you, Highness," the warden said with an unconcerned shrug. "Your friend can sit in the gallery with the rest of the observers." Of course there was no objection to Sylvia standing a few scant paces from her prince, but then, in times like these she was considered as more of a part of Isadore than a political entity in her own right. So in a way it was an odd sort of respect for Ambry to be considered important enough to bar at the door.

Ambry insisted that it would be no trouble for them to watch from the gallery. They wouldn't admit it in front of Hedley, but they were secretly relieved that they didn't need to present themself in front of the city council. They handed over their papers to Isadore, though he'd practiced his arguments enough to hardly need them, and headed up the narrow stairs to the public seating.

There were a few others already there, but not nearly enough to fill the deep rows of benches. A group of old men and women bearing noble crests on their jackets, probably political observers reporting to their lords out in the countryside. A woman who could only be a journalist, judging by her keen eyes and ceaseless pen. A scattering of cityfolk, from poor to well-to-do. Ambry searched for Sophie, the artist from Willow Street, but didn't see her. They shouldn't have been surprised. They could easily imagine how she'd scoff at the idea of taking time away from her workshop to watch the slow grind of political wheels. Then one of the men turned his head, met their eyes, and they recognized Dale.

Dale nodded a greeting and pushed through the crowd to Ambry's side. "I'm glad to see your prince keeps his promises," he said.

"Of course he does," Ambry said without thinking.

Dale smiled. "I have high hopes for this," he continued. "People have tried before, but something feels different this time."

"How have things been since the storm?" they asked.

Dale's face turned a little sad. "We're surviving. But I'm worried about Daisy and Connor and the baby. That storm destroyed her house, and she still hasn't been able to find somewhere else to live. We've been taking turns giving them shelter for the night, but that can't last forever." He gave a heavy sigh. "Saints willing, something like that won't happen again soon, if they approve this thing."

"I hope they do," Ambry said, pushing aside their doubts as the bells rang to mark the start of discussion.

They'd expected most of the proceedings to fly over their head. But after months of training in politics from Isadore and Melanie, they found they were able to follow most of it, to see through the banter to the crucial points within. Hedley and Isadore and the other representatives on their side had responses ready for all their opponents' challenges, and several times managed to turn the tables and leave the challengers scrambling for their own answers.

Ambry couldn't deny that those moments were heady and sweet. But sweeter still was seeing the representatives who had come into this undecided ask their honest questions and edge closer to Hedley with each honest answer. They thought again of their mother's priestess and wondered if Hedley had ever met her.

The discussion carried on for most of the morning before the councilors retreated into their private chambers for the final vote, where even Isadore was not permitted to follow.

The observers whispered to each other in tones ranging from cautious hope to unconcerned disinterest. The warden eyed them, ready to protest should they speak too loudly, despite the fact that there was no council present to interrupt.

The city bells rang as they waited, long enough for conversation to fade away. Finally, after what seemed far too long, the councilors emerged and their herald took to the debate floor to announce the decision.

"The Council has on this day voted to approve the proposal put forward by Representative Tara Hedley."

They had won. The gallery erupted in shouts, both angry and joyous, drowning out the rest of the herald's announcement. The warden yelled up at them to be quiet, to no avail.

Ambry cringed at the noise and made their way down the stairs, nearly walking right into Isadore and Representative Hedley, who had come to collect them.

Isadore eyed them with concern. "Are you all right?"

"I'm fine," Ambry said, then admitted, "It's too loud here."

Hedley nodded. "It's always a circus after a Council session. Let's go to my office." She ushered them through a side door and down a hallway lined with portraits. At the far end of the corridor she opened a door onto a small room. There was a writing desk, a table with a few chairs, and a bookshelf against the wall by the door. The little office ended up rather crowded with Hedley, Isadore, Ambry, and Sylvia all stuffed inside, but it was still a relief compared to the chaos of the debate hall gallery.

Hedley settled into her chair and dropped the papers onto her desk with a satisfying *thwack*. "As you just heard, we've voted to approve most of the restrictions," she said. "All new buildings will be held to the new, stricter code, and existing ones will have to comply with a slightly looser but still improved set of rules within five years."

"Most?" Ambry asked, before they let victory carry them away.

"There's going to be a few exceptions. Mostly regarding historical buildings, which I can't really argue with, but you know somebody's going to weasel their way under that protection wrongfully. Maybe they've got a fountain your great-grandmother touched once. Places like that are a dozen for a chime in the royal city. But still. It's progress."

"And the landlords?"

"Once the law goes into effect next spring, they won't be allowed to raise rents without at least six weeks' warning, and not by more than a certain percentage at a time. If they refuse to maintain their buildings, the residents can put in petitions which will be investigated at the owner's expense."

Just as the residents of Willow Street had asked. That was almost all the points Isadore had wanted.

"What about landlords having to live in the same district?"

She shook her head. "That was shot down rather quickly, I'm afraid. Representative Marcell prevailed on that." The disdain with which she said the name suggested a long-held rivalry. "Too many people own too many scattered properties for that to be viable. But it was a very worthy thought."

Ambry nodded. "I'm still happy with what we achieved." Even if their own proposal hadn't been approved – and they'd known from the start that that was unlikely – many others had, and it would greatly benefit the people of Willow Street and beyond.

⇡

Isadore and Hedley spoke a little longer, planning for another meeting in a few weeks' time to discuss the reaction to the new laws. Ambry stayed quiet for much of that, though Isadore could tell they were noting every word.

How had he not thought to ask for a letter of permission for them? Having them beside him felt so natural now that he hadn't considered it might be seen as unusual. They had only been working together for a few months, and already he could hardly imagine not having them there.

They left the council hall before the visitors – or the other representatives – could find them. Ambry seemed to have recovered quickly from the overwhelming noise in the gallery, but Isadore still made sure to take the quieter streets home. He did, though, make time to stop at a bakery he knew Sylvia liked to buy a basket of seed-crusted buns from the rather astonished baker. Ambry tore into one with no hesitation, brushing the falling seeds onto the stones for fortunate birds to come by later.

They wore Darby's formal clothing today, with their hair braided and decorated and their coat falling elegantly over their shoulders, and it suited them magnificently. April had come through on her promise to replace Ambry's worn shoes with comfortable, sturdy boots of rich brown with bronze buckles, which only perfected the image. Isadore wished the representatives could have seen it, could have heard Ambry argue their case.

They returned to the palace to receive even more good news: a letter from Lacey, Isadore's former assistant.

"She's doing very well, and so is her wife," Isadore reported as he read over the paper. "The inn's been very successful this season. They've met a lot of people who've promised to come back next year. They both love the sea.

Jasmine has taken Lacey sailing a few times. She says the best times are in the evening, when the moonlight falls on the waves and everything is calm for miles around."

Melanie smiled. "I see she's discovered her romantic side. She was never that poetic for us."

"Love does that," Isadore said.

"So it does," Melanie said, her eyes lingering on Ambry for just a moment too long to be coincidence.

He read on, through tales of memorable guests and new friends, treasures found beneath the sand and glimpses of gentle sea-beasts in the distance. Along with the letter, Lacey had sent a shell the size of Isadore's outstretched hand painted with a golden sunrise and framed with a fan of seabird feathers. The note said it was Jasmine's work. He studied it for a few moments, smiling, then set it on the bookshelf beside the other treasures there.

Later that evening, after he'd sent Ambry off early for well-reserved food and rest, he returned to the shell, gazing longingly at the image of the sunset and thinking of summers in the Crested Islands. Ambry would love it there, he thought. So many beautiful places to wander, so many fascinating plants and animals to try and catch a glimpse of.

He looked up to find Melanie watching him. "I don't think Lacey is the only one turning poetic."

He set the painted shell aside. "What do you mean?"

But she wasn't fooled. "Isadore. It's clear as day to anyone who looks at you two together that you love them. And they you."

His heart sank. "Is it that obvious?"

"Here's a hint, stop just standing there smiling when they're talking."

"Do I do that?" He'd just been listening, he thought, no more than that.

Melanie's expression told him the answer. He sighed, and sat heavily on the couch, shaking his head.

"Why is it something to be so sad about?" Melanie said. "I haven't seen you this happy about anyone in a long time."

It should be obvious to anyone, he thought, why what she was suggesting was not, could not, be possible.

"I can't, Melanie. It's not appropriate. It would be taking advantage."

"So that's where your mind goes?" She snorted. "No, it wouldn't. And besides, you know that's not the only thing love's good for."

"It's not the only thing. But I want to. I want them." He shook his head. "It's not right."

"You can't possibly have missed how they look at you," she said. "You're usually much better at reading people than this, Isadore. If you're not brave enough to tell them, I–"

He didn't let her finish that thought. If he did, he might have agreed to it.

"Melanie, I'm ordering you not to say anything," he insisted. And then, gentler, "Please. I don't know what I would do if I spoiled this."

"Ordering me?" Melanie had never seemed quite so disappointed in him before. It bit deep, but he didn't have the strength to challenge her. "Very well. But I'm telling you, you're making a mistake."

"Someday, maybe," Isadore said, and roughly pushed away the swelling hope the words kindled. "But not now. Not while we have so much else to do."

She studied the ever-growing piles of letters and newspapers on her desk. "The work will never let up, you know that."

For a long few moments, he didn't know what to say. Then he shook his head and stood. "Enough. The Ambassadors will be arriving soon, and the treaty signing is in two days. We have to be ready."

"Ambry and I have been making more than certain of that," Melanie said. She reached for a well-worn packet of papers. "Would you like me to review the schedule again? Or the menu for the feast? Or the furnishing of the guest chambers?"

She wasn't happy with him. That much was clear. He swallowed, thinking of the future.

"After the summit, Melanie. Then, I promise you, I will speak to them."

She smiled and tucked away the packet. "I'll hold you to that. Now go. You'll need to be rested if you'll be spending the day greeting ambassadors."

He took the dismissal and fled, trying and failing to push his roiling feelings aside. He couldn't afford to distract himself with such thoughts, not on the eve of such an important occasion. After, perhaps he could take the leap.

The delegation from Larsellan arrived the night before the Ambassadors were scheduled to gather, in a train of sturdy carriages pulled by strong horses. Isadore had ample warning from the sharp-eyed guards who manned the watchtower and was waiting outside the great doors to receive them.

Talland's August Teller climbed out of the carriage first, a wide grin on his large face, followed by the thinner Kestrel na'Southwind. The two of them had traveled together, ostensibly to save effort and time, but it was hardly a secret that there was more between the two men than simply diplomatic politeness. Were it any other men, Isadore might have feared their personal connection would hinder their political relationship, but relations with Larsellan were straightforward to a fault, and unlike the warring clans of Larsellan's ancient past, August and Kestrel were more than capable of finding agreement on any number of topics.

"Highness! It is good to see you again at last!" August said, clasping his hands around Isadore's. Isadore returned the greeting, and offered it to Kestrel in turn, who bowed in the Tallandi style.

From the second and third carriages emerged Sandry na'Briargate, Larse ambassador to Arrawey, and Mila na'Greenwood, Larse ambassador to Kivern. Sandry carried a sleeping infant in a sling against her chest. The two women might have been mistaken for family, at a first glance. They had the same long hair, Sandry's a soft brown and Mila's half-gray with age, and the same light scarves over their heads, but as they directed their underlings, the subtle differences in their voices and manners became clear.

Behind them their staff filed out and took the carriages to the stables. The handful of scribes and servants had only one guard with them, but unlike the other delegations, their carriages would not have attracted much attention on the journey. Larse designs were not ostentatious and never gaudy; they did what they were built for and lasted generations. Isadore suspected these carriages were the same ones the Ambassadors' predecessors had driven to meet his grandfather.

August looked around at the banners decorating the hall: Larsellan's thin gold and blue, Kivern's twin-pointed red and black with the gold crown at the center, Arrawey's vertical white and blue mountains, Talland's intertwined blue and green. "I suppose we have you to thank for all this. Not many people could wrangle Kivern *and* Arrawey into the same room, much less signing the same paper!"

"Save the praise for Beck and Miller," Isadore said. Talland's envoys to Arrawey and Kivern deserved the praise far more than he did. "They did the whale's share of the work."

"Ah, humble, is he? Queen Seraphina taught him well," Kestrel said.

"Enough of that, Kestrel," Mila said. "We are guests."

"That you are. Come, you must be hungry. Your rooms will be ready when we're done." No doubt the watchtower guards had sent word to the servants to have those preparations finished with all haste.

"Ah, we'll make do with anything," Kestrel said with a dismissive wave of his hand. "Save the staterooms for those honorable lords and ladies from Arrawey. Won't do any good displeasing *them* the night before the signing."

"And insulting them won't do any good either," Sandry warned, coming forward to greet Isadore. "Highness. I am pleased for us to meet under these skies."

"As am I. And I offer my congratulations on this little one," he said, smiling at the baby, who slept on, oblivious to the fuss around him. Evidently a mere Tallandi prince was not worth opening his eyes for.

"Thank you, Highness." She ran a gentle, calloused hand over the tufts of thin, downy hair crowning the child's head. "He arrived just after we concluded negotiations with Lady Martellan and King Daragh."

"Very good timing. When he's a bit older, I'm sure he'll have the entire Council wrapped around his finger."

Sandry smiled. "He already does! I've hardly had to ask for help at all. It's as if he summons them by magic whenever he needs something."

Isadore silently thanked his mother's long-ago decision to have several guestrooms built in the Larse style. In their homeland, the ambassadors would have lived in connected or even shared rooms with their staff during the weeks the Lands Council was in session, just as they lived with their families at home. Isadore's grandfather had once said that managing politics was like managing family. In Larsellan, that was more true than ever.

One of the servants, Patrice, Isadore thought, appeared in the doorway. "Highness, the rooms for our guests are ready."

"Thank you." Isadore nodded to the ambassadors. "Go, rest for a while after your journey. Someone will summon you when dinner is ready, or I can have food sent to your rooms."

"Thank you. We'll do our best to stay out of your way until the reception," Mila promised. Melanie would have been glad that Isadore knew better than to tell her that it was hardly the Larse guests he was worried about.

The ambassadors from Arrawey sailed into the crown city the next morning aboard a stunning riverboat, its mighty prow carved into the head of a mountain eagle. Their procession down the street to the palace, flanked by guards, drew watchers from all corners of the city.

Kivern's delegation rode up to the palace gates just after the Arraweyans were shown to their rooms. Alaric Grenner leapt from his horse, gold-edged coat glittering in the sun, and shouted commands to the servants who followed. Frederick Massan did the same. Willem Habb, Kivern's ambassador to Larsellan, was the only one who spoke quietly, but his sharp gestures brooked no disagreement. The three of them together formed a united front, an impenetrable wall. Not for the first time, Isadore admired Karin Miller for her ability to handle them.

The palace staff worked like clockwork, showing them all to their rooms and taking care of all their needs. They'd be very busy today and tomorrow, and Isadore thought to himself that afterward, something should be done to reward them for their hard work.

The celebration today was set to last long into the night, and then there was another one planned for after the signing the next morning.

"It almost seems that the purpose of all this is to have them too hungover to pose any last-minute complaints," Melanie had said of the schedule.

"And you're sure you don't want to join us?" Isadore asked, only half-joking.

She laughed. "Isadore, I spend every single day reading what these people write and listening to their assistants prattle on in meetings. I don't need to hear their polite chatter too, not when I can finally snatch an evening free for myself."

He couldn't argue with that. If he had his way about it, she'd be getting at least as much credit as the ambassadors were. But he also knew she'd appreciate time to herself much more than praise and flattery.

"I see. Well, saints willing, you should be free until we bid them farewell."

"Sometimes I wonder if we should even be rewarding them," Melanie mused. "They spend three years squabbling and get invited to a ball. While if they'd done what they were supposed to do and worked this out, it would have been business as usual."

"I'm sure Sir Valentino would have figured something out," Isadore said. "That man goes through more parties than Darby does spools of thread."

"At least somebody's enjoying it," Melanie sighed, slipping the last of her papers into a folder and tying it shut. "This will be Ambry's first official reception. I hope they have a good time. They deserve it."

"They certainly do." Ambry had been running about all day helping with the last of the preparations. Even now, in their honored position, they weren't too proud to help the kitchen staff or the gardeners. But they would be at the ball, and at the treaty signing.

To have them at his side, recognized, if only momentarily, as one of the people who brought about this historic bargain, that was enough to carry him through any doubts, any amount of tedious dinner conversation.

Just one more day, and his greatest accomplishment would be secured.

⟡

In just a few days, Delia, Ella, and Marion had transformed the palace's largest ballroom into an entirely different place from the room where Ambry had once scrubbed floors and dusted window frames. As they wandered about, careful of their every step, Ambry thanked every minute they had spent with Melanie, memorizing the names of the ambassadors.

The guests had dressed in all their finery, from the politicians to the assistants. Arrawey's Sir Valentino Bressing, Lady Claudine Pennafor, and Lady Lauretta Martellan were easy enough to spot, gliding across the floor in their long coats and flowing dresses. Sir Valentino's pointed mustache wouldn't have looked out of place on the stage of the Northwind Theater, and the two women were night and day mirrors of each other: Lady Claudine's dark skin and hair crowned with a band of opals, and Lady Lauretta's pale skin and fair hair braided with a field of silk bellflowers. The servants wore lighter-colored cloaks, each embroidered with Arrawey's royal seal, a hawk flying over a snowy mountain.

The three from Kivern, all men, were more difficult to tell apart in their identical uniforms. From what Ambry had heard from his letters, they'd uncharitably imagined Kivern's Alaric Grenner as an ugly old man, scowling at everyone around him. So it was a surprise to find him to be tall and strong, with proud, watchful eyes and a polite, formal manner. If it wasn't for the uniform, he wouldn't be notable at all, apart from the dueling scar that stood out on his cheek. Frederick Massan and Willem Habb, envoys to Arrawey and Larsellan, looked much the same, if a touch more relaxed than Grenner.

The Kivernese generally kept to themselves, always with a servant near at hand. And very few of the servants were interested in speaking to anyone outside of their party. Arrogant as it seemed, Ambry could hardly blame them. With so many people around, it was hard to know what to say, never mind who to say it to.

Ambry wore the formal suit that had carried them through the City Council meeting and noted with a swell of patriotic pride that Darby's designs could easily stand their own against Arrawey's long silver-edged blue and purple cloaks and jeweled buttons, and Kivern's sharp crimson and gold suits with decorative daggers at the hip. The Larse delegation wore more ordinary-looking clothing that some might assume would be more at home in the fields or mills, but even Ambry could tell the fabric and cut was finer than that, and likely far more comfortable than the others. And when Mila and an assistant passed by them, they caught a glimpse of the embroidery at the collar and hems, twining leaves and vines and even little birds and butterflies, each picked out with astonishing skill.

In stark contrast to those clustered groups of blue and red, Karin Miller sat with August and Kestrel, the three of them laughing over some story of Karin's that Ambry couldn't hear through the noise.

Isadore, also garbed in Darby's finest, milled about, talking merrily to each of the ambassadors in turn, thanking them for their hard work and dedication over the long years it had taken to secure the treaty.

Dominick watched him from his stern position against the wall, from which he could survey the entire room for danger. It seemed fitting that even a celebration like this couldn't brighten his severe mood.

Delia appeared, carrying a tray of wineglasses. "You don't know how much I want to take one of these for myself," she said, offering them to Ambry. "And you! You look like one of these lords yourself."

"I wish I felt like one," Ambry confessed.

"You're doing great. Just smile and tell them how clever they are, and you'll be fine."

Ambry wasn't certain about that particular advice, but accepted a glass of bubbling Larse wine from Delia's platter as one of the ambassadors did the same. Delia winked at them and swept off towards the table where Sandry na'Briargate and Lady Lauretta were discussing something or other, with Sir Valentino and a few of the Arraweyan and Larse servants listening.

"Ah, you're Ambry Jean? Isadore's new assistant?" Ambry turned to see Sheridan Beck, the Tallandi ambassador to Arrawey. And the only one of the ambassadors who was not clearly a man or a woman. "He's spoken highly of you. I must say, I never thought he'd give anyone a chance after Lacey left, but you've impressed him."

Ambry bowed to them. "Thank you. It's been incredible. Sometimes I still can't believe he chose me."

Beck smiled. "You know this already, but he makes good decisions. Sometimes it takes him a while to reach them, but he's rarely wrong. Remember that."

There were so many things they wanted to ask Beck, about how they did the things they did, about Arrawey, about Isadore, but now was not the time. Surely, they would rather talk to their fellow ambassadors or prince than a mere assistant.

Then an angry woman's voice echoed across the room, and there wasn't any more time to ask any questions at all.

"What are you doing?" Grenner demanded, rounding on the woman.

She'd been moving in Isadore's direction, but Ambry didn't recognize her. She wasn't dressed like any of the guests. A new member of the Palace staff? Isadore had been talking about asking Mrs. Hammond to hire more hands for the kitchen and garden.

She kept walking, as if she didn't even hear him. Grenner grabbed at her arm. A flash of a blade, then Grenner cried out and fell to the floor, reaching for the dagger at his hip. Before he could draw it, Dominick was on top of the attacker, shoving her to the ground. Her head hit a chair with a dull sound, loud in the suddenly quiet room, and she went still, crumpled on the floor under Dominick's weight.

"Highness, stay where you are," Dominick ordered, but Isadore was already moving, three long strides bringing him to kneel beside Grenner.

Ambry had a sudden vision of the prince at Danny's side, hands held out to heal. The same happened now. Isadore pulled the knife free and tossed it aside to clatter on the floor, and pressed his palms to Grenner's shoulder even as blood spilled over his sleeves.

"How did she get in?" one voice demanded.

"What did she want?" another asked.

"There might be more!"

Tearing their eyes away from Isadore and Grenner, Ambry glanced around the room.

Sandry and Mila's staff had formed a protective shield around them, and August and Kestrel stood together. The Arraweyans swept their elegant cloaks out of the way, and the other two Kivernese and Karin Miller had drawn their weapons.

Isadore stood, stumbled, steadied himself with a hand on the back of a chair before sitting heavily in it.

"I've healed him," he gasped. "He'll live."

The silent room burst into noise. Angry shouting, questions, cheers, tears. Frederick Massan helped Grenner clamber upright, and no sooner had he regained his footing than he was cursing aloud, demanding to know what foolishness had allowed this to happen, that he would sign nothing until he knew.

Royal guards hurried into the room, crowding Ambry back into the hallway behind. Ambry moved to push forward through, towards Isadore, but a hand on their arm held them back. It was Ella, face ashen with shock.

They could only watch as one of the Larse servants held out a damp cloth for Isadore to scrub Grenner's blood from his hands. He accepted it woodenly, eyes distant, still not rising from his seat. He didn't seem even to hear Grenner's furious accusations, or the other ambassadors' arguing.

In the midst of the chaos, Dominick reached down and tore something small and sparkling gold from the unconscious intruder's neck. A Tallandi royal badge, same as all the servants wore. That was why she had not been stopped.

He turned it over. "AJ," he read, and his stone-hard eyes fell on Ambry.

Horror bloomed in their stomach. This was their fault, entirely their fault. The noise from the other room blended into a confusion of raised voices and clattering plates. How long it lasted, Ambry did not know, but at some point Isadore strode from the room with Dominick at his back, breathing a little roughly, clothing and hairpins just the tiniest bit out of place. He looked around until his eyes settled on Ambry. He stepped forward.

"Come with me," he ordered, and swept away toward the heir's tower, not even pausing to catch his breath. Ambry followed, a growing dread tailing their every step.

Chapter Twelve

✧

Only when they were alone in Isadore's study but for Dominick's watchful presence at the door did Ambry realize they were shaking. They swallowed hard, fought back shivers of fear, dared to look at Isadore's face. Whatever Isadore had done to save the Ambassador had drained him, yet there was still a ferocity in his eyes when he turned to address them.

"Ambry. How did this happen?"

They shrank back under Isadore's suddenly-harsh gaze, that gaze they had prayed would never be directed at them. "I lost my badge when I was in the city last week," they said, the words flat and distant, as if spoken by somebody else. They reached for the one they wore on their collar now and felt it cold and hard under their fingers. "I didn't want to trouble anyone." *I didn't want to get in trouble.* "De– One of my friends had another one." Would she be blamed too? When none of this was her fault?

"You lost your badge," Isadore repeated, flatly. "And you didn't report it. And because you didn't, the Ambassador's life was put in danger, and his delegation are now claiming he was targeted, and are threatening to withdraw from the agreement."

The words struck like knives. Ambry looked down, unable to face those eyes. Sickening horror swept through them, prickling sweat and chills all at once. They might have killed the Ambassador today with their carelessness, and they had all but certainly ruined the treaty, the treaty Isadore had worked on for months.

And the way Isadore looked at them hurt worlds more than anything else. Blood pounded in their ears. This was the end of it. They would be sent away from here in disgrace, alone. Where could they go now? Surely not anywhere in the palace. What a fool they had been to think they were suitable to walk alongside the prince. There had to be somewhere to flee, somewhere to hide before this agony wrenched itself out of their chest as tears or worse, but they could not move, could not lift their feet or even their head. Ambry stood frozen as terror knotted their stomach, clawed their heart, clenched their throat.

"Well?" Isadore asked. "How did it happen? Why didn't you say anything?"

Some distant part of Ambry noted that he didn't sound angry now, but it hardly mattered amid the storm in their chest. They opened their mouth and could not make a sound. No matter how they tried, they could say nothing to explain themself or defend themself or even to beg forgiveness.

Behind them, Dominick called, "Answer him!"

Breath came faster now, short gasps that strained their lungs. This was unacceptable, this was pathetic, this would only make it worse...

"What is it?" Something had changed in the prince's voice, but Ambry could not interpret it, could not even think through the pain and the horror. They dropped to the floor, hoping it would be enough to express everything they could not say, and knelt there, shaking, ludicrously still fighting back tears even though one more humiliation on top of this could hardly make it any worse. They tasted cold, bitter truth: that they had lost Isadore's regard, that they had failed at the simplest of tasks. That they would surely not be permitted to stay. Empty days of regret stretched before them; their heart fought uselessly against the inevitable. They wanted to beg, but still they could not speak, and perhaps that was for the better because it meant they could not damage their situation any further with their foolish tongue. But silence might be just as damning.

It didn't matter. It shouldn't matter. They had failed, and nothing they could do would fix it, and yet something inside them fought, fought that failure, tearing things inside them as it writhed uselessly against their ribs.

They heard Dominick's voice high above their head, stern as ever. "Highness. Should I remove them?" No doubt he thought them disgraceful, unworthy. They waited, waited for Dominick's hands on their arms, waited to be wrenched to their feet and thrown out of the room. Sobs shook them, knife-edged, sickening things that tore their way through their throat no matter how they struggled to hold them back. Proving him right.

Footsteps. Isadore's voice, commanding: "No. Stay there, Dominick. Let me handle this." And then, softer, at their ear. "Ambry. Breathe. Please, breathe. It was not entirely your fault. We caught the intruder. The Ambassador is safe. We might still be able to mend the treaty." Gentle hands against their bowed neck, around their back. "We *will* mend the treaty. We can talk about it later. I trust you. I forgive you." Distantly, they noticed that Isadore had knelt beside them, that he had reached out to comfort them.

Dominick spoke again, disapproving, disgusted. "Such a shameful display should not be rewarded."

Ambry choked on a ragged, stuttering breath.

"Lieutenant Marshall, that is *enough*," Isadore snapped, more anger in his voice than Ambry had ever heard from him before. "You will be silent," he ordered. He pulled Ambry close, as if by shielding them from Dominick's eyes he could shield them from the all-consuming pain that grew within them like thorns.

They should have felt relieved, and yet they only felt pathetic. Still the horror shook them: disgust at their error, at their inability to handle this. The fear of Isadore's disapproval.

And shame, that while a crucial treaty lay in tatters, the Prince of Talland had to spend his time comforting a servant weeping in a useless heap on the floor. Still they could not lift their face to Isadore's, for fear of what they might find there.

"Ambry." That voice, so steady, so concerned. They wanted to run from it and hide, they wanted to bury themself in the care that it offered. "I can help. I can calm you, put you to sleep for a while. But only if you want it."

They wanted it. Gods, they wanted it. It was more than they deserved. And yet Isadore offered it so readily, tired as he was from the day's work and the disastrous reception. Ambry managed to whimper something in agreement. Coward that they were, they would take the comfort now and pick up the shattered pieces later.

Isadore ran a soothing hand over their shoulders. "I'm going to need something clearer than that. Can you nod?"

A breath. Another. And then Ambry found strength enough to choke out, "Yes. Please." Anything to end this nightmare that had stolen their voice and shaken them like a rat.

"All right. It'll only take a moment…" A touch at their temples, for one second, two, three, and then a fog of exhaustion swept through them, dulling the sharp, broken pain in their chest and sapping the strength that knotted their muscles, and they fell forward into Isadore's arms and merciful darkness.

✧

Ambry went limp under Isadore's hands, choked sobs easing slowly into deep breaths. Isadore held still until he was certain they would not easily wake, and then gathered them up in his arms and stood. Wordlessly, Dominick moved to assist him, and together they carried Ambry to the long couch and settled them comfortably onto the cushions. Isadore unfolded the blanket from where it sat on the windowsill and draped it over Ambry's back. The sleep he had induced would not be restful, he knew, but it would at least be a respite from the pain and terror that had driven them to their knees.

Dominick made as if to speak, then stepped back.

Isadore watched him, making no effort to hide his displeasure. "What is it you wish to say, Dominick?"

Dominick bowed. "Highness. You are so easily swayed. A warm heart can be a great asset. But if it becomes known that a fit of tears is all that is needed to escape reprimand... you will see more such fits in your future."

Isadore clenched his teeth against the first response that came to mind and chose something more measured instead. "I appreciate your advice. But that is not what this was." Ambry's terrified sobs still rang in his head. There had been nothing false in that terror.

"Still." Dominick tilted his head. "A suitable punishment is needed. For their carelessness in allowing a servant's badge to escape their possession, for their poor judgment in hiding that fact."

He was right, in a way. Isadore hadn't expected Ambry to be so careless. He wondered for a moment if he'd missed some sign, if his care for them had softened his judgment. But that didn't matter now. Now, they had to work with what had happened.

"That woman would have found a way in, with or without that badge. Her actions are hardly Ambry's fault alone. I think this has been punishment enough." He looked to where Ambry lay asleep on the couch, breathing steadily, hair damp with sweat. "More than enough." The pain that had exploded into his vision when Ambry fell had been so bright as to be nearly blinding, even though he had not been consciously looking. He could not often see pains of the mind and heart through his magic as he saw pains of the body, but there were some conditions, grief and terror chief among them, that left their mark in aches and tremors that blazed as bright as any bleeding wound.

Guilt stung him, for his role in causing this. He heard his own words echo in his head and regretted them bitterly. There had been no reason for him to confront Ambry thus, to all but accuse them of ruining the treaty. They were nervous at the best of times, but this had been agony. Whatever mistakes Ambry had made, they had not deserved the panic that had all but consumed them. He and Ambry had disagreed before and all had been well. But those times had not come after weeks of exhausting, sleepless days, and the weight of four kingdoms on their backs.

Dominick heard his tone and did not argue. Isadore reminded himself that Dominick had only meant to do his duty, that he did not realize how cruel his words sounded. Surely, he would not have said it if he knew. *He* had not seen the burst of pain that had sparked in Ambry's chest when he had threatened to throw them out. Still, anger swam somewhere deep inside Isadore. Dominick had never approved of his closeness with Ambry, he had sensed that much, but at least he had kept that displeasure quiet. But now, to use Ambry's pain as a reason to be rid of them? To accuse them of weakness for succumbing to a terror so great they had no chance of fighting it? Isadore took a steadying breath and as gently as he could, said, "I think it would be best if you were not present when they wake."

There was a flicker of a wince in Dominick's face, as if he had been stung, before his features settled into a stony mask. He nodded. "I understand," he said flatly. "I will send for Sylvia to take my post." He called for a page to take word to Sylvia and returned to his silent watch at the entrance.

She came quickly, soon enough after the order that Isadore knew she'd been awakened already, and hard at work investigating what had happened in the ballroom.

"Highness," she said, as Dominick silently departed. "The Ambassadors are all safely in their rooms. We have advised them to stay there for the time being, until we are certain there are no more threats."

Sensible precautions. Isadore nodded, trying not to imagine what conversations must be going on in those rooms. "Do you believe there are?"

She shook her head. "No. There's been no sign of anything more, but we will stay on our watch. The woman has not awakened yet, but the doctor says she will soon, and when she does, we will question her."

"Good." It was far from good. But he was glad the intruder was not too badly hurt to answer their questions. He wouldn't have had the energy to heal her, even if his guards had let him, and he certainly didn't after granting Ambry sleep.

"Is Ambry well?" Sylvia asked after a moment.

"I think so," Isadore said. "This was... this was unexpected. It wasn't their fault," he added, as if he needed to convince Sylvia of anything when he could simply order it of her and she'd obey.

"We'll know whose it was before long," Sylvia said, and took up her post outside the door. "And if there are any more, they won't get far."

Before Isadore could fall back into self-recriminations, the door to the inner room opened and Melanie pushed through with a platter of slim letters in her lap, each of them bearing a bright official seal.

"From the ambassadors." She passed him the tray; he turned the letters over in his hands and then put them down without reading them.

She glanced to Ambry's sleeping form and did not ask the question she undoubtedly had. He felt he owed her an explanation even so, and as briefly as he could told her what had happened after the reception was brought to a halt.

"I'm not surprised," she said, plainly yet gently, which was how he knew she had read his guilt in his face. "We've all had weeks of stress leading up to the summit. Anyone would feel terrible after something like this. And you know Ambry judges themself harshly."

"Was I wrong to trust them?" Isadore asked the air, not looking at Melanie. The words tasted foul. "Without that badge, nothing would have happened."

"For all we know, it still would have," Melanie said. "It's a serious mistake, but it's one they'll never repeat."

Never, not after how that error had hurt them. Isadore wanted to believe her. But when he tried to focus on anything other than Ambry's error, he was immediately drawn into wondering about his own.

Isadore sat on Ambry's usual chair and lowered his head into his hands, not caring how he upset his hairpins in doing so. "This is my doing, Melanie. If I had not spoken so harshly... This is why anything more than this cannot be. If they are afraid of me, afraid to disagree or resist me..."

"This was an unusual situation, Isadore," Melanie said.

He wished he could accept that answer. "I cannot risk causing them more pain."

Melanie sighed. She moved beside him, took his hand. "Listen to me, Isadore. You are the most trustworthy and caring man I know. And Ambry is strong, despite their anxieties. They know themself. And they know that you will never intend to hurt them."

"It doesn't matter what I meant if they are hurt by it anyway. It's still wrong."

"But it *will* matter to *them* what you meant by it. And if it happens, you can mend it."

He looked away. "I wish I could know that for certain."

"Well, you can't know the future. But you can trust yourself and trust them. I do."

He saw her wisdom, even if he could not yet feel it to be true. And he could not afford to lose himself to regrets now, not with the agreement in the state it was. There was work to do, and that must come before all else. He'd been taught that his whole life. He moved the chair to the other side of her desk. "What have you heard?"

She dug a few pages from the stack of notes and set them in front of him. "Everybody's a little shaken, no surprise there. The Guard searched everything, but it seems that the woman was the only intruder. Grenner is still angry. He says he won't sign the treaty without more concessions."

The words landed dully against Isadore's ears. He'd heard them already, but he hadn't wanted to believe Grenner would follow through on those threats made in the heat of a crisis.

"He can't back out now," Isadore said stupidly, hardly believing what he was hearing.

"According to his laws and ours, he can," Melanie reminded him. "But it might not have to come to that. His staff are working to calm him. As are Beck, and Miller, and Teller, and the rest of them." She looked up at him, eyes earnest, reflecting an optimism Isadore did not feel. "You impressed them tonight. I think they'll be willing to negotiate."

"We can hope," he said, a bitter twist to his lips. "Though I would prefer it if we didn't have to rework anything."

"It might be for the better, in the end."

"Perhaps." Or it might be worse. "Have they changed their minds on the Lynwood Provision?" That had been such a tenuous agreement. He would hate to see it crumble now, when it had been so close to succeeding.

She shook her head. "Not yet, thankfully. But once they think they have an inch, they'll most likely try to have that cut from the treaty. If they're going to try anything, that's going to be it."

"Right. Let's say they do." He snagged a pen from the table and made a note. "Then we'll demand to restore the Atworth Proposal, and this time, it'll be binding."

Melanie smiled. "And Grenner knows that that'll crack the whole thing right open again, and that's the last thing any of us want. We've come this far, nobody's going home empty-handed, especially over something as petty as this. If we're lucky, they'll back down and leave the Lynwood Provision as written."

"But if they try to water down Lynwood instead of removing it entirely..."

"Then we can call them out for their cowardly maneuvering in using something like this to rewrite a treaty that's been years in the making at the very last second. But first we'll give them a chance to salvage their pride."

Isadore was able to bury himself in the letters for a time, in the puzzle of searching for answers between the lines of long-winded formalities. He and Melanie quickly fell into a familiar rhythm, passing papers back and forth, preparing letters. She offered knowledge gleaned from assistants' gossip, he balanced that against what he knew of the ambassadors and their masters. He proposed plans, she finessed the wording into something that could please even the fiercest doubters.

By the time Sylvia's quiet cough heralded a messenger at the door, they had compiled a page of serviceable revisions that might just sweeten Grenner's mood. He hoped they wouldn't have to use them, but he also knew how stubborn that man was.

"Highness, the ambassadors are expecting you in the Heartlight Chamber."

Isadore sighed. "Tell them I'll be there shortly."

Melanie gathered up the papers. "Go on. I'll send a note when Ambry wakes."

"Thank you." He took the folder under his arm and cast one last look towards Ambry before following Sylvia down the stairs.

✧

Ambry woke slowly, regretting the loss of the comforting darkness as soon as they lifted from it. They felt strangely worn all over, and their throat ached as if they'd swallowed nails. And then they remembered. Remembered the flash of a knife, Grenner's blood on Isadore's fine clothes, Dominick holding up the badge. Their badge, which had allowed all this to happen. Remembered Isadore's anger, the terror that had torn through them, remembered how they had been helpless to answer for their mistake. They braced themself for another fit of that hopeless fear, but it did not come. Something warm in their chest kept it at bay. Their own exhaustion? Isadore's spell? Whatever the case, it would be best to leave now, rather than make Isadore deal with them any further. They sat up, and felt their head begin to pound.

Melanie looked up from her desk. "No, stay. Isadore wants to talk to you."

Their heart plummeted. They had behaved shamefully and now they had to face the consequences. Melanie must have seen something of it in their face, for she added hastily, "He's not angry. It upset him, seeing you like that. He's worried."

That was almost worse, wasn't it? Isadore didn't need another concern on his mind tonight, not with so many angry ambassadors to placate. Ambry bit their lip, found it already sore and scabbed. They stared at their hands, at the blanket and the beautiful curling embroidery that covered it and let the last traces of Isadore's spell drown out the drumbeat of criticism in their head. It wasn't enough, but they would take whatever comfort they were given, for they were surely not strong enough to stand without it.

"Here." They looked up at Melanie's voice. She pushed a cup of tea into their hands. Ambry sipped it, and found it sweetened exactly to their liking. They managed voice enough to thank her, and drank, letting the warmth soothe their raw throat.

They had nearly finished the cup when the doors swung open and Isadore entered. The guard who followed watchful at his side was not Dominick but Sylvia, for which Ambry was pathetically grateful. They did not think they could bear the weight of Dominick's disdain again today.

Isadore smiled weakly as he approached, and if it was meant to set Ambry's mind at ease, it did help a little, at least until Ambry saw the weariness dulling his eyes. They shouldn't have been surprised to see it, not after all Isadore had done. The long delicate negotiations, the ball, and the unending days of sleepless preparation before that. And then two major healings in one evening. Ambry wished there was some way they could be of help, instead of needing help.

Isadore took a cup from Melanie with a murmur of thanks, and after a moment's hesitation, sat beside Ambry. "How are you feeling?"

Ambry looked away. "Better, I suppose. Thank you." For his spell, for his mercy, for not sending them away in disgrace. "I'm sorry." The panic was gone, and yet the shame remained, sharpened by gratitude. For a moment they thought they would weep again, but this time, somehow, they managed to hold the ache inside. Part of them wished more than anything that Isadore would again hold them close and warm, but that was something they could not ask for now.

Isadore sighed, lowered his head. "I should not have blamed you for the mistake. I sincerely apologize for that. There are any number of ways this could have happened." Ambry could see the truth in that, though it did not make them feel any less a fool. "And Ambassador Grenner is unpleasant on a good day. I'm sure he would have used any impropriety in the evening as an excuse to demand the treaty be rewritten in Kivern's favor."

Ambry winced. "The treaty…"

"Is still on the table. We're meeting again tomorrow morning. Ambassador Miller sounds optimistic."

"And I've heard," Melanie put in, "through certain channels, that Grenner's staff were rather impressed with our prince's heroics."

Isadore opened his mouth to protest, but Melanie smiled and continued, "You saved Grenner's life, Isadore. That will be worth something in the negotiations, to the others at least if not to Grenner himself." She was the only person Ambry knew who would dare to interrupt the prince so easily. "And he might be an ass, but he won't go home to Queen Frida without the deal he promised her."

"I wish it didn't have to be. But it might well help us."

So there was hope, at least. Perhaps this could be salvaged.

Isadore gently tugged the cup from Ambry's fingers and refilled it from the pot on Melanie's desk, adding a generous spoonful of honey. Sweet-smelling steam rose up. Ambry held the cup still until their fingers started to sting from the heat. It almost felt good, pain on their skin instead of in their heart.

Of course Isadore noticed. "Stop that," he told them, too softly to be called scolding. Ambry winced even so. And then, "Have you eaten? I could have something sent up."

Ambry turned the cup in their hands. "You shouldn't be doing this. You should be worrying about the treaty and the Ambassador, not me."

Isadore tilted his head, smiled faintly. "Can't I worry about you both?"

"That's not what I—"

"I know. I know. It's all right."

Isadore called for a page and sent him to ask for a plate. There was silence between them for a while, a calm, tired silence. Melanie continued to work, preparing neat piles of documents that she handed off to her assistants and undersecretaries as they entered. Ambry wondered if they ought to feel exposed, with all these people seeing their state, but they were to a one perfectly professional and did not even glance towards Ambry or Isadore.

A few minutes later, Sylvia opened the door to reveal Ella carrying a platter of food. She paused when she saw Ambry, worry creasing her face. Ambry wondered how ragged they must look to inspire such a reaction.

"Ella. It's all right. I'm fine." Whether they deserved that was another question altogether. Ella's concern eased a little but worry remained in her expression as she set down the tray. Could they say more, or would that risk the secrecy of the agreement?

"The Ambassador is well and the treaty will be saved," Isadore said, sparing Ambry the need to decide what to say. "Tell your fellows not to worry overmuch for us."

Ella bowed. "Thank you, Highness. I'll tell them." She hesitated. "If I can speak…?"

"What is it?"

"We – the kitchen staff, that is – we were all very impressed with you tonight, Highness." She smiled. "It was an amazing thing to see, as much as we wish we hadn't had to. We're truly proud to serve you."

"Thank you," Isadore said. "But know that when this treaty succeeds, it will have been due to far, far many more people than just me."

She uncovered the dish to reveal a piece of roast chicken. The skin was no longer crisp, but they could still smell the generous sprinkling of herbs and beside it sat a generous pile of beans in a buttery sauce. Fine as it was, it didn't inspire much of an appetite. Ambry ate anyway, hoping it might ease the fatigue that ached in their bones and behind their eyes. They managed half the plate before they had to set the rest aside, making a silent apology to Ella and the cooks for the waste. Isadore didn't press them to eat more, for which they were grateful.

Isadore yawned. "Melanie, go to bed," he said, turning toward the desk. "We've done everything we can possibly do before the next meeting."

Melanie folded her notebook closed and capped her pens. "Only if you make sure you rest as well."

"I will, I promise."

She smiled. "Good night, then," she said, and disappeared through the inner door, leaving them alone in quiet, lamplit darkness. Ambry expected Isadore to stand, to dismiss them too to their bed. They wanted sleep desperately, and yet they didn't think they could bear to be alone.

Instead, he gently set his hand on Ambry's shoulder, wordlessly inviting them close. Grateful beyond expression, Ambry let themself lean against Isadore's side. He shifted to accommodate them, settled down against the cushions and cradled them against his chest. A voice inside them reminded them that they should get up, that they shouldn't trouble Isadore any more tonight, but how could they even think of moving from here? Here, they were comfortable and warm and loved. Somehow, Isadore still wanted them. If only they could live forever in this calm, and never have to deal with the world outside and their own inevitable mistakes. A sensible voice, the voice that had been all but crushed to dust by today's disaster, was starting to bloom again in the back of their head, promising that all would be well, that they did many more things right than things they failed. But it was quiet still, and they feared it would be again extinguished in another painful rush of fear.

Isadore tucked an arm around their back, rubbed the last of the tension from their shoulders with warm hands and perhaps a touch of magic. "Rest," he told them. "Just rest. Everything will be all right. There's nothing else we can do until the morning."

Here, at least, they were safe from that dark and crushing fear. They gave themself up to what Isadore offered. For the second time that day, Ambry fell into a dreamless sleep in Isadore's arms.

✧

Some time later – he didn't know how long, except that the fire had long ago burned out and he'd been drifting near sleep for a while – Isadore rose slowly and regretfully from the couch, careful not to wake Ambry. He tucked the blanket around them and knelt by the fire to rekindle it so there would be no risk of them becoming cold.

He had liked holding Ambry more than he wanted to admit. Having them sleep in his arms had felt right in a way he couldn't easily explain. He desperately hoped he had not overreached. Would they want to keep so close when they were steady and well? A memory drifted into his head, of Ambry resting their head in his hands while he eased their headache as rain poured down outside. They would have to talk about it, eventually. When this current trouble was past and the treaty finished with.

Sylvia waited silent and patient at the door. When he looked to her, grateful beyond measure that she had let him lie there without disapproving or interrupting, she only nodded, slowly, and still it told him everything. Isadore knew he should retire to his bed. He would be of no use to anybody if he did not sleep, and he knew he could not sleep well here. But he did not want to leave. He'd put them through so much strain in the past weeks preparing for the summit. He ought to have noticed before it became too much.

He sat beside Ambry, brushed strands of hair from their face, resisted the need to kiss the marks of tears from their cheek. Perhaps he should wake them, send them to their own bed, but he was loath to disturb them. They badly needed the rest, especially after Isadore's spell of sleep, which he knew left its subjects drained and muddled. And yet his heart clenched at the thought of them waking here alone and in the dark after what had happened. He fought with himself for several long moments over a sudden desire to summon Lawrence to protect Ambry, but there was surely nobody in the palace who would dare threaten them. Even Grenner's staff would not be so vindictive or so foolish as to attack someone so close to the Prince of Talland. And besides, Lawrence had a shift in the morning and it would be unfair to wake him early. He had already disturbed his guards' schedules enough by calling for Sylvia before her time.

Anger coursed within him when he thought of what Dominick had said. To imply that Ambry's helpless fear had been something invented, something worthy of shame and punishment, rather than the terrifying battle against their own body and mind that Isadore had felt so keenly from a single touch... He shook his head. He would deal with that in the morning. He loved Dominick so, but the man would insist on judging everything that passed under his eye. He sighed. All would be well, eventually. He turned his magic sight on Ambry, found no pains troubling them save a slightly sore throat. They slept deeply; Isadore doubted they would wake before morning. It was left to be seen whether this night would leave its scars on them. He prayed that would not be the case. He should not blame himself, Melanie had insisted on that, but still he could not help but feel some responsibility. If he hadn't spoken so harshly, Ambry might have been able to speak without terror. But none of that mattered now. Now, they had to deal with the situation they found themselves in with whatever they could find to help them.

At last satisfied that Ambry would be safe, and more importantly, know and feel that they were safe, he let Sylvia shepherd him up the winding stair to his bedroom. He undressed in a daze, grateful for the low fire that burned in the hearth for it meant he did not have to trouble himself to light the lamps.

For a long time, he stared out at the night sky and the city below, wondering how long it would be before the people who trusted him to secure this treaty would read about this night in their newspapers, and what they would make of it. He'd fight to keep Ambry's name out of it, if he had to. He prayed that by the time Ostberg prepared her presses with word of the treaty, it would be sealed and done.

There was nothing he could do now but sleep. His great bed, normally a welcome respite from the world and its needs and its hurts, had never before felt so cold and quiet.

Chapter Thirteen

✧

Ambry woke again in Isadore's study, curled under that beautiful quilt. Warm sunlight streamed in through the window, washing away any last traces of fear that might have attempted to rise in their chest. Their hair was a tangled mess and their throat dry, but at last they felt they stood on solid ground again. Whatever was to come, they could survive it.

That terrible evening felt like a distant nightmare now, too far away to strike again. Guilt still gnawed, for the danger they had put the Ambassador in, but it was bearable now, as if a wall stood between them and the terror that had overwhelmed them. Rested, they could see beyond their fears and their mistake to the truth. Grenner and Kivern were acting entirely unjustly, taking advantage of this incident to push their political agenda and renege on previously-agreed terms. And Isadore was far more angered by Grenner's actions than by what had happened at the reception.

While theirs had indeed been a foolish mistake, it had been only one part in a chain of mistakes for which no one person was guilty. And it would do nobody any good to linger on what they might have done, save to make better plans for the future so that it would not be repeated. The storm had passed and somehow it had left no damage in its wake. Would they fall again into that desperate, lonely place? They didn't think they could bear it again. But if Isadore was there... then they knew they would survive it.

They might have been ashamed, for all they had needed of Isadore, now that his spell was no longer there to drape a comfortable cloud over their thoughts. But they felt only gratitude. Isadore had offered it all so readily. Ambry's savage fears had dragged them into hell, and Isadore had gone to war to win them back. And of course he had. He would have done the same for any under his watch. That was one of the many reasons Ambry loved him. And they did love him. There was no use hiding it now. They hadn't recognized it for a long time, mostly because they had not wanted to admit it. It was a far deeper feeling than the sort of infatuation Delia and Ella so teased them about. True, there were many moments of that dreamy-eyed delight, of overwhelming admiration and pride, and of wanting. But mostly there was warmth and safety, peace and laughter.

But how to tell him? Isadore cared for them, and they cared for him. But they could not be certain that it was the sort of care that could lead him to hold them again, or to go any further than that. They would rather wait than risk ruining this comfortable sweet thing they had. But if they waited, would Isadore ever move, or would he forever fear to push them too far?

They could hear Melanie and Isadore talking quietly in the inner hall, but they couldn't pick out any words, only a gentle hum of sound. Lawrence stood watch by the door. He turned at the sound of the blankets rustling and gave Ambry a gentle nod and a smile almost hidden by his mustache. That tiny gesture spoke worlds more than any words could. Isadore's guards considered Ambry also to be their charge, and would protect them as such. Or at least, Sylvia and Lawrence would. Ambry did not want to think about what Dominick saw in them.

They wanted to wash and change and fix their hair before Isadore and Melanie saw them again, but with the two of them in the hall they had no way of reaching their room without meeting them, unless they went around from the main stair, which would risk others seeing them, and all the rumors that would come of that. They took a steadying breath, stepped out into the hall, and waited for Isadore to notice them.

They didn't need to wait long. Isadore turned as soon as they stepped through the door. "Ambry. Did you sleep well?"

They surprised themself with their answer. "Yes. Thank you."

"Good. You can rest today, as much as you need." They were grateful for the offer, but they thought that they'd rather work, rather feel that they were doing something useful. "I've been meeting with the palace guards to figure out how that fool made it inside."

Ambry looked away. The answer to that seemed simple enough. It was because of *them* that the intruder was able to get past the guard so easily. "I'm sorry. We– when I lost it, we were on the ferry. I thought it fell into the river. I didn't want to bother you or Mrs. Hammond for a replacement. I know I should have."

"The gate guard should have been more careful," Isadore said.

"On the ferry?" Melanie repeated, eyes narrowing. She turned to Isadore. "Didn't Dreisand's last report say that Hardy's gang was working with the ferry pilots to steal valuables?"

Isadore let out a breath. "They would have gotten their hands on a royal badge eventually, some way or another. It would only take one getting lost and finding its way to someone with devious plans. Or they might well have had pilots and pickpockets searching for someone wearing one."

He meant it as a comfort to their guilt, and Ambry was grateful for it. But it didn't lessen the weight of shame in their stomach. However it had happened, they had still made a terrible mistake. One that might have ruined everything Isadore had worked for.

"The treaty?" That was the most important thing.

"We don't know yet," Isadore said. "Grenner's been secluded with his advisors all morning, and then he's going to meet with the rest of the Ambassadors."

"I'm hoping," Melanie put in, a touch of venom in her voice, "that he's realized what a bastard he looked like last night and is hastily trying to backtrack, but we'll see if any saints see fit to grant that wish."

"And soon, I hope." Isadore said. "Are you hungry? You'll have to thank Ella again for me. She made the most marvelous little fruit tarts for the Ambassadors' breakfast. And there's enough for the three of us too." He passed them a little plate from the sideboard. "Let's go sit down. I'm expecting a messenger as soon as Grenner decides anything."

Like all of Ella's creations, the tarts were perfect. Golden shells of thin, ruffled, sugar-speckled crust overflowing with berries stewed until soft and sweet, paper-thin apple slices arranged into flowers on top. A sprinkling of oats was the only concession to the fact that this was meant as a breakfast and not as the dessert course of a banquet. How early had Ella woken to have these all prepared?

Melanie had hers half-eaten on a napkin in her lap. She nibbled at it as Isadore spoke, obviously savoring the taste. "You know what ambassadors are like," she said between bites. "They need a little pampering before they'll listen to you. And they'll do anything to save face."

Before Isadore needed to ask, Ambry hung the kettle on the fire to brew a strong, bitter tea that would suit the sweet pastries. Isadore and Melanie accepted cups with a few words of thanks, and things almost felt normal again.

"When are you going to meet with them?" Ambry asked. That's what Isadore should be doing, instead of worrying about them or eating tarts.

Melanie shook her head. "I would've sent him down already, but Karin Miller told us that wouldn't help, and might even make things worse. And she knows Grenner best."

Isadore sighed. "They are guests in our kingdom. It gives us an illusion of an advantage in this deal, for all that the details were already worked out weeks ago. Or we had hoped they were. Our best attempt to bargain with them failed. If my mother or I were to interfere again, to try to convince them one way or the other, Grenner would cry foul, and add that to his list of reasons why the treaty should be rewritten to his advantage."

"We have to let them work it out on their own now," Melanie said. "And that could take days."

Ambry nodded, and added bitterly, "And now that Grenner's opened it up again, some of the others might start asking for changes."

"The Larse probably won't try anything," Melanie said, "But Arrawey… I wouldn't put it past Lady Lauretta to try and convince the Larse to cede ground now that the door is open. We've told ours to keep to the agreed terms and nothing else, unless they see a workable solution. Of the Kivernese, Massan will back Grenner up to a point, and Habb will do whatever they eventually agree to even if he's not happy about it. And as I said, the Arraweyans will talk up a storm, but they'd only put their foot down for a plum deal."

With the treaty in as many pieces as a smashed riverboat, everything was so complicated now, and nothing was certain. If only the night had not gone so badly, but there was no way to take that back now.

"Do you know why that woman did what she did?"

"The Guard are questioning her. I've told them to send me a report as soon as they learn anything. Maybe that'll help settle the Ambassadors' tempers. It's hard enough keeping them here. Massan threatened to take his staff and leave, until Grenner called him a coward for it."

"So Grenner still wants the treaty," Ambry realized. "If he wanted to leave, he would have agreed with Massan."

Isadore nodded. "And we're hoping to rely on that to get the deal we agreed upon." He finished his breakfast and set the plate aside. Ambry put theirs on top a moment later. They hadn't thought they'd have had the appetite for it, but Ella's baking was too good to pass up.

"You don't need to stay here all morning," Isadore said. "There's nothing to be done until Grenner sends word. You might as well take some time to yourself. I'll call for you when we know something."

Once, they might have feared Isadore was sending them away so he would not be bothered with them, but now they knew that was the farthest thing from the truth. They washed, very grateful to scrub the remains of sweat from their skin and emerged refreshed. They took the time to braid their hair up off their shoulders and pin it with the jeweled dragonfly hairclip. How long would it be, they wondered, before they knew what Grenner's decision was? Ambry suspected he was delaying it entirely on purpose. Stretching out the tense wait as a way to show his power against a treaty he personally disliked. They couldn't imagine the other ambassadors were very pleased with him at this point, and the longer they were forced to wait, the less they would be willing to sympathize with his injury or listen to his demands.

Their room, while comfortable, was far too quiet and too far removed from what mattered. Somehow, they found themself back in the tower study, sitting on the couch with a book of Kivernese history while Melanie and Isadore read half-heartedly and distractedly through the latest round of notes, all wishing there was something more they could do.

"Highness," Lawrence called. Dominick stood in the doorway. Ambry froze, shame threatening to engulf them yet again. Dominick who had witnessed all their wretched tears, who thought them weak and worthless. What could he want? Surely it was far too early for the shift change…

"Dominick." Isadore stood. "Is there something wrong?"

"No, no, everything is well. But–" He looked from Isadore to Ambry, and for the first time they could remember Ambry saw a flicker of unease in Dominick's face.

Isadore must have figured out what he meant, for he nodded, face carefully neutral. "Go on."

Dominick stepped forward, took a breath, straightened his back, and then in one fluid motion he knelt before them and bowed his head.

"Ambry. I have come here to offer you my apologies. I spoke cruelly while you were in distress, and it served no purpose but to harm you further. I failed to see the truth of the situation and I judged it wrongly. I am ashamed."

Before Ambry could find an answer in their shock, Dominick spoke again, this time to Isadore. "And I am here to apologize to you, Highness. For questioning your judgment in a matter I had no right to interfere in. Through insulting someone you trust, who you care for, I have insulted you, and I regret it bitterly." He looked at the ground, waiting, shoulders bent. "I am willing to accept any punishment you deem proper."

That he would address Ambry first, before his prince, even Ambry could see how much that meant.

Isadore spoke first, still formal and expressionless. "Thank you. Stand, please."

Dominick rose. He looked to Ambry, met their eyes, and for the first time since they had met him at Isadore's door on that spring day with a basket of letters in their aching arms, Ambry did not feel that Dominick was resenting them, or distrusting them, or merely tolerating them. This felt more as if Dominick was giving to them the sort of power over him that only Isadore held and trusting that they would wield it well.

They wanted to look away from that intensity, but Dominick was offering this in earnest remorse, and Ambry owed him a response. His words still echoed in their head.

The memory made something twist sickeningly in their stomach, the sensation of him glaring down at them in the throes of their anguish like they were a brat making a scene for the sake of it, trash to be cleaned away. No, that would not help anyone. He was the prince's guard, and he did what he thought was best for Isadore's safety and dignity no matter the feelings of anybody else in the room. Ambry had been very lucky indeed that Isadore had a different idea of what was proper than most others.

And yet a small part of them was pleased, or at least relieved. Dominick's words had tipped them over into tears, and though they had no space in their head to be angry at him for it, they were glad to see he knew now how he had hurt them. But they didn't want Dominick to suffer. They had had more than enough of shame. If they were to move forward, this must be mended. Nothing good could come of it if Isadore's guards did not respect his assistant, or if his assistant could not trust Isadore's guards.

"I understand what you were doing," they said. "And I can only imagine what you saw."

Isadore put a gentle hand on their arm, freeing them from needing to decide what to say next. He stood. "Ambry. Lawrence. Could you let us speak alone for a moment?"

Ambry nodded. Lawrence bowed. "Of course."

Isadore went into the inner hall, Dominick following behind him. One of them pulled the door closed, and there was nothing more to hear.

There was quiet then, for a time, and then Lawrence spoke. "I don't claim to know what happened last night," he said, "but for what it's worth, I do not blame you. I have a daughter who has suffered from similar fits of fear her entire life. It's a heartbreaking thing to watch, and I have always wished that I could do more to help. I… forgive me, but I saw something of her in you and wondered if you suffered the same. So when Marshall came to me last night complaining of childish fits of tears from somebody who I knew was as responsible and upstanding as they come, I made my own conclusions. And I made certain to tell him exactly what I thought about it. I am glad to see that I have been understood."

So, Lawrence and the others had been talking about them? Ambry wasn't certain how they felt about that. Part of them cringed away from the thought that their collapse and their weakness had been discussed, but the look in Lawrence's eyes was pure compassion without a trace of disapproval or pity. To know that Isadore's protectors cared about them this much, that meant a great deal.

"Thank you," Ambry said at last. "You didn't need to, but thank you."

"I needed to," Lawrence insisted. "To accuse someone in such a condition of weakness or selfishness... it is the worst possible blow to strike." He paused, letting the words hang in the air. And then he continued, gentler, "Despite his ignorance and his stubbornness, Marshall is not cruel. I think he knew already when he came to me that he was in the wrong, but he needed to know he wasn't going to be able to ignore it. What you suffered is not weakness in any way," he continued, as if he had read their thoughts. "It is some wicked demon of the mind, and I would quest to the ends of the earth if only I could learn how to slay it." He shook his head. "I don't know what Marshall said to you, but I won't blame you if you didn't want to forgive him immediately. I know I would not, if he said it to my Pricilla."

What did they want? Mostly, they realized, they wanted this to be done with. "Dominick doesn't like me," they said, and winced against the jolt of pain that thought gave them. Was there anything in the world they could do to impress him?

"What Dominick doesn't like is change. And there are very few people who he believes are worthy of Isadore's attention.

It will take time, but I'm certain you'll prove yourself to him. Not that you should need to. The rest of us already know you're more than worthy." He sighed. "I've always considered myself blessed that I should serve someone with such powers as Prince Isadore. Healing, whether by spell or by medicine or by needle, now *that* is the greatest goodness in the world. And you should know that you've been very good for him. He's happier when you are near, not wound up quite as tight with worry and work. Don't ever doubt the good that you have done. We're all grateful for it." He dipped his head, not quite a bow, and returned to his statue's pose at the entrance.

Before Ambry could reply, the door opened and Isadore and Dominick came back in. What had they said? Both looked satisfied, though there was something unreadable and weighty in Dominick's expression. He paused at the door to bow to them again and left without a word.

It wouldn't be for long, of course. He would return when Lawrence's shift ended. By then, Ambry hoped they would know what to say.

Isadore sat beside them. "What are you thinking?"

Ambry let out a breath. Having Isadore close made it easier to sort through their feelings. "I don't want to make any more of a fuss about it," they said, and it was the truth.

Isadore nodded. "I understand. I only ask that you not carry shame where it is not deserved."

"Thank you, again, for everything."

"I couldn't have done anything less." Isadore leaned close, close enough to once again put his arms around their shoulders, but then he pulled back, uncertain.

"Dominick?" Ambry didn't know what they wanted to ask.

"I am still angry with him, but that is something between us, and not for you to be concerned with. I believe he now understands what happened. He will never again say such things to you, or any in this household."

Ambry winced. As upset as they were, they couldn't stop themself from remembering the crushing shame and the overwhelming pain of having disappointed Isadore. But then, Dominick was a different sort of person, not cursed with fear as Ambry was. And the way he had come before them, opening himself to their displeasure and their reprimand... it had felt in a way as if he had needed it, needed to atone before he could move past it. Like the knights in Kivernese tales, bound to their lords and taking their sustenance from those lords' approval. Isadore was more than worthy of such devotion, precisely because he never demanded it save in moments like these.

✧

Lawrence knocked at the door to announce a visitor. Isadore turned, expecting Karin Miller, or a messenger, or even Alaric Grenner himself. But it was only Postmaster Kieran, bearing a basket of newspapers.

"Here you are, Miss Melanie. Just the papers, mind you. Nothing new from the honorable guests as of yet. Young Delia and Ella are cooking them up a fine feast. Finer than those boors deserve, if you ask me, but nobody has."

Isadore didn't bother hiding his laugh. "I think you'll find plenty of agreement here," he said, accepting the basket and setting it on Melanie's desk. He tipped his hat and left, winking at Ambry as he went.

Ambry, ever diligent at their work, didn't wait for Melanie to ask before starting to help her search through the paper.

"What do they say?" Isadore prompted, fearing the answer.

Melanie spread the paper in her arms out on the desk. There was a sketch of the Arraweyan delegation's beautiful riverboat above a short paragraph noting the arrival of the foreign ambassadors, but nothing else in the many crowded headlines and mocking cartoons caught Isadore's eye, which he realized a moment later was why Melanie was smiling.

"There's nothing yet. In fact, they're surprisingly free of tawdry suspicion and rumor-mongering. Maybe they haven't heard yet. Or maybe they're waiting to learn the truth before spitting out half a story."

Isadore let out a breath of relief. "Ostberg must finally have prevailed on her editors. She's no fool. She knows that the damage that might come of undermining the treaty is worse than the gain she'd make selling a few extra papers in the scandal."

"And as Florence Ostberg does, so does the rest of the press."

"The reputable ones, at least." There were other, smaller papers, that printed salacious rumors and fantastical speculation on cheap paper that tore at the slightest breeze. Isadore didn't fool himself into thinking they didn't have a wide readership, even among those who considered themselves above that sort of thing. Melanie's staff kept eyes on them, of course. It wouldn't do to have some misconceived rumor, or worse, a mad theory built off of a kernel of truth, blindside them in their work. But she didn't trouble Isadore with that unless it was utterly necessary. Sometimes he suspected her of keeping the most amusing stories to herself, but generally he appreciated it. Better to have his focus on important matters.

He picked a few sheets from the table and paced back and forth as he read, skimming over tales of city business and petty crime, past advertisements from shopkeepers seeking customers and employees, searching for anything to keep him busy while they waited for the Ambassadors to come to a decision. Hoping not to see anything that might ruin his remaining chances at ever seeing that decision made.

Time dragged on, until Isadore turned and found Dominick waiting at the door.

Dominick bowed. "Highness. I've received word from the Guard. The prisoner is ready to speak with you. She insists upon it," he added, in a tone that made it very clear he did not think she had the right to insist upon anything.

Isadore stopped pacing and went to the door. "Thank you, Dominick. Take me there now."

Contrary to some of the stories, Talland did not put prisoners in dungeons. Dominick showed Isadore down a tight hallway to a cell built into the wall of the sturdy Guardhouse. Thin slits high on the wall let light leak in onto the woman seated on a narrow bench behind thick bars.

She still wore the dress that had passed as a servant's uniform the night before. Dark splashes of Grenner's blood stained the breast, and a spilled drink had marked the hem, but she sat proud and sad, watching Isadore and his guard approach.

The young guardsman keeping watch at the end of the hall bowed and moved out of the way so that Isadore and Dominick could face the prisoner.

"You will stand," Dominick ordered, and the woman obeyed. Isadore motioned for him to step aside, and moved forward to address her.

"What is your name?" he asked.

"Daisy Trapper, Highness. And I'm not ashamed of it. I wish I could say I was sorry for all the trouble, but that was exactly what I needed."

"I want to know why. What reason had you to disrupt the treaty? Once you were inside the gates you could have stolen anything and slipped away. Why attack the Ambassadors when you must have known you would be caught?"

"Stealing your treasures?" She shook her head. "That's not what Hardy wanted. That's not what would get my little one a better life."

"The City Council ruling–" Isadore began, and then he saw her eyes, glaring at him through the bars, and knew it was the wrong thing to say.

"You think you've helped us?" Daisy snapped. "Hardy was the only man who'd ever done anything for our little street. And then you come in and think you can save us without even lifting a finger. With a few pretty words and a few pages of law that'll take months to do any good, if anyone even obeys it in the first place. While I have no home, and not even a cradle for my baby to sleep in."

Isadore remembered a crumbling house washed out by storms; a wooden cradle smashed by a falling branch.

"You're from Willow Street."

She drew herself up. "Do you see why I wanted anything else? There's nice enough folks in the district, ones who might shelter you, at least until they get desperate too. There's never enough to go around. Only takes one thief to set everyone against each other. And the rest of the city? They talk about us like we're born out of the dirt on the street. Only fit for menial work that barely brings in a crumb of bread." Her hands made fists in her lap as she went on. "One of Hardy's men came to me while I was trying to earn a few chimes doing laundry for the women who are too lazy to do it themselves. He promised me a new life if I could make sure those papers were never signed." She shook her head, eyes welling up. "I'd done things for him before, small things. Carrying messages, snatching a few purses from folks that wouldn't miss them. I never wanted to hurt anyone. But I knew if I did, you would save them, Highness. The papers, they say you can do anything with those hands of yours. So is there truly any harm?"

"There certainly is." He forced himself to stay still, and not rub the imagined feeling of Grenner's blood from his sleeves.

Daisy lifted her chin, gathering her determination. "I'll be locked up. I know that. I've accepted that. But it'll be worth it, for my boy's sake. He'll grow up safe, even if it's without me. You'll never catch them. Hardy promised me they would be sent somewhere the Guard will never find, with enough money that they'll never have to scavenge in the gutter again."

He could not deny she had courage. Maybe more than she even knew. Isadore had met very few people who would go to the lengths she had for a slim chance at improving life for her family.

"Your husband and child did not trespass on palace grounds or injure a foreign dignitary," Isadore reminded her. "I have no quarrel with them." And, softer, "In fact, I believe there is still something I can do." Dominick would not approve, but he had already made it clear that he would not always heed Dominick's judgments.

"What can you offer me? Some plush chairs for my dark cell?"

He thought that he should have been offended by the way she spoke. He could feel the tension coming off of Dominick in waves. But he could see the fear and fury in her eyes. She was not through fighting yet. Maybe Isadore could give her something to fight for.

"If you know anything that might help the City Guard find Ellis Hardy and bring him to justice…"

"I can't do that," she said, before he'd even finished. "If he had the slightest thought I was going against him, he'd hunt me down, and my husband and our boy."

Isadore let out a breath. "It's your decision to make. I cannot promise anything, especially in light of your crime. But give me time, and I'll return to you with my offer."

"I have plenty of that now, at least," Daisy said, looking around at the cell with an ironic twist to her gaze.

"For now, you'll be kept comfortably," Isadore said, looking at the guard officer as he said it. The boy took his meaning and bowed in acknowledgement.

With that, Isadore let Dominick usher him from the Guardhouse. For once, he hoped dearly that Hardy would keep his promises. After all Daisy had sacrificed for her family, they should at least be safe. Isadore didn't often think of the saints, and rarely prayed to them, but today he silently called upon Saint Iryin, the open-handed and ever-forgiving twin of Tarya, the harsh-eyed saint of justice who carried a heavy staff she slammed on the stones to condemn criminals.

"Highness," Dominick said when they were away from others' ears. "You need not concern yourself with her wellbeing. She might have killed you."

This time, Isadore understood Dominick's criticism completely. But he thought he could see a glimmer of something beyond this dreary prison, if only he could find the right thing to do.

"She could have," he admitted. "But she did not, and she might well help us accomplish a greater good."

Dominick nodded silently and said no more.

⟡

Ambry decided they'd had enough of sitting around, doing very little except for waiting for the whip to fall, watching Isadore and Melanie and all the others struggle to mend the treaty they'd broken into pieces. No, they reminded themself, the treaty Grenner had broken.

Markus, Melanie's chief assistant, came in at one point with a few pages of legal precedent that he thought might help with the negotiations, but Melanie dismissed it after no more than a quick glance.

"If we try to tell them what to do, they're never going to do it," she said. "They're going to have to realize it's what's best for all of them, not just for Isadore and Talland."

Ambry thought of the ambassadors in their endless meetings, arguing in circles, each session ending in another round of tedious letters that used a lot of words to say very little. Saints, didn't they ever tire of hearing themselves speak? There had to be something they could do to help. Something better than reading and rereading newspapers. There had to be something Grenner wanted more than he wanted to claim offense from Talland.

A voice came from the door. "Ambry?" It was Delia. She held out a basket. "Letters from the ambassadors. They're back in their rooms for now. I don't know when the next meeting is."

"There's no agreement yet?"

"It didn't sound like it," Delia said with a shrug. "They didn't let me hear anything. The look that Lady Claudine gave me!" she scowled. And then she sighed, anger dropping away to be replaced by guilt. "The badge," she said. "I'm sorry. I only wanted to help you."

"It's all right. We're going to fix this," Ambry said.

"They're snooty asses, all of them," Delia said fervently, then glanced at Melanie with an embarrassed smile.

"You shouldn't say it out loud," Melanie told her. "But I won't tell you you're wrong."

"Oh, I know that." She smiled. "I'd better get back to the kitchen. The ambassadors are going to be demanding their next meal soon."

Ambry heard her gasp of surprise from halfway down the stairs, and a few moments later, Isadore and Dominick stepped into the room.

Isadore didn't say anything at first, only sat heavily on the couch, as if pulled down by a tremendous weight.

"What did she say?" Melanie asked, before Ambry could.

Isadore sighed. "She lived on Willow Street," he said, glancing to Ambry. "The storm. That ruined house."

"I remember," Ambry said. "Daisy? Dale said she had a baby." But what could possibly have brought her into the palace with a knife?

"They were struggling. Even with help from their neighbors, it wasn't enough. Ellis Hardy promised her money and safety for her family if she disrupted the treaty signing."

Ambry could hardly imagine a situation so terrible that working with Ellis Hardy would be preferable. But then they thought of living in Willow Street during summer storms or winter snow, without strong walls to shield them, with neighbors quickly running out of help to give. Maybe then they would consider turning to the questionable skills of a master thief and manipulator. But they hoped they'd never attempt such a crime just for promises of money.

And then Ambry thought of their little cousin Herrin's games, Isadore accusing Adrian of laughing off concern about his gambling partners, Dreisand's bitter condemnation of the violence in the city. They shook their head. "He does so many terrible things, but there's people out there who think he's a hero, and that's the message he tells his people to send out."

"He's an arrogant fool," Melanie declared. "He'll slip up someday, and the Guard will be waiting for him. Or maybe his own lackeys will finally grow sick of him ordering them about."

"But why would he want to disrupt the treaty?" Ambry started, before realizing. "The new trade laws?"

Isadore nodded. "We knew this might anger him. He gets so much of his profits from the bandits on the Larse and Kivernese borders, and the treaty had measures to keep the merchant caravans safe."

"That was one of the parts none of them argued about," Melanie supplied. "Kivern even agreed to send guardsmen along with merchants and travelers."

Isadore and Melanie were still talking, but an idea was taking shape in Ambry's mind. It might be absurd, ridiculous, impossible. But it might work, and of the three of them, Melanie was certain to know.

"All those notes we read from Grenner," Ambry said. "The way he talks. It's just like all those stories about Ellis Hardy. He wants everyone to think he's a fighter. A hero. Someone you don't want to challenge."

"What are you saying?" Isadore asked, leaning forward in interest, eyes bright.

They studied the spread of newspapers on Melanie's desk, still silent on the matter of last night's ball. "If we let the story get out to the papers that Grenner found the intruder and protected you from him…" they looked to Isadore, and faltered for just a moment before continuing, now with the surety of confidence in their voice. "If the whole city reads that he's the hero who saved the prince and all the ambassadors at the treaty reception, then he'll have to sign it, won't he?"

For a few moments their heart hammered again, and they were sure they'd said something absurd, idiotic.

Then Melanie's face slowly brightened as she considered the idea. "He would love that. He wouldn't *dare* back out of signing the treaty then. Not when it would spoil his image. The public might not care about the details of the treaty, but the Chronicle's promoted the benefits it'll have to trade and travel. They'll have few kind words to say about Grenner if he turns around and ruins it."

"That… that might well work," Isadore said, not quite believing it at first.

Melanie gave a conspiratorial smile. "It won't be hard to accidentally let that slip to the press. I'm sure Ostberg's already hungry for details, especially since there hasn't been a public announcement yet. Maybe if your friend Delia happened to wander into the city with Markus, and they *happened* to run into a young man Markus knows, who works for the City Chronicle? I think Florence Ostberg would be very pleased to get ahold of this exciting story before the others do."

She rang the bell to summon her assistant, and for the first time that day, Ambry's heart lifted in hope that the treaty could be saved.

Chapter Fourteen

✧

Whatever magic Markus could work, Ambry knew it was going to take time. Delia was delighted to be recruited into the effort, and even more delighted to escape the heat of Patrice's kitchen and the demands of twelve hungry and tired politicians and their assistants.

Markus, eyes sparkling behind his glasses, promised a report as soon as they were done. But it would take until the next morning to see the fruits of their labor. Meanwhile, Isadore, Melanie, and Ambry were left to handle the daily affairs of the prince's office, along with monitoring the ambassadors' progress. If they somehow managed to agree on a compromise before the day was out, or, saints forbid, abandoned the effort entirely, everything would have been for nothing.

That fear hung over Ambry, sharpening at every letter that came through the door. At least Melanie and Isadore had stopped fussing over them. They wanted to leave their terror behind. Thinking about it, lingering on it, could only risk summoning it back, or so they feared.

They'd forgiven Dominick for last night, and they told him so at the first opportunity. Dominick accepted it with a grateful bow, and since then his gaze had not weighed on their back.

A knock on the door. This time it was one of Melanie's assistants who stood there with a fresh basket of letters.

"No progress yet, Highness," he said.

The ambassadors had met again, and once again it had been utterly fruitless. Isadore read aloud Karin Miller's scathing letter describing Grenner and Massan holding firm on their demands for revisions, while Ambry and Melanie flipped through August Teller's apologetic tale and Sheridan Beck's pleas for hope, which were fading with each round of talks. The reports from the rest of the ambassadors were predictably terse, full of flowery requests for concessions Talland didn't want to give and bland predictions that they would surely come to an agreement if only they were given a little more time.

Mrs. Hammond came up for a flustered few minutes to give her own report. The kitchens were hard at work preparing meals for their guests, and the maids were keeping their rooms spotless. For each negotiation session, Ella brought a platter of treats to the long table. Nothing too fine, nothing to make them suspect they were being persuaded one way or the other, but hopefully enough to sweeten their moods, at least a little.

"Patrice and the others must be exhausted," Ambry said after Mrs. Hammond hurried back to her work.

"I'll be sure they're properly thanked for their support in this," Isadore vowed. "We told them to plan for three days of pampering our guests, and now I can hardly see this settled in fewer than five."

"They'll handle it," Ambry said. That much they knew for sure.

Melanie shoved the stack of letters back into the basket for her staff to take to the archives. "They will, but if this goes on much longer, I wouldn't be surprised if Mrs. Hammond had the ambassadors poisoned," she said.

"Don't give her any ideas," Ambry said.

It was pure coincidence that it was that very moment that Ella appeared at the door with plates of roast chicken for lunch. She did a good job of pretending she hadn't heard Melanie's remark, but Ambry could see the grin she was desperately trying to hide.

"Thank you," Isadore said. "Are the ambassadors as unhappy in person as they sound in their correspondence?"

"They're not very pleased, Highness. But there haven't been any fights yet."

"I'm sure the good food is helping with that," he said.

A blush touched Ella's cheeks. "I hope so. We won't stop until they come to a decision."

Even if, Ambry thought with a wave of anxiety, that decision was to go home empty-handed. But no, they reminded themself. The ambassadors had worked so hard for so many years. It would be a disgrace to leave the treaty on the table now. And Grenner knew that. That was why he was hoping that if he waited long enough, the others would budge and at last bend to his will.

They just prayed that the standstill would last long enough for Grenner to falter. Long enough for that tale of the ill-fated ball to appear in the City Chronicle and appease his selfish pride.

Dominick cleared his throat. "Highness, the Captain of the Guard is here."

Isadore stood up, leaving the letters onto Melanie's desk. "Come in."

Captain Dreisand strode into the room. This time, she didn't question Ambry's presence before she gave her report. "Highness. I received the Royal Guard's report about Daisy Trapper."

"You wouldn't be here if you didn't have news. What do you know?"

Dreisand raised an eyebrow and took the chair Melanie offered. "Very observant, Highness. One of my officers overheard another accept a bribe to allow a man and an infant unquestioned passage on a ship bound for Larsellan. She won't give up the name, but I'm fairly certain I know who it is."

"Has the ship departed yet?"

"Yesterday, unfortunately. But it won't be difficult to find."

"You can't do that," Ambry interrupted, before they realized what they were saying. Dreisand turned to them, a question on her face. Ambry looked to Isadore. "You told us she said Hardy would kill them if the Guard interfered."

"We are fully capable of subtlety if needed," Dreisand said. "Justice doesn't always come on thundering hooves. But if we do not move soon, we will need to work with the Larse outlands patrols."

"That may well be the best way to keep them safe. I will have to speak to the Larse delegation before I can be certain," Isadore said, "but I have thought of a way we can handle this that would please everyone involved." He smiled. "Except Ellis Hardy, of course."

"And what is this plan?"

"After what she has done, I would not disagree with you if you said that Daisy Trapper is no longer welcome in this city." At that, Dreisand made a harrumph of agreement and let Isadore continue. "But I cannot see what good she would do in a prison, far from her family. Since she was trusted with this mission, which Hardy clearly holds in high importance, we can assume she has experience with the comings and goings of his inner circle. If we can leverage what she knows about Hardy's gang, we might be able to bring them to justice at last."

Dreisand nodded, but it wasn't yet an agreement. "And in exchange?"

"In exchange, I will ask the Larse delegation to take her to Larsellan when they depart and make all efforts to reunite her with her husband and child."

Ambry should have expected that from Isadore, whose compassion seemed endless. But it surprised them all the same. Dreisand frowned in thought, and for a moment

Ambry feared she would reject the idea out of hand, and demand something harsher.

"I see," Dreisand said at last. "It is not something I would have suggested. But, I believe it might have a chance of working where all other efforts have failed." She stood up. "Take me to her. I know everything we have about Hardy's gang, so I'll be able to tell if she's lying, and if she is, she will regret it."

Isadore and Dominick led her down to the guardhouse, leaving Ambry and Melanie to keep reading through the letters.

"I didn't expect Captain Dreisand to agree to that," Ambry said after a while. "It's very good, what he wants to do. Is she really going to let him let Daisy go?"

Melanie smiled. "Dreisand is tough. But she's been chasing Hardy for years. Letting a criminal go free might be a price she's willing to pay for the chance to take him down for good. Maybe if Daisy been captured by the City Guard she'd have resisted more. But within the palace, the Royal Guard answers to Isadore and Queen Seraphina. Dreisand knows better than to make demands where she cannot."

Could they truly capture Ellis Hardy, and put an end to his influence in the city? It seemed too good to ever come to pass. But then, so had this treaty. Both still hung in the balance. But as every moment passed, Ambry found more reasons to hope that they would be successful.

Delia and Markus returned a short while later, both looking very pleased with themselves.

"Ben's going to take it straight to Florence's desk," Markus announced. "It'll be in tomorrow's paper for certain."

"Good work, both of you," Melanie said.

Delia looked at Ambry. "We didn't tell him about the badge," she reassured them.

"Whatever the reason, the Guard isn't going to be happy that the public knows they fell down on the job," Markus said, with a touch of remorse.

"Then it'll encourage them to never let it happen again," Melanie said, utterly unapologetic.

Ambry and Melanie worked for a while longer as the sun crept below the horizon. When it became clear that Isadore and Captain Dreisand wouldn't be returning any time soon, she sent them to bed.

"Get some rest. There's nothing else we can do until the morning."

"You should too," Ambry reminded her.

"I will, I will," Melanie said, suppressing a yawn. "There's one more letter I want to draft, and I need to talk to Isadore, and then I promise I'll sleep. You're getting as bad as he is, did you know that?"

Ambry decided to take that as a compliment.

✧

It took until late into the evening that Captain Dreisand was finally satisfied that Daisy Trapper had told all she knew about Ellis Hardy, his lieutenants, his plots, and his lines of communication. Dominick stayed long past his shift to watch it all with an icy stare, as if the woman in the cell was still a threat to his prince.

If only they could be certain that the Guard could trace the ship Hardy put her family on. If only they could be certain that Larsellan could keep her family safe. The fear and hope in Daisy's eyes when he offered her the bargain was almost too much to bear.

While Dreisand worked, Isadore drafted his request to Kestrel and the others twice, three times, and finally came to the conclusion that this was a message he was going to have to convey in person. And that was something he could only do once the treaty was signed, lest Grenner accuse him of unfair manipulation. As if Grenner's own actions had been as just and heroic as the morning papers would proclaim them to be.

As much as he resented giving the old fool any credit, he had to admit Ambry's idea could well be what sealed the treaty. They were so clever, and so determined to fix things, even when it truly hadn't been their fault that the treaty had come so close to falling apart. And still could, if this didn't work.

He didn't doubt that his mother would be having long conversations with the guards who'd been on duty that night. Speaking in their defense might well push Dominick into madness, so he didn't even consider it, but he hoped silently that they kept their posts. They'd watch all the better in the future.

When Dreisand finally finished her relentless questioning and strode from the guardhouse, her face proud and her pockets full of notes, Daisy dropped exhausted onto the cell's shabby bed. Isadore returned to the heir's tower just as Melanie was leaving. She gave him the good news, and both of them went to their beds, praying that Ostberg would come through, and that it would be enough to change Grenner's mind.

The ambassadors surely weren't happy to stay another night with no agreement. At least Ella and the servants were keeping them comfortable. Isadore was almost beyond caring, even though he knew that pampering them through their stubborn complaints was a far better option than threatening to send them home when they might take that offer and dash all of Isadore's years of work to the ground. And he reminded himself that most of them were as much victims of Grenner's whims as he was, and didn't deserve the resentment.

He woke early the next morning, too early for Kieran to have brought the papers yet. The heir's study was empty when he stepped inside. Through the window, he could see the gardeners already hard at work sweeping up fallen leaves to mulch for the vegetable beds next year. He watched them clear one bit of ground, and then another, and then he wandered over to the bookshelf and idly ran his hand over the spines of the books, pausing first at the histories and then the book of sea stories that sat behind Lacey's seashell. He wondered what she would say to all this. She'd probably be glad it wasn't her bag of ferrets to wrangle, Isadore thought with a smile. He'd get to tell her himself soon enough. If the treaty went ahead. If the Queen allowed them to sail.

"Highness," Lawrence said softly from the doorway.

"Are they here yet?" Isadore set the shell back down.

"Not yet. But I wanted to tell you that I believe the treaty will succeed."

"Have you heard something?" Lawrence would never say something like that unprompted without a reason behind it. He was not a man for groundless hope.

"I spoke to two of the guards who were monitoring the treaty negotiations. It seems the Arraweyan delegation have given up trying to push the others for changes and will be satisfied with the document as it was, if only Kivern agrees. And Frederick Massan is not as staunch an ally as Grenner had hoped. They haven't come to blows yet, but there have been raised voices."

"So Grenner is truly on his own now," Isadore realized.

"I suspect he fears mostly for his reputation at the moment. As he should be." And which would play right into the headlines soon to arrive on his desk.

Lawrence gave a wry smile. "It is also no small help that Kivern and Arrawey celebrate Saint Hilan's Day in a week's time, and if they do not settle this quickly, they won't arrive home in time to attend the festivities."

"All the better."

Melanie arrived a moment later. Today she was using a cane painted in Talland's royal colors. Isadore decided to take that as a good omen.

"Nothing yet," she said, before Isadore could ask. "But it should be any minute now."

She was right. She'd barely gotten her pens and notepaper prepared when Ambry rushed through the door, carrying a basket of letters. And on top, a copy of the City Chronicle, almost still hot from the press.

And right there, in a bold panel on the right side of the front page, exactly what they had been waiting for. Isadore listened as Melanie read it out, forcing back a bitter scowl at the praise heaped upon Grenner.

"This is good," he said.

"You mean it makes you look like a fool," Melanie sighed. "But that'll soon be forgotten."

"Gossip changes fast," Ambry said. It was something Melanie said often. Clearly, they were learning from the best.

Isadore breathed a sigh of relief and set the paper down. "I wish I could thank Ostberg, but that might give the wrong impression."

"Stay out of her business," Melanie agreed. "If she even thinks you're trying to use the paper for your own gain, she'll make sure they never say anything nice about you again?"

"Like what she's saying today? That I was so distracted I didn't notice an intruder approaching with a knife?" He'd tried not to care about what the papers said about him before, but it was never pleasant to be seen as a dullard. He shook his head. "Enough of my pride. Have the Ambassadors met yet?"

Ambry nodded. "They're just about to. Ella brought a tray of tarts to the room. The papers will be there when they arrive."

"And in the meantime, there is still plenty of work to be done," Melanie said, holding out a hand for the rest of Ambry's basket.

Isadore was grateful for it. As they worked, he found his eyes drifting towards the door at every little sound and sometimes at none at all, but he owed the rest of the work his attention and his effort, and he did his best to give it.

Shortly before noon, someone finally came up the stairs. Sheridan Beck, followed by Karin Miller and August Teller. Isadore needed only the first glimpse of their proud, relieved faces to know Ambry's gambit had worked.

"He's agreed to sign it?"

Beck nodded. "Just as written, no changes. I won't ask what you did, but the old mule is finally happy about something."

"As if he deserves it. Another session of that and I might have stabbed him myself," Miller said, earning herself a glare from Beck. "He'll be insufferable all the way home, I'm sure of it, but that's Massan and Habb's problem now."

"When is the signing?"

"As soon as we return," Beck promised. "We came to invite you to witness it."

"I'll be right there. You have all the papers?"

"Ready and waiting. No changes needed, not even a comma. Saves your printers some effort," August said with a smile.

"Good. Very good," Isadore said. He held out his hand. "Ambry? Do you want to watch?"

Ambry took the offered hand. Isadore hoped they noticed Beck's proud smile. The ambassadors, for very good reasons, would never know what part Ambry had played in securing the treaty. But Isadore wanted Ambry, and the tiny slice of the world that waited in that meeting room, to see that they *had* played a part in something that would reach around the world and make things better in so many different ways that Isadore never could have accomplished alone. That was well worth all those long months of work.

Together, they made their way down the stairs and towards their victory.

⟡

Four copies of the treaty lay on the table, scrolls pinned flat by jeweled weights. Only the most important of official documents were printed on scrolls. For the sake of Minerva Corey's archive staff, Ambry was grateful they weren't handwritten.

The four kingdoms' diplomatic emblems stood out on the papers in colored ink. A green riverbank for Talland, a blue mountain for Arrawey, a red castle for Kivern, and a golden field for Larsellan.

The ambassadors offered polite greetings to Isadore as he entered. They mostly ignored Ambry, but they secretly preferred that to having to find responses to each of them. They noticed Grenner standing by the window, face stern but satisfied. He wasn't going to put up another argument, even if he sorely wanted to. The other Kivernese delegates were much more cheerful, and obviously relieved that the treaty had finally been restored. On the other side of the table, Lady Lauretta and Lady Claudine picked glass-tipped pens from a velvet tray held out by one of the Arraweyan assistants. A similar tray waited by the Kivernese ambassadors, holding three-pointed metal pens engraved with coiling bronze patterns.

Isadore stepped forward. "Ambassadors. I hear you've reached an agreement?"

"A little delayed, but it's done," Ambassador Kestrel said.

"Some of the best things take time," Ambassador Sandry told him. She carried a sleeping baby against her chest in a sling. Ambry suspected some of the ambassadors and assistants envied the infant the ability to nap through tedious meetings.

"We walked all around the mountain and came back right where we started," said Kivern's Willem Habb. Massan made a noise of agreement, but Grenner offered no response.

"Well then, let's get this done with." Sheridan Beck strode forward and signed their name to each of the papers in turn, followed by Karin Miller and August Teller. The Arraweyans followed. Even standing a few paces away, Ambry could admire Lady Claudine's looping calligraphy. As it came time for the Kivernese to do their part, a palpable tension rose in the air. But the doubt only lasted a moment. With decisive flicks of his pen, Grenner signed each copy of the treaty and stepped aside to allow Massan to follow.

As the Larse delegation finished signing the papers, Sir Valentino leaned against the table, the picture of relaxed pride. "Didn't I tell you it would be done today?" said to his companions. Their polite responses told Ambry he hadn't said that at all.

"At least we'll be home in time for Hilan's Festival," Lady Lauretta said. "My nieces would have started throwing things if their favorite aunt wasn't there to give them sugar-gems."

Miller crossed her arms in mock severity. "My father would have smacked me if I'd asked for sweets on Saint Hilan's day. In his mind, it was a day for severe reflection and labor."

"Oh!" Claudine's face filled with pity. "But she was such a happy saint!"

"Who worked hard all her life and gave every penny of her earnings to her foundling-house," Massan said. "So we honor her by living as she did for a day, or even a week, for the especially devout families." He smiled, and added in a conspiratorial whisper, "The sweets are saved for the next day."

"We've certainly had enough sweets to make up for a week of work," Mila said, glancing at the tray of sticky crumbs that had once held some of Ella's finest treats.

They talked for a little longer, while they waited for the ink to dry. Then, one by one, the delegations gathered the proof of their efforts. Without needing to be asked, Arraweyan and Kivernese servants swept forward and rolled up their treaties, while Mila handled the Larse copy. Sheridan Beck plucked the weights from Talland's copy of the treaty and rolled it tight with a deft flick of their hands, tying a green ribbon around the center before passing it to Isadore.

"Highness," they said, with an elegant bow and a glowing smile. "Despite everything, it was well worth the journey."

Isadore accepted the scroll with a grateful nod. He turned it over, studying it as if he hardly believed he was holding it at last, and then passed it to Ambry as if bestowing a holy gift.

"Ambry. Take this to the archives, and then go deliver Melanie the good news."

"Yes, Highness," Ambry said. It was almost odd to go back to that formality after so many months of eschewing titles, but it felt right. Once again, they were reminded of the responsibility Isadore trusted them with, and what an honor it was to carry.

As they walked through the door, they heard Isadore say, "Kestrel, can you stay a moment?" and then they were down the hall and they didn't hear any more.

✧

"You did well, Isadore," Seraphina said, after the last Larse carriage had passed through the city gates. "Not only the treaty, but a lead on Ellis Hardy that the City Guard has been hunting for years."

"I only hope they find him," Isadore said. "Kestrel, Sandry, and Mila agreed to take Daisy with them to Larsellan. They'll do what they can to reunite her with her family, and the border scouts on both sides will be on high alert for any interference by Hardy's forces."

"And the treaty will allow that very thing. I must say, I find myself impressed. You managed to accomplish something I had truly not thought possible."

Isadore frowned. She had never admitted that particular fact before.

"If you didn't believe the treaty was possible," he asked carefully, "why did you tell me to pursue it?"

"Because it is best for you to learn as early as possible that some ambitions are not possible to achieve. It seems you shall have to wait to learn that particular lesson."

Isadore considered that he already wished for something that would never be possible, but that was hardly the sort of thing he wanted to bring up to his mother now, especially when they would be spending the next weeks in close company.

He sat in one of the fine chairs in Seraphina's study, trying not to show his unease. There was truly no reason for it. The summit was over, the papers signed, the ambassadors all alive and as satisfied as they could be under the circumstances. But it would be no use saying any of that. He'd learned when he was very young that his mother did not appreciate boasting from anyone.

"We came very close to losing it," he admitted instead. "Most of the credit belongs to Melanie and Ambry. They worked out how to convince Grenner to come back to the table and agree to our terms."

"Your assistant?" Seraphina studied him. "Yes, you've praised them almost every time we have spoken for the past few months. I should like to meet the person my son thinks so highly of. Especially if I am to spend two weeks with them on a ship at sea."

Isadore fought to keep his face still, not to give her a hint of reaction that she'd read perfectly in an instant. "I'll arrange that."

"Do that. I'll expect them tomorrow morning, after my meeting with Ambassador Beck."

Isadore wanted to ask what she needed Beck for, but that was no longer his place. If it was relevant, he'd learn soon enough. He'd had more than enough of foreign politics for now, he thought.

◇

"Ambry," Isadore said when he returned to the tower study. "My mother wants to meet you before we leave for the Islands."

Ambry took a moment to find their breath. "The Queen?"

Isadore must have seen their face go pale. "It's informal. You're not being knighted or anything. Yet."

"Oh. That's disappointing," Ambry said, still a little stunned by the request but unable to resist the joke.

"Don't be afraid of Queen Seraphina," Melanie said. "She might never smile, but she won't eat you up either. Just don't say anything foolish and you'll be fine."

She made it sound so simple. Ambry vowed to themself to say as little as possible.

"She'll invite you to have tea," Isadore said. "When you sit down, don't look as if you expect her to pour it, or touch it yourself. Wait for her maid to do it."

Melanie smiled. "If you wait for her to do it, you're arrogant and rude."

Ambry caught her meaning. "And if you do it yourself, you're greedy?"

Isadore nodded. "But if you let the maid do it, you're patient, polite, and you understand how work belongs to those most suited to do it." It sounded like he was quoting something his mother had said. "I've never agreed with the test, but she's always been fond of it."

Ambry carved that particular advice deep into their memory. "When?" they asked.

"Tomorrow, midmorning. I'll bring you up, but I don't expect she'll allow me to stay. You shouldn't worry," he added with a reassuring smile. "I can't see any reason for her to dislike you. Especially after you saved our treaty."

Ambry let the praise wash over them, and didn't point out that their idea had only been one part of the work that had gotten the treaty signed.

Isadore was silent for a moment, looking into the fire, face sad and thoughtful.

"Melanie," he said at last, "did you know the Queen expected the treaty to fail?"

"Nobody expected the treaty to even get to the table," Melanie reminded him, untroubled. "There's precious few politicians who can get two of our neighbors to cooperate with us, never mind all three. That summit would have been historic even if Grenner hadn't tried to cock it up."

"I suppose I shouldn't be surprised my mother gave me what she thought was an impossible task," Isadore mused. "She's always made it her goal to humble people, family and politicians both."

"And you succeeded," Ambry said. "That has to matter to her."

Ever since they'd met, Ambry had seen Isadore fight against the demands to hold himself above his people and their problems. They thought of Daisy and the desperate, unfortunate act she'd been driven to. They hoped she was safe now, and that she would find her family again.

Somehow, and they'd never know how, they managed to get a full night of sleep before they were due to meet the Queen. As Isadore led them to her door, and they saw the guards standing watch at either side, a tongue of that fear that had swallowed them after the attack on Grenner lapped at their heart, and they took a steadying breath, wishing desperately that it would help more than it did.

"You'll be fine," Isadore reassured them. "You're honest. That's all she wants." And with that, he ushered them into the room with a hand on their shoulder, and then the hand was gone, and the door closed behind them.

At a round table in the center of a sunlit room sat Queen Seraphina. She might have been a statue, she was sitting so still. The only part of her that moved was her eyes, following Ambry. She wore a red gown traced with royal bronze. Golden rings glinted on the thick braids that draped over her shoulders. If she stood, she'd be almost as tall as Isadore, but she did not need to stand to make her confidence known.

Somehow, Ambry managed to speak. "Your Majesty. Good morning." It wasn't the wisest thing they could have said, but at least it was far from the most foolish.

"Ambry Jean," she said. "Sit, share tea with me."

Ambry found themself obeying, moving across the floor to the table. Towering bookshelves lined one side of the room, windows the other. Elegant golden lamps hung at the corners, unlit in the morning's daylight. Ambry perched on the offered chair, before remembering Isadore's confidence and sitting straighter, praying they could channel even a fraction of that faith.

If all the stories of Seraphina's magic were to be believed, she would know at once if they lied to her. Ambry tried to reassure themself they had no reason to say anything untrue, but the possibility still hung heavy in their mind as they took their seat. The Queen waited a moment, still watching them, and then made a tiny gesture that Ambry almost didn't catch, so distracted were they hoping she didn't see any lies in their face, and a maid appeared from somewhere behind her and poured tea for both of them into fine cups marked with Talland's seal, their petal-like rims like the bends of the kingdom's rivers.

The Queen put hers to her lips, and Ambry followed her lead. They barely tasted it, but at least they didn't choke.

Seraphina set her cup back down. "Isadore tells me you were instrumental in finalizing the treaty."

Ambry nodded, then forced themself to sit still and speak. "We– we had to please Ambassador Grenner without giving up any of our terms. I thought if we gave him something to boast about, he would back down." It sounded foolish, spelled out so plainly, but they reminded themself that it had worked where nothing else had.

"So I saw," the Queen said. "I am pleased that Isadore did not let his own pride stall that effort."

"He's worked so hard for this," Ambry insisted. They knew they shouldn't speak so forcefully in front of the Queen, but this was the truth and she had to see it. "He's never let pride stop him. In– in the city, he listened, even when they criticized him."

"Hmm." The Queen looked thoughtful. "I see he has inspired much devotion in you."

"He deserves it." If nothing else, the Queen had to understand that. That in so many ways, Isadore was everything a leader should be, and in all the rest, he was working day and night to meet them.

The Queen did not answer that, only went on to ask more questions about Isadore's efforts and about Ambry's work, about their interests and the duties Isadore gave them. So they supposed they couldn't have offended her too badly. Sometimes they'd find the perfect way to answer a question, and sometimes they fumbled for words and came out with something that sounded so much flimsier than they meant. The Queen gave barely any hint of approval or reproach, only those almost imperceptible thoughtful flickers of her dark eyes. But by the end of the interview, Ambry thought that she at least did not despise them or think them unworthy. They didn't dare reach for the arrogance of hoping she approved of them.

When Ambry at last escaped her gaze, they fled back to the heir's tower and dropped onto the couch, as exhausted as if they'd been running messages all night and all morning. Isadore and Melanie offered warm greetings, and didn't make them tell what the Queen had asked of them. The two of them refused to believe they'd given anything other than a favorable impression.

And surely, if she had thought them terrible and weak, she would not have allowed Isadore to invite them on their sailing trip to the Islands, and as the handful of days before their departure passed by, no such interdiction arrived.

✧

They'd had this debate before. Isadore hadn't won it then, and he knew he wouldn't win it now, but still, he wouldn't feel right if he didn't at least try to invite Melanie to come with them on their voyage to the Crested Islands. Melanie did not share Isadore's love of ships and sailing, and besides, she said, someone needed to be there to answer letters and keep an eye on the comings and goings in the capital.

"But you should join us," he pleaded. "You deserve the rest." And there would be plenty of space for her on the royal ship, since Abigail and Celeste had decided to stay at university rather than miss some of their classes. He'd miss them, but he'd see them for the New Year's Festival. He admired their dedication. When he'd been in school, he'd skipped class more than a few times, for almost any excuse he could get, and sometimes for none at all.

"Not this year, Isadore." Melanie shook her head. "You don't need me hounding you with letters. You take Ambry and enjoy yourself, and you won't have to listen to me complaining about everything. It's a perfect compromise."

Still, he didn't want to leave her behind while he enjoyed the sea. "But if your knees act up while I'm gone…"

She gave him a sharp look. "I've survived my whole life with my knees before I met you, I think I can manage two weeks on my own. Besides, there's a doctor here now I can consult if I need to, remember?"

Isadore winced and looked away. "I'm sorry, that was arrogant."

She smiled. "No, it was sweet. You think it's your responsibility to fix everything wrong in the world. But it isn't, and you deserve some time to relax. I think you're more worried about being without me than I am about being without you. You'll be fine." A laugh, and a devious shine in her eyes. "I can tell Ambry to bring a few folders of import tax proposals if you're really that desperate."

It was no use arguing further; she'd made up her mind and she would not be swayed.

Isadore tilted his head. "Promise me you'll at least take some time for yourself?"

"I will, I promise. There's a few plays I want to see, and a new exhibit of Mountain Era art in the city museum. All the reviews I've read in the papers say it's magnificent."

"Good. You'll have to tell me about it."

"Oh, I will, until you're sick to death of it and begging me to read you more patrol reports."

"Keep wishing, because I don't think that's going to happen. At least until they get someone with an actual sense of humor to write them." The patrol reports somehow ended up being even more tedious than tax ledgers, and usually less significant. "They should get that fellow from the Chronicle," Isadore mused.

"I'll look forward to that when the sun turns green and birds fly into cookpots," Melanie scoffed. "Nobody in the Guard has a sense of humor. I think it's a job requirement not to."

Isadore glanced at Lawrence, who raised an eyebrow. "I cannot tell you that, Highness. It is a deeply-kept secret that we are sworn never to reveal."

"Such a pity. But the Guard can keep its secret methods if they keep turning out officers as fine as you."

"I shall be certain to tell the commanders that. They will be relieved to hear it."

He let Lawrence's rare humor warm him for another moment before turning back to Melanie, and the piles of letters on her desk.

"I fear to ask, because I know I'm not going to like the answer, but what else needs to be done before we set sail?"

"You might be pleasantly surprised. Most of the lords are using the good weather as an excuse for a holiday, so they haven't been pestering us with as many letters as usual. The Guard's sent us some more reports on the Bavenites, but I think those are going to go right to the Queen."

Isadore's expression tightened. "What are they up to now?" The Bavenites, born of a particularly conservative branch of the already intolerant Southern Order, had been a thorn in their side for years, bitterly protesting every little reform Queen Seraphina proposed. Not content with hating the vulnerable within their own communities, they'd spread their hatred outward, condemning the world for daring to embrace difference.

"The usual," Melanie said, voice sharp with scorn. "Preaching to anyone who'll give them half an ear about how the people of Talland are profaning the purity of genders and encouraging aberrant behavior, letting our women and children run free without beating them into obedience." She scowled. "Where do they get these ideas? If there was something sinful about allowing people to be different than those boring old fellows in their holy books, you'd think we'd have been smited by now."

"There's no sense in it," Isadore agreed. He thought of what Ambry had said of the temple in the city built by those who'd escaped the Church's lies. "We just have to keep on living as we are in spite of them and hope they come to understand someday. Or at least hope that their children will someday come to understand."

Melanie nodded. "Wisest thing you've said in a while. I'd have thought you would want to fight them."

"Oh, I do, but it would only inflame that idea they have that they're the ones under attack. If only they could see the pain they cause…"

"They'd be proud of it. To them, anything is worth it if it drives people away from sin."

"Where is the sin in loving another? Or in living as yourself?"

"It's in disobeying their expectations. In listening to your own soul instead of the word of god."

"Their god must be looking in the wrong direction if he can't see that different sorts of people exist in the world."

"I can't say you're wrong about that," Melanie said. "But when you step onto that ship? I'll remind you that a lot of sailors pray to the saints of the Southern Order, including Baven. And just like you said, it wouldn't be good to offend them." Her expression shifted. "Unless they say something first, of course. But if they value their posts, I doubt they'll say anything cruel in your presence."

"I know. Not all of their saints are so awful. I used to love that story about the saint who tamed the sea serpent. Kelyn, was it?"

"Karta. Kelyn was the one who summoned a waterspout to chase off the pirates. And neither of *them* told their adherents to shun people who haven't hurt anyone."

"I only wish more of them would listen to that."

"Enough drowning in things you can't change," Melanie scolded. "I've already told Ambry to pack their things. At this rate they'll be ready before you are."

"As you command," Isadore said, and took himself off to his bedchamber to finish preparing.

Chapter Fifteen

✧

They left early the next morning in a train of carriages bound for the river where the royal ship waited for them, decks scrubbed and sails ready to be unfurled.

Ambry rode with Isadore, accompanied by Dominick, Sylvia, and Lawrence, behind the carriage carrying the Queen, her stone-faced guards, and two of the palace maids, who would attend to both of them for the journey.

"I almost don't know what I'm going to do without ambassadors' letters to read," Isadore said, watching the sunrise from the carriage's window.

"Delia made me pack some books," Ambry said. Some was an understatement – she'd shown up at their door with a towering stack of them, some new and some old, more than they could ever fit in their bag. They'd chosen three of them, two of Delia's favorites and one notebook filled with her own hand-written tales, and promised to tell her all their thoughts when they returned. "I think she mostly wanted an excuse to give me a gift after we all survived the treaty signing." And for letting her talk to Isadore and be part of the plan. "It'll be strange to not have work to do." They loved their work, and they loved working with Isadore, but they couldn't deny it would be very good to have all these days away from letters and newspapers and meetings and politics.

"We'll need to savor it," Isadore said. "Melanie will probably have piles of work for us as soon as we get back."

Ambry didn't doubt that for a moment. Sitting across from them, Lawrence gave a little snort of amusement. Dominick glared, but he didn't seem to notice.

The carriages slowed to a halt by the riverside. The royal ship sat at the dock, flag waving proudly in the morning sun. Ambry bundled their bag into their arms and climbed out of the carriage after Isadore and paused for a moment to just look up at the ship.

Lawrence stopped beside them. "There's even more to see when you're aboard," he said, mustache not quite hiding his smile.

Ambry took the hint and followed after him.

The Queen's guards went aboard first, and she strode after them, gaze sweeping the deck as the sailors bowed. Evidently, she didn't find anything to complain about, because she gave a single nod, then swept off to her cabin, maids hurrying behind.

Isadore ushered Ambry in front of him. They stepped onto the ship, felt the shifting of the wood under their feet, so different than the tiny river ferries, or the canoe one of their uncles had taken to the lake long ago and rowed each of the children out one by one.

As soon as everyone and all their bags and chests were onboard, the captain called out to the sailors. They leapt into position, shifting sails and hauling ropes, and barely a minute later, the ship pushed off from the dock and set off down the river.

Months ago, they never would have believed that they'd be invited on the royal family's ship. How had they grown so accustomed to working with Isadore, standing alongside him? No, they'd never forget the honor of their position, or the generosity Isadore offered them. But it was no longer quite so bewildering as it once had been. Now, it was something they hoped they would have for the rest of their life.

✧

Isadore stood on the deck of the ship, watching the banks of the river go by, city streets turning to fields. Every so often a stone marker stood up from the land, counting up the distance from the capital.

Another day would bring them down the river and out into the southern sea, and from there, it was another three days of clear weather to the Crested Islands. He knew the journey well. When he was a child, this had been his favorite time of the year. A chance to escape the palace walls and his stern teachers and explore places that for all the rest of the year he only got to see in the adventure books most of those teachers so fiercely disapproved of. Except of course for Theodora, who'd snuck them in with his schoolbooks whenever he'd done especially well in lessons.

If Celeste were here, she'd already be following the sailors around, pestering them endlessly for stories of their travels in whatever language they wanted to tell them in, and practicing her own speech at the same time. The rumors said her command of other tongues was flawless, and Seraphina saw no reason to challenge that tale. But her family and teachers knew that her magic only made it easier to catch someone's meaning and understand the patterns of what she heard. An incredible talent, but one that was served by her patient ears and endless curiosity rather than the other way around.

Last year, Abigail had spent hours sketching the sails and waves in her journal, and hours more fishing with the sailors, studying each creature they pulled from the sea. Isadore still had one of her drawings in his desk. It was one of him standing next to a vine-covered ruin on one of the islands. His hands might be a little spindly, and the rocks not quite touching the ground, but it was clear at a glance what it was.

Years ago, he'd brought Lacey Penner with him. She'd loved the ship and the sea and the shore, and more than that, she'd loved the young innkeeper they'd met at the shore. He'd been sad to lose both her daily companionship and her skills at handling the avalanche of paperwork that came daily through his office. She'd always found some way to lift his mood or at least make the work go faster. But he couldn't regret that she'd gone to live with the love of her life. Jasmine had followed her home, but she'd never liked living in the city and had always longed to return to the shore. When Lacey asked to go with her, how could Isadore refuse her?

Maybe, he thought, turning to where Ambry sat on a bench, looking out at the landscape, a notebook lying forgotten in their lap, they'd both found a precious someone in the bargain.

Melanie had given him more than one pointed look over the past few days, but he still could not bring himself to say anything that might reveal his true desires. Not while they were stuck at sea together.

"What do you think?" he asked.

Ambry started and looked up. "I'm sorry, I was distracted."

"No need to apologize. It truly is beautiful out here." His kingdom, which he had all too few precious chances to travel through.

"I haven't been this far from the city since I moved here," Ambry said. "I forgot how beautiful the forests were."

If they ever had the time, Isadore vowed, he would take Ambry all around the world, just to see their face at the sights.

"When I was younger, a sailor once told me that there were fairies living in the forests, and if I sat still enough, I might be able to catch a glimpse of them." Isadore smiled. "He probably only wanted to keep me from running around for a while, but it certainly worked. I thought I saw one once, but it was only a bird."

"I collected stones from the river," Ambry said. "My uncle told me if I found enough, a fairy would come and trade them for gold. I never found any gold, or any fairies, but sometimes he let me trade a few of them for enough chimes to buy some sweets."

"Which were your favorites?"

"Anything with lemon," Ambry said. "Ginger too, but those were expensive. I didn't like mint, but most of my cousins did, so I'd always get a bag of those to share."

"I always wanted the roasted sugar sticks," Isadore said. "The darker the better. My sisters preferred candied fruit and cakes to most of the sweets, so I had most of them to myself." He carefully tucked away Ambry's favorites in his memory, ready for the first chance he had to fulfill their wishes and walked around the ship to greet the captain and the sailors.

Two of the male sailors leaned against the railing, strong arms working at the ropes, checking everything over before they reached the sea. And tattooed on those strong arms, Isadore noted, was the emblem of the Southern Order.

Isadore wasn't certain of all the saint-marks that accompanied the symbol, but he recognized the sign of Saint Baven, known for harsh judgements about women and their place in the world. But Baven had said many other things as well, things that any sensible person would agree with. About working hard, and defending your kin, and using your strengths to serve your family and neighbors. He reminded himself of what Melanie had said. That he shouldn't insult them unless they belittled Ambry, and if they had any sense they wouldn't try that on the Queen's ship. The sailors noticed him looking and saluted. He nodded in reply and went to greet them. They introduced themselves as Reed, the taller one, and Arius, the stronger one, and went about their work with all the respect Isadore had been raised to expect. No, he would not say anything yet, but he would be keeping an eye on them.

When he returned to the bench where Ambry had settled, they'd taken out one of Delia's books and they were smiling at something in it, so he left them to their reading. They deserved the rest after all those months spent working with hardly a break, and the debacle around the treaty. By the time they returned to the palace, he was sure that Ambassador Grenner would have found something new to complain about. Yes, Ambry deserved the rest, and so did he.

The rest of that day and the next passed in a comfortable, timeless blur of sitting in the sun and watching the world go by, of reading books and dozing on the deck. They reached the shore just before dark on the second day.

"Can you smell the sea?" he asked Ambry as they looked out at the crashing waves.

"I can." Ambry lifted their head, letting the sea breeze brush their face and tease bits of hair from their braid. "My grandfather told me about it, but I thought that was just part of the stories."

"Wait until you see the Islands. They're truly something out of a story."

Jasmine's inn stood at the top of a grassy dune that swept down to the golden beach. The setting sun touched the sea in a blaze of light, painting the sky in streaks of pink and orange and casting the clouds in purple.

An aged wooden sign hung over the front gate, proclaiming the inn's name: The Seahorse Derby. The capital S was painted to look like a seahorse, with a curling tail and fluted snout and spines down its back. Lacey's letters said the inn was named after an old sailors' fairytale. Isadore had once thought he'd heard all the stories the sailors had to tell, but he'd since learned that there were always more.

Lacey and Jasmine waited at the dock, hand in hand. Where Lacey's hair had once hung in long golden waves, she now had short little curls on the top of her head. Little shells hung on golden chains from her ears.

"It's so good to see you again," he said, pulling Lacey into a tight hug.

"And you. And Lawrence, of course," Lacey said, smiling at him. Lawrence gave her a cheery salute.

"You've cut your hair."

She ran a hand through it, flipping the little waves this way and that. "It's easier this way. Not so much sand."

"It suits you. And Jasmine! I see your inn is thriving."

"Your Highness." She ducked her head in a bow. Jasmine's family had come from southern Kivern, and she carried their close-cut dark hair and pale brown skin. She wore practical clothes very much like the sailors did: a light shirt, and thick trousers tied at the legs in a material that would keep off the water and salt and sand.

"None of that," Isadore scolded lightly. "I'm a friend, I hope."

"If you're a friend," Lacey warned, "you'd better be ready to wash some dishes. Jasmine's been working for two days straight to prepare." Her proud face told him it was going to be a feast to remember for years to come.

"I hope we haven't pushed any of your guests out of their beds," Isadore said apologetically. Not that there was much he could do about that if he wished to house himself, Ambry, his mother, and all their guards and servants and sailors safely.

Jasmine dismissed that at once. "Nonsense. There are enough places here for wandering travelers. Maybe they'll be sad they won't get to stay at the best of them but let that be that." In Isadore's mind, Jasmine's pride was completely deserved.

"How is Melanie?" Lacey asked.

"As genius and demanding as ever," Isadore said. "I've lost count of the number of times she's saved me from certain peril, or at least from serious embarrassment."

"I told you you'd survive just fine without me," Lacey said.

"I wouldn't have done nearly as well without Ambry," Isadore admitted.

The Queen approached behind him, and he stepped aside to let her make her own laconic greetings. Jasmine led her through the door of the inn, guards going before and behind, and the maids carrying bags bringing up the rear. Ambry followed after them, carrying their own bag, joined by Dominick and Sylvia. Isadore ushered Ambry over.

"You're his new assistant?" Lacey asked. "The one who so heroically saved one of the kitchen staff?"

"It was Isadore who saved him," Ambry said. "He's told me a lot about you. It's a lot to live up to."

"I never thought I'd find someone to fill your shoes," Isadore admitted. "But it turned out I just wasn't looking closely enough."

"I didn't expect you to languish away forever," Lacey scolded. "I might even be disappointed it took you so long." She turned back to Ambry. "And from the looks of it, you're doing very well. You finally managed to get Kivern and Arrawey to agree on something! Come in, and you can tell us how it happened."

Isadore and Ambry followed her through the door. The Queen and her guards were still surveying the place as Jasmine showed them around, studying each beam in the ceiling and each plank of wood in the floor as if it were a complicated page of a lawbook.

At least if they were handling the security matters, Lawrence, Sylvia, and Dominick might be able to enjoy themselves for a change. Dominick most of all. Isadore was sure he hadn't taken any time for himself in weeks.

Well, even if his guards wouldn't relax, Isadore certainly wasn't going to spend his holiday judging everything he saw. The inn was simple, yet welcoming, all pale wood and clean paint, just as Lacey had described it in her letters. Decorations made from painted shells and seaglass wrapped in wire hung from every hook and beam, tucked into every corner. They'd pulled the dining tables together in preparation for the royal visit, and plates and cutlery sat waiting.

The smell of salt drifted through the air, stirring his appetite. Jasmine's cooking was something else Lacey had described at length in her letters, and Isadore was looking forward to trying it.

A chalkboard covered most of one wall, murals of underwater scenes spread across its surface. Isadore wondered if this building had once been a school. He could see why Jasmine had decided to leave it up. They must have had children visiting recently, because the bottom third of the wall, where little hands could reach, was covered in messy but enthusiastic doodles of shells and fish and seaweed.

Ambry paused to study a drawing of the seaside story that must have given the inn its name. A row of seahorses swam as fast as they could around a track made of coral and seaglass, while on a floating platform above, a crowd of mermaids wagered handfuls of pearls on the outcome.

"Do you know the story?" Jasmine asked. When Ambry shook their head, she pointed to the smallest seahorse, a little green creature with rounded spines and fluttering fins. "That one's Pebble. He's the hero, but he doesn't know it yet. The big ones over here, they've bullied their way to the top, and everyone's certain one of them is going to win. But just before they reach the finish line, they start fighting with each other, and they knock over a huge pile of rubbish from a shipwreck and get themselves trapped inside it. Pebble's the only one who's small enough to go inside the rubble and help rescue them. He gives up winning the race to save them." She smiled. "My papa would tell me that story when I was upset about being too small to play with the boys. I always thought I'd be a hero someday, but sadly there haven't been any shipwrecks to rescue anyone from."

"Nonsense," Lacey said, coming up behind them. "You were a hero to that couple who got caught in the storm, weren't you?"

Jasmine snorted. "And I wouldn't have had to if they hadn't gone out when it clearly wasn't safe, at least to anyone with eyes and brains. But one thing I've learned out here is to never be surprised by how much sense some people lack. Especially when they've come from the city."

"I want to hear that story," Isadore said. The three of them turned to look at him.

"I'm sure *you've* got some sea sense," Lacey said. "You've been out here often enough to pick up a few things. You said you always used to talk to the sailors when you were a boy."

Isadore shook his head. "A wide-eyed little prince wandering into their hard work? I'm sure half the stories they filled my head with were lies and nonsense. Unless you've seen some three-headed sea monsters with a taste for children?"

Jasmine laughed. "I'm going to try that one the next time someone's younglings won't stop running into the surf when there's a storm coming."

"It'll work. I had dreams about those dripping fangs for years," Isadore said.

Someone called out from an inside door. Jasmine waved to him, and then ushered her guests towards the table. "Dinner's ready."

They gathered around the table, not just the honored guests but all the servants and sailors too. Seraphina wouldn't have it any other way. That was one aspect in which Isadore knew his mother wasn't nearly as stern and cold as she so often seemed. She might not often lower herself to speak to anyone who was not family or staff, or an advisor or lawmaker, or the occasional lucky petitioner, but she would make certain that all around her enjoyed the rewards of their work, no matter how lowly they were.

Jasmine made sure there was plenty to go around. Steaming bowls of clams went down the table, followed by platters of crispy fried fish, roasted meat cooked with fruit, and dishes of some sort of seaweed that tasted fresh and sweet despite the dusting of salt on its dark green fronds. And all of that accompanied by jugs of another one of Jasmine's secrets: a sweet, strong wine made from fruit brought in from the Crested Islands.

Nothing went to waste. Seraphina let her maid choose her portions and set them on her plate, but she ate as heartily as the rest. Isadore watched Ambry's face shine in wonder at each new dish. Jasmine had every right to be proud of this place.

As they ate, Jasmine and Lacey told stories of their adventures and the interesting people who had come through their door. As the meal went on and the jugs of wine drained lower, the tales got stranger and stranger, until Isadore was certain some must have been invented wholecloth, but he didn't complain. Nor did the sailors, who interjected here and there with their own accounts of terrible storms and prophetic travelers.

He and Ambry listened rapt to a story about a girl and a raft pulled by trained dolphins, which suddenly ended in a dirty punchline and raucous laughter from the sailors. Ambry, ears pink, grinned and reached for the last few pieces of sugared fruit from the plates that had appeared when the rest were taken away.

Not everything had been taken away, though. Empty shells clattered along the table. Two of the younger sailors must have had a few too many cups of Jasmine's brew and tried to set up a game of knock-down with shells and goblets, which Seraphina pointedly ignored.

After the meal finally drew to a close, they made their way to their rooms. The beds were small, but comfortable, and with the soft sound of the sea coming in through the window,

Isadore could think of few places he would choose over this. For a moment, he wished they could stay longer, see more of Lacey and Jasmine's life, but that would only inconvenience them.

A night here was a gift, and he would treasure it. And in the morning, the open sea waited for them.

✧

There was no work to be done here, the sea and sky around them were utterly beautiful, and Ambry couldn't enjoy any of it. The motion of the waves was hardly violent, yet it threatened to knock them to the deck with every step. How could this be so different from the calm motion of the river? They'd eaten precious little for fear that their roiling stomach wouldn't be able to hold onto it. All of their adventure novels had taught them that the feeling would wear off quickly, but it had been most of a day and still they longed only to curl up somewhere on steady dry land until it went away. It was monstrously unfair, they thought, that the only characters in those books who ever seemed to suffer from seasickness were villains and the most unimportant of the hero's friends.

They found a shaded bench where they could sit and not be in anyone's way and tried very hard to think of solid, stable things. Mountains, castles. Very large trees. They looked up when Isadore sat beside them.

"Seasick?" he asked gently.

Ambry nodded. "Is there something you can do about it?" they managed to say, letting a little bit of pleading into their voice. It didn't take much effort; they probably looked as miserable as they felt.

Isadore shook his head apologetically. "I'm sorry, my magic can't do anything for that. Trust me, I've tried." Ambry's heart sank. Before they could resign themself to possibly feeling this awful all week, Isadore added, "But there is a tea that might help. I'll have some prepared."

He returned a few minutes later with a wide-bottomed cup that tapered up to a smaller opening. Ambry wondered at the shape but decided not to spare the voice to ask. Isadore answered their question anyway. "It's designed so it won't spill if it's sitting on a table and the ship rocks. It's such a clever little thing for how simple it is."

Isadore so loved things like that, simple items or ideas that could solve far larger problems. Ambry sipped the tea, careful not to disturb their stomach any more than it already was. They tasted mint and ginger and something else that they couldn't name, bitter and medicinal but not unpleasant enough to overshadow the rest. Isadore sat beside them as they finished it and pulled the cup away when they were done.

"Sleep for a bit and see if you don't feel a bit more steady when you wake." With a hand on their shoulder, Isadore guided them down to the quarters that had been set aside for them, a tiny space with barely more room than was needed for a bunk and a chest. But it was private, and it gave them a little distance from the sight of the rolling waves.

"I'll come and check on you in a little while," Isadore promised. Ambry didn't bother latching the door when he closed it, only pulled the tie from their hair and curled into bed.

Now that they were horizontal, the motion of the ship was somewhat more bearable, a gentle swaying that they no longer needed to fight against for their footing. They weren't tired enough to sleep, so they lay there comfortably for a time listening to the muffled noises of sailors working on the deck and the sounds of the water splashing against the sides of the ship.

They did start to feel better later that day; whether it was the effect of the tea or simply that they were becoming used to the motion of the ship, they were at last able to watch the glittering sea without fear of losing their stomach or of toppling over the rail.

By the time dinner was served, they felt steady enough to join Isadore and the Queen in the state room. They had worried that it would be uncomfortably formal, that they'd have to figure out how to not embarrass themself. But just like at Jasmine's inn, Isadore ate alongside Lawrence and Sylvia, and the Queen's maids chattered happily as she listened and occasionally offered an opinion. By the time the chef set the second course on the table, Ambry felt confident enough to offer some words of their own. They didn't miss the way Isadore smiled listening to them.

The food was, as always, absolutely delicious. Ambry's plate was soon piled with roasted fish caught just that afternoon and rare tropical fruits shaved into fine ribbons and cooked in a sharp and salty glaze. Then there were the fresh vegetables loaded on just a few days before, and pickles stuffed with something they didn't recognize, but savored all the same.

Two days later, the distinctive shapes of the Crested Islands came into view on the horizon. Isadore joined Ambry at the railing and pointed out a jagged shape.

"There, on the easternmost island, do you see that? It's the remains of a tower built by some force that tried to settle the island centuries ago."

"From Talland?"

"Kivern, we think, but they didn't leave any clear records. There's a whole range of theories about who it was, and why. Some think they wanted an outpost for trade with Melira, across the sea, but the ruins are too old for that. The most common theory is that they were simply explorers, led by a particularly proud lord, who wanted more lands to call his own."

"I've heard that's what the scholars think," one of the sailors said from behind them. It was Arius. "I've also heard that it was a ship of outcasts that went there, either on their own or because Saint Baven's priests sent them away. Perverts and layabouts. Not the finest of folk. They lived long enough to build that there fort, and then died out, from a curse or a storm or because there weren't enough of them fertile to breed." His eyes settled on Ambry as he said it, but the moment Isadore moved, he looked away, studying the distant ruins. "Or it might have been the snakes that got them. It's said they can smell sinners."

But his meaning was clear enough. Ambry recognized the story. Their grandfather had told them a version of it when they'd dared to tell him who they'd discovered themself to be, except in his telling there had been no islands, just a camp in the forest where found-people gathered. Saint Baven asked them three times to repudiate their knowledge, reclaim their shed names. They refused and were struck down by lightning for their arrogance.

Ambry had crept away in tears when they'd first heard that cruel tale. Now, they stood proud, and tried not to hope that the sailor didn't know what he said.

"I hadn't heard that particular version," Isadore said, a chill in his voice that surely even the sailor could hear. "However it happened, it was a terrible tragedy that so many people died in an attempt to build a new home."

"Of course," Arius said. "If you'll allow me, Highness, I have work to get to."

Isadore nodded. "Go," he said, dismissing the sailor with a wave of his hand.

When the sailor was out of earshot, Isadore let out a heavy breath. "I'm truly sorry you had to hear that, Ambry."

"I'm fine. I've heard worse," Ambry said. And then they wished they'd said something else, because it did nothing to reassure Isadore. The grief in his eyes only grew deeper.

"Yes. Of course you have. I shouldn't have said anything."

"You should," Ambry insisted. "It means a lot to people like me." To them, and Marion, and Darby, and so many others. "That you believe us and support us." They took a breath and watched the islands until they could speak again. "Amalia Tobin told a version of that story about the island once."

"Amalia – your mother's priest?"

Ambry nodded. "Hers was about Saint Astrenn." They ran their fingers over the mark of Astrenn on their collar. They'd been so happy when they'd discovered how Darby had included it as part of the design. "The saint gathered the found-people who'd been sent away from their homes and gave them shelter on a mysterious island only they could reach. Some priests chased after them to try to drag them back, and they were turned into snakes and stinging insects. Astrenn's people lived happily on the island until they were lifted into heaven."

"A better tale than Baven's," Isadore said when Ambry was done. "My family has never followed the sorts of saints who judged people for that. I don't know why people trouble themselves to care what strangers do. Maybe it's strange if you've never met them, but if you look at the records, there have almost always been found-people working in the palace. Cooks, servants, teachers." He smiled. "And archivists. I suppose they made sure their kin were remembered."

"It's good to be remembered," Ambry said. They looked out on the distant outline of the ruins again and wondered who had truly made them, and what had become of them. "Maybe while we're out there, we can find out who those islanders were." It was only a wishful fancy, but it was a better feeling than lingering on Arius's tale.

"I always hoped I'd stumble on some ancient book or stone tablet out there," Isadore said. "I think Minerva Corey would sell her heart to get her hands on those records, if they exist. We'll make landfall tomorrow. I'll show you my favorite places. And maybe some of the silly stories I came up with…"

Anything he had to tell, Ambry wanted to hear it.

Chapter Sixteen

✧

By the time Ambry roused from dreams of watching sea dragons weave and dance through slowly-waving forests of seaweed, the ship had already dropped anchor at the closest of the five Crested Islands. They pulled on some clothes – old ones, they didn't want to risk getting Darby's sailing outfit dirty while exploring the ruins – and went out on deck.

Isadore was already awake, watching the sailors run about with ropes and eating one of the little buns Jasmine had given them when they'd sailed away from the inn. He handed Ambry another one with a smile. It was a bit stale, but still tasted good.

Eventually the two sailors from the Southern Order, Reed and Arius, came by to tell them they could go ashore whenever they wished.

"Watch your feet out there," Reed warned. "It's the season for goldstrikes, and they're not the only beasts crawling about that'll do you harm any chance they get. Should be clear enough by the ruins, at least."

Arius chuckled. "If you get to it first, give it a rock to the head and stake it over a fire. Gives a man strength." He held out a thick bundle tied fast with leather straps. "Some supplies, for you and your friend. You get hungry fast out on the Islands." He pushed it into Ambry's arms. They fumbled with the straps for a moment, then got it comfortably over one shoulder.

Maybe he'd had a change of heart. Or he'd realized that antagonizing the prince's assistant was an idiotic move aboard the royal ship. Either way, Ambry would be happy to be away from him for a day.

They hardly needed the extra supplies. Partway up the overgrown ridge leading away from the ship, Isadore suddenly ducked into the bushes and came out with handfuls of brown nuts. A better snack than grilled snakes, Ambry thought.

"You'll need to shell those," Sylvia said, pulling out her knife. She took the nuts and crushed them against a stone with the back end of the knife, cracking them so that Ambry and Isadore could easily peel away the shells and eat the sweet insides. It seemed the change of scenery and the escape from the pressures and routines of the palace was bringing out the softer side in Isadore's guards. Or in Sylvia and Lawrence, at least.

They continued along the ridge, brushing past low trees with giant fan-shaped leaves and clusters of red fruit underneath. Every so often a little carved figure stood up from the path. They all had the same round eyes and small pitted nose, but the markings on the tops of their heads were all different.

"Are those saint-marks?" Ambry asked.

"If they are, they're not saints anyone alive remembers," Isadore said. "But I think Saint Karta's sign was found on the next island, alongside a carving of a sea serpent."

Up close, the walls of the ruined fort were even larger than Ambry had expected from the shore. The sandy rock was pitted from endless years of rain and wind, but most of the structure still stood proud.

"Let's go this way," Isadore said, pointing to a section of wall that ran a few paces from the cliff. "Careful with your footing, some of it might crumble. But there's a magnificent little place at the end with even more carvings."

Isadore climbed up onto one of the massive stone blocks and reached out a hand to help Ambry up. They crawled along the wall, then sat on the edge, looking out at the bay below where fisherbirds wheeled over the ocean. Every so often one would turn from its circling and dive sharply into the water, only to come up again with a wriggling fish clamped in its beak.

Arius's story hung in Ambry's mind, but even after centuries it was more than clear that whoever had built this place had not been weak or crude in any way. Just to haul the bricks from the side of the western mountain must have taken years of work by hundreds of builders.

"When we return to the palace," Isadore said when they voiced their thoughts, "I can find you some books about the Islands. One of my old tutors wrote a paper guessing at the settlement."

"What did they believe?" Ambry asked.

"She never found an answer she was completely happy with, but she didn't think a tragedy happened here."

"Did she have another theory?"

"There are graves here, but tidy ones, under holy symbols. There's nothing to indicate death on a massive scale. So, either the islanders sailed away and foundered… or they returned to the mainland."

"But why? It's beautiful here. They could get food from the fish and the trees, and there's wood and stone to build with." Whoever the settlers, whether merchants or runaways, had planned it in detail, organized extensive effort. What could have inspired them to leave?

"There could have been a famine season, forcing them to sail further out. Maybe the grandchildren of the settlers were curious about the mainland. Or they felt guided by some sign from the saints."

As if guided by signs of his own, Isadore didn't sit still for long. Bare minutes had passed before he was clambering along the wall again. Sylvia followed closely from ground level, sharp eyes watching the stones and trees for danger.

Finally, he came back closer to the ground, leading Ambry through a curtain of vines into a little round area surrounded by the ruins of stone columns.

"I must have given my guard Theodora hell back when I was a child," Isadore said when Ambry caught up with him. "Always climbing over anything I could find, chasing after every pretty feather or shiny rock."

"I would have been worse," Ambry said. "I used to build fairy houses out of rocks and sticks and mud. And I'd cry if anyone tried to move them." The fairy houses had probably looked like nothing more than piles of rubbish, but to Ambry's eyes they'd been finer than the castle of the Sea King in their grandfather's stories.

"That's sweet," Isadore said. "And at least you'd only need to be washed, and not fetched out of a tree or fished out of a gully."

"You couldn't have been that bad."

"Oh, I was. You didn't know me before Melanie beat some sense into me."

"I can imagine that." That was a story they hoped to hear someday.

"What, Melanie beating sense into me?" Isadore laughed. "You see that every day."

"You, exploring," Ambry said. "You always like hearing about Captain Michaelsen's reports from the north."

"If only I could go out there myself," Isadore sighed. "Think of it, lands covered in ice the entire year."

"I'd rather stay in the warmth," Ambry said, letting the sun wash over them.

"This is a good place to enjoy the sun. Time for a rest?"

Ambry agreed heartily with that.

"Shall we?" Isadore motioned to the bundle Arius had given them.

"Please. I'm hungry already."

"Put it here," Isadore said, sitting on one of the longer stretches of unbroken stone blocks. "This'll make a fine enough table."

They set it down and Isadore unfastened the ties. As the bag fell open, something moved inside it, darting towards Isadore's arm. Before Ambry could make sense of what it was, Isadore cried out and threw the bag to the ground, spilling packages across the sandy soil.

Sylvia leapt forward, pushing Ambry aside. They fell against a rock and scrambled back upright in time to see a sandy, black-speckled tail lash once, twice, and then lie still under Sylvia's knife. She looked from the dead snake to Isadore's wrist and the two wounds there.

"A goldstrike," she said. "How…" Her expression turned dark.

"It was in the bag," Ambry realized, heart pounding. "But it couldn't have crawled in. It must have been there when Arius gave it to me. He said something about hunting them."

The fury that blazed in Sylvia's face at that was enough to frighten demons.

Isadore shook his head, holding his wrist. "It hurts, but I think…"

"We need to get help, Highness, and soon," Sylvia said. "Ambry. Help me get him back to the ship, quickly, and when we're near, go ahead and call for the doctor."

Both of them obeyed without a hint of doubt, stumbling over the ancient stones of the wall and towards the path. Isadore made a strange sound and started to sway on his feet. Ambry took his arm and guided him down the path, step after step, praying that there was something more they could do. That help would be waiting for them. They couldn't think about what would happen if there wasn't a cure.

✧

The ship seemed so far away now, and his body so tired and aching that he knew he could never cross the distance. His feet dragged in the dirt. The sun beating down on his back felt like an assault from the saints themselves. How far were they? Why couldn't he just sit down for a moment by the side of the path and gather his strength? Even breathing was a struggle. Something pounded in his head, matching the pounding of terrible burning pain in his arm.

"Please, Highness, keep moving." Sylvia's voice, harsh with worry. He tried to reply to her, but he couldn't get any words out past his dry lips. "There's a doctor on the ship," she went on. "He'll know what to do."

Ambry was on his other side, their hands supporting him. The sun dazzled his eyes as he searched for the sight of the shore, the ship, and finally found it. For what felt like endless hours, the ship drifted in the distance, worlds away, and then Ambry broke away from his side and raced up the ramp, feet pounding on the wood.

"Help, please!" they cried. "There was a snake…"

"A goldstrike!" Sylvia called after them.

But Isadore could barely hang onto his senses, never mind his feet. He let Sylvia drag him where she would. Someone joined her. Lawrence's hands on his arm. Then there were voices, thundering footsteps, people talking, someone moving him, sudden darkness and coolness.

Something soft under him, damp with sweat. A light, over his head, fuzzy and dim, and then too bright too bear. Even with his eyes closed, the light seared into his head. After another eternity of swimming through tangled thoughts and too-hot sensations, he realized it was his own pain, pulsing out from where the snake had plunged its fangs into his skin, along all his nerves and veins and into his heart.

He let it consume him. He could do nothing else. And then something bright within him pushed back against the pain.

He chased it, giving that power all the strength that he could, even when he was sure he had nothing left. His magic swelled inside him, burning through his waning reserves of energy, keeping the pain from swallowing him entirely.

Isadore lay there, hearing nothing of the voices around him, doing all he could simply to live, simply to avoid falling into the darkness that he knew awaited if the venom worked unchecked. It was far worse than that climb back from the ruins. Harder than anything he'd ever done before. At times he couldn't even remember who he was, just that he hurt terribly. And then Ambry's voice reached him, and he remembered the ship, the ruins, the flash of Sylvia's knife in the sun. He turned over and reached for Ambry. Pain shot down his arm, blinding him again.

He could feel the magic fighting the venom burning through his veins, every moment growing hotter. He was lying still; he was sure of it. Something soft, a bed somewhere on the ship. But he felt as if he was running as fast as he could go, fighting against a weight so great he had hardly a hope of pushing through it. He couldn't do it. He was going to burn himself out, and there was nothing he could do to fight it.

✧

"His magic must be fighting off the creature's venom," Lawrence said. "I can't say how long it will last, but if he can keep up his strength, he may well be able to fight it off."

Isadore reached out with weakened arms. The doctor had looked him over with a grim expression, saying little, and gone back to his little cabin for supplies. He returned with a poultice for the wounds and a potion he said would ease the pain and fever.

Ambry stood aside to let him work. When he was done, he left as quickly as he'd come, pulling Lawrence outside to speak with him. What was it he had to say that he didn't want them to hear?

Isadore turned over and made a confused, frightened sound. "Ambry? Is that you? I can't… everything's too bright, I can't see. I don't know where I am."

He was keeping his voice level, but it was slipping. Ambry knew him well enough to see that he was terrified and trying desperately to hold onto sense. What could have done this to him?

"We're on the ship. Sylvia and Dominick are here, and Lawrence is talking to the doctor."

Isadore sat up and grabbed for their hand. "Stay. Please. Stay with me."

"I'm here," Ambry said. They sat on the bed beside him, not sure what else to do, but needing to do whatever they could.

"There's… there's something I need to do, isn't there? What is it? Melanie always has more letters."

"There's nothing else to do today. You've finished everything," Ambry said, forcing through their alarm to put as much certainty in their words as they could, trying to think of what Isadore would say were their positions reversed and it was them in this strange, lost torment.

Isadore made a noise of protest and struggled to rise from the bed before falling back onto the sweat-soaked sheets.

"Isadore. You're safe here," Ambry promised, pushing aside that hopeful hitch in their heart at the feeling of saying his bare name.

Isadore nodded, unconvinced, frightened. It scared them, to see him in such fear and distress when usually he was confident, composed, steady. But they could not afford to be afraid now, not when Isadore needed them. Needed their strength.

"I'm cold," Isadore said plaintively. But he didn't do anything to amend that, only sat still and unhappy on the bed as if frozen by a fairy spell.

Ambry dug through the chest by the bed and drew out a worn woolen blanket that smelled of sea salt. Isadore was still sitting on the bed, staring at nothing. Ambry climbed up beside him and wrapped the blanket around his back. He barely moved as they did.

"Is that better?"

He took the fabric in his hands and held it like it was a strange and foreign thing. "I think so," he said.

Before they could move away, Isadore reached out for them again. They let him, moving as close as they dared, feeling him shivering beside them. For once, they did not care that Dominick was watching.

"I'm here. Keep fighting. You're going to survive this." He had to survive this. Ambry could not imagine otherwise.

Isadore pulled them close. "Stay here. I need you here."

They stayed, wrapping their arms around Isadore, doing all they could to keep him comfortable as his magic warred against the goldstrike's venom. He pressed against them, searching for warmth, and finally, finally, eased into sleep in their arms.

Delia might have found this impossibly romantic in a story. Ambry too had enjoyed reading things like this. But here and now, not knowing for certain whether Isadore would recover or when, seeing him so frightened and lost… Ambry wanted only to protect him from that, no matter what it meant.

After a time, there was a sound from the doorway. It was Dominick, turning to greet Lawrence as he came back inside.

"Marshall, Ambry. They've found him," Lawrence said. "The sailor who did this. One of his fellows came to us with his suspicions. Sylvia is questioning him now."

Arius. He'd planned this. Slipped the snake into their bag so it'd attack them out on the ruins. Ambry burned with anger, but there was no time for that now.

"How is His Highness?" Lawrence asked.

"Better, I think," Ambry said. "He's sleeping now. I think his magic is still working against the venom. But the fever's broken."

"Good, good," Lawrence said, with a breath of such relief that Ambry nearly sobbed. "Her Majesty wants to see you, Ambry. Just for a minute."

There was no way they could refuse that summons. Ambry kissed Isadore's damp brow, then slipped from his limp arms as gently as they could and crept towards the door. Then they stepped out on the deck and into the presence of the Queen of Talland.

She studied them with that same stern gaze she had worn when she summoned them for tea weeks before. At last, she spoke.

"Tell me, how fares my son?"

Ambry fought back a shiver at the Queen's forbidding expression. "He's sleeping. The– the doctor said it wouldn't last more than a day. His magic is doing something to help him."

Once again, Ambry remembered the Queen's truth-seeing magic. They'd told all the truth they knew, but would it be enough? She studied them, dark eyes holding thoughts Ambry couldn't begin to guess at.

"What's happening?" they dared to ask. "Arius–"

"Lieutenant Marwen is keeping watch on the prisoner," she said at last. That was Sylvia. "He made little effort to hide his reasoning for such a cowardly and foolish plot. He meant to harm you, for what he calls your perversion of nature."

She said it so simply, but even so her disgust was clear. A shock went through Ambry, cold and unpleasant, stabbing into their heart. Isadore was suffering because Arius hated them?

"He will face my justice," the Queen went on. "You can be certain of that."

Ambry was, and they knew they would not regret a moment of it.

"Tell me when he wakes," she said before they could reply, and swept off back to her cabin, guards following at her side.

Dominick and Lawrence waited for Ambry inside Isadore's cabin. Ambry told them what they'd heard.

Lawrence shook his head in dismay. "How terrible," he said. "I'm truly sorry he thought such a thing, and more sorry that he thought it a reason to harm you."

"Pathetic fool," Dominick spat. He looked to the door, torn between protecting his prince and going after the man who had harmed him. Then he turned to Ambry.

"Stay with him," Dominick said, and for just a moment his expression softened, and then that fearsome mask was back in place. "Her Majesty will see to the rest of the sailors. We will learn how he did this, and if he had any helpers, they will suffer for it." He sounded grimly pleased at that eventuality, and Ambry couldn't disagree.

Dominick stormed off through the door, leaving Ambry and Lawrence with Isadore. Lawrence gave Ambry a small nod of approval and turned back to his watch.

Isadore shifted on the bed, reaching out yet again, before falling back into uneasy sleep. Ambry stayed by his side for all of it, easing him with gentle words when his face twisted in pain-haunted dreams.

Dusk was falling when Isadore finally awakened in the dark cabin. Sylvia was on duty at the door, and Ambry knew Dominick and Lawrence were close by. Not even the Queen could convince them to rest at a time like this, and Ambry knew none of them would be able to even if they tried.

"Ambry?" Isadore sat up, running his hands through his sweat-flattened hair.

"You're awake. How are you feeling?" Isadore looked terrible, but he was alive, and from what Lawrence had said, that was far better than what happened to most victims of a goldstrike's bite.

Isadore groaned. "Exhausted. Aching. But I think I have my senses now." He rubbed at his bandaged wrist and winced. The swelling and bruising extended past the pale fabric, staining the sweaty brown skin with lurid colors.

"I'll let you rest. The Queen and her guards are trying to find out how it happened. It was Arius. He put the goldstrike in the pack he gave us." They fought back a sudden wave of guilt that they'd carried the thing all the way up into the ruins.

"The sailor from the Southern Church?" Isadore surged upwards, and fell back to the bed, strength spent. "He must have wanted it to bite you. I saw he wore Saint Baven's marks. And what he said about the Islands. But I believed he wouldn't try anything aboard the royal ship. I should have been able to stop it."

"You couldn't have known," Ambry insisted. They couldn't let him blame himself for this. "I'm safe with you, Isadore. The snake didn't come near me." Before, they might have shivered at the thought of what Arius would now face from the Queen and the royal guard, and from his fellow sailors. Now, they felt it wholly deserved. "I'll ask what they know. And Sylvia needs to rest…"

"Wait," Isadore said, reaching weakly for their arm.

"What is it?"

"Ambry." He looked away, uncharacteristically nervous. "I don't quite remember everything I said. If… if I have overstepped, I am truly sorry…"

Ambry couldn't let him keep talking like that. "No. You haven't, you didn't. I was proud to help." Doubt fluttered in their stomach, settled into a deep, heavy pool that could not be moved. "If anyone's guilty of that, it's me. You were weakened and confused and I didn't really think about what you would have wanted in your right mind."

"You were everything I needed. I'm truly grateful."

Warmth blossomed once again in their chest. But they could never have expected what Isadore said next, or at least, they would not have dared to hope.

"I suppose there's no use avoiding it anymore," Isadore said. "I've come to love you, Ambry. I promise that was not my intent when I hired you. I tried to ignore it as it grew." He took a breath, hesitating. "I need to know if you–"

Ambry couldn't bear to hear his doubt any longer. "Yes. Yes, I feel the same," they said, all in a rush, and surged into Isadore's arms. "Delia– the others always talked about this. About falling in love with you. They were certain I had. But when it actually happened, it felt different." Why had they doubted this for so long? It seemed so clear now. "I'm sorry that it took me so long to tell you."

Isadore sighed. He moved to let Ambry sit beside him. "No. You were being cautious, and you had more reason to than I." He stared out the tiny window, then sighed and shook his head. "When I was studying at the University, my closest friends were Adrian, who you've met... and Lord Cedric Farndale."

That was one of the names whispered in disgust around the servants' table. "I've heard of him. But not good things."

"I didn't see it then," Isadore said, as if confessing something terrible. "I thought he was a good man, who understood care and decency and the power he held over his household."

All those whispered rumors about Mrs. Hammond came to Ambry's mind. They almost asked. The words came to their lips. But then they swallowed them back down. Whatever had happened there, the reason Isadore had hired her as his housekeeper was between them, and not for Ambry to know.

"You've never been like that," Ambry told him, needing him to believe it.

Now that they knew, some of their old imaginings came into their mind. Especially here, on the bed, in the quiet and the dark. But it wasn't the right time. Isadore's face shone with sweat, and his eyes were sunk dark with exhaustion and pain.

"Do you need anything?" Ambry asked. "I can fetch some more water."

"Please."

They got a cup of water from the barrel, stopping only to report Isadore's improved condition to one of Queen Seraphina's guards, and returned to the prince's cabin. Not even Dominick protested when Ambry spent the rest of the night beside Isadore.

The next day passed in an odd haze of tending to Isadore and sitting on the deck, watching the ripples of waves pass by. Between the terror and exhaustion of the goldstrike attack and Isadore's confession that had finally answered their own heart, they almost feared the entire thing had been a dream. But one look at Isadore's tired eyes and bruised wrist, or the sailors' silent attention to their work, proved otherwise.

Isadore slept most of the day under his guards' careful watch. They weren't the only ones looking out for him, Ambry noted. One of the ship's cats had come out of hiding and taken up position on the foot of his bed. When Isadore wasn't sleeping, he read one of the books Ambry had brought, or talked quietly with them. Delia's handwritten tales went a long way to distracting him from the lingering pain from the bite and the exhaustion of having drained his magic to survive it. They spent hours discussing the stories. They didn't talk about Arius or the goldstrike. So much was still the same between them, despite their newly confessed love, and

Ambry knew they wouldn't have wanted anything else. This was all they wanted, and the thought of returning to the palace as Isadore's lover set their heart pounding with joy.

Ambry hadn't planned on speaking to Reed. But on such a small ship, it was all but impossible to avoid one man forever. They found him scrubbing salt from the deck near the bow, and their feet brought them forward.

"Why did he do it?" Ambry asked before they could stop themselves.

"I'm not the one to ask about that," Reed said, voice low, without looking away from his work. But his hands tensed on the brush and what Ambry could see of his face grew shadowed. "He was a fool and an idiot."

"How did he manage it?"

"Must have gone out early and found one of the beasts in its slumber," he all but growled. "Some folks do that. The only strange part was bringing it back alive. They can be good eating if you know how to handle them. Most sailors won't risk it, but some think they bring luck."

"He must have known he'd be caught."

Reed shrugged, feigning ease. He didn't turn to look at them. "He thought His Highness too soft-headed and soft-hearted to figure that out, I judge."

"And you didn't?" Ambry asked. They didn't know what power drove them to the words, but they had to know.

This time, Reed turned around. A strange look came into his eyes as he studied Ambry. "I don't like what you do," Reed said plainly. "Saint Baven says women and men should treasure what they're given. They should stick to it and teach their babes the same." He raised his arm and tapped on the saint-mark tattooed there. "But it's not for me out on this ship to say what you do in the palace or the city, and to set a goldstrike on you for it, well, if Baven wanted that done, I figure he'd have done it himself. Whatever Her Majesty wants with us now, that's landsman's law. Not for sea folks like me to challenge."

"I don't know what they're going to do with Arius," Ambry said. "But you weren't responsible. You don't deserve any punishment."

"Deserve, now, that's for the saints to decide," Reed said. "I hope I've done my best." He turned away and strode off back to his work before Ambry could reply.

Ambry thought to themself that Reed could have done far better than he had, but saying that would do no good. They walked away from him and back to Isadore's side.

✧

Isadore sat on his bed in his cabin and rubbed the salve over his wrist. It was still sore even days later, the marks of the creature's fangs radiating purple bruises over his swollen skin. But that was far, far preferable to what might have happened if he had not had his magic to save him. If it had been Ambry…

His hands tightened in fury, and he didn't care that it made the pain flare bright again. He wished he could storm into that cell and throw the man overboard with his own hands.

The Queen would see to Arius's punishment. She approved of very little in the world, but there were few things she disapproved of more than those who harmed others simply out of hate and nothing else. And anyone who threatened her family was sure to face the worst of her wrath and her power.

He wondered briefly if she would do the same if the goldstrike had attacked Ambry as Arius had intended. Seraphina might not count Ambry as part of their family yet, but Isadore certainly did.

He'd been taught too much logic and philosophy to say with certainty that it had been Ambry's presence, their touch, their voice, that had allowed him to survive the goldstrike's venom when few others had. But Ambry had made it bearable. He might have lost his mind in that roaring abyss if it hadn't been for Ambry beside him, offering comfort and a path out of his muddled dreams and back to reality. And if that suffering was what it had taken for the two of them to admit the love they'd been trying so desperately to hide, he could accept it as some sort of divine payment.

At dinner, Seraphina studied Ambry with a sharper eye than they deserved, and the look she cast upon Isadore told him she knew exactly what had happened in that dark room after the torment of the serpent's bite. Was it disapproval? Or judgement? No, he reminded himself. She only wanted for him to succeed and find loyal allies.

He could hear Melanie's voice in his head, telling him that he had to be patient and let his mother come to her own conclusion on Ambry's worthiness. But still he wanted nothing more than to come to their defense. She would not have that treaty without Ambry's help. Or the Council agreement on the landlords in the city, or any number of other accomplishments in which Ambry had been instrumental, or at least of great help.

Ambry had won over Dominick, after all. No doubt they could win over the Queen as well. It was just a matter of how long that would be. His mother, like Dominick, thought him soft-hearted, inexperienced, open to manipulation. It would be all too easy for them to imagine him allowing Ambry to shift his policies, his political aims. And sometimes they did, but only when they brought Isadore's attention to an issue or an approach that he hadn't seen before. She didn't see that sometimes he had disagreed with Ambry, and they'd accepted it. And she didn't see the times when they'd worked together on an issue, and Ambry was the one who offered Isadore the last key he needed to make something work.

But with the way things were, it was all he could do to convince his mother not to turn back towards home that very day. Arius's arrest had done nothing good for the crew's morale, and when they'd learned what exactly he'd done, it was a wonder no fights broke out. From the sound of it, some of them got very close to coming to blows. The captain had come to beg at her feet for forgiveness, which she had granted in a few formal words Isadore knew would do little for the man's guilt. Reed kept to his work throughout all of it, refusing to speak a word about his friend, good or ill. Isadore wanted to interrogate him, demand to hear what he knew, if he'd had any idea of his companion's plans and let him do it. But that would accomplish nothing. If he had been at all complicit, Sylvia and his mother and the others would have uncovered it by now.

There were better things to think about, after all. He had Ambry, and the Islands, and he was determined to enjoy them both in the few days they had left.

Chapter Seventeen

✧

Isadore insisted on going back to the ruins two days later. Dominick grumbled in protest, but Isadore said that he certainly wasn't going to spend the entire time hiding in his cabin. To Ambry's surprise, though perhaps it shouldn't have been, Lawrence backed him up.

"The ruins are no more dangerous than they were yesterday or the day before," he said. "And this time you will bring your own things, instead of accepting gifts from vile rats who think it their duty to do the saints' will."

"We should at least retrieve the pack before some beast decides to take it for a nest," Isadore argued. And his guards eventually conceded, on the condition that both Sylvia and Dominick accompanied Isadore and Ambry.

The extra caution wasn't necessary. Nothing else, man or beast, tried to harm them as they wandered through the forests and climbed over the ruins and hills. But more than once, Ambry caught Dominick smiling at the beautiful landscape around them, and Isadore saw it too. Ambry had almost thought that there was nothing in the world that Dominick enjoyed, and now they knew for certain that wasn't true.

They'd worried that Dominick would not approve of their new relationship with his prince. He must know by now. But even when he did watch them together, he never glared or grumbled. Once or twice Ambry felt a protective eye on their back, and when their feet slipped on a patch of crumbling stone, it was Dominick's strong hand that reached for their arm and steadied them. Coming from him, Isadore whispered to them one night as they watched the clouds drift through the sky, that was as good as an oath of service.

After that long night at Isadore's side, Ambry slept in their own cabin for the rest of the journey. Both of them wanted more, but they'd agreed it was best to wait until there were not so many sailors around to hear and gossip. And when they did not have access to the potions that would prevent the risks of such an activity. So Ambry was not too sad when all too soon, it was time to depart.

The Islands shrank into the distance behind them, and then disappeared over the horizon.

"Next year," Isadore said, "perhaps we will find some new signs from those ancient people."

It was only a fantasy, but Ambry smiled. "I hope we do."

It rained on the second day of their voyage back to the mainland. Not a storm, just a steady shower that raised a fog on the sea. Ambry almost imagined they could catch glimpses of sea dragons swimming beneath the waves. The sailors set up barrels to catch the water and adjusted the sails to better catch the wind.

They'd read about sailing in so many stories of daring captains and clever stowaways, ferocious sea monsters and beautiful mermaids. They still didn't know the names of every spar and sail, but from watching and talking to the sailors, they knew a little of how it worked. Enough that they knew Delia would be pestering them for months asking after details for her stories. And they'd give her what they could, just so long as she let them read the stories as soon as they were done. If they had any time between meetings and letters, that was. But Isadore would make sure they had that time.

Coming back to the palace with clear eyes suddenly seemed almost as much an adventure as their voyage to the Islands. There was still so much for them to share with Isadore, so much for them to learn. And they knew they would savor every moment.

✧

Just as Isadore suspected, he and Ambry weren't able to keep their secret for long.

Very soon after they came up the stairs to the heir's study, Melanie's face broke into a delighted smile. "You two! I suppose you've finally worked all that out?"

"Indeed we have, and we're a lot happier for it." He'd tell her about the snake someday, but there was no point worrying her now. Right now, they had something far more important to think about.

"You knew?" Ambry asked.

"I didn't get to this position by being oblivious to people's secrets," Melanie said. "Especially when they're as blatant about it as you two were. If it had taken you any longer, I might have tied you together like the lovers in that opera about the ruined castle."

Isadore accepted the teasing without complaint. She had the right to be a little pleased with herself after watching them dancing around each other for so many months.

"I had to be sure," he said. "And now I am."

"And your mother?" Melanie asked, with a touch of doubt creeping into her face. Isadore felt Ambry shrink down ever so slightly beside him and touched their hand.

"She is not certain yet," he said. "But I believe we have time to convince her."

"Sometimes it's for the best that she doesn't interfere with your life," Melanie reasoned. "She'll see the truth soon enough. I'm sure of it."

Isadore was less sure, but Melanie had rarely been wrong before.

"Now, I have more good news for you," Melanie said, a gleam in her eye, holding up an envelope marked with Kivern's royal seal.

"Oh?"

"Queen Frida dismissed Alaric Grenner," she announced, savoring every word. How long had she been waiting to tell him this?

He stared at her. "You're not joking? How? When?"

"As soon as she heard, it looks like. One of his assistants told her what exactly happened at the ball. She's sent her personal apologies for his behavior at the summit." She handed him the letter to see for himself.

He read over the words in their formal calligraphy, hardly daring to believe them. Kivernese politicians rarely apologized unless they truly thought it was necessary to save face.

"He didn't tell her himself?" Isadore mused. "I would have thought he'd have wanted to boast about how heroic he was."

"Apparently not. He must have known she'd disapprove. I expect we'll hear more details later. The new ambassador will present himself to you in about a month's time."

Isadore could have laughed for relief. He shook his head, marveling over the revelation. "I'm glad we won't have to deal with him again. Nor will anyone else. But I regret the shame to his family…"

Melanie shrugged. "His children are grown and his wife is dead, so there's not too much harm to be done there. I wouldn't have much sympathy for them even if that wasn't the case. Diplomatic posts in Kivern earn a lot of money and prestige. He can always sell one of those gold-edged coats of his if he needs funds that badly."

"And maybe buy something more fashionable and less gaudy with the proceeds," Isadore said, lip curling in sharp amusement. "That's good at least. Can we expect any repercussions?"

"I doubt there's much he can do on his own. He'll probably try and spread rumors if nothing else, but we'll have to see if anybody believes a disgraced politician they already know to be an unpleasant ass. I'm sure our spies over there are already looking out for any trouble from his allies. I haven't heard anything yet. No news is good news on that front."

"Good, good. As much as I want him gone, I don't want to prejudice our relationship with Kivern any more than it needs to be." Politics must come before personal feelings, at least where Kivern was involved.

"Oh, Karin Miller will see to that. She says she'll send us a report after she meets with Grenner's replacement. We don't have word on who that'll be yet, but I think Queen Frida will be a lot more careful in future about her appointments."

Ambry wasn't as optimistic. "You just wait, I'm sure the next fellow is going to be even worse."

"Somehow I doubt that," Isadore said. "It would be quite an accomplishment to be more of an ass than Alaric Grenner."

"Whoever it is," Melanie said, "it should be some time before we have anything as fraught to discuss as that treaty. Grenner should be grateful his name's still on it."

Isadore felt the same, but he couldn't bring himself to worry about it any longer. "I don't care whose names are on it. It's enough that they all signed it to begin with."

"Hopefully next time we ask the ambassadors to agree on something," Ambry said doubtfully, "they'll remember they worked together once before."

"That's expecting a bit too much of their memories," Melanie said. "But we can hope. Without Grenner in the mix it should be a little easier next time."

She put the envelope away in the drawer she reserved for notable correspondence, and then read through a few more much less interesting reports from Sheridan Beck and August Teller.

"I can handle things here for a little longer," she said when the basket was empty. She cast Isadore and Ambry a meaningful look. "You two should rest. You've had such a long journey."

He knew perfectly well it wasn't rest that she meant for them to enjoy, but he could hardly say anything to challenge her. Ambry rose from their seat, eyes bright.

"Yes, we should. Come with me," Isadore said, and led Ambry through the inner door.

✧

A few paces past the entrance, Isadore pulled aside a worn tapestry Ambry had never thought much of before when they'd come back here to help Melanie or Markus with some task or other. Behind it hid a set of stairs up to the heir's bedchamber.

"For security," Isadore said, smiling at the wonder Ambry didn't bother to hide. "When it was my mother's room, I thought it was hidden by magic. But it's only a secret latch," he said, showing the pin on the back of the curtain that kept it in place unless the seeker knew the right way to hold it.

That knowledge was the finest invitation Ambry had ever received. Their heart pounded in almost dizzy anticipation as they followed Isadore up the spiraling stairs and onto the small landing outside his door. A window looked out onto the walls below.

As Isadore pulled them inside, Lawrence took up his silent post by the door. Of course Isadore's guards went wherever he did. If Ambry had thought about that reality before now, they might have been embarrassed at the idea. But now, they were grateful. The attack in the tavern in the city, and then during the summit, and on the ship… Isadore's life might be luxurious, but it was far from safe. But no matter the danger that came with standing beside Isadore, Ambry was proud to be there.

Isadore's bedchamber was a mirror to the study below. The same six walls, the same wide window, the same well-used hearth.

In place of the study's dragon tapestry hung one woven with a river scene, where fishers and washers worked their trades on the winding banks and children launched little wooden boats into the current, each attached to a beautiful kite that flew proudly overhead. A figure standing untouched amid the waters might have been Saint Avira, one of the protectors of Talland's rivers and lakes.

There were two bookshelves in the room, both filled with books and decorated with little charms and figures, and a heavy desk with a silver pen stand, and a door leading out onto the castle ramparts, from where Isadore could see the gardens and walls and the city beyond.

And in the middle sat a great bed with plush pillows and an embroidered quilt at the foot. A wall-hanging behind it displayed Talland's royal seal in silver and amber on a field of green.

They'd held off on this on the ship, for any number of reasons. Too many people too close, small beds, too much else to do and see. But now, they had all the time and privacy they could want. The guards would not tell tales, nor would the maids dare interrupt.

Isadore took their hand. "And you're certain?" he asked, a flicker of doubt coming into his eyes. Ambry's answer was to reach out and pull him onto the bed. They'd waited more than long enough for this.

It wasn't like Ambry had imagined. They were bolder than they'd thought they'd be, and there was far less fumbling than there had been with any of their schooldays encounters, but it certainly wasn't magic. They didn't know each other in this way yet, had yet to discover what each other liked. It involved a lot of asking and trying, sweet words and quiet pleading. In all of their imaginings, Isadore had been silent but for a few words of praise. How could they never have thought of his voice, smooth and warm and all for them?

There wasn't time now, either to think or to doubt. Not while Isadore pressed warm kisses to all the sensitive parts of their body and they reached for him in reply. Each touch filled them with dozens of ideas for more things they wanted to do, which evaporated just as quickly as pleasure filled their thoughts to the exclusion of all else.

The two of them moved together, laughing and moaning by turns, needing more and more but at the same time wanting this to go on forever, chasing those waves of delight, searching for the surge that would bring them both over the edge.

Isadore pressed closer, and Ambry squirmed around him, letting the sweet sensation drive away all traces of thoughts and worry and doubt.

That peak faded slowly, leaving them awash in warmth and love. Ambry didn't know how much time passed, lying there against Isadore, until finally thoughts began to return.

"What a treasure," Isadore breathed. "And right here in the palace, for so long!"

Before they could stop themself, they were already imagining play-acting that very thing, spinning a story where they were still a servant in the kitchens, and then Isadore would discover them, and admire them, and invite them up into this tower, where they'd enjoy each other all over again. But even in Ambry's imaginings, they didn't stay strangers for long. Their prince was more than a beautiful face and kind hands that could wash away pain at a touch. He was compassionate, and curious, and determined, and always willing to consider another point of view, or look at someone all but forgotten by the world.

They didn't need any imaginings now, not in this moment of bliss they never thought they'd experience.

The two of them stayed there, curled together, for a little longer, until they couldn't justify it any longer, and Isadore brought them into his well-stocked washroom to clean off before making their way back downstairs to work. Ambry carefully put away any more thoughts of that large bath for later and turned their focus diligently to letters and documents.

Melanie, to their relief, didn't say anything, but the small smiles she kept casting them said more than enough. Ambry figured she had more than enough reason to be so pleased, if she'd been waiting for this longer than the two of them had even known this was anything more than a brief infatuation.

Melanie wasn't the only one. Oh, Delia was never going to let this go. She'd know the moment she saw them. And she was going to ask them for every detail. But of course they'd never share. This was for them and Isadore alone.

✧

Isadore should have expected that Melanie's perceptiveness would extend beyond his new relationship with Ambry. Even though the bruises had faded, somehow she still knew that it hadn't simply been the beauty of the Islands that had brought his secret longing out into the open.

When Ambry left to unpack their things, she turned to him and asked, "Isadore, what else happened when you were in the Islands?"

"What do you mean?" he asked, holding onto the vain hope that she wasn't asking what she so clearly was.

"Don't pretend it was nothing. I know you would never have admitted your feelings without something to push you to it. And your guards have been twitchier than ever," she added, with a glance at Lawrence by the door. "What happened to make them so concerned?"

He sighed. There was no use hiding the story now. "I didn't want to worry you. I... I was bitten by a goldstrike."

Melanie's face went pale. "They're deadly. How–"

"My magic, we think. It was– it was awful." He ran a hand over his face. "We– Ambry and I, we were out by the western ruins in the Feather Forest."

"I thought the sailors would have taught you how to avoid the nests," Melanie said, frowning.

"No, it wasn't like that. One of the sailors put it in Ambry's bag." He told the story in as few words as he could. He didn't want to relive that day even in thought, despite the good that had come from it. "He thought Ambry was wrong for living as they do. He thought I was wrong for supporting them."

Melanie made a sound of anger. "Idiots, all of them. What did he expect to gain from that? That you would suddenly become a devotee of Saint Baven and persecute those he deems perverted?"

Isadore shook his head. "Even his own faithful weren't on his side. The sailor who gave him up was also from the Southern Order. And a devotee of Baven as well."

"Admirable." Melanie didn't sound particularly impressed. "If only he could have stopped it before it happened."

"I don't think he knew the other truly meant to do it, and he wasn't just making a joke."

"A poor joke, even if it was."

"I know."

"And the sailor? What are they going to do with him? If Saint Tarya doesn't come down from the heavens to smite him first." The look on Melanie's face said very clearly that she would like nothing more than to deal with him herself.

"He's been taken in by the Guard. I don't know what they plan to do."

Melanie studied him. "You'd be well within your rights to dictate his fate. But you won't?"

For just a moment, Isadore thought of exactly what he would like to do to that hateful coward, and then he forced himself to be calm. "I could not be fair or just. Let the Guard and my mother decide, and I'll be pleased to never think of him again."

"That's one of the wisest decisions you've ever made," Melanie said with a wan smile. "I wish you wouldn't, but it's right."

He accepted the praise, still wishing he could do more.

✧

Just as Ambry anticipated, Melanie wasn't the only person to sniff out something new in Ambry's demeanor upon their return. The day after they arrived at the palace, Ambry went down to the kitchens to join their old friends for dinner, and to tell them the news. They and Isadore had decided it would be more trouble than it was worth to keep it a secret any longer. Those closest to them wouldn't judge, and anyone who did could be dealt with in their turn.

But there was no judgment here, only joy. Delia and the others were just as delighted at the news as Ambry had expected.

"I told you this would happen! Of course he loves you," she said, after nearly smothering them in a tight hug.

"You told me a lot of things," Ambry protested cheerfully. "Not all of those came true." They'd been careful about what details of the voyage they shared. If she ever got wind of what had happened at the Islands, she'd never let them go without wringing the entire story out of them, and they weren't sure they wanted to tell it just yet.

"But the important ones did. I'm so happy for you."

"You're not upset I kissed a prince before you found a princess?" they joked.

"Oh, I'm still planning on that," she returned without even a moment's pause. "You just wait. They'll be talking about the wedding for decades."

Ella insisted on baking a celebratory cake. As long, of course, as Ambry helped dust the cabinets and shelves, a duty which they accepted without complaint. Patrice, Marion, and Alice offered their own congratulations, while Erik leaned on a broom in the doorway and clucked over the exuberance of youth.

"You're not so old yourself there," Patrice scolded. Erik made a clownish kissing face at her, which set Danny laughing. She sighed, and didn't protest.

"Are you going to move into his bedroom?" Delia asked, stacking washed and dried dishes to put back in the cabinets. "What's it like?"

Ambry shook their head. "I'm keeping the room at the bottom of the tower. It's not far away, and I like the space."

"A wise decision," Patrice said. "Even if I loved them that way, I'm sure I couldn't handle having a man hanging around me every minute of the day." She gave Erik a look as she said it.

The cake was one of the best Ella had ever made. It might have been better than the treats she'd made for the ambassadors, or it might just have been that Ambry could eat it without the strain of worrying whether the treaty would ever be signed. Delia once again accused Ella of keeping the good ingredients for herself, to which she gave no response, but the shine in her eyes said enough.

Delia nearly stopped breathing when Ambry told her that Isadore had enjoyed her stories. It was one of the few times they'd been able to get more than a few sentences out without her interjecting at every turn.

"The one about the hunter who turned into a tiger was his favorite, I think," Ambry said. "And the one where the fairies caught the thieves."

"I'd like to read those," Alice said. Danny nodded in agreement.

"Buy me the paper and ink, and I'll copy it out," Delia promised. When Ambry told her that Minerva Corey and Markus in the archives might be able to help her make printed copies, she looked like they'd said she really was going to marry that imaginary princess.

"I could sell them in the market," she said. "And maybe with a royal seal of approval?"

Ambry laughed and shook their head. "I don't think he'd go that far. But I know he'd be first in line to buy copies."

"Oh, I'll give them to him for free. But the rest of you better get your chimes ready."

"Ambitious girl," Patrice said approvingly. "Print and sell all you want but be sure you don't forget your cleaning."

"If I sell enough, I'm going to move into a little cottage and hire someone to cook and clean for me while I write all day long," Delia declared.

"And we'll all miss you when that happens," Patrice said. "But for now, there's floors to sweep and dishes to wash, so finish up and get back to it."

Delia gave a tragic sigh, but Ambry could see that she was still smiling.

✧

"Isadore!"

Abigail leapt from the carriage, braids flying behind her as she flew down the path to tackle Isadore in a tight embrace. Celeste followed behind at a more reasonable pace, adjusting her bag on her shoulder, but her smile was no less bright than her sister's. Snowflakes landed on her dark cloud of hair, dusting it with white.

Isadore held out an arm to bring Celeste into the hug. "I'm so glad to see you two," he said. "You must have a lot to tell."

"And you need to tell us about the Islands," Celeste insisted. "How did you manage without us?"

"Let's go inside before you freeze and become a wandering winter spirit," Isadore said, brushing snow from Celeste's hair. "And I have someone for you to meet."

"You said in your letter. A lover, Isadore?" Abigail teased. "Tell us everything!"

Isadore shook his head, smiling. "Come and meet them first."

Celeste hurried back to the carriage to help her maid with her bags, despite the maid's protests that she shouldn't trouble herself. Once they were inside the palace, she finally conceded and let the maid bring them to her chambers, while the twins followed Isadore to the Queen's tower.

Seraphina's maid served tea, and the two princesses gave measured recountings of their studies and friends and adventures. Over the past two years, Isadore noted, their stories had gotten more calculated and careful, in the hopes of avoiding their mother's disapproval. He'd had to learn the same after earning several stern lectures after letting things slip about his first year that he probably shouldn't have. On the other hand, he told Melanie everything, even if it sometimes took him a while to admit it, and her advice had guided him through more than one difficult situation.

So, he wasn't at all surprised that his sisters waited until they were alone in his tower to tell him their true thoughts. Celeste, who'd been all but silent during their tea with their mother, recounted a breathless tale of her friends rescuing a kitten from a professor's dog and keeping it secretly in their cottage, hiding it every time the matron came by.

"They thought she would never find out, but there was fur everywhere! Lena tried to tell her it was just her hair, and she said, 'Miss Cassey, are you telling me your black hair turns calico in the night?'" Both of them burst into giggles at Celeste's impression.

"She took the kitten for herself," Abigail said. "We were so sure she was going to leave it out in the wild. But the next time we saw it, it had a little bow on its neck and a cozy basket in the window!"

Isadore had heard from his female school friends that Matron was secretly kind, despite her sharp voice and gnarled hands and her insistence at picking out every violation of the rules, no matter how tiny. But he'd never believed it until now.

"I still don't know what I want to study," Abigail said, picking idly through the tray of pens Melanie had left out on her desk. "Or maybe it's more that I want to study everything."

"You can study as much as you want," Isadore told her. "At the University, or the archives here. Or you could travel. Didn't you say you always wanted to visit the Great Library of Arrawey or the Temple of Learning in Kivern?"

"I do," Abigail sighed, eyes going distant at the thought of those faraway places. "But I want to do something with it. Not just stash it all in my head like some oracle in the forest."

"You could still go there," Isadore said. He was determined she wouldn't deny herself that just because she wasn't sure of her goal. "Talk to the people there. Maybe something will inspire you, something you've never even heard of before."

She thought about it and nodded. "Yes. I'll do that."

"And are you still painting? The mountains in Arrawey are supposed to be an artist's dream," he added.

Abigail laughed. "Enough, Isadore. If I paint anything, I'll make sure you get to see it, just don't push."

He thought of the set of fine brushes he'd bought for her New Year's gift and smiled.

A knock came at the door. Isadore looked up and welcomed Ambry in. The twins leapt to their feet and surrounded them.

"Oh, they're just as handsome as you said!" Abigail said, making Ambry's ears turn pink.

"Give them some space," Isadore said. "You'll have the whole month to get to know them."

He needn't have worried. By the time Melanie came through the door with a basket of letters and a snowflake-patterned cane, Ambry had told them a few of the happier stories from their voyage to the Islands and Abigail and Celeste had already conspired to invite Ambry to an afternoon at the princesses' favorite teahouse. Clearly, they planned to try and wring all sorts of secrets from them about their brother. He found he didn't mind that as much as he thought he would. He was glad to have his sisters home again, and even more if they could be friends to Ambry. He could endure a little sibling teasing for his lover's sake.

"We'll find you tomorrow," Abigail said as she pulled Celeste through the door. "I don't care how much work Isadore wants to give you, this is more important."

"I won't complain about that," Isadore said. "As long as you bring them back in one piece."

"We will, we will," Celeste promised, and the princesses vanished through the door, no doubt off to the archives to hide among the bookshelves until their mother summoned them again.

Chapter Eighteen

✧

A few days after Ambry's outing with the princesses, the first major storm of winter blew in from the mountains, stripping away the last of the autumn leaves and leaving the bare branches covered in a glittering layer of ice. It was far from the worst storm the city had seen, but it was early enough in the season that many people would not be prepared for it. Isadore had warm clothing distributed to the palace servants. Queen Seraphina ordered the City Guard to provide fuel to the people of the city to protect them from the coming cold.

Business had slowed as shopkeepers and traders closed up their stores midday and went home to their families, but the work of government never ceased. Isadore and Melanie had spent much of the day in the archives searching for answers to a thorny legal issue. A generations-old contract made reference to an even older city statute that had since been destroyed in a fire. Months of searching had revealed no copies of the text itself, only vague references, so the parties involved had asked Isadore for help, hoping the palace archives would provide the answers they sought. So far, they had found nothing but dusty half-destroyed pages that told them nothing at all of use.

"I'm half-tempted to tell them to just split the company and be done with it," Isadore grumbled, setting down one packet of papers and reaching for another. "At least that way they won't be arguing about how to run it."

"It might well end up that way," Melanie sighed. She shut yet another box of papers with a derisive snap and handed it to Ambry to return to the shelf above her head. "It must have been filed in the wrong box, or maybe it was lost ages ago and nobody thought to report it. Markus and I can keep looking. You and Ambry should return to the tower and see if there's any news from the city."

Isadore didn't expect much, and when he, Ambry, and Lawrence returned to the tower study, all that Kieran had delivered fit into one small basket on Melanie's desk. That was one good thing that came of the weather: that all but the most urgent couriers would be kept from their routes. Later in the season they would be ready to endure even the worst storms, but for now, the roads lay empty.

Then he spotted the one letter that had been set apart from the rest. The one that had been delivered not by Kieran but by a palace page. It was unmarked, but Isadore knew at once that it had come from his mother. He opened it to find his suspicions correct. And then, as he read the short, direct lines, he found something he hadn't expected at all.

"What is it?" Ambry asked. "Bad news?"

"Not at all." Isadore set the letter aside and smiled. "My mother wants to invite you to our New Year's dinner after the speeches." She ought to have sent a message to Ambry themself, he thought, but this was a good sign. With one small gesture, the Queen had signaled that she finally might have come to accept Isadore's choice of partner. He wondered with a smile if his sisters had had anything to do with that.

"I'd be honored to attend," Ambry said. Isadore saw their interest where once there would have been only anxiety on their face. So much had changed since the two of them had first met, and he still felt as if he was learning new things about them with every day, every word, every kiss.

He studied the rest of the envelopes, each decorated with an assortment of seals and crests, all of them demanding immediate attention. But some would have to wait, Isadore decided, glancing at the snow clinging to the frosty windows.

"There's no way we can get replies out tonight, not in this weather. I'll pick out the most pressing so we can have them ready for tomorrow," he told Ambry. "Can you go around and see if there's anything in the palace that needs help?" He'd rather go himself, but he could only imagine how disruptive that would be. Ambry nodded and hurried off. While they were away, Isadore began to sort through the letters. He read through maybe half a dozen of them, noting down possible responses for Melanie to review later, then pulled his eyes away from the endless papers and settled onto the couch to rest a while. Outside, the snow fell in fat fluffy clumps that piled on the rooftops and statues and fountains, draping them in a thick mantle of white. Far better that than a storm of ice that would make the roads and canals treacherous or impassible. When the winds died down, the city's children would enjoy this snow. It was the sort you could dance in, catch on your tongue, shape into little houses and littler people to live in them. And the break from lessons would certainly be a cause for celebration. For the first time in a long while, he thought of the old winter estate where he and his mother and sisters had spent long festive weeks before politics had made that impossible.

"Isadore?" Ambry stood at the door.

Isadore looked up. "Anything to report?"

They shook their head. "Nothing major. The fires are all going strong and there's wood to spare. The kitchens are stocked." They smiled. "Jonah's excited. He wants to build a snow castle once he's allowed outside."

"Good, good." He had seen Marjorie's son only a handful of times in the past years, at first as a swaddled infant and then as a charming child more interested in his doll than the prince he was brought before. Soon he'd be old enough to join the other children at their lessons. Since his great-grandmother's time, the children of the staff and guardsmen had been permitted to join the diplomats' children under the care of the palace's best tutors, and now even the snobbiest of nobles could imagine no better way to manage their younglings while at court.

He sent Ambry back to the kitchens for mugs of hot spiced wine and a platter of currant teacakes. When they returned, he invited them to sit. They had both been working all afternoon, but Ambry had woken before him and their lunch had been cut short. It wasn't fair that he should rest when Ambry could not.

Ambry curled beside him on the couch and accepted the second mug when Isadore passed it to them. The winds outside whistled against the windows while the fire roared heartily on the other wall, casting the room in a warm glow. The oldest of the palace cats, a tawny striped creature not much more than fur and bones, had arranged itself on a cushion by the fire and lay there purring happily.

"When I was young," Isadore said, "we'd spend our winters at the old Lord Brennan's winter manor."

"Lord Brennan?" Ambry questioned. Of course. They must be imagining the cruel man who now held those lands.

"His father," Isadore clarified. "Oswald Brennan. He was a friend of ours, and nothing like his son. We stopped when the younger Lord Brennan took over, because we couldn't abide his policies – or his personal behavior, for that matter – and obviously we didn't want to be seen to be favoring him." That, and the younger Brennan's angry response, had been a political battle he did not care to revisit. There were still regional officials, allies of Brennan, who no longer trusted the Crown.

"What was it like?" Ambry asked. They took a cake from the platter and nibbled around the edges. Their face when they realized it was stuffed with jam was enough to take away all of Isadore's angst over the Brennan affair.

"The winter manor was wonderful. Everything glittered with icicles and snow. The forest looked like something out of a storybook. I spent ages exploring, pretending I was a scout searching for a fairy village." More memories rose up as he spoke, warm and inviting. "The lake froze over every year. Old Brennan's wife taught me to skate on it. Or tried to. It took me a very long time to figure it out. I once found one of the groundskeeper's cats out there, trying to catch the fish under the ice!" He smiled at the memory. And then sighed, at the sadder tale that came into his mind.

"I was thinking of one of my last years there. I was ten, full of dreams of leadership, of how I'd be the best and most beloved king in history. Kind to everyone, with no need to resort to the violence of past times." How sure he'd been that such a thing was possible, back then. "My mother thought it was time for me to learn the harsher side of ruling. So she brought me out to the courtyard where Brennan's guard was going to whip a cook who'd been caught stealing and selling expensive ingredients."

Ambry winced. "That's terrible." Isadore was gripped with a profound hope that they had never seen anyone face the same. He could hardly imagine that they could ever do something that anyone but cursed old Grenner might see as worthy of such a punishment, but he wouldn't ask now.

He nodded. "I thought the same. I begged the guard not to, but she wouldn't be swayed. That day, it was snowing far worse than this, and the wind was enough to half-flay your face if you turned into it unprotected. It was only supposed to take a few minutes, not nearly enough for the cold to be dangerous. The guards stripped him, and she raised the whip... I saw this blinding flash tear through my vision like lightning. I didn't know what it was at that point, only that it frightened me. I heard the cook scream. And I ran. I don't know where I thought I was going. There was nowhere to go, not in that weather. I reached the frozen lake and decided to turn back. And that was when I slipped off the dock and broke my leg on the ice." Isadore heard Ambry's breath catch.

He shivered at the memories of pain and cold and fear, and took a warm sip from his mug, letting the heat sink into him. "Looking back, I'm very lucky I didn't fall straight through. I somehow managed to crawl back to shore and find a little bit of shelter, but even at that age I knew it wouldn't be enough to last me the night. I waited for someone to come, or for the storm to end, but all I could hear was the roaring wind. It was so cold that every inch of my skin stung with it, and I couldn't stop shivering. I truly thought I was going to die out there."

He gazed out the window, watching the flakes cling to the glass and melt there, grateful once again for the warmth of the fire and the comfort of the cushions. "Dominick saved me. All the other guards my mother sent had gone off into the forest, but Dominick remembered how I had liked the lake, and argued with his sergeant to be allowed to search alone. It was the only time before or since that he's ever argued against an order." And Isadore owed his life to that. "He found me hiding half-frozen and barely awake in the boathouse and carried me back to the manor."

Isadore remembered only flashes of that: the light of Dominick's lantern through the door, his voice rough-edged with relief. The world falling away as Dominick lifted him into his arms. Waking bundled in blankets beside a roaring fire with two of the manor's cats curled heavy and warm against his side, Theodora sitting watchful nearby. She had begged his forgiveness and Seraphina's for not being able to run after him, even though it had been Seraphina's guards who had stopped her, for as skilled a caretaker she was, the cold would surely have threatened her health and left her as vulnerable as her charge.

He hadn't learned until later what Dominick had suffered in rescuing him. "He gave me his hat and gloves, and because of that he lost a fingertip and most of an ear to frostbite." The sting of guilt at the thought had long since faded, but an echo of it remained there still. "I felt terrible. I apologized to him as soon as I was well enough to. And he told me not to worry about him, because it was his duty and honor to protect me."

From the doorway, Lawrence gave an almost imperceptible nod. He had joined Isadore's guard the year after that terrible winter, but no doubt he had heard the story from Dominick.

Isadore chuckled. "I still worry about him, of course, but I try to be quiet about it, to respect him."

He smiled at the flicker of surprise on Ambry's face. "You didn't expect that? He's a good man. Frightening, of course, to a misbehaving boy expected someday to take up the mantle of leadership. Too stern, sometimes, true. And rigid against change even when change might be needful. But deeply loyal, and strong. I trust him with my life. And I'm certain he would protect you too, were you threatened. Any of my guards would." Which would never need to happen, if Isadore had his way.

Across the room, Lawrence was smiling, a subtle thing that Isadore was sure Ambry could not see. He sighed and reached for another teacake. "Mother was far from pleased. Grateful of course that I was safe, but angry at the fuss I'd caused. And then there were the weeks in bed... my tutors made the most of that, at least. By the end of it I could recite most of the Ballad of the Mountain Army from memory." He took a breath and sang the opening lines, "*In the darkness rose a fortress, built far from watchful eyes. Behind its walls a cruel lord ruled and heeded not the cries.*" He was far from an expert musician, though he could follow a tune well enough. Celeste might be the true musician of the family, but Seraphina had made certain her children were taught in all the common ballads, as well as several historical ones she thought important.

"You were recovering for that long? You couldn't use your healing magic?"

Isadore shook his head. "The gift hadn't fully developed at that point. Since that lash, I realized I could see pain, others' and my own, but it took me a long time to work out how to blot out the vision when I didn't want to see it. It sapped a lot of my energy. I didn't learn how to heal until months later. And even if I had known then, it's far more effort to use it on myself than it is to use it on others. My teacher said that's because healing draws on the subject's internal energy as well as the healer's. To heal myself, I need to provide both."

"It doesn't seem fair," Ambry said. "You can take away other people's pain but you're left to suffer your own."

"It's not all that bad," Isadore reassured them. "I *can* heal myself, it's just more difficult and tiring. And if I need to, I can call on the best doctors in the land, so I suppose I don't have any reason to complain."

Ambry looked for a moment like they wanted to argue, but said nothing.

"At least there was one good thing that came of all that," Isadore continued. "We don't whip people anymore. I insisted on that as soon as I was old enough that Mother would listen, just before I went to the University." He smiled and glanced at the bookshelf. "She made me earn it, though. I had to research the issue and present my evidence before she'd consider revising our rules, even just within the palace staff and Guard."

He and the Queen disagreed on many things, but she'd taught him to argue well and listen better, and she'd always done the same in return.

"I spent a lot of time in the archives that year. That's how I met Melanie. I couldn't have made my case without her help. But she made me work for it." She'd never given him a direct answer to any of the questions he'd asked. At most she'd lead him to the right book, or author, or maybe suggest a philosopher or politician that might be of interest, but she'd never done his work for him. At first, he'd hated it. By the end of the project, he'd known he wanted nobody else but her as his personal secretary. He'd asked, and she'd given him the first direct answer she had all year – a yes.

"I learned a lot about how the other kingdoms punished wrongdoing. Have you ever heard of knifeblade vows?"

"That's in Arrawey, isn't it?" Ambry asked. "I remember that from *The Tale of the Buried Stone*. The lords and the servants swore oaths to each other over a ceremonial knife, and if one of them broke the oath, the other cut him with the knife to leave a scar."

Isadore nodded. "Talland used to have the practice too, but it died out over the years."

"That story made it sound almost romantic. I didn't know it was a real practice."

"It's much rarer now, but it still happens, especially in the northeast. Scars are still thought to be shameful in Arrawey. They usually hide them with clothing or makeup. When I read that, I asked Melanie if those stories sounded strange in Kivern. They see scars as honorable." He thought of Grenner's dueling scars, and once again thanked the saints that he would never have to see him again. "She laughed at me and gave me a book on Kivernese military training. It was written by Karin Miller's father. He's Kivernese, and he spent decades writing their history so foreigners like us could see them in their own words."

"I read some stories about ancient horse warriors. They seemed... brutal."

"They were, but according to what I read, a lot of our stories about them aren't quite right. Miller said they only punish with a whip as an act of redemption. It might come from the story of Saint Seryan and the lost ring, or the story might have been rewritten to match the practice. Whichever way it happened, it meant that a soldier's willingness to suffer for their errors made them stronger, in that philosophy. It was intriguing. But of course that did nothing to support what I wanted to do." He took a drink of wine to ease his throat; the fire was low and giving off ash, but he was comfortable and warm with Ambry beside him, and he didn't want to move just yet. "Of everything I read, the accounts from Larsellan helped the most. They'd done away with beatings and whippings centuries ago. The historical texts said it was a practical measure. Injured workers aren't of as much use in the fields and workshops, and the resources that would be spent treating wounds and infection were better left for illness and accidents." He smiled, reliving those glorious moments when he'd first felt an argument come together on the page, stitching history, philosophy, and rhetoric into an argument that might at last convince the Queen to shift her stance. "And that was the largest part of the speech I made to Mother."

"And it worked," Ambry said, looking at him with such pride that Isadore treasured his victory all over again.

"It did. She and I drafted the new policies, and we announced them the next month. The Guard gave us some trouble about it, but I wouldn't back down. And do you know what happened? Things started working a lot more smoothly. I wasn't sure exactly why until I talked to the old housekeeper and the captain of the Royal Guard. People were reporting issues that they saw. Before, they'd ignore things that didn't seem like their responsibility out of fear that they'd be blamed and beaten for bringing them to light, or that their friends would be." He just wished he'd stayed involved in the day-to-day running of the palace after he went to university. He'd come back assuming everything would just keep working the way it had done before he'd left, and his work in the heir's tower with Melanie had kept him from seeing what was wrong until Ambry had so daringly brought it before him.

Ambry nodded. "I understand that. I mean – I won't hide anything, not again. But–"

"I wouldn't blame you if you had, back then," Isadore said. *And I still do not blame you for your stolen badge*, he thought, but didn't say. No need to make Ambry remember that terrible night any longer than necessary. "I won't use pain for punishment," he said, some of that ferocity leaking into his voice though he knew there was nobody here he needed to convince.

"That's a very good thing," Ambry said. "I used to work in Lady Mohren's household. Her housekeeper was very quick to punish people for any reasons she could find. I learned there's a certain feeling in the air when people think they'll be hit for mistakes. Sometimes we'd protect each other, cover for problems so nobody was punished. But mostly people tried to protect themselves and let others get hurt as long as they didn't take the blame."

He hadn't known. "I've met her a few times. Adrian courted her daughter for a few months right after we graduated. I never thought she would treat her staff that way."

"I don't think she cared," Ambry said. "She never said anything to the servants that wasn't an order."

"It's no excuse." The fire had all but burned itself out; Isadore got up and threw another log into the hearth. "If only I could do something about it. But I doubt she would appreciate my bringing it up." And he would not risk somebody coming to harm if he did pry into her household affairs like that. She was a proud woman who would certainly seek revenge on anyone she thought might be telling stories that tarnished her reputation as a beacon of pious charity.

He took another sip from his cup. There was so much in the world that he couldn't fix, Crown Prince or not. Better to focus on what he could, or at least that was what Melanie would say. And he reminded himself that with Ambry's help, he has already fixed so many broken things, both in the palace and beyond.

"How did I talk so long about that dreary topic?" he said, half to himself.

"I'll always listen to history," Ambry said. "Especially if you're telling it." They stood and leaned up to kiss him.

"History is the most important thing in the world, because it is the world," Isadore quoted. "My mother likes to say that. But I think we can leave it aside for a while, and do something else? It'll be a while before Melanie and Markus are ready for us."

Ambry took his meaning without another word, and the two of them went together through the inner door and up to the heir's chamber.

⟡

Ambry returned to their room to find that one of Isadore's maids had piled wood ready in the stand by the hearth. They pulled the curtains closed and stripped out of their jacket and boots before lighting the fire. It took a while for the flames to catch, but finally Ambry had a warm blaze going. They sat in an armchair with a book, intending to read a chapter or two, but their thoughts kept drifting from the words and back to the warm things they had shared with Isadore earlier. They hoped the coming holiday would give them even more chances to sneak away with their lover. At last they gave up trying to focus and curled into bed, where their distracted imaginings could wisp away into sleep.

They woke to dull skies and a chill in the air, and the sight of yesterday's snow blanketing the gardens outside made them very grateful for the warm shirts Darby Allister had sent for them in the last package of Isadore's winter clothing. They were as plain as Allister could manage without utterly breaking their own heart in letting anything that might pass as ordinary leave their hands. The soft fabric still betrayed hints of color around the hems, and Allister hadn't been able to resist embroidering two sprigs of tiny leaves in gold and green at the collar.

They spent the morning listening from the couch as Isadore paced back and forth before the great window, reciting the words Melanie's staff had written for him for his New Year's speech. He'd claimed them as an impromptu audience, freeing them from their other tasks for a short while to listen. Ambry hadn't thought before about how much planning and effort went into this part of the celebrations. It had always sounded so natural to them when Isadore and the Queen spoke, though of course part of them had always known that the words were all prepared and rehearsed beforehand. The Queen and Prince hardly had time to write their own speeches, though they had input in their content. Hearing Isadore practicing, occasionally stumbling, suggesting modifications here and there, Ambry could appreciate the artistry in it.

"...always in search of greater prosperity, greater opportunity, to create a rich and meaningful life for all... can we change that?" Isadore looked up from the paper. "It sounds like I'm saying their lives aren't already meaningful."

Melanie rolled her pen in her fingers. "Hmm, I think it sounds good as it is. We will have to rework that paragraph on the beauty of the land, though, it sounds a little trite after that last round of storms in the Wrightwood Forest."

"I agree, we shouldn't brush over that so easily. I'd still like to talk about beauty, but not in a way that'll make people who lost their homes feel ignored."

Ambry had been there when Melanie read the reports of the damage. Nobody had been killed, thankfully, but a lot of houses had been destroyed and the waterways muddied with debris.

"You could talk about resilience instead," they suggested. "How the storms won't stop the forest growing back, and they won't stop the people who live there."

"I like that," Isadore said, gracing them with a brief smile that set their heart pounding for just a moment before they managed to bring themself back to the present. He cleared his throat and read another page, his beautiful voice rolling through the words and turning what might have been boring and routine into poetry. "...it is our duty to bring about bright changes for this kingdom and its people," he finished.

Marion's comic came into their mind and Ambry couldn't help laughing.

"What is it?" Isadore peered at the paper as if expecting a joke to magically appear in the text, and then turned to them, puzzled.

"I'm sorry. Er," How to explain it? "There's this comic serial that's really popular in the city. A dirty comic. It's called Bright Changes." Melanie was looking at them now. "I don't think you should use that phrase." They could just imagine how the others would react to hearing that in a speech, especially when it was pure coincidence.

Isadore made a face Ambry couldn't quite read, somewhere between amused and chagrined. "Ah. I see. That would have been embarrassing. Good job catching it."

Melanie, on the other hand, didn't bother hiding her amused smile. "We'll change the wording," she said, taking a note. "I'd never heard about that. Thank you, Ambry."

"It's not the sort of thing I like," Ambry added quickly. "But my friends like to talk about it."

Isadore paused. "You can read whatever you like, you know. I won't tell you that you can't or judge you for it. I might actually be interested in that. You should see some of the stories my friends at university read. And wrote. Those were absolutely filthy." He grinned, making Ambry laugh again.

"You can keep that between you and Adrian," Melanie said, looking over the top of her paper just so Isadore could see her rolling her eyes.

"I never said it was—"

"Yes, but I've met him. Several times." She waved a hand dismissively, smiling. "Go back to reading, Isadore."

Concern flickered in Isadore's eyes. "He hasn't done anything inappropriate, has he?"

"What, Adrian?" She shook her head. "No, he wouldn't. He's charming, but a little too young for me." She nodded at the speech. "Keep going. I want to be able to finish the next draft by tomorrow night."

Ambry tried to pay attention to the rest of the speech, but their thoughts had caught quite firmly on the image of Isadore sharing dirty comics with his friends. What sort of things had he enjoyed? The vast majority of Ella and Marion's favorites had been far too absurd to get any reaction from Ambry besides embarrassment, but there had been a few books Delia enjoyed that they had found pleasing, and a few others from the hidden back shelf of their favorite bookstore. Elegant pictures of people in intense pleasure, their personalities shining through in every line. The stories blushingly erotic but also somehow sweet instead of dirty, rich and passionate and warming. They hadn't suggested anything of the sort yet to Isadore when they were in bed together, never mind trying it, but they couldn't deny they had thought of it.

"Ambry?"

They looked up, realizing they had heard nothing of what Isadore had been saying for the past few minutes. "I... er... it's very good so far," they lied, knowing it wouldn't help. Their pink ears surely gave them away.

"I'm boring you," Isadore said, but he sounded more amused than chagrined. He raised an eyebrow at Melanie. "Maybe we need to rework this part? I wouldn't want the crowds falling asleep in the square. Imagine what Ostberg would say."

Ambry shook their head. "No, no, it's good. I'm sorry, I was distracted."

"That's all right. To tell the truth, I'm rather tired of it too."

"You've only got a page left," Melanie said, unimpressed. "Read that and then we can do something else. I've got some tax ledgers that need reviewing."

"On second thought," Isadore said, "I wouldn't mind more speechwriting."

This time, Ambry made certain to listen as Isadore read out the last page of the speech. But if they focused more on the sound of his voice than the words he spoke, he didn't need to know.

Chapter Nineteen

✧

All of Talland celebrated the New Year, even those parts that disdained the other seasonal festivals as frivolous distractions from honest work. And the royal city celebrated in the grandest ways of all. Every available surface not already dusted with snow had been draped in garlands or decorated with good luck charms. Snow foxes for good fortune in the new year, pine needle poppets for good health, fat-bellied cats for hopes of wealth.

The Spring Festival celebrated new growth, the Autumn Festival celebrated the harvest, but the Winter Festival overshadowed them all with the sheer size and energy of the celebration. It fell close enough to the turning of the year that the two had blended together into two long weeks of uninterrupted celebration, beginning when the festival torches were lit and ending when the sun set on the first day of the new year.

Ambry had always loved the Winter Festival. At the first signs of cold winter winds, their mother would hang painted wooden snowflakes in the windows. When the family gathered, she baked little cakes for the cousins to share. However empty their cupboards might be, somehow there was always enough for everyone to be satisfied with their share.

Their oldest aunt always brought a basket of little packages wrapped many times over in colored paper. The children passed them around in a circle, each taking off a layer, until the last one came off and revealed the prize to its lucky winner. Half of the fun had been in guessing what was inside, seeing who could figure it out with the most layers still untouched.

Most of the others tore the paper off as hastily as their little hands could go, leaving scraps littered across the rug, but Ambry had always peeled theirs off carefully and kept the paper for other games.

Sometimes their cousins would fight over the toys. Ambry remembered one time when they'd snatched a wooden horse from one of their cousins. They'd felt guilty as soon as she started crying, and tried to give it back, but their mother had already seen and she hadn't been happy with them.

Most years the children had traded the prizes among themselves afterward so that everyone got their favorite. They'd only later learned that the gifts had been cunningly wrapped with just enough layers to ensure that each person in the circle ended up with one prize.

Now that they were grown, the holiday was less about games and toys and more about choosing the perfect gifts for their friends and writing letters to those they hadn't spoken to in a while.

Even in stern Lady Mohren's household, there had been time for celebration and good food. She'd always seemed kinder and more forgiving around those weeks, though Ambry had suspected that was more due to the ancient superstitions that those who were angry during a festival would be cursed with bad luck for the coming year than out of anything to do with the goodness of her heart. But that hadn't mattered, not when it meant that busy days of decorating, polishing, and baking that filled the halls with the scents of spice and sugar alternated with long days of rest and storytelling and gift-giving.

But none of that could compare to spending the New Year in Talland's royal palace, with their friends preparing endless trays of treats, spending it at the side of their prince and lover. And if the cold weather meant they sought out each other's warmth more often in the evenings, that was yet another blessing.

They'd worked for weeks to find a suitable gift, passing by table after table in the never-ending winter market with Delia and Ella and Marion. Only after they'd turned down a dozen suggestions did they realize why nothing in the glittering spread of treasures called out to them. They passed by the artist who'd made the dragonfly hairclip they still wore most days. His table was hidden under a forest of little trees and an army of wire insects and animals. Butterflies with gems threaded onto their lacy wings, cats toying at dangling beads, flowers that spilled little rainbows when the light hit the glass inside their petals.

And Ambry remembered the little amber tree that still waited on the desk in their room. They'd bought it for Isadore, back before the treaty summit, but they'd lost courage before giving it to him, and then in the rush of the treaty and the trip to the Crested Islands, they'd all but forgotten it.

The artist smiled at them as he worked at some half-finished creation in his hands. After making sure that Delia and Ella were busy at another stall, Ambry bought one of the cats, the one with the coiled tail and the jade ball between its outstretched paws. Delia would adore it.

"You look happy," Ella said when they met up again. "Found something for your prince?"

"I did," Ambry said.

"And you're not going to tell us what it is?" Delia said, with an attempt at a pout that was washed away as soon as the scent of frying dough reached them. "Let's get snowdrifts before the line gets too long," she said, pulling Ella along with her.

Ambry agreed. They'd always loved snowdrifts, the craggy golden treats piled with mounds of sugar. Especially the lopsided ones Aunt Polly made. Their mother had somehow mastered the art of eating them without getting even a speck of sugar on her clothing, a trick none of the rest of the family could ever manage.

Patrice fussed at them when they arrived back at the palace a little later than they should have, and threatened extra work, but she relented when Delia offered her the gift of a new scarf to hold back her hair in the kitchen.

"What makes you think I'm susceptible to bribery, girl?" she scolded.

"It's a New Year's gift," Delia said innocently.

"Four days early?" Patrice said. Then she sighed. "Off with you. There's enough that needs doing to keep you busy for a while, I'm sure of that."

Grinning at her victory, Delia hurried back to work.

Inspired by Delia's irreverence, Ambry went to their room to fetch the tree and put it back in its box before climbing the heir's tower to Isadore's study. When they arrived, they found Isadore sitting by the window reading a report. There weren't many of those to go around during the holiday celebrations, so Isadore had insisted Melanie take a free day for herself.

"Anything important?" Ambry asked.

"Not especially," Isadore said, sitting up and stretching. "This came from Captain Dreisand. Mostly the usual. A few thefts, a few drunken fights, some market stalls that were caught selling stolen or harmful goods."

"Any word on Ellis Hardy?"

Isadore shook his head. "None. The Guard is still seeing his people lurking about, but only a fraction of what there was before. Dreisand believes he's fled to Kivern and is running his operations from there."

"Are the Kivernese trying to find him?" It was a tremendous relief that he was gone from the city, but not if it meant he'd only start causing chaos elsewhere.

"Dreisand has informed the border scouts, and I'll send a message through Ambassador Miller, but I don't believe it'll come to much. There's too many places in the mountains where he could hide away." Isadore slipped the report into Melanie's desk. "At least we can take some pleasure in the fact that he's about to find out that bandit caves are not nearly as comfortable in life as they are in the stories."

"I hope so," Ambry said. It was a reassuring thought, at least. They held out the box. "I know it's early, but there's so much planned for the next week that I don't think we'll have any time."

"Wait," Isadore said. "I have something for you first. Sit down."

Ambry took his place on the couch, and Isadore went through the inner door and came back a few moments later, carrying a large rectangular box and placed it in Ambry's lap. It was fairly heavy, and looked a little like the ones Darby's winter clothes had come in. Had Isadore commissioned them a coat or something of the sort? But no, Darby's mark was missing from the corner. They'd never have sent anything without their name proudly upon it.

Ambry lifted the lid from the box. A sea dragon's face stared back at them, all curving horns and silver scales and one bright jade-green eye, each color a different sort of bright fabric. A stream of milky bubbles surged from its mouth, melding into the rushing surf above.

They'd seen something like this only once before, when they'd visited Willow Street after the storm.

"That's Sophie's work," they said, standing up to spread the tapestry to its full size. The dragon's sinuous amethyst and silver curves spiraled through a sea picked out in a dozen shades of blue, and a rainbow of little fish peeking out here and there from behind rocks and strands of seaweed.

"It is." Isadore beamed as Ambry's eyes explored every inch of the artwork. "When we returned from the Islands, I went to her with a special request."

"And she listened to you?" Of course she had, since Ambry was holding her creation now, but it still surprised them that she'd take any sort of command from Isadore after criticizing him so harshly.

"She did. It helped that I was able to pay quite a bit for both the work and materials. And that I have other requests in mind for the future."

Ambry was about to ask what those were, but he caught the look in Isadore's eyes and knew he wouldn't be telling that secret just yet. They weren't at all unhappy to wait.

"And this is for you." Ambry reached for the paper box and held it out. Isadore accepted it, and gently unfolded the tabs. The amber-tipped tree sparkled in the thin winter sunlight.

Isadore turned it in his hands, running his fingers along the whorled curves of its trunk and branches.

"That's beautiful. Where did you find it?"

"In the market. The same artist who made my hairclip."

"I can see the similarities. Thank you. I'll treasure this." Isadore admired it for a few moments longer, then reluctantly set it on the bookshelf, next to Lacey's painted shell. "And now, there's one more to attend to."

A moment later, Ambry understood what he meant. Their gift might not have come from Darby Allister, but another box had. Isadore pulled it out from under Melanie's desk and shared a conspiratorial smile with Ambry before calling Sylvia into the room. Inside the box she found gloves that would keep her hands warm while not impeding her motion. And sturdy boots far more comfortable than the ones the Guard offered. She pulled on the new boots and found that they fit perfectly. She bowed, smiling, and tucked the gloves into her belt.

"Thank you, Highness. These are wonderful."

"Don't tell the others. I want it to be a surprise."

Sylvia nodded. "They'll be pleased. Thank you for thinking of us."

She was right, and she kept her promise. When Lawrence and then Dominick came on duty, Isadore gave them their own sets of gifts. Lawrence accepted his with a jolly laugh and heartfelt thanks, and Dominick made a half-hearted effort to refuse before at last accepting and praised at length the quality of the materials and stitching. Ambry had the sense that this was a scene they reenacted every year and smiled to themself at the thought.

And that wasn't the last of the gifts. When Melanie returned to work the next day, she found on her desk a bottle of wine and a set of Arraweyan glass pens from Isadore, and a tin of spiced shortbread from Ambry, each piece decorated with a winter scene in colored icing.

"I hope you don't expect me to share again after this," she said, holding it out so they could each take a piece.

"No fear of that," Isadore said, biting into an image of a rabbit hiding in a snowbank. "Patrice and Ella will keep us in treats until the Spring Festival, I'm sure of it."

Ambry nibbled their own cookie, savoring each bite, waiting as long as they could before touching the winter dragon's icy wings.

✧

On the day before the last of the year, Isadore and Ambry put on their winter coats and boots and went out into the city to see Adrian. A light snow was falling, dusting the newly-cleared streets with a thin layer of white that crunched pleasantly under their footsteps.

Adrian and Rose waited by the palace gates, hand in hand. Rose's long hair was tucked under a knitted cap. Adrian had a thick scarf already speckled with snow but no hat. Isadore wondered if he'd lost it already or simply decided not to wear one despite the snow and chill. His pale cheeks and nose were marked with red from the cold, but he was smiling as if it was a summer's day.

"Isadore! You've been avoiding me."

"I've been busy," Isadore claimed. "There were a lot of letters waiting for me after we came home. And the situation with Hardy…"

Adrian sighed. "The same excuses. I'm telling you, you need to get more creative. You were so good at it when we were in school."

And he'd learned a lot about responsibility since then. So had Adrian, even if he rarely showed it. Isadore decided it wasn't the day for a lecture today. Adrian had enough to talk about without needing any prodding. And he was certainly willing to lighten his judgments when Isadore presented him with a box of sugared Crested Island fruit. Jasmine's creation, and it had taken some effort for him to persuade her to take fair payment for it.

Rose boldly plucked a sliver of something sparkling and honey-gold from the box and chewed on it, letting Adrian kiss the sugar from her lips. Isadore vaguely hoped his own romance didn't look nearly so syrupy. But Ambry was too practical for that, he thought with relief.

"How was your adventure in the Islands?" Adrian asked when he was done with this display. "Did you find true love this time or is that an honor reserved only for your assistants?" he said, smiling at Ambry. "I see this one didn't run away to live on the beach with a mermaid."

On second thought, maybe they were that sweet after all. And that obvious. "Well, you see," Isadore said, putting an arm around Ambry. "I think you'll find that honor was bestowed upon both of us."

Adrian crowed with delight. "Didn't I tell you they'd be perfect together?" he said unsubtly into Rose's ear. She giggled and smiled at them.

"Saints, did everyone know?" Isadore asked, shaking his head. Ambry laughed.

"You've always been obvious when you were in love," Adrian told him. "It's just that you've never waited so long to say something." He turned to Ambry. "You're lucky to have him. If you can ever pull him away from work, that is."

"We've been handling that together," Ambry said.

"And bending the world to your whim, I'm sure."

"You'll have to tell us how it happened!" Rose insisted.

"Yes, yes, in time," Isadore promised.

"I'll hold you to that." Adrian shook the snow from his coat. "Now then. Should we get a drink to celebrate? There's a place here that has the best cider, and winter stew with more sausage than turnips."

"Lead on," Isadore commanded, and Adrian was all too happy to obey.

Halfway to North Moon Square, they found Darby and April skating on a frozen pond. Darby's fur-lined lavender gown appeared to sweep the ice with every twist and turn of their long limbs, but it never seemed to tangle or pick up dirt. If Isadore didn't know better, he might have attributed Darby's gifts to some sort of magic. But of course it was entirely their own skill, and their dedication to studying everything they came across, from Larse embroidery to the pattern of a wintermoth's wings, for later use in their own creations. Beside them, April's rose-colored coat was the perfect companion to Darby's. As she twirled, creamy scarves spun out behind her like the tails of a winter dragon. The two of them seemed utterly lost in their own world, but it was only moments before they noticed they were being watched, and by whom.

"Highness!" Darby cried, dancing across the ice and scrambling up to perch on a low wall in front of Isadore. "So you've decided to escape your tower for a while to come out and enjoy the snow? And dear Ambry too!"

"The snow, and the season, and the company of friends," Isadore said, as April came to her partner's side. They held out a hand to help her balance on the uneven ground.

"How did your guards find my gifts?" they asked, raising an eyebrow towards Dominick, who was watching the passers-by on the street with a glare as cold as the weather.

"Very serviceable," Dominick said, with a respectful nod. "I'm very grateful for the gift. Under the proper care, they should last for years."

Darby's face broke into a wide grin. "Ah, that's a high compliment, coming from a trained soldier such as you."

"We were on our way to the Swimming Turtle for some lunch," Adrian said. "Join us?"

"We would be honored." April and Darby traded their skates for the winter boots stashed in a bag by the wall, and together the seven of them made their way through the snowy streets to the tavern.

Somehow, they managed to all crowd around a table at the back of the Swimming Turtle, just by the rusty old axes the proprietor had hung on the wall to honor his grandfather's labor in building the place decades ago. Isadore ordered cider for all of them, and while Dominick refused the drink, Isadore insisted he sit with them at the table.

This time, nobody showed up to interrupt them. And the stew was just as tasty as Adrian had promised.

"How was the opera?" Ambry asked Darby. "The one with the bird costumes that you were so concerned about."

"Oh, I survived, with the scars to my pride to show for it," Darby sighed. "The dancers looked just as foolish as I'd always said they would, but the music was impeccable, so at least it will not be remembered as a tremendous disaster."

"The crowds didn't find them foolish, my dear," April said, reaching for a seed bun and tearing it in half to share with Darby. "I heard that some of them watched it twice, just to see those feathered wings."

Isadore smiled, and didn't offer an opinion beyond, "I'm sure it was a magical sight." He'd never quite managed to pin down what Darby found ridiculous or sensible or beautiful or ugly. Certainly many of their creations looked absurd at first glance, until they were worn on a living body instead of a stiff mannequin, and then they moved like magical creatures.

"We saw that show," Rose said. "Adrian took me to one of the last performances. It was beautiful. When the general's daughter fell on the battlefield, holding out her wings until the last moment to warn the others away from the trap... that was very poetic. And they couldn't have done it without the costumes."

Darby shook their head. "I suppose I should be honored to be so appreciated. Even for work that was far from my best."

Nonsense, Isadore thought. Darby was incapable of doing anything but their best, no matter the assignment. And nothing in the world could stop them from basking in praise.

"Do you know what show they're putting on next?" Ambry asked. Isadore made up his mind to be sure they got a chance to see it, whether as the prince and his honored companion or disguised as common folk.

"A retelling of *The Island Princess*, I believe," April said. "By a new playwright from Arrawey."

"That's one of my favorites," Ambry said. "Do you think they're going to pair her with the pirate queen, or her loyal maid?"

"Who can guess?" April said with a delighted flick of her hand. "Either would be terribly romantic. But if I had to put my lind on it, it would be the maid. Arraweyan operas are always about loyalty in the end, and the pirate queen is loyal to no one. It's a wonderful story either way. Have you read the one by Aubrey Marks?"

"My friend Delia made me read it. And all the stories she wrote about them too."

"Maybe it'll be her tale on the stage next time," Adrian said. "They never get tired of the same stories."

"And you love them," Rose reminded him.

The conversation moved from opera to the Crested Islands. Isadore and Ambry told most of their tale, leaving out the part about the goldstrike. No need to bring up such a terrible thing now, when they were all so happy.

When they finished, Darby and April insisted they come to the Northgate and see the garden of ice sculptures carved out of blocks taken from the frozen river, and from there they stopped for hot spiced wine and skewered fritters and followed the sound of music to a little wooden stage tucked behind an inn where half-drunk actors performed a delightful, if muddled, take on *The Snow Rabbit*. They didn't have the Springleaf Opera's orchestra or Darby's fantastical costumes, but the performance was still one of the most entertaining Isadore had ever seen, and by the end of it all of them save Dominick were cheering for the little rabbit as he tricked his enemy, the hungry wolf, into the frozen river and pulled him out again as a friend.

They returned to the palace long after dark. Isadore and Ambry fell into bed together, and stayed there until well after the sun rose the next day. Isadore couldn't bring himself to regret any time they lost lazing about. It was the last night of the year, and they'd need the strength to stay awake until dawn.

✧

Melanie's chair wouldn't be of much use in the snow, so today she sat atop a sleigh pulled by two of the palace horses, sturdy brown and white creatures who didn't mind the noise of the city, the bells on their bridles chiming brightly as they paced through the streets. Sylvia followed alongside them on her own mount, warm in her new gloves and boots, her only concession to the joyous season a large furry hat tucked around her ears and topped with a puff of yarn.

Today Isadore did not try to hide who he was. He went among his people almost unremarked. On the first day of the year they would honor him and gather to hear him speak, but today they celebrated alongside him, respectful but not overawed.

His sisters, he told Ambry, had other plans. Dressed in plain winter cloaks, they attended the festivities not as princesses but as anonymous travelers, free to enjoy the games and dances and treats on their own terms. Their guards walked beside them as friends, their blades carefully hidden against their unlikely need.

Ambry, to their surprise, found they liked riding alongside Isadore. They'd expected the attention to be overwhelming, but there was so much else going on that they didn't feel singled out for special focus. And it was undoubtedly a benefit that they didn't have to navigate noisy crowds or wait in long lines or fear slipping on icy paths.

The first few days of the year would be full of games and pantomime plays for the children, mulled cider and dances for the adults. Children ran about waving little flags and shaking wooden noisemakers, sticks with beads on the ends of strings tied onto the tip, meant to mimic the wands the winter spirits used to call back the sun to light the new year. They darted between brightly-colored stalls that offered games played for little prizes, most often cloth dolls or sweets.

These games were simple things: throwing balls at targets or guessing which box held a toy or picking a black stone from a basket of white while blindfolded, but Ambry knew how much allure they held to children. The entire festival was a golden time for them. Finally, they could enjoy a time when parents would not scold them for running through the streets or cheering too loudly. Ambry hadn't been a particularly noisy child anyway, but it still had been fun to watch their friends use the freedom to their advantage.

A row of stalls offered treats of every sort imaginable: sizzling sausages cooked over open flames, pastries fried and drenched in syrup, little butter cookies cut in the shape of snowflakes and dusted with sparkling sugar. Isadore leapt from the sleigh and came back moments later bearing cups of spiced tea rich with cream and honey.

Ambry savored theirs in small sips while Melanie wrapped her hands around her cup and drank deeply. She sighed. "Mmm. This is my favorite part of the holiday. It almost makes the cold worth it."

"You're not warm enough under all that?" Isadore eyed the mountain of furs burying her.

"It's nice, but it's still not perfect. Let's get closer to the fire." She pointed to the figures that stood bathed in the flickering light of the tremendous bonfire in the center of the square. Young children stepped as close as they dared to the roaring flames, warming their hands in the glow. Others approached with coiled scraps of paper in their hands that they tossed into the fire: wishes, to be sent to the gods on the smoke that drifted towards the sky.

Isadore smiled. "As long as you don't set my carriage on fire."

"Are you sure?" she teased. "It would certainly be exciting."

"I think there's enough excitement planned for tonight already," Isadore said.

"Oh, very well." She reached for Ambry's plate of sugar-and-nut dumplings and took two, pausing over a third. Ambry bit into another one before she could change her mind and offered the last to Isadore. The sticky filling melted in their mouth, all warm syrup and rich flavor.

Back in their home village, they'd gathered in the church with their cousins and aunts and uncles and listened to the priest tell stories of the gods' first winter, where the world they'd created nearly froze over in the bitter cold. All had seemed lost as the sun sank deeper and deeper into the dark. But a trickle of life flowed in the depths of the frozen river, and on the darkest day it burst forth to grasp the drowning sun and thrust it back into the sky. There had been songs too, somber ones and joyous ones. But it had been only a whisper compared to the singing that came from the musicians walking through the crowd, lamps held above their heads on poles, bobbing up and down as they moved. These weren't solemn prayers, lists of rules and tasks, or tales of the horrible fates that befell naughty children. These were bright and happy songs of games in the snow and parties in warm houses, tales of trickster clowns and daring animal heroes who helped chase the stars across the sky and into their dark underground realm and out into the sky again. And this year, as they always did, they succeeded in bringing back the light.

Ambry watched the lanterns dance through the streets, saw the faces of the crowd illuminated by their glow. These were the people Isadore governed and guided. The people he and Ambry worked for every day. There was a lot to be proud of. The treaty, the city council rulings. And there was so much more to do in the new year. It should have been a staggering weight, but Ambry wasn't afraid. Whatever lay ahead, they knew they could face it. Now, though, was a time to celebrate.

By the time the first sunrise of the new year cast its first glimmers of pale light on the snowy fields, Ambry was draped half-asleep against Isadore's shoulder, warmed through by strong wine. He wrapped one of the blankets around them, ran his hands through their hair, leaned over to kiss their forehead. Ambry hummed in contentment and shifted closer still. They could live forever like this and be utterly happy – warm and loved, mind drifting far from anxieties, the distant sounds of music floating to their ears. Isadore's breath and heartbeat and steady hands close by.

As the palace bells rang out into the dawn, Isadore pressed a kiss to their lips.

"To the New Year, my love."

About the Author

Kate Diamond lives in Madison, WI, with a cat who would very much like to be a co-author but whose contributions so far consist mainly of rolling over and looking cute. Kate enjoys writing about hopeful worlds, beautiful settings, and alien friendships.

Printed in Great Britain
by Amazon

Printed in Great Britain
by Amazon